ELEVEN

CLOUDS OF SOLITUDE

VOLUME 2

by

J.J. Bende

and

Carisa Holmes

ELEVEN:
CLOUDS OF SOLITUDE
VOLUME 2

Pensiero Press, LLC.
PO Box 533
Dublin, Ohio 43017
www.PensieroPress.com

ISBN Number: 978-0-9847305-3-7

For more adventures and information on Eleven, visit:
www.QuestofEleven.com

On Facebook at:
Facebook.com/QuestofEleven

DEDICATION

I dedicate this book to my 5 month old daughter, Jersey.
My wish for you as you grow up is that you never hesitate
to imagine and to create; your dreams can only take you as
far as you carry them. Your sweet smile inspires me to
keep striving and someday I hope you will enjoy reading
what your father has created.

~J.J. Bende

I dedicate this work to the warrior child within all of us,
the medicine within the sickness and the glimmer
of light in every dark place.

~Carisa Holmes

ACKNOWLEDGEMENTS

The co-authors would like to acknowledge the following contributors:

Thanks again to Danielle Kaheaku
for your hard work on the project.

And a humble thanks to all of the creators of stories
and art for your courage and inspiring works.

Thanks again to all the supporters of the series at home and far
away. Your enthusiasm for the tale is humbling.

A MESSAGE FROM J.J.

Thanks to my wife, Nicole, whose continued love and support has never wavered throughout the years. A special thanks to my son, Amedeo, for keeping me on my toes and always being up for an adventure. Lastly, to my friends and COC partners including, but not limited to, Bas, Jake, and Jm; thanks for the support and promoting skills.

A MESSAGE FROM CARISA

Love and gratitude to my family members, both here and beyond the veil, for your loving support and encouragement through these difficult times of birth and renewal. Thank you to Suzanne Roberts for your wonderful work and for helping me to finally free myself. Thank you to Scott Conway for your amazing friendship and continuing support, to Karen Bradford for reminding me to dance and be happy and free, and to all of the wonderful writers, artists and musicians who renew my spirit and continue to inspire me to create.

ELEVEN

CLOUDS OF SOLITUDE

VOLUME 2

by

J.J. Bende

and

Carisa Holmes

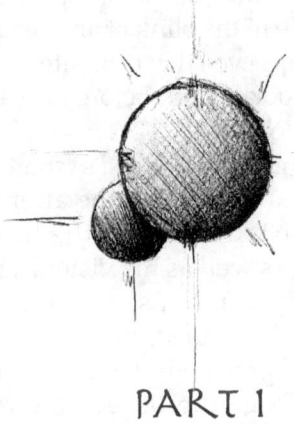

PART 1

A SECRET COMES TO LIGHT

Lium stood at the edge of the Utara territory, looking north to the border of Jonquil and Verde. Utara now hung low in the sky, and from this vantage point Lium could see beneath the clouds and mist that hovered in the higher elevations of Jonquil. The golden sandscape below ended abruptly at the bluffs of Sukai, where desiccating winds rushed up the sheer face of the rock.

A sudden gust lofted Lium's fair hair up and around his face as he shifted his gaze beyond Sukai, to the line where green met gold. The southern region of Verde sprawled out before him, blossoming to life with Jonas' return. Emerald hills blushed with color, and rivers reflected the clear blue above. The black fog that once haunted the valleys had cleared and the Land flourished, loved by the suns. Lium shut his eyes and tried to squeeze the contrasting images from his mind's eye. He stood, quite literally, on the cusp of great change.

Lium reached into his vest and took out the emanator Esod had given him. It felt cold and hard in his hand, and the weight of it reminded him of the burden he now carried.

Vivid scenes of the violence at the battle of Thatch flashed in Lium's mind. Choices made in the blink of an eye had forever altered the course of his life, perhaps even that of all life on Graha. He would now walk the dark and crooked path before him, knowing what he had done could not be undone.

Lium had long struggled in Esod's shadow, fighting for recognition, then eventually winning the attention of the great warrior himself. He hadn't known it at the time, but Esod had admired his gift of sight, as well as his vision. Though Lium had set out simply to create for himself some shred of the notoriety and wealth that Esod had attained, his ambition would be his poison. In time, desire and greed blinded Lium, and as dark forces took over the Lands, he began to believe the intelligent choice was to work *with* Corpus, not against him. The shift in power had been palpable in even the safest of havens. Only a fool would have continued such a fruitless endeavor as to fight for the resistance, and Lium was no fool.

And so he had given up on hope and turned his face from the light. He had embraced his dark benefactor, and knowingly walked with the group into the trap at Thatch. Lium had been the reason why the dark forces had always seemed to be a step ahead of the group throughout the entire mission in Verde. It was he who had betrayed the resistance, and regret now ate away at him like a cancer. The stress of the deception rattled Lium, and his nerves were scraped raw. Though he had taken great care to cover his intentions, he had nearly been caught once in the Harita forest, when Mila had suddenly returned through a doorway and almost discovered him speaking in secret with Corpus. Though he managed to conceal his communication, as he took the girl's hand, he had found that his own was trembling.

Lium swallowed hard as an intangible something tightened around his ribs, preventing a satisfying breath. The feeling had become familiar to him in his travels with the group. It dogged him at every turn, from a sideways look from Thornhill to a sneer from Rosette. In his sensitive state, every glance came from a place of suspicion, and all eyes were upon him. Being known as a man of spoiled integrity was a bitter enough thought, but the idea of Esod—his most admired mentor—learning of his weakness was impossible to stomach.

* * *

Violent images of the battle of Thatch again intruded upon Lium's memory. He could hear Esod shout in pain from the knife wound as if the man was right next to him. The sound echoed inside his head, and he reeled from the reverberation. Shades of rusty brown moved through his aura, and he shook his head in an attempt to clear his mind. Had he known that Esod thought of him as a true protégé, he might have found the strength to stand against the dark forces. To walk at Esod's side as his equal, to be admired as a Prime Warrior of Jonquil; could he not find a single thread of courage to fight for that reward? Lium had known full well Corpus awaited them in Thatch—what had happened to his mettle?

He had allowed himself to be captured during the battle at Thatch, knowing the Dark One would quickly free him, and Corpus had done just that, praising Lium for delivering the group to him. Corpus had then given him another assignment, one that sat like a whetstone in his belly. Lium remembered with shame how he had done his master's bidding at Thatch.

Rosette is Deceived

At the battle of Thatch, Lium and Rosette took cover behind a pile of rock and soil. Esod was nowhere to be found; Lium, freed from his captors, had rushed to aid Rosette in her fight. The two had managed to take advantage of chaos and infighting among the captors of Thatch and had slipped away unnoticed from the scene. Rosette crouched beside Lium, ribbons of crimson twisting through her green aura. For an instant, Lium's eyes met hers, but she quickly averted her gaze.

Lium tucked a blade into his vest and turned to Rosette. "I know you don't care for me," he said, "but I also know what it is you seek."

Rosette shot a glance at him, then tucked a stray strand of dark hair behind her ear.

"I know you hunt the one who destroyed Verde and cast out her king. He is here." Lium turned his eyes skyward. "Corpus hovers over Thatch even as we speak."

"Where?" Rosette rose quickly and peered into the clouds above, blade in hand.

"You alone cannot destroy Corpus. He is far too powerful for even a warrior of your caliber. If you can tolerate working with me, together we can defeat him."

A nearby blast sent Rosette back behind the rock pile. "How?"

"We will need to combine forces. A single warrior, even armed with an emanator, is not enough. You would only weaken Corpus and he would return again." Lium raised a brow, looking directly at Rosette. "His minions would find you."

Rosette flinched as she thought of Briar, her finest warrior, wrapped in the clutches of the shadow being. "What do we do?"

"If we both focus our energy and direct our emanators at Corpus, he would not be able to survive the hit."

For an instant, blood red flushed the entirety of Rosette's aura. Her fingertips tingled at the thought of destroying the being that had taken her warrior from battle—and stolen Jonas away from her heart. "Are you sure it will work?"

"Gishon of Jonquil told me of this technique. He is the creator of the sohoyin emanator, and is one of the wisest Magisters of Jonquil. Though no one has had the chance to put his theory to test, I believe it will work." Lium stared at Rosette, eyes glinting. "Will you join with me to hunt Corpus?"

Rosette thumbed the blade of her knife, leaving a slight tinge of red along the edge. She stared coldly at Lium. "Let's do it."

Lium looked out from behind the rock pile and scanned the horizon. "Corpus is moving off into the south toward Jonquil. If we are to keep pace with him, we must go now."

Rosette looked to the south, then checked the battle area again. It appeared that each of the other members of their group, save Mila, had been taken by captors. Only she and Lium remained. Rosette frowned at the tightness growing in her belly. Leaving the others to make an alliance with Lium was unthinkable, yet if she stayed to fight, she would almost certainly be captured—perhaps even killed. If she did choose to leave with Lium, there was a chance for retribution. If they succeeded, Corpus would be destroyed and Solanum would have little power to hold the group captive any longer. She could easily rescue them if they did not manage to free themselves. She clenched her fists and fixed her eyes on Lium, who waited beside her, poised to flee.

With a nod of agreement, they were off.

As they fled the battle, a familiar form caught Lium's eye. Esod lay motionless on the ground, chest barely moving. His body faded as his kumu drained steadily into the surrounding soil, marking the exit of his life force. Lium gasped and droplets of sweat instantly formed on his brow. His aura flickered, and all of the energy within him seemed to short-circuit at the sight. Lium's heart pounded as he left Rosette and rushed to Esod's side. He fell to his knees and grasped Esod's hand, shaking it as if to rouse him, but the great warrior's face was gaunt and expressionless. Lium tried to speak, but panic would not allow the apology to cross his lips. The one person who had seemingly believed in him more than he believed in himself was dying. He watched as the moment slipped from his grasp like sand through fingers, powerless to ebb the flow.

The sound of Esod's last breath hung in the air like smoke, and it swirled mercilessly in Lium's ears. The warrior's body finally faded away, leaving behind only the pale residue of kumu. Lium himself could barely draw a breath, and the tears that welled in his eyes blurred his vision as his body stiffened and his lips set to a grim line. He sensed Rosette behind him, but did not move to address her.

Despite the high position of the fallen warrior, there would be little time for ritual or remorse, for the battle raged on around him. Lium quickly took the lintu from Esod's pocket, the its jewel-encrusted metal surface glinting in the light as he opened the compartment. Lium shut his eyes and breathed as deeply as his stiffening ribs would allow, sweeping his hand to and fro as he gathered Esod's kumu. Within moments, the task was done and Lium shoved the lintu into his vest and dashed away with Rosette.

Lium and Rosette fled Thatch undetected and headed south in pursuit of Corpus. Swift and silent as shadows, they stopped only to rest in the night. For weeks the two pursued Corpus over harsh terrains, concealing themselves so as not to be discovered. All the while it appeared to Rosette that they were tracking a target that wished to evade them. The truth, however, was a different matter.

Eventually they arrived in Sukai at the mouth of the Tenpi desert, where a skilled pilot named Kazel resided. Infamous in Jonquil, he was rumored to be blessed by the suns and impervious to wind, the ideal candidate to fly them into Jonquil in pursuit of Corpus. The two stopped at the front door of the lone tavern in Sukai, and Rosette paused to brush the accumulating sand from her eyes. "Why do we need this Kazel to fly us over Tenpi? Are you not a pilot like every other Jonquilian?"

"It's true, my dear, that I can pilot a sanlifter, but Jonquil is not what it used to be. It has always been unforgiving, but in these times the territories are crumbling and sinking into the desert below. This territory of Utara is particularly treacherous, and we will need an expert pilot if we are to have a chance to survive."

"How are we going to find him?"

"From what I've heard, Kazel is either in the air or at the bar."

Rosette rolled her eyes as she pulled open the door. "Come on, let's hurry."

The two stepped inside and paused for a moment to allow their eyes to adjust to the meager light. The room was quiet and a smoky aroma tinged the air. Nearby, a lanky young man leaned heavily on the bar, methodically finishing his fifth measure of kvass, his yellow-ochre aura flickering weakly, like a candle in a breeze. The light from the open door broke the dim mood of the room, and the man wavered as he turned to look at the newcomers. Partly intrigued and mostly drunk, he leered at the attractive woman and her well-dressed companion—this would be interesting.

The man stepped forward, straightening himself. "Ah! Welcome to Sukai!" he said loudly, bowing dramatically in an overly formal manner. "Corso," he called to the bartender, "bring your finest bottle for my fancy new friends!"

Rosette narrowed her eyes. "That won't be necessary."

"Our time runs short," Lium said. "We must find the pilot Kazel and obtain a sanlifter as quickly as possible."

Corso snorted, and his glow momentarily flashed bright green. "Kazel? Who aims to run into that dunebuster on purpose?"

The drunk man swore at Corso, laughing. "You want Kazel, you found him. At your service."

Kazel sloppily clicked his heels together and tilted his dusty cap.

Lium's eyes widened, and he lifted an eyebrow. "You hardly look capable of walking, let alone piloting a sanlifter over Tenpi."

"You dare question the famous *Kazel*?" Kazel hiccupped, lifting his sixth drink to his lips. "The kvass lubricates my reflexes."

Corso set down his smoking pipe and laughed heartily, a rasping sound building within his sickly lungs. Kazel smirked at him, then turned back to Lium. "Where in Jonquil are you headed?"

"We are in pursuit of someone and we are not sure how far along they are at this point. We must leave immediately."

"A chase, eh?" Kazel paused in thought, licking his lips. "Sixteen silvers and twenty."

Lium's mouth fell open. "Are you mad?"

Kazel frowned. "Have you forgotten who you're talking to? I *am* the famous—"

"So be it," Lium sharply interrupted, withdrawing a pouch from his vest. He took out the necessary payment and marched to Kazel, placing the coins firmly in his hand.

"Let's fly!" Kazel shouted, downing his kvass and slapping the bar top in celebration. He then shuffled toward the rear of the building and began fumbling with the locks.

Rosette eyed him suspiciously. "Can't we find someone else to fly us in?"

Lium sighed, shaking his head. "No other pilot in Sukai is reckless enough to fly in through the pass of Tenpi these days. It has always been dangerous, but now the wind patterns and falling debris have rendered it nothing short of perilous."

Kazel finally managed to unlatch and open the door; he stood silhouetted in the light from outside. "Just c'mon already, this is nothing for me!"

Rosette frowned. "There's a reason why they say there are no old, cocky pilots…"

"He may be cocky and well-lubricated…" Lium looked woefully upon their drunken pilot as he tripped over the door threshold and staggered out into the yard. "But he's our only chance. Time is wasting."

Rosette breathed a heavy sigh and reluctantly followed Lium and Kazel through the rear door and to the hangars.

Kazel stumbled as he entered the hangar and then scowled at the ground as if it had somehow sabotaged his steps. He looked around the cavernous space and seemed to lock on a spot to the far left, then made his way over as Lium and Rosette followed. He stopped beside a sleek metal machine with four in-line seats and wings folded back at rest. The polished body tapered to a pointed tail with a fin covered in sturdy fabric. Kazel kicked at the wheels, ensuring they were in good condition. He reached inside the cabin and drew back a lever. At once, the port wing of the craft extended outward and locked into flight position. Kazel tugged firmly at the wing to ensure it stayed securely in place. He then flicked the lever forward, and the wing neatly folded itself back onto the body.

"This one will do," Kazel said.

Rosette glanced at Lium. He shrugged, moving to help Kazel push the craft out of its resting place. They wheeled it carefully around the other craft in the hangar and out to the head of the run-way, which looked discouragingly short. It seemed only a hop from the bluffs of Sukai to a sheer drop-off into the mouth of the Tenpi desert that sat nearly a quarter spatial below. Though the drop had once been a great aid to pilots, affording them time to gain altitude in the steady winds that blew up the cliff walls, it now loomed ominously. Unpredictable gusts threatened to dash a craft to bits on the rocky bluffs below. The winds of Tenpi howled ferociously as they rushed up the cliff face, and sand whirled into the air, wisps of it snaking across the runway like gossamer serpents.

"Winds are wild today," Kazel grunted. He turned to Rosette and said, "You're lucky you ran into me." He then looked the warrior up and down, his eyes lingering on her graceful form. "Anytime you need to fly, you just let me know. I'll take you anywhere."

Feeling no need to respond to such a proposition, Rosette squinted at Kazel, then turned her gaze to the sandscape beyond the bluffs. An endless ocean of dunes stretched out as far as she could see, the crests and troughs undulating in the winds. Black fog hovered in low areas and skimmed the tops of the dunes.

Rosette detected movement and looked to the sky in the distance. Something had fallen through the patches of clouds and mist that cloaked sections of the higher elevations. She narrowed her eyes and saw a twisted clump of metal on the sand below. Several such clumps were within view, standing as both remnants of the creation and symptoms of the decay of Jonquil. Save these few landmarks, there was only a vast and empty desert.

Rosette turned from her observations as Kazel pushed the sanlifter into position, aligning it with marks that had been made in the runway. He clambered awkwardly into the pilot's seat, only now feeling his sixth and most unnecessary beverage. Lium and Rosette climbed aboard and settled into their seats, placing their goggles over their eyes for protection; it seemed their pilot had not deemed it necessary to choose a sanlifter with a dome cover.

Kazel drew back the two levers on either side of his seat and the wings of the craft unfolded, extending fully to gather the energy from the suns. He grumbled to himself as he began pedaling and the craft crept forward. He swiveled round to Lium, who sat directly behind him. "Utara territory, right up there," Kazel said, pointing. "All kinds of junk falling from the sky. Hang on in case I need to make a move."

Lium nodded and relayed the message to Rosette. Kazel continued pedaling and though the sanlifter picked up speed, as the end of the runway came into view, Rosette felt certain they should be moving faster than they were to get into the air. Before she could protest, Kazel pulled his goggles over his eyes and shouted, "Here we go!"

At once, a blast of wind hit the craft, easily lifting the wheels from the ground. Kazel pulled back hard on the yoke just as the sanlifter came to the edge of the bluff. The craft cleared the rocky edge and then hovered, lofted by the powerful air currents from below. The sanlifter teetered slightly as it began its ascent over the bluffs, and Rosette could feel the hum of the propulsion system as it came to life, rapidly increasing their airspeed.

Despite his pickled state, Kazel had managed to lift off safely. But no sooner had he reached for the handles to tuck the wheels into their flight position when he caught sight of something shining in the light just ahead of them: a sizable section of metal had torn loose from the underbelly of the Utara territory. The winds had caught the section like a sail, sending it far into the distance and now, careening directly toward the sanlifter. Kazel knew he was already low, but he would need to swoop lower still to avoid a collision. Panicked, he turned and warned Lium, "Hang on!"

Kazel punched the yoke forward and the sanlifter dove erratically, tossed about by the winds. The metal debris hurtled downward and northward, as if seeking to take the craft from the air. Kazel gnashed his teeth and his arms tightened as he forced the yoke further forward. The nose of the sanlifter tilted sharply down in response, plummeting toward the dunes. Kazel swore loudly and watched as the chunk of debris flew past, just inches above them. Though he swiftly brought the craft to a level position, the downdrafts near the ground proved brutally strong. Despite his best efforts, he was losing altitude.

Kazel shook his head and wrestled with the yoke, coaxing the craft higher. "C'mon now, come up, come up, come up..."

Though the sanlifter gradually began to ascend, Kazel soon fearfully realized it would not be enough, and there was good reason to avoid flying low over the dunes outside Sukai. Just ahead, an enormous, eyeless face began to emerge from the sand. The head, measuring nearly three times the length of the sanlifter, appeared to be mostly mouth; though blind, the creature had sensed the presence of something moving above its sandy lair. Unfortunately, the sanlifter had flown in low enough to rouse the beast and dozens of tentacles now whipped about in the air, reaching out expectantly for prey.

Kazel's eyes nearly popped out of his head. "Ocnityl!"

Two thick tentacles suddenly broke away from the rest and moved in tandem toward the sanlifter. Kazel opened the throttle and turned the yoke hard to port, rolling the craft. He growled as he struggled to get sideways in the gusting winds, the creature's tentacles inching closer and closer together, rapidly closing the window for escape. Kazel let out a long cry as he finally pulled the wings to full vertical position. The passengers clung tightly to their seats as the craft slipped through the opening between the two tentacles just before they slammed together.

"Son of a..." Kazel started, glancing backward at the near-miss. "Ah!" he shouted as yet another tentacle slashed through the air to the starboard side, so close that Kazel could see the hooked suckers swiveling menacingly over the length of it. The great arm rose into the air once more and Kazel sent the craft into a full barrel roll, spiraling down toward the dunes. The creature missed its target once again and the pilot fought to right his craft before it crashed into the sands. He swooped low into the blast of the unfavorable winds near the ground, then fought vehemently to get back up and away from the horrible beast that lurked below.

He had nearly gotten away when he heard an alarmingly loud *thunk*. The very tip of a tentacle had wrapped around the rear wheel, and the sanlifter slowed ominously. Below, the gaping mouth of the ocnityl opened, eagerly awaiting its meal, the waves of the creature's call tangibly buffeting the sanlifter.

"Quick," Kazel screamed, "somebody do something!"

Lium turned around and saw Rosette already in motion. She jumped out of her seat and shimmied backward down the tail of the craft, weapon drawn. She slashed deftly with the curved blade, severing the tentacle just below the wheel. The craft dipped wildly, and Rosette slipped from her position and wrapped her arms around the tail section as she fell, latching on just as the craft leveled and Kazel regained control. She threw her legs back over the tail section and righted herself once more. She crawled back into her seat and looked back at the frustrated creature, now digging itself into the sand. "What was that thing?"

Lium only panted with eyes wide, unable to respond. Kazel, his knuckles white with fear, leaned his head over the starboard side and vomited up the remains of his last kvass, then quickly gathered himself. "It was an ocnityl. They live in the sand. They keep those arms spread out just under the surface and if you walk over one, or fly too low, it can feel you there, and then it wakes up."

"Yes, the beast grabs its prey and then tosses it into its mouth to digest it slowly...in acid." Lium finally added.

"That's why they say *fly low, die slow*," Kazel laughed. "I'm sober now!"

Rosette shook her head. *One more reason to stay out of Jonquil,* she thought. She glanced back at the tail section of the craft as Kazel moved the wheels into flight position. The tip of the severed tentacle still clung to the rear wheel, writhing in vain.

The sanlifter continued to gain altitude and climbed ever higher, through the clouds of the upper elevations and into the clear blue beyond. Rosette found herself once again in awe of the unfathomable size of the discs Queen Zehn had placed her creation upon. The land itself sat upon metal discs that hovered in the air by way of a featherlight gas that Zehn had sealed inside. In the past, her presence in the Land along with the lift from the gasses kept the discs of the Land of Jonquil afloat in the sky. In her absence, the discs were deteriorating and sinking toward the sands below, some now even hanging below the clouds and dark mist, shedding sheets of metal as the winds tore them loose from their pinnings. The once-brilliant sheen of the pale golden metal was now dulled, tarnished from neglect, and Jonquil was a sagging and faded remnant of what it had been when Rosette last saw it.

She shook her head and continued scanning the sky for signs of their quarry. "Can you see anything yet?"

Lium's eyes flickered as he intently focused his gaze. "He is moving very quickly. I've never seen any being move at such speeds. It's almost as if he has acquired Queen Zehn's gifts." He pointed right ahead through the front viewing glass. "He's headed directly south. Stay your present course, Kazel."

"Right, just don't ask me to fly low," Kazel replied, still rattled from their close encounter with the ocnityl.

Lium kept their final destination to himself. He knew exactly where Corpus was headed.

The Palace of Gosai

The journey had lasted longer than Kazel expected. His rations were running low, and it had been much too long since his last measure of kvass. He turned to Lium with a frown. "Any sign of them? I'm not flying outside Jonquil. If we don't find whoever you're chasing soon, I'm dropping you in the nearest territory and heading back to Sukai."

"We are very close, I can see that he has stopped moving now. He is hovering over the Selatan territory, so take us there," Lium replied.

"Selatan?" Kazel worriedly ran his hand over his aching head. "But that's where the Palace of Gosai is. That place is crawling with raiku; if we fly in there, we'll be ripped to shreds!"

"Just take us to the water gardens near the entrance of the palace. From there we'll be able to watch for raiku. If one of them makes a move, we'll have time to take off and get away." Lium reached into his vest and withdrew several coins. "And here are five silvers more, to ease your anxiety."

Kazel's eyes lit up as he took the coins from Lium and tucked them into his pocket. He continued flying south and before long, the sanlifter coasted toward the disc that housed the Palace of Gosai. Unlike the other territories of Jonquil, the Selatan territory was not connected to any other Lands by bridges or walks. The palace floated on its own royal island in the sky at a slightly higher elevation than all other territories. As the craft floated through the veils of mist that surrounded, the grand palace came into view. The graceful curves of the structure rose from the land in perfect arcs. Queen Zehn had crafted it from the same precious metal as the discs, and it gleamed in the light. The stone walkways that led through the water gardens and to the entrance were studded with jewels that sparkled brightly, despite the decay of the Land. In places, the domed crystal skylights still welcomed the warmth of the suns and wide windows of colored glass tinted the rays of light that streamed inside.

Other sections of the palace, however, had not been so well preserved in Zehn's absence. These sections were infested with swarms of the raiku, winged creatures larger even than the hoverdales. These normally solitary beasts had been forced to flock together in Selatan in Fincher's service, causing their naturally aggressive dispositions to turn most foul. Unfortunately, the beasts continued to behave much as they did when they roamed their natural habitat in the Timur territory, harvesting sheets of metal and shredding them, forming them into nests they violently protected. Long, powerful beaks lined with sharp teeth and claws armed with serrated hooks made the raiku as destructive as they were frightening. In parts of the palace, the animals had torn away gaping sections of the structure, replacing them with giant nests of shredded metal, and no sane person dared discourage them.

* * *

Queen Zehn had been an enigmatic and private woman, and the palace had always been an exclusive destination seen by only a privileged few Jonquilians. Lium had been fortunate enough to see it once, as a guest of Esod. He had always imagined the interior would be a sight to behold, but had not been prepared for the striking beauty that surrounded him. The edifice was opulence in its highest form, the finest sandplaster work, sumptuous silks, and precious metals gleamed in halls lit by expansive skylights that revealed the bright blue sky above. Now, however, the pristine beauty of earlier days had been spoiled by evil.

Kazel carefully set the sanlifter down in the courtyard of the water gardens in front of the palace, positioning it so that if necessary, he could make a quick getaway. Several raiku closely watched the craft from their perches above. Any one of the creatures could easily swoop down and tear the sanlifter and its occupants apart, but they only watched as the craft came to rest in the courtyard. Lium slipped out of his seat and stood next to the flyer, stretching the stiffness from the length of his lean body. He looked to the palace entrance, then turned to Rosette.

"Corpus is inside," he said, removing his goggles. "Come now, we mustn't delay."

Kazel raised his goggles and shook his head. "Look, I said I'd bring you to the gardens, but I'm not gonna stick around to be eaten."

Lium smiled. "You may go, I'm certain there will be a suitable sanlifter here for us to use. Thank you, Kazel."

"Good luck!" Kazel laughed, once more placing his goggles over his eyes.

Rosette climbed out of the craft and the two cautiously entered the palace. Rosette noted that the raiku watched intently, but seemed to have no interest in attacking them. As the two passed below their nests and into the palace, the creatures remained eerily still.

Without delay, Kazel began pedaling his craft into position for takeoff, finding the winds steady and strong. No sooner had the craft taken to the air than several raiku left their roosts and began circling the sanlifter. Kazel felt a lump growing in his throat and found his hands tightening on the yoke. What had provoked the creatures into motion? He nervously wiped his brow and pulled the wheels up, anxious to put some distance between himself and the infested kingdom.

At once, a large male broke away from the circling formation and drew his wings straight up, then forcefully down again as he began the hunt.

Kazel caught the motion in the corner of his eye and turned to see the screeching beast barreling toward him. Kazel's heart leapt wildly in his chest and his mouth fell open. Unable to react in time, he could only watch as the creature's toothy beak connected with the wing of his craft. With three powerful strokes of its wing membranes, the animal snatched the sanlifter off its course and pulled it back over the garden courtyard. The raiku slammed the flyer violently to the ground and landed astride it. Kazel screamed and scrambled from his seat, intent on abandoning the craft, but a rival male raiku landed in front of the first, his shrill call piercing Kazel's eardrums.

With limbs weakened by terror, Kazel tried to flee, but instead fell quivering to the ground. The two animals dove their beaks down simultaneously to claim their prize, each grasping one of Kazel's legs. Shrieks tore through the silence of the garden as each raiku consumed its portion of the meal, and within minutes, both the sanlifter and its pilot were no more.

Oblivious to the carnage outside, Rosette and Lium moved further into the halls of the palace. The silent stillness of the corridors caused Rosette to take pause, the hairs on the back of her neck standing up in warning. She quickly looked around, but saw no immediate threat and continued down the hall with Lium. As they entered the grand throne room, Rosette heard shuffling sounds coming from either side. Her fingertips tingled, and she quickly drew a blade from her belt. At once, seven Guardsmen dressed in Jonquilian silks burst into the room. Rosette glanced at Lium and noticed that he looked inappropriately calm. She turned quickly at the presence of a soldier to her left and struck him with her elbow, dropping him to the floor and then spinning to her right, the tip of her blade threatening another soldier that approached. He leaped backward in surprise and before he could strike again, she had kicked him against a metal pillar and knocked him unconscious.

Out of the corner of her eye, Rosette saw that Lium was not fighting but had moved away, his gaze fixed on a point in the back of the room. She turned toward where he looked and saw a lone man entering the room. Tall and striking, with jet-black hair pulled tightly into a long tail, he walked in with his hands clasped behind his back, as if taking a casual morning stroll. As the man approached, Rosette reached for her emanator lash, and just as she made her move, the man unclasped his hands and held his right one toward her, palm up. An invisible energy burst from his fingertips and instantly reached Rosette's eyes. Shocked by the burning pain, she grunted and fell to her knees, hands grasping her face. After a few moments, she opened her eyelids and found the room just as black as when they had been closed.

Rosette stumbled to her feet and into a defensive posture, striking out in vain at unseen enemies. She heard the tall man moving closer. "The odds of one blind woman, however fierce, defeating six sighted men are desperately slim," he observed, staying out of the way of her wild strikes.

The tall man nodded slightly and the Guardsmen swooped in on Rosette, overwhelming her. They bound her at the wrists and ankles with a metallic cord that tightened as she struggled against it, cutting into her skin. Realizing the hopelessness of her dilemma, Rosette chose to save her energy and cease struggling.

Lium finally stepped forward out of the shadows and addressed the tall man. "Fincher, what will you do with Rosette?"

"That decision is for Corpus to make," Fincher said flatly, clasping his hands once more behind his back. "I want to thank you for delivering the woman and so smoothly executing your orders, Lium. Corpus will be most pleased."

Lium bowed dutifully, and then winced as he saw Rosette writhing on the floor, teeth bared and jaw set tightly, growling in rage. She had never liked Lium, but now she had just cause for pure hatred. The Guardsmen grasped Rosette by the limbs and carried her toward the corridor. Though blind, Rosette managed to sense Lium's proximity and directed her sightless gaze at his eyes. Lium took a step backward and turned away, the image of her eyes, red with fury, indelibly burned into his mind.

Fincher cocked his head and made his way toward Lium. "Now then, for your payment. The rewards of serving the Dark One are many. There is no question that, as promised, you will have your own private territory in Jonquil under my rule, and riches beyond measure." Fincher stepped a few paces away and unlatched the lock on a bejeweled golden chest that sat up against the wall. "Allow me to begin with this modest token of appreciation."

He lifted the ornately carved lid, and Lium saw the chest was filled with shining coins. Fincher reached inside the chest and withdrew a sack. He latched the chest again and brought the sack to Lium, who took it with a bow.

Lium tried to tuck the bag under his arm, but it was too weighty for a casual grip; it would require two hands. He cradled it carefully and felt the coins inside. They were larger than silvers, and if they were of the denomination he suspected, it was more wealth than he had seen in all his years. He took a nervous breath and cleared his throat as Fincher reached into his robe and withdrew a cylindrical metal object that dangled on a chain.

"This key is for the sanlifter nearest to the hangar doors. You will find a bottle of kvass and some dry goods in the cargo hold for your refreshment."

As Lium reached to take the key from Fincher, the heavy bag of coins slipped from his grasp and fell to the floor with a clunk. Lium quickly took it up again and gripped the neck of the sack firmly in his fist. He looked up at Fincher and smiled sheepishly.

Fincher blinked slowly. "According to my calculations, the weight of your treasures will slow your craft, but will not significantly impede flight. You should arrive safely at your home by nightfall."

"Thank you, Fincher," Lium managed. "What duty would you have me do now? Has Corpus any assignment for me?"

"Corpus was here briefly, but has already left for Lapis to initiate the next phase of his plan. You are to return home and await his instructions."

Lium nodded. "If there is nothing else, then I will be on my way."

The two men bowed slightly to each other. Lium turned and walked toward the door.

"Cooperation with Corpus is the only logical choice," Fincher called after him. "Wisdom compels us to submit to the certainty of logic and the elegance of a simple equation."

Lium paused and glanced back at Fincher. Though he did not fully understand the vague mathematical references, he did not want to ask too many questions. He simply nodded, then made his way out the door and to the hangars at the back of the complex.

The cold thin air outside seemed to amplify the creeping numbness that intruded upon Lium's senses. He focused on it in an attempt to extinguish the pain that now burned in his chest as he entered the hangar and found the sanlifter Fincher had prepared for him. The craft did not disappoint; it was one of the best models and looked to be in pristine condition. Lium carefully placed the sack of coins in the cargo box. Even the bag itself was a treasure—the finest silk with embroidery sewn by an obviously skilled artisan, yet somehow none of it seemed payment enough for the sacrifices that had been made. The image of Rosette's normally lovely green eyes blazing red haunted his memory.

Lium inserted the key and pedaled the sanlifter out to the flight yard. The craft rolled smoothly and the wing handles shifted back and locked into place with almost no effort. Lium shook his head and pointed the craft into the wind for takeoff. As he navigated the sanlifter around the front of the palace and toward home, he noticed the raiku, still perched motionless atop their nests. The creatures looked identical to when he had first arrived, save the blood-red streaks on their beaks.

Farewell Esod of Jonquil

Lium finally pulled himself out of his memories, blinking hard to clear the lingering image of Rosette's flaming eyes. He walked the short distance from where he stood to the very edge of the Utara territory, tucking the emanator back in his vest and taking out the lintu that held the remains of Esod's kumu. For a moment, the clouds above parted and the light of the twin suns struck the jeweled surface of the lintu. Crystalline gems of azure and yellow broke the light into sparkling fragments that seemed to float away on the breeze.

The clear air breathed life into Lium, and he finally found the words he had searched for at Esod's passing. "Esod of Jonquil, a

Prime Warrior of golden integrity, whose remarkable gifts were a light and an inspiration to all. Go in peace my teacher, my brother..." Lium paused as tears choked his words, "...my friend."

Lium crumpled to his knees. "And please forgive me for what I have done."

The waves of the storm he'd long held back broke through and finally flooded his heart. He gripped the lintu with trembling fingers and wept in mourning of all that had been lost.

Eventually, Lium stood and wiped his face, composing himself once more as he shut his eyes and recited the ancient incantation:

> *Op mod vinden*
> *Tilbage til sandet*
> *Kumu evige*
> *Aldrig ender*

With those words, he dedicated the essence of Esod to the wind, the suns, and the sand. He held the lintu delicately in his fingertips, as if in reverence of the contents. The wings glinted as the light was absorbed, and he watched as the energy of the suns pulled it from his grasp. The lintu would fly for a time, then release the kumu held within to the wind and sands below. Though a fitting farewell by Jonquilian standards, Lium could not help but feel that something was missing.

Just as he finished the ceremony, Lium sensed a dark presence about him. He looked into the distance, seeing nothing, but then heard his master's voice in his mind:

"Servant Lium, hear my voice. You must seek out the Sankari Sano. The child has returned to Graha and is preparing to travel to the Kanluran territory of Jonquil. You must stay close and report her movements to me. I will send my minions to finish her."

Lium bowed. "Yes, master."

Lium's mind grew quiet once more and he stood up. The time for tears had passed; there was work to be done.

A successful man must risk much in pursuit of his goals, he thought. There were bound to be casualties along the way.

The cold numbness crept into Lium's heart once more and he drew a shallow breath, blinking hard as he focused his eyes south to Kanluran. Remembering his master's words, Lium readied himself for the arrival of the prophesied one.

PART 2

RETURN TO SAMERA

Mila emerged from the doorway and took a few halting steps forward onto the bulwark in front of the castle in the Samera Kingdom. Her white glow reawakened and grew brighter as she got her bearings once more, smoothing back a stray strand of dark hair that had escaped from her ponytail. She looked around and was intrigued by the scene before her. As she had left her slumbering friends in her bedroom on the other side, she had wondered where the doorway would open. Would she wind up in a dark forest again, or would Thornhill be in a completely different area of Verde she'd never seen before? For just an instant, she'd imagined arriving in front of the castle, looking out over Thatch. Though it was now dark and she couldn't be completely sure, it appeared that she had arrived exactly in the place she had pictured in her mind. Mila shrugged, brushing off the curious piece of happenstance as coincidence.

Hearing voices in the distance, she looked down the bulwark in their direction. At regular intervals, soft light seemed to emanate from the very rock of the wall itself. She walked forward to one of the glowing areas and inspected it closely. She hadn't noticed before, but atop each of the lights, a rounded area smooth as glass had been set into the stone. *Maybe they're solar lights,* she thought. Mila turned from the lights and walked in the direction of the voices she'd heard.

Just a few moments later, King Jonas himself rounded a corner and came into view, and Mila was again struck by the splendor of his aura. Vivid tones of green swirled about in an orb many times the size of other Verdeans. Streams of it seemed to pour in from the sky into the top of his head, and ropes of emerald snaked down into the ground below him.

"Jonas!" Mila exclaimed as she ran forward to greet him.

He smiled broadly as he saw the girl approach. "Ah, Mila!"

She threw her arms around him, and Jonas chuckled in his easy way. "It's good to see you, too. Have you just arrived? Did you have any trouble finding me?"

"I just got here a second ago, you were right here."

"And just in time. I am on my way in for a small plate before bedtime. Are you hungry?"

Mila smiled. "I'm always hungry."

Jonas chuckled softly. "Come, we'll dine together then."

The two made their way down the bulwark and entered the castle through a side door. The hallway inside was illuminated with lights similar in appearance to the ones she'd seen outside on the bulwark.

Well, these can't be solar lights—they're inside, she thought.

Mila decided some other power source was at work, one that must have been restored when Jonas returned. She looked down the hall, then turned and looked in the other direction: strangely, there was no sign of Thornhill. She glanced at her wrist; though the watch remained strapped securely to her arm, it seemed that it had not opened the doorway in close proximity to Thornhill as it always had before. She tapped the face of the watch and looked up at Jonas. "Where's Thornhill?"

"He journeys here from Cypress. He has been toiling away there, restoring his chamber garden and helping the townspeople rebuild. He will return to Samera by morning."

Mila slumped a bit in disappointment and Jonas patted her shoulder reassuringly. "Don't worry. I'm certain he will be the first to greet you when you wake."

After a few paces, Mila and Jonas entered a cavernous dining hall with plastered walls and wide windows that, during daylight hours, must have afforded a striking, panoramic view of Thatch and beyond. Mila scooted her Chucks on the smooth stone floor, enjoying how the squeaking sounds seemed to echo endlessly in the spacious room. Long wooden tables with benches divided the room into a grid of aisles and islands. At the back of the hall, a set of double doors stood ajar, and Mila could tell the room beyond was a kitchen. King Jonas went to an enormous table that stood in front of the central window, and as he gestured for Mila to sit, the chair slid backward, as if by magic.

Mila was at first surprised by the movement, but soon remembered that Jonas, like everyone she'd met in Graha, had unique gifts. She plopped down on her chair; the woven material of the seat felt softer than she imagined it would. The uneven tabletop looked to have been hewn from the full length of a massive tree, with the knotted bark still attached along the edges. Mila ran her fingers over the satiny surface worn smooth by the touch of many hands. It smelled faintly of evergreen. Just then, she heard a woman's voice happily humming in the adjoining kitchen.

Jonas smiled and turned toward the voice. "What have you got for me, Madra?"

At once, a round face framed by wavy brown hair popped through a set of heavy drapes that obscured the view into the kitchen. "Oh, we're having two, then?" the woman said, quickly closing the drapes again. She soon emerged from the doors carrying a dark loaf of bread on a wooden tray. Her plump form moved merrily across the room, with long skirt brushing against the floor as she went. Her cheerful green glow swirled playfully in front of her smiling face—Mila thought Madra was one of the happiest people she had ever seen. The woman set the bread tray on the table and smoothed her apron. Mila's eyes widened when she spotted a cup with the pinkish spread she had tried in Cypress some time ago.

Mm, yum!

The woman's eyes flashed brightly as she got a closer look at Mila. "And who might this lovely young lady be?"

"This is Mila, the girl who has been such a help in restoring Verde." Jonas paused, a sweet smile crossing his lips. "The one who saved me from myself. Mila, this is Madra, the golden-voiced Queen of the Galley."

The woman giggled and her cheeks flushed pink. "Oh goodness, well, I'm very pleased to meet you, Mila."

"Good to meet you, too."

"Shall I bring another bowl out for Root?" Madra asked.

Jonas shook his head. "He's gone to bed early tonight...thank goodness."

Madra chuckled knowingly. "All right then, I'll be right out."

The woman scurried back into the kitchen and came out again in nearly the same motion, two green bowls in her hands. Steam rose steadily from them as she set them atop the table. Mila leaned forward and saw they contained some sort of soup or stew.

"Will you join us, Madra?" asked Jonas.

"Hmf! No, no, I've got to get things shut down for the night. You two enjoy."

"Thank you, my dear," said Jonas, eagerly taking a spoonful of soup.

"Very welcome, you just call if you need anything."

The woman rushed away once more and Mila turned her attention to the fragrant bowl in front of her. It smelled of herbs, and she leaned over the bowl and drew a long breath. "Mmm, smells good."

Jonas nodded in agreement, his mouth too full to answer. Mila took her spoon and whirled it around in the soup. Roughly chopped chunks of what looked like vegetables floated up and around in response.

Remember, Mother had often said, *the uneven shape and size of chopped vegetables means the meal is homemade.*

Mila smiled and took up a spoon of soup, blowing on it gently. The broth had a subtle sweetness, and Mila guessed the vegetables were some sort of root. "This is really good," she mumbled.

Jonas smiled at her, his eyes sparkling. "The food is getting better every day. For so long, Madra had little to offer anyone in the way of nourishment. Now that the Land is being restored, she is happy to get back at her creations again. Just yesterday she baked fifteen loaves!"

"Wow, she must have a really big oven!" Mila said. She tore off a section of the loaf Madra had brought out and coated it generously with the spread as Jonas spoke.

"I so look forward to our first Harvest Carnival. In ancient times, all Lands would gather here in Verde to feast and celebrate. Over time, the gathering became limited to only those from Verde. Then there was nothing at all. To bring people from all Lands together again to feast..." Jonas paused in thought, gazing out into the blackness beyond the window.

"It feels weird eating in this huge room when there's only two of us," Mila laughed, dunking the bread into her broth.

Jonas smiled and nodded. "Yes, it is very different from dining here at official mealtimes, but I do love to eat here when the room is empty. It gives me an opportunity to sit quietly and think about the issues that face my kingdom. The empty seats are a constant reminder that in all my decisions, the people of Verde must be considered. It is my duty as king."

"I hope our president does the same thing as you," Mila said, slurping a hot spoonful of broth.

A few minutes later, Mila and Jonas both had reached the bottom of their bowls. Mila nibbled on the last scrap of her bread and brushed the crumbs neatly into a pile.

"Have you had enough to eat?" Jonas asked.

"Yeah, that was a good midnight snack."

"Then it would be wise for both of us to go to bed. You have a big day tomorrow with Thornhill. Come, I'll show you to your chambers."

Jonas got up from the table and started away, then glanced back at the mess they'd left. Jonas closed his eyes. A burst of grassy green flushed his aura and flowed out from his hands, engulfing the tabletop. As if touched by invisible hands, the empty bowls stacked themselves atop the bread tray as it lifted into the air, hovering just before them. Jonas turned his focus and the tray floated toward the galley.

"Madra, eyes peeled, my dear!" Jonas called.

Mila crossed her arms and smiled, reminding herself once more that people did things a little differently in Verde.

The two left the dining hall and Mila followed Jonas up a winding stairwell to the second floor. Light fixtures similar to those she'd seen below gently lit the hallway, and Mila noticed that Jonas' glow appeared especially bright in the space. Jonas stopped a few doors down, glancing into the room as he opened the door. "Here we are," he said, gesturing for Mila to enter.

Mila stepped inside and saw a substantial bed with four hefty posts that stretched from floor to ceiling. A colorful woven rug covered most of the stone floor, and a straight back chair sat in the corner by the window.

"If you need anything, just call. Madra's chambers are just down the hall. Thornhill will come to wake you in the morning. Sleep well, Mila."

"Goodnight, Jonas," she said as he slipped the door shut. Mila walked further into the room and sighed. The space already felt comfortable, almost like it had always been her room. Returning to Graha this time had felt a little like coming home. Mila went to the big bed and drew back the covers, pressing her hands into the overstuffed mattress. It yielded easily, and her hands sank into what felt like a warm cloud. She eagerly kicked off her shoes and tossed her hoodie on the chair in the corner. She pulled the band off her ponytail, her dark hair falling just above her shoulders, and slipped the band around her wrist for safekeeping. As she crawled under the blankets, she felt nearly as comfortable in this strange bed as she did in her own.

But though the bed felt heavenly, a certain purring spot of warmth was noticeably missing: Santo would not be there to snuggle with her this night. Mila sighed again and closed her eyes. Soothed by the luxurious bed and nourished by the warm soup in her belly, she quickly drifted off to sleep.

Familiar Faces

"Wake up, child."

The voice came from a foggy place, and Mila wondered if it had been part of a dream. She blinked a few times and listened for it once more.

"Come now, the suns are rising."

Mila recognized the familiar voice and pulled the covers away from her face. "Thornhill!" she croaked.

"Good morning, Mila! It's good to see you again. I am sorry I wasn't able to meet you when you first arrived, but I understand

Jonas took good care of you in my absence."

Mila nodded slowly, one eye still shut. "We had soup."

"Well, if you've still got your appetite, there's a morning meal to be had."

Mila rubbed her eyes and smiled, her glow gently pulsing.

"The wash room is just one door down from here. You may use it and then come down to the dining hall when you are ready. Do you remember where it is?"

"Yeah, I remember."

"Good. Bring all of your things with you when you come down; we will depart shortly for Sukai."

Mila nodded, eyes now fully opened. "Understood."

After refreshing herself and changing her clothes, Mila strapped on her backpack and found the dining hall once more. It looked even more spacious in the light, and the view outside the wide windows was nothing short of breathtaking. The twin suns rising over the Harita forest beyond the valley brought the entire landscape to life with a thousand shades of green.

King Jonas and Thornhill sat at the same table where she'd enjoyed her soup the night before.

Jonas turned in her direction as she approached. "Good morning, Mila. Did you sleep well?"

"Yeah, that bed was awesome!"

"You will not often sleep in a bed so fine as that one," Thornhill chuckled, motioning to the chair next to him. "Come, sit and have something to eat."

Mila obliged and the three waited for their first meal of the day. Within a few minutes, a fair-haired boy that appeared to be Mila's age came from the galley, pushing a shelved cart. The lower shelves held dishes loaded with food, and on top sat a silver kettle and three matching cups.

"Ah, thank you, Anther, and please tell your mother she is welcome to join us, as you are." Jonas said.

Anther smiled and bowed. "Yes, King, I'll tell her."

The boy hurried back into the galley and Jonas shook his head. "I don't know why I bother to offer. There will be no prying Madra out of that galley for quite some time."

Thornhill laughed and poured hot liquid from the kettle into the cups. He passed one to Mila, then took one for himself and another for Jonas.

"This is arbata, and a nice hot cup is perfect for mornings such as this. I am so thankful it grows freely once again in the fields," Thornhill said, lifting his cup to Jonas.

Mila took up her cup and carefully swirled the pale green liquid. She gingerly took a sip; it tasted something like the tea that she had so often enjoyed in the Chinese restaurant her family frequented. In that moment, she wished she had a fortune cookie to dunk.

"I am grateful not only for arbata, but also for this bounty," Jonas added, lowering his head in gratitude.

Mila smiled and rubbed her belly. "Me too, I'm really hungry!"

Thornhill shook his head and polished a turryn against his jacket. "Certainly nothing wrong with your appetite."

As the three enjoyed their meal, Mila looked outside. Below them, the town of Thatch was waking up for the day. She could sense a feeling of revitalized hope and optimism that tentatively bubbled up from the places where such things had been repressed for an age. Before long, the town bustled with people busily cleaning and clearing, socializing and laughing. A group had gathered on a street corner near the edge of town to play music and dance. The melody drifted up the hill and into the castle, just barely audible through the thick window glass. The dreary brown-gray veil of silence that had been draped over the town had lifted, and Thatch was again buzzing with color and activity. In fact, every part of Verde within view—the valley, the Harita forest on the hilltop, and the meadows to the south—glowed with renewed life. When she'd left a few weeks before, the Land had been blushed with spring; now it blossomed into the fullness of summer.

"It looks even prettier than when I left. All the colors are brighter and it looks like flowers are growing everywhere!" Mila said, pointing out the window. The light from outside struck the face of her watch and reflected into her eyes, reminding her of a question. "Thornhill, when I crossed over this time, I ended up here at the castle, not where you were. I think my watch might be broken or something."

"Hmm, I hadn't thought about that," Thornhill replied, stroking his beard. "There may be an important reason why that happened, child. Let us not assume that something is broken."

Mila nodded thoughtfully and watched once more as the morning light danced off the face of the watch.

The three soon finished their meals and walked out onto the bulwark to observe the sunrise unobstructed. The morning air was crisp and cool, and Mila briskly rubbed her arms to warm them. Thornhill took notice. "Are you too chilled, Mila?"

She shook her head. "Once the sun comes up—I mean, the *suns* come up higher, I'll be fine."

Thornhill smiled and turned his attention to the town in the valley below them.

"We've made progress since you left us. Much of the plantlife has been restored, and the houses and halls are being rebuilt. We've even managed, in most places, to restore our power system. Most of the workings of it are below ground, so Corpus simply disregarded it."

"You have some kind of underground powerplant?" Mila asked.

Thornhill lifted a brow, not entirely understanding the inquiry. "Well, child, did you notice the lights throughout the castle and on the bulwark here last night?"

"Yeah, I saw them. Are they solar lights? You know, sun power?"

Thornhill nodded. "Many of the outdoor fixtures are powered by the light of the suns. In fact, the energy of the suns is one of our primary power sources here on Graha. The other, as I mentioned, is underground." Thornhill pointed to a hill just outside the town of Thatch that seemed to stand out from the surrounding landscape. Though covered with the same lush grasses as the rest of the meadow, it simply looked out of place. "Do you see that mound there?"

Mila nodded. "Yeah, I see it."

"That is an amplifier. It picks up the subtle energy of the planet, amplifies it, and then transmits it through the ground to other amplifiers in the surrounding areas. Each town can then tap into the power coming from these amplifiers to run lights or power devices. Since the energy source is the very kumu of the planet itself, it never runs dry."

Mila raised her eyebrows and nodded approvingly. "We sure

could use some of those things on Earth."

"It's not a perfect system," Thornhill cautioned. "But then, nothing ever is."

"That is true, my friend," Jonas agreed. "Things are never perfect, but I am most pleased with the work you have done in Cypress. It is a world away from the ruin it was a short time ago."

"Ah, Cypress. Mila, you would barely recognize it! It was the first town that Jonas chose to regenerate after you helped bring him back to Graha. It is returning quickly to its former regal bearing."

Jonas turned to Mila. "I chose to begin with Cypress because it is inhabited by citizens who wish to work closely with me for the good of Verde. Many of my most trusted and faithful constituents call Cypress home." Jonas suddenly looked up and smiled, his aura swirling energetically. "Here are some of them now."

Mila turned to see Woodson and Bract approaching. Young Root followed them, his tiny hand engulfed in Bract's. Upon seeing Mila, Root broke away and bounced toward her. "Mila!"

"Ah, I see Master Root is finally out of bed and has found some new friends," Jonas laughed.

The excited child hugged Mila wildly, hopping up and down on his toes. In that moment of bubbly exuberance, he reminded her of Madison.

"Hi, Root!" Mila smiled.

"Good morning, Jonas!" Root said, waving to his caretaker. Then, as quickly as he'd arrived, he was off again, skipping across the bulwark and throwing his hands joyfully into the air. His blue-green aura pulsed and expanded as he jumped and played. Though on the surface he seemed to be a typical child, Mila could sense there was something more to him.

Just then, Mila heard Jonas' voice in her head, *Root is very gifted indeed, Mila. In fact, he will begin his teachings now instead of at the age of eleven. Already he is displaying great power, and he needs guidance to learn to control it.*

Mila smiled up at Jonas and then quickly turned at the sound of giddy laughter. Root had found some winged creature and it flitted about his face, teasing him.

"Ha-ha!" he laughed, flinching as its delicate wings brushed his skin.

Mila laughed along with him and then paused, as if remembering a thing long forgotten. "So, where is Aux?"

"Aux is in his home Land of Crimson," Thornhill replied. "He is spreading word of the prophecy and our adventures together, and how you have helped us." He grinned playfully. "Mila, you are becoming quite famous."

Mila's eyes widened in disbelief. Famous was the last thing she ever imagined she would be.

Thornhill continued, "Having seen the Sankari Sano with his own eyes, Aux has charged himself with the difficult task of convincing his fellow Crimsonites that the prophecy is true."

Mila furrowed her brow as she remembered that some people in Graha seemed to believe she was much more important than she felt. She tilted her head to the side and felt her cheeks grow warm. "And what about...Lium?"

Thornhill shook his head, his aura dimming. "Both Lium and Esod have been missing since the ambush at Thatch." He scratched his beard in concern. "Nor do we know the whereabouts of Rosette."

Mila was then startled by a sudden wave of uncomfortable feelings. Sorrow and longing colored the currents, and she immediately recognized Jonas as the source. She sensed that though he was truly happy with the rebirth of Verde, he remained burdened with worry over Rosette and missed her terribly. She then heard his voice in her mind once more.

She is my heart, Mila. I can never return to joy until that place within me is filled again.

Mila lowered her head and nodded respectfully.

"I must continue preparing for our journey to Jonquil. I need to gather some more supplies before we depart. Friends, I shall return." Thornhill said.

Jonas patted him on the shoulder and Thornhill walked away, disappearing down a stairwell. Mila watched as he went, but was soon distracted by shadows that moved swiftly over the bulwark. She looked up and saw the familiar forms of three hoverdales—two full-sized and one smaller—overhead. She squinted and cocked her head. "Is that..."

"Botan!" Jonas called, holding up a hand.

Mila smiled broadly and shielded her eyes, watching as the

creatures circled and came in for a landing nearby. She could now see Botan atop the largest hoverdale, waving his arm. As the creatures came to rest, Botan dismounted, approaching Jonas.

"Jonas, my king," he said, bowing slightly.

Jonas laughed, reaching forward to shake Botan's hand. "I see you've recruited the hoverdales to help with the trip to Sukai."

"Yes, with our departure delayed as it has been, travel on the hoof would have taken much too long. Time is running short, and the hoverdales were happy to help," Botan smiled, turning to gesture to Eo. "The youngster was particularly excited about the mission."

Mila ran up to Eo and threw her arms around his neck, laughing aloud. "Eo! I didn't think I'd ever see you again!"

At first, the animal was surprised by Mila's bold gesture; the girl seemed to be gaining confidence. He quickly relaxed, though, and shared with Mila telepathically, *My home is so much better now that our king is back. All the plants are growing again, and there's lots of food to eat! Thanks for helping us.*

"Sure, no problem," Mila casually replied.

Jonas and Botan approached Mila and Eo. "I see you've found your old friend, Mila," said Botan. "It appears he is just as happy to see you as you are to see him."

Eo lowered his head and crouched down before Mila, purring loudly.

Botan laughed. "I think he's ready to leave for Sukai right now!"

Mila smiled at Botan. His wavy brown hair seemed a bit longer than it had the last time she'd seen him. The ever-busy Thornhill rejoined the group, having gathered the necessary supplies for the trip. He brushed his hands together and exhaled heavily. "All has been prepared, and we mustn't delay any longer than necessary. Every hour that passes may be a danger to Queen Zehn and Rosette."

Jonas agreed, though a pained expression briefly took the place of his smile. Mila looked up at him in concern, and soon heard his voice in her mind.

Because Rosette is a part of Verde, I can feel that she yet lives, but there is much danger surrounding her and us all. Do take care, and as soon as you know anything, please tell me.

Mila stood a bit straighter and nodded. *I promise.*

Botan approached Ganymeade and Thornhill went to Cyliene. Both hoverdales willingly stooped. Thornhill pulled himself into position on Cyliene's back, but before Botan could mount Mila tapped him on the arm, having promised to relay a message. "Botan? Ganymeade wants to tell you he's glad you picked him. He says that carrying Aux was the hardest thing he's ever done, but that it made him stronger, and now he's the strongest hoverdale alive."

Botan smiled and patted Ganymeade on the shoulder. The animal arched his neck, purring in gratitude. "Ah, you are most welcome, my friend. Let's mount up and get going. We've a long day ahead of us."

Mila sighed and ran her fingers along the grooves of the scales that covered Eo's shoulder, wondering what lay ahead.

A Golden Child

Golden rays struck the stones of the bulwark as the suns climbed higher in the eastern sky. Soon, three shadows interrupted the light as the hoverdales took to the air once more. With three powerful strides, Eo had lifted his body from the ground, and the animals sailed over the edge of the wall. The ground fell away as they cleared the hill and soared over the town of Thatch below, swift as arrows. As they passed, a few of the townspeople looked up in surprise, and Mila was tempted to let go, just for a moment, to wave. She soon thought better of it, realizing a fall from such a height would certainly be her undoing. Instead, she carefully straightened her backpack with her elbow and held on to Eo's neck feathers.

The hoverdales glided past the edge of town and then swooped down, picking up speed as they skimmed low over the ground. As the group traveled south, closely following the lay of the valley, Mila observed the flourishing Land below, so different from when she'd last seen it that she barely recognized the vista. The surrounding forests guarded by majestic trees, the meadows thick with grasses and flowers...all glowed with rejuvenation.

As Mila focused on the beauty of the Land, she began to hear the thoughts of the people of Verde, as she had when she first crossed into Graha. The collective message she'd heard then had been of fear and hopelessness, with a gray sadness haunting the background of every thought. But now the heart of the Land radiated hope, and the minds of the people were filled with joyful noise.

Through the chorus, one man's thoughts seemed to stand out from the rest. Excitement colored his tone in anticipation of some positive thing to come. Mila soon figured out the voice was of Thornhill, his close proximity ensuring his thoughts came through loud and clear. She determined that much of his anticipation was due to seeing Salvitor. Having spent so many lonely years in hiding, Thornhill was most ready to reunite with long-lost friends, especially his dear Sal. Their friendship had been one forged from early childhood and nurtured by commonalities that ran deep in both men. Mila was intensely curious; she'd heard so much about this Salvitor, and even used some of the devices that he'd created. She wanted to know more.

She took a few deep breaths and focused on Thornhill. His white hair swirled behind him, and soon she found herself being pulled into Thornhill's memory, and the story of Salvitor.

Salvitor was born far below Jonquil, in the dunes of Tenpi. A desert birth, forbidden and rare, was one no Jonquilian would choose. An expectant mother would never willingly descend at such a sacred time as childbirth, unless there were secrets to be kept. And so Salvitor's mother bundled her shame in scraps of silk and set it under the roots of a tree, leaving the child to an unknown fate in the harsh elements. Part of her wished for someone or something to rescue him—he was, after all, only an innocent babe. But there would be no way for her to raise this child as her own, having been born of such circumstances.

High above the scene, near the edge of the Kanluran territory, Miriam of Jonquil sat outside her home in meditation. She could not seem to quiet her mind this day, and her eyes refused to relax and close. Annoyed, she sighed and gazed out over the desert below, still cloaked in pre-dawn darkness.

Miriam narrowed her eyes and blinked; something seemed to stir in the dunes, and she could detect just a hint of faint light moving through the dim. Miriam quickly shut her eyes in denial. She was only imagining things. No sane Jonquilian would descend to the desert just before sunrise, when the raiku were most active. She breathed deeply and again attempted to hush the chatter in her mind, but her eyes popped open once more. The faintest cry drifted on the wind, and though she could not say whether she'd actually heard it or simply sensed it, she was certain something was out there.

Soon, the lesser sun crested the horizon and rays of gentle blue washed over the dunes. For Miriam, the dawn brought no solace. Troubled by the things she'd seen and heard, she soon went to her partner, Etu. After a long discussion and a bit of coercing, Etu reluctantly gave in; they would investigate the place where she'd detected the strange lights and sounds.

The sanlifter bumped to a stop at the crest of a dune, and Miriam and Etu hauled themselves out onto the sand. The wind whipped around them and Miriam pulled her silks in around her face to shield her eyes from the grit. She glanced around worriedly, sensing some manner of trouble nearby. Wringing her hands, she walked up and over the crest and down to a banjam tree that huddled at the foot of the dune, the exposed roots forming a twisted mass that clung to the shifting sand. As Miriam drew closer, she saw a section of violet fabric tucked among the roots, moving in a way that could not have been caused by the wind. She dashed forward, at once curious and terrified, and knelt in the sand under the banjam tree. Her eyes filled with tears and her mouth fell open when she finally saw what had been left there in the night—a tiny baby boy. "My stars. Etu!"

Her partner ran to her and was stopped dead when he saw what she'd found.

"He's just been born," she cried, taking the baby into her arms.

Etu shook his head slowly in disbelief. "Who would have done such a thing?"

"I don't know, but we must bring him home and get some nourishment into him." Her voice quivered, and a tear drifted down her cheek. "Whoever he is, he doesn't deserve to die like this."

And so Miriam and Etu took in the child and named him Salvitor. By his bright golden aura, it became apparent he was truly a child of Jonquil, but something about him did not fit. His eyes lacked the gentle slant most Jonquilians possessed, and his sandy brown hair was quite unlike the jet black or pale blond normally seen on those people. Though Miriam and Etu raised the child in the traditional Jonquilian ways, he always seemed a stranger in his own Land.

In childhood, Salvitor was perpetually fascinated by mechanics and engineering. Rather than playing with his toys, he loved nothing better than to take them apart and put them together again, ever curious about their inner workings. As Salvitor reached the Turning Age of eleven, he found that he was able not only to understand how mechanical devices worked, but also to remake them into more than what they had been originally. He discovered he could channel kumu, the universal source energy, and use it as fuel for his mechanical devices. His gift, at its core, was his deep understanding of the formless energy, and how to combine it with mechanical devices in the realm of form. Though each citizen of Graha was able to use kumu in his or her own way, young Salvitor was able to harness and control astonishing amounts of it, incorporating and storing it in physical matter. His gifts were nothing short of remarkable.

Like all children reaching the Turning Age, Salvitor was due to be sent off to Development where he would learn about the beginnings of Graha, the Founding Four, and the appropriate use of kumu and his own personal gifts. Salvitor, true to form, expressed a somewhat unusual desire to travel to Verde for his education. Being the heart of all the Lands, Verde boasted the finest Development in Graha, and Salvitor wanted to study there for the best and broadest education. Though it was merely a choice he made for his own betterment, it fueled rumors that he had been born a mixed breed, with one parent from Verde and the other from Jonquil. After all, he did not look like other Jonquilians, and sideways glances had oft been cast his way. Salvitor, though, could not understand why such a fuss was made over his origins. Was he not of Graha, like every other child?

Eventually, Salvitor was granted permission to study in Verde. Once there, he thrived and excelled in every aspect of his studies, at times even beyond the attending Magister's ability to understand. Sahler, a High Magister of Verde, soon took notice of the brilliant young Salvitor. Recognizing the endless potential of his gifts, he took Salvitor under his wing to ensure he received the best chance to attain his highest development. While under Sahler's tutelage, Salvitor met another gifted young man named Thornhill. Though they had been born in different Lands, the two became the best of friends.

In their years together in Development, Salvitor and Thornhill learned many things that children of Graha must know— the workings of the natural systems of the planet, how the Founding Four, at the age of eleven, created the Lands, and how the source energy, kumu, would serve their every need once they mastered it.

Every student in Development learned many lessons beyond the traditional written curriculum. Salvitor and Thornhill, ever curious and thirsty for understanding, soon learned of the alleged existence of mystical doorways. Rumors abounded that, in random places throughout the planet, a doorway opened each time the clock turned 11:11. It was said these doorways led to another realm of pain and tribulation, and all who were drawn in through the openings would be doomed, lost to its clutches forever. The rumor of the doorways intrigued both Salvitor and Thornhill, but Salvitor became completely fascinated. He continued to pursue the mystery of the doorways, and later in life he became consumed in their study.

A sudden blast of hot, dry air shook Mila from the visions in Thornhill's mind. She looked around and saw that the formerly green landscape had been replaced by sand and scrubby plants. She glanced over at Thornhill, and he returned her gaze with a wink and a tilt of his head. Mila wondered at first what his gesture had meant, but soon realized he had known she was eavesdropping. She smiled sheepishly at him and held fast to Eo as the hoverdales slowed and prepared to land.

Thornhill, Mila, and Botan bid the hoverdales goodbye and approached the town of Sukai on foot. Humble cottages stood along a road that moved in an arc around the main square, and Mila could see tall buildings with wide doors beyond. Sparse vegetation dotted the dry ground and only a few people milled about, with no discernible sense of urgency or purpose. Sukai seemed perched at the edge of a cliff, the golden sand of the Tenpi desert stretching endlessly beyond. Though the sky directly above was starkly blue, Mila could make out cloud formations hovering in the distance.

The three made the short walk to the tavern at the edge of town, where Thornhill stopped and turned to Mila. "This is the town of Sukai. In days past, when the segregation of the Lands had just begun, the Prime Advisors to the royalty would come to meet here to discuss the growing troubles of the Lands. It was the ideal meeting place; the townspeople tend to keep to themselves, and the tavern has a private meeting room, very well protected. Since the kings and queens could not leave their Lands, they entrusted this task to their Prime Advisors. For Jonas, it was I, for Queen Zehn it was Salvitor, Bobbin spoke for Queen Helena, and for Mason..." Thornhill's eyes flicked left, then right. "For Mason, another," he said dismissively, obviously withholding something.

Mila raised an eyebrow, but Thornhill turned and moved forward. The three stepped inside the tavern, shaking the sand from their feet onto the mat by the door. The old tender looked up from counting his coins and dropped five silvers in surprise. His aura swirled and his eyes lit up when he recognized the white-haired man. "Well, if it isn't Thornhill of Verde!"

"Corso, my old friend," Thornhill said, smiling warmly. "It's good to see you again. This is Botan—"

"Oh, right, right, I remember you, Botan, been a while," Corso interrupted. "Where's your big friend?"

"Aux has returned to Crimson, so we have a smaller friend with us in his stead," Botan motioned to Mila. "This young lady is Mila. She has come to help us in our quest to rebuild."

"Mila...*Mila*? Jonas' Mila?" Corso said in surprise. "Goodness, it's an honor to meet you."

He limped around the corner and shook Mila's hand. "I'm not sure what you did, but I can see changes. Since King Jonas returned, it's a little nicer here. Sukai has never been paradise, but things are getting better."

Mila smiled. "You're welcome."

With a great deal of effort, Corso climbed atop a stool and motioned for Thornhill and Botan to join him. As the men talked, Mila wandered off to a corner of the room near the shelf wall that led to the private room upstairs. She took note of the trinkets on the shelves. There was a green glass bottle with a decorative metal collar, a carved wooden box, and a figurine of a woman hewn from smooth white stone.

Mila turned from shelves and noticed a marking that had been burned into the leg of a nearby table. She went to it and crouched down, her eyes widening as she saw that it was the eleven symbol now so familiar to her. She remembered seeing it on the adoption letter her mother had shown her, and on the turryn tree she had revived when she had last been through Verde on the hoverdales. It was the very same symbol that was etched on the back of her watch. Thornhill had told her it symbolized unity, but she could not piece together the true meaning. Mila briefly closed her eyes and received a brief vision of young Salvitor creating the symbol, then destroying it in defeat.

"Mila, child, we must find a sanlifter."

The voice broke her from her thoughts and she glanced over at Thornhill, who held out his hand to her. She rejoined the group as they made their way to the hangars.

The three followed Corso through a windswept field and into the hangars, dusty metal domes with wide, rolling doors. As they approached the doors, Corso paused to catch his breath, running a hand through his sparse gray hair. "Normally, I would recommend that you hire Kazel fly you in to Jonquil. Utara territory is more dangerous now than ever. But nobody's seen him for some time... probably passed out in a flagon of kvass somewhere." Corso let out a raspy laugh, his dark green aura flashing as he slid open the door and stepped inside.

"I have piloted a sanlifter before, and I know to take special care to avoid the debris fields. I plan to fly along the western edge of the territory and to approach Kanluran from above," Botan replied.

Corso nodded, and the four then began weaving through aisles of flyers. Corso shuffled ahead of them, and soon stopped near the middle of the room. "Ah!" he said, rapping his fist against the body of a nearby sanlifter. "This is the one you want, four seats, new wheels, and not so much as a scratch on the glass dome."

Botan stepped forward to inspect the craft, and after a few minutes of testing levers and checking locks, he nodded approvingly. "It's a good craft, worth the price. We'll take it," he said, shaking Corso's hand.

After making the transaction, the three men then pushed the craft out of the hangar and into the sunlight. Mila followed close behind, a bit nervous about what the rest of the journey would bring.

Treacherous Winds

Mila sat in the third seat of the sanlifter, squinting at the wind that blasted across the runway and pelted her face with grains of sand. To her, the sanlifter seemed rudimentary at best: it had no bathrooms or in-flight movies to watch, and only a simple domed glass hatch to protect their heads from wind and rain. But she trusted Botan and Thornhill to keep her as safe as possible, and if this was the next step of the quest, she would take it. The two men pushed the sanlifter into place at the start of the runway and Thornhill carefully crawled into the second seat. Botan reached into the cabin and pulled back the levers, and the sanlifter's wings extended out.

Mila gazed out over the vast sea of dunes that seemed to stretch endlessly to the horizon. Far in the distance, a section of metal tore away from the Utara disc and fell to the sands below. Mila shook her head. "Gosh, how can anything be alive in there? It just looks like a big empty desert and some junk."

"Most of Jonquil is up, not down," Thornhill replied, pointing to the clouds. "But there are some creatures that do make their homes in the sands of Tenpi."

"That's right," Botan cut in. "The ocnityl live below the sand throughout the northern territories of Jonquil. They will swallow almost anything, so we have to be careful not to fly in too low, lest we rouse one of them."

Mila gulped. There always seemed to be some hungry thing waiting to eat her. "So, the octo-whatever is big enough to eat us?"

Botan frowned. "And then some."

Mila sighed and buckled her lap belt as Botan hopped into the pilot's seat and prepared for takeoff. He began pedaling, and the sanlifter crept unenthusiastically forward in response, the edge of the cliff looming ever closer with each turn of the wheels. Mila leaned over and looked past Botan and Thornhill at the shortening runway before them, fearing they would simply plummet to the bottom far below once they came to the end of it.

Strong winds rushed up the face of the cliffs, and just as the sanlifter's wheels came to the edge, the craft was instantly lifted into the air. Botan's aura flashed brightly as he adjusted the yoke, skillfully tilting the wings to maximize lift. Mila looked down, but within moments, they had risen high above the tavern, yet had not moved forward very much. Soon, the propulsion system gathered enough kinetic and solar energy to begin pushing the craft along, and the sanlifter picked up airspeed, moving onward and upward.

Mila smiled in relief as the town of Sukai began to disappear into the background. Thanks to Botan's skill, the sanlifter had gained enough speed and altitude to avoid rousing the hungry ocnityl waiting in the sands below.

Not long after departing Sukai, Mila caught her first glimpse of Utara, the northernmost territory of Jonquil. From below, she could see vast spiral cloud formations that cradled massive metal discs. Though the primary disc occupied most of her field of vision, the swirling pattern of the layout of discs and clouds was still evident. Mila craned her neck for a better view and was struck by recognition: something about the formation seemed vaguely familiar. Mila focused on Botan, watching intense flashes of emerald green brighten his glow. He seemed to be in a state of high concentration as he carefully guided the sanlifter up and into the west.

"I am taking us into the shore stream current. It will carry us south along the western shore of Jonquil. When we get closer to Kanluran, you may even be able to see the Western Sea," Botan said, pointing.

Mila looked out to where he pointed, but she could see only sand and empty sky. Faced with such a blank and desolate slate, her mind began drawing images of what the inhabited places of Jonquil must be like. She imagined stately homes and lush gardens thick with exotic plants. Perhaps there were rivers that flowed from some magic source and tumbled over the edge of the discs in magnificent waterfalls. Had the people somehow managed to bring animals up into the city in the sky? What would they eat?

* * *

Some time later, Mila was quite literally shaken from her thoughts as they approached Kanluran. Turbulence suddenly struck the sanlifter, tossing it violently about in the air. A powerful downdraft forced the craft to lose much of the precious altitude it had gained—and in Jonquil, altitude was everything, for the lower winds were unpredictable and rarely worked in a pilot's favor. Mila looked up at Botan in alarm. His glow pulsed rapidly as he shook his head and tightly gripped the yoke.

"Hold on, I've got to get us higher!"

Mila grasped the handles on the sides of her seat. His aura swirled energetically, and though he fought valiantly to climb once more, the turbulence had forced them too far down. They approached Kanluran from below instead of above, and would be flying directly into the path of any falling debris. Botan narrowed his eyes and watched carefully for threats, his brow moist with sweat. The sanlifter dipped and tilted on the air currents as the pilot fought for altitude and control.

Botan flinched as a flash of pale gold crashed toward them. "Cover your heads!" he shouted.

At once, a storm of metal began cascading all around them, falling from Kanluran like deathly rain. Botan used his gifts to navigate the craft into safe places in amid the fallout, but even he could not steer clear of it all. The sanlifter soon took a crippling hit to her port side, metal tearing through the wing and leaving half of it dangling.

"Ah!" Botan yelled, fighting to regain control. He pulled back on the yoke, wrestling the craft higher, involuntarily banking hard at the same time due to the wing damage. The injured wing tore loose and slammed into the rear of the craft, cutting through the fuselage and shattering the glass dome. Mila screamed as crystal fragments rained down. The wind howled in her ears.

The sanlifter dove erratically and the rear half of the craft waggled. They were very close to the edge of the disc, and Mila prayed that Botan would be able to clear the jagged rocks at the border. The broken sanlifter eased higher in the air, and though Mila could just see the flight yard ahead, she squeezed shut her eyes in dismay. They were not going to make it to the runway.

The sanlifter's nose pitched sharply down, and the craft smashed into the rock and metal at the edge of the disc. The awful grinding pierced Mila's eardrums and sent sparks flying all around them. Mila heard something snap and break loose, then felt herself slide backward as the craft slammed to a stop.

As the mist cleared from around the wreck site, Botan looked back in horror to see that though the front half of the craft had lodged somewhat securely in a rocky outcropping, the tail section and Mila dangled precariously over the edge. The two thin metal cables that held it in place hummed as tension forced them closer to snapping.

Mila quickly unfastened her lap belt. "Help! Get me out of here!" she screamed, reaching desperately toward the severed front half of the craft.

Botan and Thornhill leapt from their seats and into action. With Thornhill holding fast to the back of his jacket, Botan thrust his hand over the edge, carefully balancing himself on the craggy rocks. "Reach for my hand, hurry!"

Mila stretched her fingers to the point where it seemed they would pop from their sockets, but Botan's hand was just out of reach. "I can't reach!" she cried.

Botan frowned, a flash of hot panic flushing his body. There were no plants around for Thornhill to call on, and no way for him to use his gifts to help her. They could only watch helplessly as one of the cables snapped and the tail section of the sanlifter shifted ominously to one side.

Mila shrieked.

The craft began to swing and roll, and the one remaining cable steadily frayed where it scraped along the rocks. Mila's heart pounded so hard that she could feel it banging against her ribs. Her hands trembled as she clung to her seat, pushing herself up once more after having been dislodged by the sudden movement. Thin threads of wire began to unravel as popping sounds indicated the last cable was giving way. Botan grasped the jagged metal where the tail section had sheared away, pulling at it with all his strength in a futile attempt to lift Mila to safety, deeply cutting his hands in the process.

"Thornhill! I can't get to her."

Thornhill looked around the crash site in desperate hope of finding someone to help. Movement in the mist caught his attention. A tall, lean figure raced toward him, a coil of rope in one hand. Thornhill blinked in disbelief when a moment later he recognized the man. It was Lium, and his aura expanded in flashing waves of yellow as he approached.

"Lium!" Thornhill shouted. "Quickly!"

The fraying cable snapped, and the tail of the sanlifter plummeted toward the sands far below. Mila screamed, and the call cut through Lium's ears like a hot blade. Having seen the events of the crash from where he'd been standing a few moments before, Lium knew exactly what needed to be done. In one deft motion, he took the end of his rope and secured a slipknot to the undamaged wing of the craft. He dove over the edge and down through the thick clouds, snatching Mila from the falling wreckage just moments before she would have fallen out of reach. He held her tightly with one arm, the end of the rope clutched in his other hand as they swung out over the sea of dunes below.

"Gotcha," he said casually.

Mila clung to her savior, panting, still too panicked to identify him. A few moments later she gathered herself enough to recognize Lium, and she was overcome with a wave of relief and admiration.

"Hold onto my back so I can climb back up," Lium said.

Mila was unsure of the best way to hold on, so she positioned herself like she had when her father gave her piggyback rides. She buried her face in Lium's blond locks and squeezed her eyes shut, terrified by the dizzying height at which they dangled. They hung just below the clouds, and Mila had made the mistake of looking down.

Steadily, Lium began to haul them up, hand over hand, his biceps straining against the load. He could feel a subtle warmth flowing through his body. It was more than just the surge of adrenaline, more than the physical demand of pulling such their combined weight up a rope. It felt like a strength that had long since escaped him, and his ribs seemed to release a portion of the stiffness that had cursed him for a time.

Lium climbed through the coolness of the cloud bank and emerged to the sight of a very relieved Thornhill and Botan looking down upon them. The two men began hauling Lium and Mila up the side, and much to everyone's relief, both were soon safely on solid ground. As Mila let go of him, Lium felt a tingling over his entire body, and had to fight a sudden and most powerful urge to burst out laughing. Instead, he gave Thornhill and Botan a casual nod. "Fancy meeting you gentlemen here."

"Haha, Lium!" Botan laughed, vigorously shaking Lium's hand.

"Ah, careful now," Lium hissed, withdrawing his rope-burned palm.

Botan felt a twinge of pain and realized his own hands were badly cut. He took out some cloth from the remains of the sanlifter cargo box and began wrapping his wounds.

"Oh, that nearly ended me," Thornhill gasped, embracing Mila.

"Thought we were going to lose you, Mila," Botan said. "Thank stars for Lium, who came out of *nowhere!*"

Lium bowed slightly and dabbed the blood from his raw palms, noticing that, curiously, his body still tingled with warmth.

Mila finally gathered herself enough to speak. "Oh my gosh, thank you, you saved my life!" She embraced the one whom she now had all the more reason to admire.

"Oh, let's not make a fuss over it. I was just in the right place at the right time," Lium replied, patting Mila on the head.

Thornhill then looked at the girl and noticed that her glow seemed especially bright, and swirls of it curled around Lium like serpents in play. The light from her smile seemed to merge with that from her eyes, and sparks flickered along the borders of her aura. She was beaming.

Thornhill cleared his throat. "Tell me, Lium, how was it that you were able to escape the ambush in Thatch?"

A flash of brown muddied Lium's glow as he paused, carefully considering his response.

"Esod and I were badly beaten by a gang of six men. At some

point I fell unconscious, and I don't remember much until some time later, when I awakened. I had been left for dead and so had Esod, who lay close by." Lium swallowed hard. "Unfortunately, he was..."

"Was what?" Botan shot back.

"Dead. Esod is dead."

Botan's mouth fell open. "No..."

Lium's voice faltered as he continued. "I'm afraid it's true. The greatest warrior of Jonquil is gone. The reason I saw your sanlifter crash is because I was standing at the edge of the territory here, performing Esod's final dedication. I had just moments before released the lintu containing his essence when your craft came into view. Even in death, he somehow manages to protect others." Lium turned away from the group, unwilling to reveal the cracks in his stoic facade.

Mila could sense he was indeed very sad, but a dark chasm of emotion hid just beyond her view. There was guilt in it, and that rift was tearing Lium in two.

At the edge of Kanluran, Mila had gained a new understanding of the danger of their mission. Hungry creatures that stayed hidden in the sand were one thing, but the untimely death of a group member hit much too close to home. Esod had risked his life, and lost it, for the sake of the their resistance. In a way, she felt that she should have done more to help him. She crossed her arms over her chest and lowered her head.

"This is horrible...it's all my fault," she said tearfully. "If I hadn't gone home during the fight, I could have helped Esod like I helped Jonas when he got hurt. I could have saved him."

Thornhill frowned and shook his head vigorously. "*No*, child, you mustn't blame yourself. You did exactly as you were told. Your safety is paramount and there was nothing you could have done to save Esod that would not have put your own life, and our entire mission, in jeopardy."

"Esod was a brave man who died with honor for the highest cause," Botan added. "None among us could ask for more than that." He looked tenderly at the child, into hazel eyes dotted with blue-gray. "Do you understand?"

Mila looked over at Lium, who nodded slowly in agreement. She blinked the tears from her eyes and took a deep breath. "Understood."

Mila leaned against the mangled remains of the sanlifter and looked up into the gaping blue of the sky. A winged animal circled above them in wide loops, surveying the scene. Far removed from the drama of the crash, it hovered in detached observation, curious and silent. Mila squinted as the creature turned and she lost sight of it in the glare of the suns. Though she knew it must still be there, to her eyes it had simply vanished.

Having crash-landed short of their original destination in Kanluran, the group found themselves stranded a fair distance from Salvitor's workshop. The group rested on the ground near the wreckage and discussed the conundrum.

"What was your destination?" Lium asked, polishing the side of his boot.

"Salvitor's workshop. I must find out what he knows of Queen Zehn's whereabouts, and I'm hoping he'll also know something about Rosette."

Mila noticed that Lium's aura suddenly flickered, and a wave of brown washed through it. "You're sure that Salvitor has this information?" Lium said.

"Nothing is certain, but if anyone knows, Sal does." Thornhill's eyes softened. "And to see my dear friend again would make my heart glad."

Mila sensed conflicting feelings within Lium. He seemed like a coin that flipped in the air, one moment presenting its face, the next, its backside. It reminded her of the feeling she often experienced of being in two places at the same time, and she thought perhaps she and Lium had something in common. The thought made her smile, and a swirl of white curled out of her aura and moved toward Lium.

"I can lead you to Salvitor's workshop. I have been there before," Lium said.

Thornhill lifted his brows and glanced at Botan. "That sounds like a fine idea."

"It's good to have a native Jonquilian to guide us on this

journey," Botan said, placing a hand on Lium's shoulder. "You are most welcome."

Lium smiled, but flinched slightly at Botan's touch. He stepped forward, clearing his throat.

"We'll need to carry as much as we can with us," Lium instructed. "This section of the territory is quite barren."

Thornhill nodded in agreement and turned to see Botan had already pried open the broken cargo box and taken out the canteens. One was leaking steadily, and Botan quickly finished the last swallow of water that remained. "Thankfully we've got plenty of water; too much, in fact. I think Thornhill and I were a little apprehensive about getting dehydrated in the desert."

Thornhill chuckled. "Did the turryns and the loaf make it through the crash?"

"All here," Botan replied, stuffing the food into his pack.

"Mila, are you hungry? Do you need water?" Thornhill asked.

Mila hadn't even thought about eating. "No, I think I'm good."

Lium once more found his jacket, having removed it while running to rescue Mila. He brushed the dust from the shoulders and shook it to dislodge the clinging sand. "If you are ready, we must go now. Any delays would have us traveling through Kanluran in the dark, and we don't want that."

"Indeed, let's be on our way. Come, Mila."

The group left the crash site and headed south. Though still somewhat shaken, Mila felt quite safe traveling with Botan, Thornhill, and her beloved hero Lium.

As they walked, Mila looked out over the extraordinary Land, floating among the clouds. The Kanluran territory was essentially an immense metal disc upon which the rock and soil of the Land accumulated. The landscape stretched in wide expanses of short grasses, punctuated by the occasional tree with crooked limbs frozen in a strange dance. As they made their way deeper into the territory, a few homes came into view. Mila was intrigued; sleek and dome-shaped, the houses looked very different from the simple cottages of Verde. The tops of the domes were glass, and the supporting structure below looked to be crafted of plaster made from the very sand of the desert below. As the light hit the sandplaster, the minerals within sparkled like countless diamonds.

As they came closer, Mila could see that the home nearest them had likely been abandoned. One of the windows had been broken out, and a small animal scuttled into the opening as they passed. A walkway of step stones led up to the metal door, which looked to be made of the same golden metal as the disc. To the left of the entrance, the twisted trunk of a dwarf tree rose from the sandy soil, its thin canopy of leaves casting a lacy shadow on the sandplaster behind. Though Mila expected an abandoned house to be quiet, the silence that surrounded in this place was deafening.

"It's so quiet here. Where are all the people?" Mila asked, gazing up at Lium.

"Jonquil was never a crowded place, but now that evil occupies the Land, emptiness prevails."

The group walked on for a time and came to the southern border of the disc. Mila looked out and saw a long and graceful expanse of pale golden metal stretching out to the neighboring disc. The striking bridge seemed to go on forever. A series of countless beams arranged in pyramidal clusters formed the gentle arch of the structure, which swayed almost imperceptibly in the wind. As the group crossed onto the mesh walkway of the bridge, Mila noticed that the golden metal showed coppery undertones and was blackened with tarnish in places.

"Is this bridge made of gold?" Mila asked, tapping on one of the beams.

"It's radentium, the highest order of all metals. In the past, it shone brilliantly but it has tarnished from the black fog that haunts the air," he said bitterly, rubbing his fingertips over a spot of black. "This would never have been allowed to accumulate when Queen Zehn ruled. Every part of Jonquil is sacred, a reflection of the Source. To allow any part of the Land to decay is akin to watching your own body rot away with sickness. We are a part of Jonquil as much as the bridges, the sand and sky. It is shameful what has happened to this majestic place, and our people."

Lium hung his head and continued walking ahead, albeit at a slower pace. Mila shook her head and blinked a few times, looking out over the elegant bridge and the pale golden discs that floated in a sea of clouds. She shrugged and smiled. To her eyes, Jonquil was like heaven.

The group finally crossed the mighty bridge and traveled along the rim of a great rift in the Land. Mila looked out over the steep canyon cutting through the landscape, framed by towering buttes. The rift widened considerably in the distance, and the painted rock along the bottom undulated, artfully carved by the wind and sand.

"Wow," Mila remarked, "it looks like the Grand Canyon, only smoother."

She cautiously leaned over and peered below where she spotted two large homes that sat on opposite sides of the rift. Their domes of metal and glass gleamed in the light, even through the tarnish.

"Those houses are much bigger than the first ones we saw," Mila said.

"Yes, the home just below is owned by a very wealthy woman, and her brother lives across the canyon in the other." Lium pointed down toward the woman's dwelling. "You see, radentium is precious. The more of this metal you see in a structure, the more it costs. The homes we saw earlier had only metal doors, but these here have several metal domes, very expensive. The Palace of Gosai, where Queen Zehn once dwelled, is nearly all radentium and crystal glass. It is the jewel of the Land."

Lium paused for a moment, focused his gaze on the horizon, then turned once more to the others. "Soon you will see some of the plots where we raise our silk nondo and grow fine medicinal and culinary plants. Come, this way."

Lium felt his ribs stiffen once again as the air forced its way into his chest. Through his renewed fellowship with the others, he felt an increasingly strong desire to join the resistance for good, to cut his ties to Corpus and work to restore the majesty of his home Land. He had felt like a hero while saving Mila, and when he touched her some feeling had overcome him that seemed to urge a change of heart. He instinctively knew that valor was a gift that Corpus, no matter how dominant, could never give him. He would have to find it within himself.

PART 3

THE CALL TO GLORY

After long days of travel through northern Verde, Aux finally crossed the Maront bridge over the border of Verde and Crimson. Though heavily guarded on the Verdean side by soldiers of Maru, he passed without incident, as Botan had sent word of his coming. The Soza River churned below him, the rapids crashing and tumbling over rocks hidden just below the raging surface. As he crossed, he noted the stark contrast between Verde, renewed at the return of her King Jonas, and his still-broken Land. Though they had always been vastly different places, the contrast was jarring.

Undaunted, Aux arrived on the other side of the river. He would journey throughout the central Lands of Crimson, telling of the prophecy and the coming of the Sankari Sano. He would inspire his people to stand once more and fight, not merely for the sake of battling, but for the sake of Crimson and her king.

Aux obtained a kontross from a nearby keeper and mounted up for the long trek. The beast seemed sincerely pleased to be called upon, having stood idle for too many days in lean pastures. The animal steadily plodded along, its enormous head bobbing as its cleft hooves found sturdy holds in the mountain trails. In his mind, Aux plotted out the path he would take throughout the Lands surrounding Glauck Lake. He would first travel to Flux, then north to Vaux, on to Nomen and Sulex, and finally down to Robir. *I'll make Vires my last stop,* he thought, for after seeing that place, even someone as strong as Aux would be inclined to return home to rest.

In each town, Aux spoke passionately to small groups in taverns, halls, and gathering places of all kinds. He brought a message of hope, inspiring strength and burning away apathy with the flames of courage. He told the people that though King Mason was lost, he was not gone forever, and like King Jonas, he could be returned to his people. Indeed, there was yet hope for Crimson to regain her former glory. The miraculous rebirth of Verde stood as hard proof that the prophecy was true, the Sankari Sano was real, and the time had come to stand and fight.

Tired and cross, Aux now neared the end of his journey in Robir. His kontross seemed to sense his frustration, stamping at the ground as it went. Though Aux had spoken with sincerity and conviction at each stop around Glauck Lake, he feared that his fiery words had fallen on deaf ears, and all his rants were but wasted breath. Still, he pressed forward to the last few villages near the border, intent on his cause.

Aux crested a hill and then saw a tavern standing a few paces from the road. Welcoming yellow light poured from the windows and laughter spilled out of the open door. Aux nodded; it seemed a good place to stop, so he tied his kontross nearby and entered the tavern. Empty wooden flagons littered the stone floor, and groups of people gathered around wide tables. At one, a half-eaten roast sat on a platter, the surrounding men jostling energetically as they pulled pieces of meat from the bones. Though they shoved and shouted, each seemed to enjoy the process, and much ale was consumed by all.

Aux walked to the bar and caught the tender's eye. "Flagon of ale," he grumbled, placing a coin on the bar top.

The tender nodded and soon served the dribbling cup to Aux, who finished half of it before the man had turned to put the coin in his bucket. Aux grunted approvingly, then looked up as a man from a nearby table approached.

"Aux?"

Aux met the man's eyes and nodded. "In the flesh."

The man's face seemed to brighten and he held out his hand. "I am Lokk. It's an honor to meet you. Rumor had it you were dead."

Aux shook the man's hand and laughed. He pushed his wiry red hair away from his dusty face.

Lokk gestured toward the table and the roast. "Come and feast with us."

Aux's mouth began to water as his belly rumbled loudly, reminding him that the journey had been long and the rations scarce. "Thank you, brother."

The men gathered around the table, feasting on flesh and ale and sharing boisterous conversation. Aux stuffed himself, glad to finally sate his appetite.

"We heard that you died in a battle in Verde. Some others claimed you were in Jonquil on some kind of quest. The Guard is so scattered and divided now, nobody knows what to believe or whom to fight. So we sit, and wait...and drink!" Lokk roared, lifting his ale high before taking a greedy gulp.

"As you can see, I'm not dead," Aux said, ripping off a sizable chunk of roast. "And you should know better than to think I would be floating around in the clouds in Jonquil. I went to Verde to join the resistance, to help bring King Jonas back to Samera. We did that—you can see it for yourselves. Just go to the border and look at what's happening there."

"What's happening?" an older man asked, wiping the foam from his lips as he finished his flagon.

"When King Jonas took back the throne, the whole Land came back to life. It looks like it did long ago, before evil crept in."

"I thought Jonas was dead, like all the other kings and queens?"

"*No.* The kings and queens are not dead, they are only lost. They are trapped on the other side of..." Aux hesitated, glancing round the table, "...a doorway."

The older man frowned and leaned toward Aux. "Doorway? You expect us to believe that?" He shook his head. "Just a giant pile of kontross crap."

"The doorways are real!" Aux boomed. "What the prophecy says is true! The Sankari Sano has come. I have seen it all, with my own eyes."

The older man sat back and crossed his arms. "Let's just say what you claim about the doorways and the prophecy is true." He casually plucked a piece of meat from between his crooked teeth. "What do you expect us to do about it?"

"Fight!" Aux shouted, pounding the table and sending flagons of ale jumping. "We have a chance to bring Mason back to the throne and restore Crimson. We must gather our strength and come together to fight for our king!"

The older man's glow began to simmer with surly shades of burgundy. "We don't believe in storybook tales and false hopes. King Mason is dead."

Aux shot up from his chair and smashed his fists into the table, cracking it in two in a red-hot blast of rage. A pile of bones slipped through the gaping crack and hit the floor, splashing into a puddle of spilled ale.

"King Mason is yet alive! You fools will battle each other for no cause at all, but when the time comes to stand for justice, you'd sooner drown yourself in ale than fight for Crimson. Cowards, all of you!"

Aux grabbed the edge of the broken table and overturned it, sending the remains of the roast and ale crashing to the floor. The men stood and protested loudly, but none so much as laid a finger on Aux as he stormed out of the tavern in a blaze of red. Fools they were perhaps, but not foolish enough to take on a Prime Warrior in that state.

Once outside, the enraged Aux approached his kontross. The beast, spooked by the angry energy swirling around Aux, reared up, snapping the reins in half as it tugged against its master's grip. Aux cursed the animal as it broke free and ran away toward the mountains. "You, too?"

He hurled the torn bits of leather to the ground and kicked a stone after the retreating beast. It appeared he was on his own.

Aux walked in solitude the cold and crumbling path to Robir. The snow-capped peaks of the Rodhas mountains stood stark and silent in the distance. The desolate valley at the foot of the range turned its barren face to the gloom above, cloaked in shadow. Though Crimson had never been a lush or easy place, the Land now felt dead beneath Aux's feet. He began to believe that his people had forgotten valor, and that Crimson would never again stand proudly as she had before. He stumbled as he rounded a corner on the path, and felt a weight descend on his chest as he caught sight of the village of Robir just ahead. He paused, unconvinced that the tiny settlement was worth his time, yet duty soon moved him forward.

As he entered the village center, he caught sight of a rough-hewn platform of rock. Intrigued, he went to it, and saw that atop it sat a metal plaque etched with words of tribute to King Mason. By the look of it, Aux guessed that someone had fashioned the piece after King Mason had been cast out and chaos descended upon Crimson. Aux stood a bit taller and gripped his weapon belt. Though a crude monument, it rose defiantly above the black fog that swirled around it, speaking of a strength that still remained. The overt symbol of patriotism sparked a fire in his belly, and Aux felt the warmth return to his blood. "I will never forget," he said, dropping to one knee in reverence.

His aura bloomed with crimson and scarlet, and his breath began to move vigorously through his chest. He clenched his fists tightly, raising them to the sky as he growled. He then lowered his head before the monument in silence, eyes closed. He felt the fire of the Land in his body once more, and the voice of the king seemed to ring clear in his mind. Having gratefully received the strength he needed to complete his task, a renewed Aux stood and left the monument, walking a narrow path that snaked up a hillside to a cluster of homes.

He came upon a young man performing training exercises with a whelix and a stump. The man appeared to have been trained well, and had a good measure of power in his stroke. Aux approached the man and cleared his throat before he spoke. "You've some skill with the whelix?"

The young man did not stop striking as he responded, "I stay sharp. I want to be ready if I get the chance to fight for Crimson again." He scowled as he struck the stump a bit harder. "Probably just wasting my time, though. Seems that all the warriors have withered away."

Aux grunted. "You may yet get your chance."

The young man paused his exercise and cut his eyes at Aux. "Who are you?"

Aux stood tall and lowered the pitch of his voice. "Aux, Prime Warrior of Crimson."

The man's aura brightened in surprise and he set down his weapon, nodding respectfully. "I'm Galt, Guardsman of Crimson," he said, approaching Aux with an outstretched hand.

Aux looked the young man over as he gripped his hand tightly.

"My father Brux is a Guardsman, as was his father before him. I am honored to meet you, Aux."

Aux straightened. "I'm going to tell you what I have told many others and hopefully you will hear. The time has come for Crimson to unite. I have seen the Sankari Sano with my own eyes. The prophecy is real, my brother. King Mason will reclaim the throne."

Aux paused and waited for the disbelieving response that he had heard so many other times on his journey. He waited to see Galt shrink before him and for the smell of apathy to turn his stomach. Instead, the young Guardsmen brightened and stepped closer.

"You've seen the Sankari Sano, the prophesied one?"

Aux nodded slowly. "I joined the Sankari Sano and the others in the resistance to return King Jonas to Verde. You can see it for yourself; go to the border and look at what's happening there."

"I have been to the border and seen the changes in Verde." Galt lifted his head and straightened his stance. "Whether the prophecy is true or not, I don't know, but I am ready to fight and die for Crimson. The blood of the Guard runs fierce in my veins."

Aux growled in approval. "Good. I will continue on through Crimson, telling others. I need you to stay here and gather together any who will fight with us."

"I will. You will find us there, on the plateau," Galt said, pointing to a raised stretch of grassland to the north. "Look for our fires. We'll camp there until you return."

Aux fought the urge to smile and instead nodded in agreement. The two men gripped each other's hands tightly, and Aux set off alone for Vires.

The wind drifted aimlessly about the square, dusting the rough cobbles with dry soil, then blowing them clean again. The town center of Vires had once been a lively gathering place for the finest warriors of Crimson, though now it stood empty and quiet. Aux looked here and there, searching for life, or at least an indication that someone had recently passed where he now did. But Vires rested in a cold, slow sleep, without so much as a flicker of the fire that had once given it life. Though he now knew the importance of restoring all Lands, not just his own, knowing that Verde thrived while his home lay crippled was a blade in his heart.

Aux marched slowly into the central square and came to the statue of the great Prime Warrior, Poe, who had called Vires home. The memorial spoke of how King Mason had once exalted Poe as his most ferocious warrior. Aux had spent many nights of his youth at a roaring fire, listening to tales of Poe's strength and courage. He could picture so clearly the warrior's face, his brow set with determination and lips curled over battered teeth. Aux would puff his chest out as he listened, imagining that one day he could be like Poe — a hero of Crimson and a servant to the throne.

Aux shook his head as he beheld the statue, frowning disapprovingly. The lone memorial to this revered warrior had fallen into disrepair, the stone crumbling away. Debris collected in the basin below the platform. Was there no reverence for fallen heroes anymore?

Aux reached down and brushed the litter and fragments of stone away, clearing out the basin. He placed a palm over the warrior's armor, lowering his head in respect. Having finished his work, Aux climbed back down, looking to the east. He would travel now to Cadire, his home by the harbor, to rest and search for others willing to stand with him against Corpus. He looked to the statue of Poe once more and lifted his whelix high in salute, pausing to honor Poe and all great warriors that had passed.

Stowing his weapon, Aux turned and marched east to the sea.

An Eternal Legacy

Lium led the group on the final stretch to Salvitor's workshop. The steep and narrow canyon they had flanked for a time had now widened into a striking vista of pale stone set ablaze by the light of the setting suns. On the opposite side of the rim path, a windswept landscape of smooth boulders and dark catacombs stretched out into the east. Though Lium dutifully led the group to the workshop as he'd promised, he had pledged the greater portion of his allegiance to another.

Corpus.

When handed all the wealth in Jonquil, would that reward be worth the sacrifices made?

He looked down at Mila, who lifted her hazel eyes to his in response, a shy smile spreading across her young face. The child had come back to Graha to help rescue Rosette and Queen Zehn, though she had nothing to gain in doing so. No riches awaited her at the end of the journey, no prestige or fame. As far as he could tell, not a single person from her own world was even aware of her travels to Graha. Yet here she remained, risking everything for nothing.

Despite all her hopeful striving, at the end of the path, Lium would lead Mila to her doom. He would lead her to Corpus, as he'd brought Rosette to Fincher. Lium winced as he remembered once more the eyes of Rosette, blazing red with fury at his betrayal. Lium coughed at the growing tightness in his chest. At once, the thump of Thornhill's arm across his chest stopped his forward motion.

"Look there," the old man said, pointing.

Mila turned and gasped when she saw shadowy ghosts hovering behind a butte, their focus fixed on the group. "What are those things?" she whispered.

"Watchers, minions of Corpus," Thornhill said, sighing heavily. "They cannot touch us, but they are relaying our whereabouts to their master. We must move quickly."

Thornhill looked to Lium, who nodded in agreement and quickened his pace.

As the group neared Salvitor's property, the cloud cover below began to clear and they were afforded a panoramic view of the west. Mila could just see the blue ribbon of the Western Sea below in the distance, crashing and breaking against the golden shore. The sands of Tenpi seemed to dive into the surf, as if seeking to quench the thirst of an entire desert there on the beach.

The group soon came upon a dilapidated sandplaster dome, huddling among a few sorrowful-looking trees. The structure leaned slightly, as if bracing itself against the winds blowing in from the western edge of the territory, and the narrow, dust-laden windows seemed to squint at the light of the setting suns in the distance. Beyond the building, a labyrinth of rock stretched eastward, riddled with buttes, cliffs, and catacombs. As they drew closer to the dome, Mila noticed that the sandplaster had begun to chip away from the exterior; chunks of it blowing along the ground. "Looks like nobody's been living here for a long time. Are you sure this is it?"

Thornhill nodded. "Yes child, this is Salvitor's workshop, I'm sure of it. Though it doesn't look like he is here right now."

Thornhill turned and began running his fingertips over the cracked sandplaster wall to the left of the door. He moved as if reading the texture of the plaster, and paused when he found a particularly wide crack. "Ah, here it is," he said. He picked at the crack with a fingernail, and a section of the plaster swung away from the wall, revealing itself as a hidden door. Behind it stood a panel of interlocking wooden and metal shapes reminiscent of the inner working of a mechanical clock. Thornhill hummed, tugging at his white beard in thought. "Let's see, right left right, or left right left..." He brushed the cobwebs away from the panel, then pulled a lever downward. It clicked into place, freeing up a metal gear. Thornhill hesitated, then turned the gear to the left, to the right, and then left again. Another click sounded and Thornhill's fingers seemed to move automatically, as if by memory. The panel slid back and revealed a secret compartment below. Thornhill smiled in satisfaction and reached inside, withdrawing a jangling mass of keys on a cluster of rings. He rummaged through the tangled metal until he found a slender, cylindrical key with a hook on the end. "Key number one...of thirty-four. There are *thirty-four* locks here that we must open to get into the workshop."

"Thirty-four?" Lium repeated.

"Thirty-four," Thornhill confirmed. "Salvitor is very concerned with privacy, but I believe that he simply loves keys. There are at least a hundred on this chain, and he knows what every one of them is for." Thornhill turned, smiling, to unlock the first of the many locks, but to his surprise, the battered wooden door creaked open at his touch.

"That's odd," he said, stepping to the side and looking around anxiously. "Sal would never leave his door open like this. He's very secretive about his work; he protects his shop and his devices like a mother animal protects her young." He peeked in through the cracked door. "Be very careful. This open door could lead to trouble."

The group entered the building and stood in a room that looked to have been ransacked by burglars. Papers were strewn on the floor, scattered on tabletops, and stacked in dusty piles on shelves. Lium rushed to the center of the room and quickly drew his blade. "Someone has robbed Salvitor!"

Thornhill shut his eyes and chuckled. "Relax, my friend. It always looks like this."

Lium blinked and shrugged, tucking his blade back into his vest.

The group then began poking around the disheveled workshop. The musty smell of old books hung in the stale air, and precious little light struggled in through the grimy windows. Mila looked up and noticed a model of a flyer hanging from the ceiling in a corner. The tail and wings were shaped differently than those of the sanlifter they'd crashed earlier that day. *Must be a new idea for a better one*, she thought, wishing the improved model had been available for their ill-fated flight. She moved on to a section of shelves stuffed with books and loose papers. Botan joined her and delicately leafed through the papers, shaking his head. "I can't imagine how much information must be in this room," he said quietly. "It's like a deconstructed library."

Lium raised a brow at Botan and looked around the disgrace of a workspace. Though the knowledge and devices Salvitor had tucked away in the space were priceless, to Lium the shop was not worth the soil it was built upon.

Thornhill walked over to a substantial worktable that stood under one of the horizontal windows. Several unburned candles were clustered at either end, as if waiting to provide light for the great mind that often worked long hours into the night. A length of paper had been unrolled across the table, the beginnings of a sketch drawn across its surface. Thornhill's brows shot up in curiosity as he then saw something more—a torn envelope and the letter that had been inside laid to the left of the sketch.

"What's this?" he asked, picking up the letter and reading it aloud.

"Soon the shadows will come for me, and I will find no escape. I cannot cross again into the inner realm for refuge, nor can I send word of my circumstances to Thornhill by ramara. My message may be intercepted, and I must not put him in danger. And so, dear Pixie, this message I relay to you with dire urgency."

Thornhill stopped reading halfway through the letter and furrowed his brow. "Sal had told me of a young girl that visited him frequently at his workshop. In his messages he spoke of her as more a nuisance than a companion." He thumbed the edges of the letter in contemplation. "Sal never took on apprentices and certainly was not prone to socializing or seeking companionship. Solitude was his only mistress. But this Pixie...must have been important to him."

Lium fidgeted where he stood, and glanced once more at the worktable. With his gifted sight, he sensed residual heat pooled near the tabletop. He moved closer and saw that one of the candles had been nearly burned down. He reached out to touch it, and found that the top still felt warm, and a pool of melted wax slowly solidified on some papers underneath. Before Thornhill could resume reading the letter, Lium drew his blade again. I'm telling you, someone was here, and may still be here," he said, cautiously looking around the room.

"What is it?" Thornhill asked.

"The one candle there. It's been lit quite recently."

Lium tiptoed to the back corner of the room where a closet door sat slightly ajar. He paused, tuning his ears, and could just hear someone breathing inside. Lium lifted his blade, and just as he reached for the closet door handle, yellow light burst from the closet and zoomed to the table where Thornhill stood. In the next instant, the form of a young girl appeared next to him. She snatched the letter from Thornhill's grasp.

"Gotta go!" she cried.

Before the startled Thornhill or anyone else in the room could react, the girl bolted for the front door at top speed. She did not slow down—if anything, her speed increased as she approached the door. Mila's eyes widened. *Is she going to run right into the door?*

As the girl finally reached the door, her aura flashed a brilliant yellow and she seemed to vanish into thin air. Lium and Mila rushed to the door and threw it open to see the girl had re-materialized on the other side, speeding off into the distance as fast as her feet would take her.

Thornhill rushed forward. "She has the letter. Don't let her get away!"

All four raced out the door in pursuit of the girl. She headed east and swiftly disappeared into the maze of buttes and grottos beyond the workshop. Botan watched her intently, then wheeled round. "Thornhill, I can sense where she is in space if I'm close enough. Lium, I know you can see her from afar. Let's split up and make sure we stay with her. Thornhill, come with me. Lium and Mila, head that way. Go, quickly!"

The group split up and Mila pushed herself to keep up with Lium, who ran like an antelope. At times his lean form briefly disappeared behind a rock formation or a bend in the path, and Mila was forced to follow the receding glow of his aura to find him again.

After a time, he paused the chase and focused at some point in the distance. "I can see her glow just ahead of us, she's ducking in and out of the rock formations there," Lium said.

Mila nodded. "I can hear some of what she's thinking, too. She wants to find a good place up high to hide."

"Let's keep up," Lium said, striding away once more.

Mila tried her best to keep Lium in her sight, but his long legs soon took him too far ahead.

Though somewhat uneasy to be alone in a strange place, Mila could still sense the girl's thoughts, and had a good idea of her general location. Mila walked slowly in the direction she was guided, her eyes and ears tuning in as she realized she could see and hear more clearly in this heightened state of awareness. It seemed that everything stood still, save her thumping heart in her chest, and at once, a voice entered her mind.

White? Why does she glow white?

"Hello?" Mila called, turning around. She continued a few paces down the path and saw to her left an area where the face of the rock had split in two, creating a wedge-shaped cleft that ran from ground level and widened as it went up. Mila peered down the length of the cleft to where it seemed to disappear in shadow. Though she could see no one, she had the distinct feeling she was being watched.

* * *

The girl saw Mila coming from her high vantage point at the mouth of the cleft. She'd shimmied up, one foot on each side, and had wedged herself between the two rock faces high above the path. Though she'd left Sal's workshop in a panic, she now felt more curious than afraid. The dark-haired girl seemed to be alone; the men who had been with her were nowhere in sight. As Mila drew near, the girl decided to reveal herself.

"Boo!"

Mila gasped and looked above to where she'd heard the voice.

"Looking for something?" the girl said, waving the letter in the air just above Mila's head.

Mila jumped to grab the letter, but the girl pulled it away at the last second.

"Hey!" Mila protested.

The girl laughed and scooted higher out of Mila's reach. The girl's yellow aura, along with the ambient glow from the setting suns, allowed Mila to see her quarry. The girl was just a little older than Mila, probably fourteen. She wore tall boots and leggings, and her short, white-blond hair stood straight up in spikes.

"I'm not gonna hurt you. Why don't you come down from there?"

The girl glared at Mila, her eyes flashing. Though the younger girl carried a strange white glow about her, she did seem to be more friend than foe. The blonde turned her toes outward and nimbly slid down the two rock faces to the ground. She eyed Mila carefully as she walked up to her. "Hey!" the girl suddenly exclaimed, grasping Mila's arm and inspecting the watch. "Did you steal that?"

"No!" Mila shot back. "An old man gave it to me when I was running on the beach. I told him it wasn't mine, but he just disappeared."

The girl raised a brow. "What did he look like. Did he have crazy white hair?"

"Um, I think so. I only saw him for a minute."

The girl turned over Mila's arm and saw the mark on her wrist, perfectly framed by the links of the watch. The blonde ran her finger over the mark and looked up at the girl with the strange white glow. "Who *are* you?"

Just then, Lium, Botan and Thornhill rounded the corner and found the two girls. Alarmed, the blonde disappeared in a golden yellow flash, reappearing higher where she had been between the two rock faces. Mila called up to her, "It's okay. These are my friends, Lium, Botan, and Thornhill."

"Thornhill?" the girl asked. "Thornhill of Verde?"

Thornhill nodded, panting. "Yes, child, I am Thornhill of Verde. Salvitor is a dear friend of mine and of Botan, and I worked closely with him. We both carry the mark."

Thornhill turned his back to the girl and lifted his white hair off the nape of his neck. Botan also turned and parted his dark locks. Both men had marks on the backs of their necks that matched the eleven symbol—the one Mila had seen on the leg of the table in Sukai, the same one etched into the back of her watch. Mila cocked her head. Why would the symbol be marked on Thornhill and Botan, and why hadn't they revealed this until now? Before she could gather herself enough to ask, Thornhill had turned and walked closer to where the blonde girl perched.

"Are you Pixie?" he asked.

The girl hung silent and defiant for a moment between the two rock faces, then slid down once more and joined the group.

"I'm Pixie," she confirmed, nodding. "Salvitor was my friend, too."

Thornhill squinted. "What do you mean, he *was* your friend?"

Pixie took a deep breath and cast her slanted eyes downward as she spoke. "I come to Sal's workshop all the time. He used to teach me stuff and I helped him with his projects. Lately he's been gone a lot to the Inner Realm and he told me not to hang around his shop while he was gone, because he was being followed. He said there were these things, these shadow things that kept trying to get him, and he had to keep going to the Inner Realm to get away from them."

"Minions of Corpus," Thornhill said.

"He told me to stay away from his shop, but I never went too far. I was always close enough to see when the shadows would leave, and then I would come back to the shop to find Sal. But a couple weeks ago I saw the shadows come, and then I heard this... awful screaming. As soon as the shadows left again, I ran in to the shop and then I..." She trailed off.

"Speak, child," Thornhill whispered.

"I saw a faint glow on the floor where they left him."

"What?" Thornhill breathed.

A single tear slid down Pixie's pale cheek. "Salvitor is dead."

Thornhill's knees hit the ground and he slumped forward, clinging to Botan's coat. "It cannot be..."

"I'm sorry, Thornhill," Pixie whispered.

Tears erupted from Thornhill's eyes and his face twisted in pain. As the waves of grief came, he shuddered as if chilled to the bone. Botan sat beside him, embracing him as he wept, his own tears coming quickly. Thornhill's body seemed thin and frail, and Mila thought he looked more like a ghost than the man he had been moments before. When his glow had receded to an almost imperceptible flickering, Mila crouched beside Thornhill, setting her hand lightly on his shoulder and allowing her glow to pulse gently into his body. Unsure of exactly what to do or say to soothe him, she decided to simply be near.

Soon after, his sobbing ebbed and Thornhill finally caught his breath and gathered himself enough to speak. "Botan, what do we do now? Without Sal's knowledge, how will we find Queen Zehn and continue the mission?"

"We will find a way," Botan said. "There *must* be a way. The prophecy speaks of *one* who defeats Corpus and restores Graha. So long as there is that *one* among us, there is hope."

Thornhill shook his head and slowly got to his feet. "I'm not sure what to do next, friends. Who do we turn to? What do we look for? I am...deflated."

Pixie uncrossed her arms and held up the letter Salvitor had written her. "Well, in this letter, Sal was telling me he has a hidden stash of devices he made for you, Thornhill, and that one day it would be time for you to get them. But he wouldn't tell me where he hid them. He said that the only person besides him who knows where they are is the Sankari Sano." Pixie swiveled her head and focused her flashing eyes on Mila. "He said that *she* has a map that shows where he hid them."

Mila's mouth dropped open and she pointed to her chest, shaking her head. "Me?"

"Where's the map, Mila?" Pixie asked.

"I...I don't know, I never got any map," Mila stammered, glancing at the watch on her arm and lifting it to Pixie's eyes. "Is it inside the watch somehow?"

"No, that's just a timetick," Pixie said dismissively.

"Well, I don't have the map—"

"It's right here in the note," Pixie interrupted, shaking the letter in front of her. "It says that Salvitor left the map in the Inner Realm for you, someplace you'd know to pick it up."

Mila shook her head slowly, searching her memory but finding nothing. Thornhill turned to her. "Mila, the map is likely hidden in some way. It may be in a form that you do not recognize." His voice grew stronger as he spoke. "You know, Salvitor loved patterns, especially ones that repeated in certain ways. Perhaps the map itself is hidden in something with repeating patterns."

Mila shrugged, still clueless as to the location of the mysterious map.

Thornhill sighed. "It's all right, child, you will find it soon enough. You *must.*" He stood up straight, turning to the others. "But now, we must pay our respects to he who has made the ultimate sacrifice for the resistance. Come."

Thornhill led the group into the sunset, the light setting his white hair ablaze in a halo of orange fire.

Goodbye Old Friend

The group soon gathered together near the boundary of Salvitor's property, overlooking the western edge of Kanluran. The lesser sun closely followed the greater, which had hidden most of its face below the horizon for the night. Blue-violet light illuminated the carved landscape of stone, rendering it almost unrecognizable from the vista they'd seen in the warm light of the earlier sunset. Thornhill stood before Botan, Lium, and the two girls, wavering under the weight of his task. He soon cleared his throat and brought his hands together before him. "Open your hearts and tune your ears, friends. I now tell the story of my dearest friend, and of his life's work."

Thornhill looked to Botan, who nodded encouragingly. He took a deep breath and began the dedication.

"I remember the first time I met Sal. It was the second day of Develoption and I was just a young boy, nervously pacing the halls and trying not to draw too much attention to myself. Suddenly, a flash of gold appeared in front of me, and papers seemed to explode into the air in all directions. When the fallout cleared, I realized I had bumped into another lad about my age. He glowed gold, so I knew he must be from Jonquil, but he didn't look like a Jonquilian. His appearance was fascinating to me, and I struck up a conversation with him as we both worked to gather all his papers again. He struck me as distracted, but something about him was magnetic, and through the coming months I often found myself in his company. We became the best of friends."

Thornhill took a deep breath and lowered his head as sadness forced him to pause. "Through the years, we would sit and talk about things, matters that we viewed as more important than what was presented to us in Develoption. We talked about physics, mathematics, the nature of our universe...and especially the doorways. The Magisters presented the doorways as more myth than fact, but together we learned that the doorways were real. Sal became obsessed with their study. The discoveries he made as a result of his obsession would prove more valuable than any revelation any person from Graha would ever have."

Thornhill paused once more, wiping a tear that drifted down his cheek. "When we completed Develoption, I was appointed as King Jonas' Prime Advisor, and Salvitor was appointed by Queen Zehn. As her Prime Advisor, he traveled throughout Graha as much as he could; my, he did explore! Soon, though, the darkness crept into the Lands and segregation began. Times were changing quickly, and the kings and queens declared new laws that forbade all but the Prime Advisors from leaving their home Lands. With this divisive force at work, the Lands came to mistrust and despise one another, and bitter feuds littered the borders with the casualties of violence. The trouble in our world vexed Sal. He was inconsolable and so distraught that he lost his desire to serve as advisor to the queen. He could no longer subscribe to what he felt was a tainted vision for Jonquil and Graha as a whole. Eventually, he withdrew from his position as Prime Advisor and began gathering an underground resistance. He and his group traveled around Graha in secret, branding the symbol of eleven, the symbol of unity, everywhere they could in protest of the segregation and subsequent destruction of the Lands."

Thornhill turned, parting his white hair and revealing the symbol marked on the back of his neck. "Salvitor crafted this symbol as a mark of a coming of age. Just as children of Graha reach the Turning Age at eleven, he used this same number to signify a coming of age for Graha, when great change would bring the people of this world to their fullest potential. And though great change is a necessary part of the evolution of this world, it is always preceded by great unrest."

Thornhill faced them again. "The symbol also harkened to the time of creation in our distant past, for at the age of eleven, the Four Founders were chosen to begin creation of this world. Though Salvitor did not consciously know it at the time, it is also a symbol of the future, for the Sankari Sano was prophesied to come to us at eleven. And so past, present, and future are all woven into one symbol of unity, the mark Sal chose to convey his message of hope, in this world and beyond."

Mila lowered her head. At last she understood the meaning of the symbol that had become so familiar to her—a symbol that crossed the border between two worlds, a harbinger of hope and a warning of danger.

She glanced down at the watch the mysterious old man had given her. At once, the puzzle pieces fell together in her mind. The old man on the beach must have been Salvitor, and he had likely been involved somehow in her adoption process. Though she'd come to believe in her own significance, Mila was puzzled. *Why me?* Mila glanced up at Pixie, who returned her gaze for a moment, then looked away to the ground, crossing her arms over her chest.

Thornhill spoke once more. "Despite Sal's efforts to heal this world, much hatred and evil had taken hold. The people of the Lands forgot the dire importance of unity—they forgot their oneness. They destroyed the symbols whenever they were found, and Sal's resistance eventually disbanded. In defeat, he abandoned use of the symbol and focused his efforts elsewhere. He began talking of using the doorways to spend long periods of time in the Inner Realm, looking for solutions to the problems we faced. He felt in his heart that somehow the answers must be on the other side, but he had never mastered long stays in the Inner Realm. I feared for his life, but he would not be swayed. One afternoon I went to talk with him to convince him to listen to reason, and found he was already gone."

Thornhill paused and took a deep breath. "I did not see my friend for decades. He lived a lifetime in the Inner Realm, and though part of me feared he was gone forever, another part could always feel his presence somehow, and it brought me a measure of comfort. When Sal finally returned to our realm, the situation here had deteriorated. Sal became more motivated than ever to bring what he had learned of technology in the other realm to bear against the enemies of this Land. We began working together, I with King Jonas and he with Queen Zehn, until both Jonas and Zehn vanished."

Thornhill turned to Pixie. "The lintu, please."

Pixie pulled the glittering lintu from her jacket pocket and carefully handed it to Thornhill, then turned away to hide her sadness. Thornhill held it up in the failing light, his heart heavy with the thought that all that remained of his lifelong friend was encapsulated in that cold cylinder of metal and gems. "And now we gather here to mourn, to honor, and then somehow march forward without Graha's most miraculous mind. A man who lived boldly, if not gracefully; one who explored and discovered and invented and dared to love his Land so much as to risk his own life for its evolution. Salvitor of Jonquil, I thank you, and I now release your most precious essence to the winds and the sands you fought to protect."

As Thornhill recited the ancient incantation and released the lintu, Lium could not help but think of Esod's dedication. He remembered the weight of that lintu, heavy and unyielding in his fingertips, and he remembered the bitter tears and the guilt that descended and tightened over his body. Overcome by darkness, he lowered his head in shame.

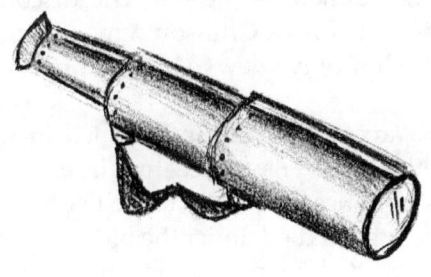

PART 4

CHANGING TIDES

After an exhausting journey through Crimson, Aux finally stood in the deserted harbor of his home of Cadire. The harbor carved an arc into a high, rocky peninsula; on a clear day, one could look south and see the eastern shore of Verde meeting the blue surf of Lapis. This was one such clear day, and as Aux looked out over the sea, it struck him that he stood in exactly the same place as he had when Botan first recruited him to join the resistance. Much had come to pass since that day, and he soon fell into a nostalgic daydream.

Aux looked out over the harbor as moonlight played on the dark swells that rolled in and crashed dramatically onto the rocky coast beyond. In the days when King Mason ruled, Cadire had been an abundant market with the freshest seafood in all of Crimson. The harbor town thrived thanks to the peaceful relations it maintained with the people of Lapis, the ocean Land just off the shores of Crimson. In those times, the Lapisians allowed the finner ships of Crimson to sail their waters and share in the endless bounty of the blue, but old alliances no longer held water. Ships of Crimson that sailed near Lapis were now overtaken by Lapisian Guardsmen and sunk, their crews claimed by the sea. The discord had begun so long ago, no one in Lapis or Crimson remembered how or why it had even begun. They only knew to blindly oppose one another, no matter the cost.

As a Prime Warrior of Crimson, Aux led his Guardsmen into daily battles with Lapis. His hatred for the Lapisians grew more intense as he lost countless comrades to the perilous sea. His home of Cadire had withered and died under the blight of violence, and most of the residents had fled inland, giving up their seaside homes for the relative safety of the mountains. The only people that remained in Cadire were the bravest of warriors and their leader, Aux, defiant and determined to defend their city from the invading Lapisians.

At the end of another day of battle, Aux stood motionless, glaring at the sea. For a time he heard nothing but the crashing of the surf against the rocky coast. Footsteps sounded nearby, and out of the corner of his eye, Aux saw a man approaching. His smaller size and green aura told Aux he was from Verde. Aux did not acknowledge this Verdean, whom he considered more a nuisance than a threat. The man drew ever nearer, then stopped a short distance away and dropped his pack.

Without turning his gaze from the sea, Aux spoke. "Seven ships...*seven* ships with warriors of Crimson sailed this morning, and not one returned." Aux spat on the ground in disgust. "Soggy grubs got them all. Why do you come here, Verdean?" Aux finally turned to the man and stared coldly into his green eyes. "And what do you want of me?"

The man swallowed hard, taken aback. He had carefully prepared just the right words to say when he finally met the great Prime Warrior Aux, but now found himself speechless. The man took a deep breath and finally spoke. "I am Botan of Verde, assistant to Thornhill of Verde. I have journeyed a great distance on the Ignis trail through the Acala mountains to find you."

Botan waited nervously for some response, but Aux stood still and silent as stone. Botan continued, "I have no words of comfort for you in the wake of your loss, but I do come with a message of hope, or at least, a call to die with great honor."

Aux lifted a brow and took a few paces toward Botan, crossing his arms over his massive chest. "What do you mean?"

"A select group of fine warriors are called now to gather in Verde. We ask each to take an oath to fight the evil forces that have spoiled Graha and help restore the throne of each Land. We seek to recruit only the best for this arduous task."

Aux squinted at Botan. "What exactly is the mission?"

"We of the resistance believe, as the prophecy says, that there is hope to restore the kings and queens of Graha to their thrones and to heal the Lands. The prophecy speaks of this gathering of warriors, and of the Sankari Sano, who is key to the success of the mission."

Aux turned once more to the sea, seemingly uninterested in a futile battle with strangers from other Lands.

Botan continued, "You may think of me as a simple Verdean who knows nothing of your culture. But there was a time when I had fellowship with a great warrior — Poe of Crimson."

Aux's ears perked and he turned to Botan. "You knew Poe?"

Botan nodded. "He once told me of a few young warriors here in Crimson that would be ready to fight in years to come. He told me the most promising of these young warriors was one named Aux, and if ever Crimson needed to call upon him, he would serve her well."

Aux's aura swirled with tones of scarlet and pulsed energetically outward. "I never met Poe, I didn't know he spoke of me." Aux balled his fists at his sides and fought the waves of emotion that rippled through his heart. Gathering himself, he turned to Botan. "In honor of Poe, I will join this resistance. My home of Cadire may be lost, but if I am to die with honor, I should rightly die fighting in some useful way. Fighting Lapis here is like wrestling a rising tide."

Botan approached Aux with an outstretched hand, smiling optimistically. "Then you will join us?"

Aux went to reach out his hand, but paused. "As long as there are no Lapisians in the group..."

Botan shook his head. "None from Lapis," he confirmed. "Lapis has been especially affected by evil influences. It seems that most Lapisians have been imprisoned within their kingdom, with only a few refugees that escaped and remain in hiding." Botan paused, shaking his head at a memory. "I have been warned to stay out of Lapis. Join us, Aux."

Aux finally grasped Botan's hand and shook it firmly. "All right."

"Thank you, my friend," Botan said, raising his sword. "To Graha restored."

Aux then drew his whelix, holding it high overhead. "To Graha restored!"

Soon after, the pair set off on the long trek south through Verde and on to Sukai, seeking Lium and Esod—the great warriors of Jonquil.

A sudden gust of wind broke Aux's daydream. Though he stood in exactly the same place he had so long ago with Botan, much had changed since then, both in Graha and in his own heart. He now realized that blind hatred of other Lands would only create more destruction, and that the time had come for all to unite as one against Corpus.

Aux huffed as he looked south past the border to the shores of Verde, narrowing his eyes. Something about the water there seemed unusual; the breakers that had ceaselessly curled onto the coast had now calmed, and the tide had drawn too far back. Even from where he stood, the rushing of the surf had grown hushed, and all around him descended an eerie silence.

Aux reached into his pack and pulled out his ocuscope for a closer look. From his high vantage point, the device allowed him to easily see the shore where the waters of Lapis met Verde. There, in the receding waves, a number of Lapisians emerged from the water. At first only a handful assembled, but as each wave of breakers rolled in, more Lapisians surfaced and made their way onto the beach.

Aux stepped forward and instinctively drew his whelix, holding his breath. He had never seen so many Lapisians come ashore in Verde, and something seemed wrong about their appearance; their auras were drenched with gray, and the swirling waters that surrounded were blackened with shadow. A few even rode in on green kraktau, giant crab-like creatures with snapping claws.

Botan told me most of the Lapisians were being held in their homeland...why are they here?

Aux shook his head and struck his fist hard against his chest, mustering his strength as he realized that any plans to restore the throne of Crimson would now be delayed. The newly restored Verde was in grave danger, and Lapis, under Corpus' influence, sought to undo what Aux and the resistance had worked so hard to restore.

Aux left the shore and made haste to the stable of Cadire. He knew that time was running short for Verde; they must be warned. He would travel to the border and bring word to the Verdean Guardsmen of trouble on their shores. He would promise to return with his warriors to help defend Verde and King Jonas against Corpus, at whatever cost. Aux quickly found the strongest kontross in the herd and rode like the wind for the nearby border of Crimson and Verde.

The Fierce Urgency of Now

On the plateau in Robir, many had gathered together with Galt; not only Guardsmen, but other men, women, children among them. They had heard the rumors of a call to war and now waited there for truth. The suns were rising, and Galt looked east to the road at the border of Robir. Far in the distance, a long trail of dust rose into the air. Galt squinted and gripped his whelix as the pounding of hasty hoofbeats drummed in his ears.

A massive figure atop a kontross crested the hill and came into view. Galt at once knew it was Aux, and quickly called the others together.

Aux arrived at the edge of the plateau and found Galt with a few of his men. Aux dismounted, and handed his kontross to one of them. "See to this animal's health. He has served me well."

The man nodded, taking the reins and leading the exhausted beast away as Aux looked at the group that had gathered. There were more than he'd imagined would show, though by their appearance, he doubted the battle-worthiness of half of them. Aux grumbled, stepping up on a stone in front of the group. Hushed whispers and gasps erupted as some recognized the great Prime Warrior Aux, while others simply gaped at possibly the biggest man they had ever seen. Aux stood straight and tall, the light of the rising suns casting an even more imposing shadow behind him. The early light revealed his stern expression, and just as the gathered became restless, Aux's voice rose like thunder.

"I remember Poe, a madman and a warrior. One who took enemies with his bare hands, thinking weapons a waste of time, one who fought ferociously and valued nothing over victory. All Poe knew was to fight, and he died doing just that, with honor, for Crimson and King Mason. Yet it seems he and the others before me have fought and died in vain, for now, so many years later, Crimson is still not free."

"For ages, we stood invincible on our mountains and guarded in our valleys, sure that Crimson would not fall, *could* not fall; that other Lands were weak but we were strong, and by our strength, we would survive. And so we isolated ourselves and lost our king, and paid the highest price for our arrogance."

Grumbles rose in the crowd, yet Aux seemed to stand even taller, scarlet determination flashing in his eyes. "I have come here today to tell you of the fierce urgency of now. Though you have come here to defend Crimson, you must know that open war is now upon the Land of Verde. Just days ago I saw Lapisians coming ashore in numbers to invade Verde. King Jonas and the Guardsmen of Verde alone cannot save their Land from this evil force, and all that has been mended there will soon be undone."

Aux looked over the expressionless faces of the gathered. Some even shrugged at the seeming irrelevance of the situation in Verde. Aux furrowed his brow. "You may think what happens in Verde is of no concern to Crimson. Let Verde fight her own battles, yes? But this can no longer be our truth. By separating ourselves and turning our backs on our brothers, *we* caused the fall of Graha into darkness. Now is the time to rise from the ruins of segregation and join with the other Lands to fight this one doom. The days of striking at whoever is before us, even if he be from a neighboring Land, have ended. We must lift the veil of blind distrust from our eyes and see that no Land alone can rid itself of this evil. Our destinies are tied together. To survive, Graha must unite."

Aux thumped his broad chest with his fist. "I believe in a Graha where no man sees his home Land as separate from another. I believe in a Graha where our bonds are so strong, an act of evil against one Land would be seen as an act against all. I believe that it is time to take our courage and strength and put them into right action. We must not sit idly and drink our ale and let evil undo what the Four Founders created. We must protect our world; we must join with the other Lands and right the wrongs upon Graha. Alliances with other Lands are not a sign of weakness, but a show of strength. Unity is the highest power."

Aux looked out over the crowd. They were quietly attentive, but not yet infused with the fire of valor. "Poe himself believed that King Mason would one day return to the throne. I know there are some among you who believe it, too, but will not speak it aloud for fear that others will not agree. What Poe believed was true. I have seen, with my own eyes, King Jonas return to his throne. It was not the people of Verde alone who brought him back, but a group of warriors from many Lands who came together, with the prophesied one, to win victory."

Aux paced to and fro, sensing a shift within the crowd. Eyes that had been clouded with doubt began to clear, and hope seemed to breathe itself to life in the hearts of the gathered. An ember had been lit, and Aux fanned the flame, his voice booming through the red orb of his aura. "This is what we must do! To restore our Land of Crimson and return King Mason to the throne, we must work to renew all Lands as one. Right now, the greatest need is in Verde. An army is assembling on her shores as I speak, and Verde will not win victory without help from other Lands. We must help our brother, and call our brother to help us in return. We must unite!"

Aux hoisted his whelix high above his head, the light of the rising suns glinting off the blade. "Now the question is, will you stand and fight for Graha, or will you shrink and shrivel and hide in your flagons and wish in vain for better days? I, for one, will fight! I offer my gifts, my whelix, my life, to Graha restored!"

As if pulled along by a powerful current, all of the gathered threw their fists into the air, weapons held high, shouting and burning with the flames of inspiration. Aux could feel his heart pounding, his fingers and toes tingling with their energy. Young Galt was among the first to step forward, weapon hoisted high. "I will fight for Graha restored!"

Soon after, two strapping brothers came forward. "You have my kalvia!" said the first.

"And my blade!" the second shouted, knife in hand.

A one-eyed man with a streak of gray in his wild red hair raised a whelix in each of his massive hands. He bellowed unintelligibly, his aura swirling with jets of scarlet.

Aux nodded approvingly. "Then let the enemy know that the warriors of Crimson still draw breath!"

More cheers erupted from the group before the gathered finally settled again to hear Aux speak. "Now, at the dawn of this new day, who among you rides with me, and who will journey through Crimson to spread word of the coming war?"

They began to talk amongst themselves, organizing into two rough groupings. The mothers with small children gathered those who planned to stay behind in Crimson, while Galt and the one-eyed man summoned the men and women who would ride to Verde. Aux took a rough count and tallied about fifty that were to ride with him. *Fifty warriors against a nation of people possessed by Corpus' shadow.* Aux shook his head at the odds. No matter; he and his warriors would still march. He walked to the group of people who promised to help in Crimson, thanking them and providing instructions.

When he reached the group that would ride to Verde, he struck a stone on the blade of his whelix to get their attention. "Now, I know that all of you gathered here are true warriors in your hearts; your presence here proves that. But who among you are Guardsmen?"

Five men raised their hands in response, and Aux nodded slowly. "I see. Come forward, you five. The rest of you go to the stables and get as many kontross as you can, hopefully one for each of us. Do it quickly."

The others moved off, leaving Aux and the five Guardsmen to plan the details of the mission.

As the lesser sun reached the top of the sky, the group returned with many beasts with cleft hooves and huge spiraled horns. The kontross marched across the plateau with determination, as if aware of their part in this pivotal event.

Aux and the five Guardsmen chose the strongest among the kontross for their mounts and rode slightly ahead of the rest of the group. Galt rode at Aux's right hand, proud to occupy a position of such honor, and a big silent man rode on Galt's right. On Aux's left was the old one-eyed man, Charg, and beside him the two brothers, Tannis and Bronnis, with the elder Bronnis on the outside.

Observing the gathered, Aux called for a halt. "Galt, I have seen your skill with a whelix. What gift do you have to add?"

At once, Galt's glow built to a deep maroon shade. In response, a sharp spike of stone rose from the ground, stretching nearly as tall as Aux. "I can create these, in defense or as a weapon."

"Hmm," Aux said approvingly, turning to the silent man. "And you, state your name and your gift."

"Blitz," the man stated, dismounting from his kontross and stomping over to the stone spike Galt created. He held his hands to it, his aura pulsing brightly. His hands seemed to turn to the same kind of stone, his biceps straining as he lifted them overhead. He growled, then slammed his hands into the stone spike, shattering it to bits. He stomped back to his kontross in silence, his hands slowly returning to flesh and bone.

Charg huffed and laughed under his breath, seemingly unimpressed by the display. Tannis cut a glance at him. He could feel anger building within him, red and jagged in his gut. As Aux spoke with Bronnis, Tannis leered at the old man, who sneered at him in return. Tannis could feel himself losing control, the desire to kill the old man nearly overwhelming him. He quickly turned his attention to his brother and Aux.

"Bronnis, I know your name and I have heard tales of your skill with the kalvia, so let's see it," Aux said.

Bronnis nodded and removed a handful of arrows from his pack, drawing his kalvia. The device hummed as he drew back the pull, the sound and vibration of it like a meditation. He coaxed his kontross into position and turned to Aux, who waited a distance away. "Hold your hand out with your palm toward me, and spread your fingers," he said, holding up his own hand to demonstrate. "Like this."

Aux hesitated, then grunted and held out his hand as requested.

"And hold still," Bronnis added, closing one eye as he aimed the kalvia. In the blink of an eye, Bronnis managed to fire four arrows so accurately, each one passed through the spaces between Aux's fingers in perfect sequence. Though startled, Aux was duly impressed. His aura flushed burgundy and pulsed before returning to its normal shade. "Good."

Bronnis dismounted, retrieving his arrows from where they had pierced the ground. "Thank you, Aux, but that is not my true gift—

that's the result of practice. My gift is to put out flame. Anything threatened by fire, I can make safe."

Aux lifted his brows, nodding once more. "Good to have you with us."

Old Charg hummed in approval, then turned to focus his eye on Tannis. "Your turn, boy." He crossed his arms over his chest. "If you've got anything to show."

Despite Tannis' valiant efforts to stay calm, he boiled with rage. He felt certain his older brother was showing off unnecessarily, and the old man had seemingly been taunting him for ages. Finally, Aux addressed Tannis. "Young man, state your name and gift."

"My name is Tannis. As for my gift…" he turned to Charg. "I could turn you into charcoal if I wanted."

Bronnis tuned in to his brother's anger, "Tannis, calm yourself…"

"Stay out of this, Bronnis," Tannis interrupted. "This old one-eye has done nothing but look down on everyone's gifts. What would be wrong with teaching him a lesson?"

Bronnis sighed heavily. "We are all Guardsmen, Tannis."

"But he needs to respect us! Why can't I show him —"

"You talk too much, boy." interrupted Charg. "Where's the action?"

At that moment, the thin barrier of control within Tannis cracked under the pressure of his emotion. His aura flashed a brilliant orange-red as he reached his hands toward the old man, who was then instantly engulfed in flames. Spooked by the sudden flash and the intensity of his anger, Tannis' mount bucked wildly and threw him to the ground, trotting a short distance away.

Tannis looked up to see Charg still astride his kontross, somehow unscathed by fire. Tannis' eyes widened as the flames simply died, and Charg sat completely unharmed, casually patting his seared garments, laughing heartily.

Tannis shot an accusing glance at his brother. "Is this your work, Bronnis?"

Bronnis sat atop his kontross, shaking his head. The old man finally stopped laughing. "Before you attack your enemy, *know* your enemy," he chided.

Aux, who had watched the entire exchange, looked to Charg. "So you are immune to flame?"

"And to other elements," the old man replied.

Tannis' face burned with anger. He balled up the rocky soil in his fists and felt it scrape his palms raw. Bronnis rode over and took the reins of his kontross, shaking his head. "Tannis, I told you about losing your temper! Your gift is just that, a *gift*. It is not to be misused—"

"Oh, get off me, Bronnis, he had it coming," the younger brother interrupted, hoisting himself up from the dirt and dusting off his clothing.

Aux moved to the front of the group and spoke. "Playtime is over. We must ride now to Verde."

The Guardsmen grunted in response, moving into formation as Aux lifted his whelix, signaling to the larger group of soldiers. "Ride!" he growled, and watched as the collective aura of the group pulsed blood red.

Aux and the Guardsmen then galloped forward, leading the group to Verde and their most urgent task.

After many days of travel, Aux and his troops approached the border of Crimson and Verde, where they were met by five Guardsmen of Verde. As he watched their green auras flashing in alarm at their approach, he remembered crossing into Crimson after King Jonas returned to Samera. Thankfully, Botan had been able to smooth his crossing, but the Verdean was too far from them to be of any help now. Rocky relations between Crimson and Verde meant they would need to take care not to incite a battle. Unity would be their only savior against this enemy.

Aux slowed his kontross and called for a halt, pointing to the Guardsmen watching their approach. "The Guardsmen there on the border probably think we are here to attack. We must not start a fight. Wait here while I explain our mission."

Aux dismounted, handing the reins to Galt as he did. In a display of trust and goodwill, he removed his weapon and handed it to Galt as well.

"Everybody wait here and..." Aux paused, suddenly aware of the grim appearance of his group, "...try to look harmless."

He began walking toward the Guardsmen stationed at the border, palms held out to show he was unarmed. At his approach, the five Guardsmen came forth to meet him—a stocky, fair-haired man and a slender man with sea-green eyes in front, and three others behind them. The men finally met in the open field, standing but an arm's length away from each other. The stocky man steeled himself before looking up at the massive man that stood before him. "Who are you, and what business brings you to the border?"

Aux spoke carefully. "I am Aux, Prime Warrior of Crimson, friend to Botan of Verde and to King Jonas and his Prime Advisor Thornhill. They can explain this fellowship later, but more urgent matters are at hand that require cooperation between Verde and Crimson."

"Cooperation?" the stocky man snorted.

"Yes," Aux shot back. "Not long ago, I witnessed Lapisians coming ashore in eastern Verde. Even as I watched, their numbers increased, and by now there could be many gathered there. I believe they are planning to attack Verde."

The stocky man frowned, shaking his head. "We have heard nothing of this from the coastal towns."

"I speak the truth," Aux boomed. "Verde is in danger and you must ride with us to meet Lapis."

The man held up his hands, as if to calm Aux. "I do not doubt your words, but we must stand guard and wait for orders from Samera before setting out on such a mission."

Aux grunted. "You cannot sit and wait for word from Samera. Gather together whatever Guardsmen and able-bodied Verdeans you can and ride now. We must protect Verde and stop this Lapisian invasion from destroying the Land."

The stocky man narrowed his eyes at Aux. "It seems odd that a Crimsonite would care so much for the woes of Verde." He looked to the slender man that stood quietly beside him. "Holant, does he speak the truth? What does the Land tell you?"

Holant hesitated at first, then bent down and held his palms to the ground. His aura flushed a pale shade of green as he listened with his hands, eyes gently closed. A few moments later, he nodded. "He speaks the truth. I can feel there is flooding and destruction along the shoreline."

The stocky man seemed to grow pale and looked up at Aux in alarm. "What do we do?"

Aux stood tall and lowered his voice. "We unite."

"Unite?" the stocky man asked incredulously. "Crimson and Verde?"

"The foe that you face is far beyond any of you. Unite, or die."

The stocky man looked to Holant, then nodded, holding out his hand to Aux, who grasped and shook it. "We choose to unite."

Aux grunted, motioning to the Crimsonite troops waiting a distance behind. "Those are my people. They are ready to fight and die for Graha. Gather as many like-minded Verdeans as you can. We ride for Samera!"

The Verdean Guardsmen raced back to the border station as Aux marched back to his troops. In all, fifty warriors of Crimson and fifty Guardsmen of Verde soon gathered and prepared to ride to Samera by way of Cypress, where they would rest, gather more troops, and warn the citizens of the coming attack. With the communications systems there restored, word would spread quickly, and King Jonas would soon know the danger that lurked on the shores of his creation. The stage had been set and the players assembled, awaiting the light of fate.

The Mazurin Gon

Rosette meandered through a peaceful garden, gazing up at a violet sky. A gentle breeze wafted the scent of grapa blossoms across her path and branches draped gracefully about her, dripping with white blooms so vibrant, they seemed illuminated from within. She breathed deeply, and was at once startled by a presence. She turned round and saw the face of her beloved Jonas, and her heart leapt inside her chest.

Jonas moved closer and embraced her warmly, his aura engulfing her in emerald light. Rosette pulled away, wanting to look into his eyes, then glanced up at the anomaly above. "Why is the sky so unusual today?" she asked, her arms resting about his shoulders.

Jonas chuckled knowingly. "Things are always a little different in our dreams, my love."

Rosette pulled away from him, her brow tight. *A dream?*

* * *

Rosette woke with a start. *It was just a dream,* she thought in despair, catching her breath. For a moment she thought it was still night, so dark were her surroundings. She then remembered Lium's betrayal, and how Fincher had blinded her and taken her prisoner the day before. She huffed and sat up, drawing the thin, cool air into her lungs, noticing a slight tinge of evergreen. The ground she sat upon felt cold and artificial, and she ran her hands over it. Solid metal. By the faint whistling of wind and the warmth of early sunlight on her face, she sensed that she was outdoors, or perhaps in some roofless enclosure. Rosette began to suspect that she had been placed in the Mazurin Gon of Jonquil, a labyrinthian maze full of perilous trials and impossible riddles. She had heard many tales of this place, and often fantasized about taking on the beast, but her disdain of Jonquil had kept her away.

Long ago, the Mazurin Gon had been used as a proving ground for the most clever and agile of Jonquilians — those who sought to become Prime Warriors. In the Gon, each would test their skill, finding their way through confounding illusions and obstacles that seemed insurmountable. The Mazurin Gon sat behind the Palace of Gosai, and Queen Zehn would watch from the observatory platform high above, carefully grading the tested. They would make their way through the twisted metal maze, pushed to the very limit of their abilities. If a warrior slipped even once and fell into a trap, the safeties would ensure they escaped with their lives, but they would suffer a fate worse than death: they would not be considered for Prime Warrior status.

As years passed and the kingdom fell into ruin, so did the Mazurin Gon. The safeties were not maintained and eventually broke loose, falling to the sands far below. The course itself, once a pristine spectacle of intricacy, had fallen into a frightful state of disrepair.

When Fincher came to rule Jonquil, he began using the Gon as both a prison and device for his own amusement. Though Fincher recognized the need for a holding place for the captured, he despised the thought of a simple prison structure. To a low-minded prisoner, such a place would seem inescapable, and they would quickly submit to their fate, a pitifully tiresome thing to observe. By contrast, a clever prisoner would likely calculate a way to escape a simple holding cell, and Fincher would not allow anyone to outsmart him. As a result, he created a prison within the maze, one that gave indication that it could be escaped somehow, if only a prisoner could figure out the grand riddle of how. In reality, his creation was a trap that no person, however clever, could ever escape. Since putting the deadly Mazurin Gon to use as a prison, he'd been afforded hours of riveting entertainment, watching the prisoners from the observatory platform at the back of the palace. Though each one courageously faced the beast, not a single one had escaped with their life.

Within the enclosure, Rosette heard stirring and swiftly scrambled into a defensive posture, facing the source of the sound.

"Easy lady, I'm not gonna do anything," a man's voice grumbled.

Rosette backed up a step and balled her fists a bit tighter. "What is this place?"

The man squinted at the woman before him, barely noticing her blank stare. He coughed, clearing the night's dusty congestion from his chest. "The first chamber of the Mazurin Gon. You're in prison."

"First chamber?"

"The holding chamber they put the prisoners in when they first get here." The man sat up, his dim green aura flashing as he finally got a good look at his new companion. "I've seen lots of people come through here. They all want to try their luck and break out of the chamber. I see how they do it, but I don't know why." He coughed once more and scratched at the long scar on the left side of his neck. "Not gonna get out with their lives. The Mazurin Gon is just one big death trap. Live wires, hungry raiku flying about, and bottomless pits that drop you through the disc and right down to the sands of Tenpi." The man stared up at the brightening sky through the open ceiling of the chamber. "I've taken that path before, I know where it leads. Now I just stay here in the chamber and wait for the joli to bring food to me. It keeps me alive, at least."

His voice echoed slightly in the metal room, though Rosette only half-listened. She could think only of escape. "How do I break out of this chamber?"

The man crossed his arms over his chest and sighed. "You'll

never get out of this maze, lady. It can't be done. The ones who've tried are all dead now—"

"Just tell me how they broke out of here," Rosette interrupted angrily. Upon considering the vulnerability of her position, she softened her tone. "Please."

The man paused, scraping his fingernails over his stubbly beard. "All right, I'll tell you how to get out of the chamber, but there are two guards posted just outside. Gonna have to deal with them before you can even try your hand at the Gon."

Rosette relaxed her defensive posture and squatted down where she estimated the man to be. He leaned toward her, speaking quietly. "This chamber is open. It's got no ceiling, but the top of the wall is electrified, and if you touch it..." The man stiffened his body, his face twisting in a pained expression. He chuckled. "It's all hot except for this one spot here, in the corner, where the power comes in. I've seen the others climb up there, whatever way they know, then if they keep on their tip toes at the corner there, they don't get cooked."

Rosette frowned. She rose and made her way into a corner of the room. "This corner?" she asked.

The man nodded. "That's the one."

Rosette ran her hands over the metal wall, testing the slickness of the surface. The smooth metal would provide little traction, and her eyes would be of no use. She straightened her arms with palms flat against either wall, then took a carefully measured step backward. She took another metered backward step, repeating the process until she had marked off seven paces from the wall.

She tilted her head to the side, knees bent, and at once dashed toward the wall. The man watched in wonder as Rosette ran up the wall at full speed, then jumped right, left, then back again off the opposite walls of the corner, ascending as she did.

As she reached the top of the wall, she felt the light of the suns on her face and reacted instantly, drawing her legs inward toward her center. She felt her right boot tilt forward as the toe found the top of the wall and rolled over, landing safely in the area that had not been electrified. Rosette cantilevered her left leg back as her body teetered forward, balancing herself on the narrow wall top. She inhaled deeply, calmly allowing her muscles and bones to align, feeling the harmony in her form. She slowly lowered her left leg, touching it gently down beside the other, and in the next moment, somersaulted into the air with a powerful leap. She rotated her body effortlessly as she dove down, landing with cat-like stealth and crouching on the ground just outside the chamber. The wide-eyed man within the chamber could only scratch his head at the feats he had just witnessed.

Rosette soon stood and leaned against the outer wall of the chamber, as if trying to camouflage herself as part of it. Her ears came alive, and every tiny sound sent tingles through her body. She could hear the guards speaking casually at their posts near the chamber door, the timbre of their voices resonating in her body. She would need a way to catch them by surprise, for in her condition, she could not face them as she normally would; she needed to be calculating. Rosette slumped her body forward and slowed her gait, moving cautiously toward where the guards stood watch.

"Help me, I can't see, will you help me?" she called helplessly, stumbling to the ground.

One of the guards swiftly wheeled round. "Hey, the blind girl!" He stepped forward with sword drawn. "How did you get out here?"

"I don't know what happened. I leaned up against a door and it opened and then I was out here."

"A door?" he cocked his head, puzzled. "The door's been locked since we got here."

Rosette furrowed her brow in feigned confusion. "Will you just lead me back inside?"

The guard shrugged at his partner and both quickly came to scoop her up, stowing their weapons upon approaching the blind and seemingly harmless woman. As they grasped her arms to lift her to her feet, Rosette smiled secretly, then swirled her wrists, quickly freeing herself from their grasp and securing her grip on them in one smooth motion.

She wrenched the men's arms behind their backs, and as they called out and wavered in pain, she forcefully knocked their heads together, rendering them unconscious. Rosette carefully stepped over the men. She blinked hard at the dark veil that blocked her view and found a pinpoint of light in the center of her visual field — it seemed there was hope that her sight might return.

Rosette rubbed her eyes, contemplating the best strategy.

Perhaps she could simply wait until enough of her vision had returned for her to make her way safely through the Mazurin Gon. Just then, one of the guards moaned in pain, writhing as he returned to consciousness. Rosette snapped her head instinctively to look at the awakening guard, realizing once more that she would not be able to see her enemy when he awoke to fight. She quietly shuffled away as quickly as she could manage. She could just barely see a halo of light forming around the pinhole of her visual field, but not enough to allow her to confidently navigate. Despite her condition and the odds stacked against her, she pressed urgently on, ever aware that the guards would eventually come looking for her.

Rosette made her way down a sloping metal ramp and scooted slowly along a path of the same material, her boots skimming the ground as she went. Though she had noticed the surrounding air carried the slight scent of evergreen for quite some time, the smell had intensified. Rosette paused, groping about to feel for whatever change had occurred. She found the path had narrowed considerably, and as she blindly extended her arms, she felt the prickly leaves of the brush wall on either side scratching her fingertips.

Gaining a sense of security from the proximity of the brush, Rosette increased her pace, using the flanking brush walls as her guide. As her fingers brushed against the foliage, it released a pungent aroma that spiced the light breeze wafting around her. Rosette found the fragrance quite pleasing and drew the scent deep into her lungs, yet as the breath moved down past her chest and into her belly, she felt a sinking sensation. She slowed, tuning in to the signals of her body, then stopped, troubled by a thought. *Beware the illusion of safety and the myth of peril.* She turned the words over in her mind, searching her memory, then finding their source. Sahler, the great Magister of Verde, had once told her those words in an effort to convey that things were not always what they seemed.

Rosette continued forward, cautiously and mindfully, as the path took what felt like a right angle turn, then straightened out once more. Within moments, the gentle rustling of the wind shifted to a steady howl as the air before her rushed downward. Startled, she stumbled and felt her body being pulled forward and down with the current. Rosette wavered, arms flailing as she tipped forward into a swirling air mass. She felt the toe of her boot tilt forward, as if the path before her had fallen away. The whirling helix of wind tugged at her. Fighting for her balance on just one leg, Rosette finally managed to fall safely to the ground, scooting backward and away from the anomaly. *What was that?*

She gathered herself and crept forward, carefully inspecting the area before her with her hands. Her fingers soon found a gaping hole in the metal of the maze; had she nearly tumbled from some precipice? She held her hand over the edge and felt a powerful vortex of wind rushing into it, drawing in anything that came within its grasp. As she felt her way around the edge of the hole, she found it a perfect circle covering the entire width of the path. Judging by the torrents of wind, it likely dropped straight through the bottom of the disc to the desert below. Had she continued walking carelessly forward, spurred on by her false sense of security, she would have been drawn into the vortex and down to her death on the sands.

Rosette huffed and leaned back, contemplating a way around this obstacle. She crawled over to the brush wall, tentative hands feeling along the twisted trunks of the brush. She tugged at the plant, checking the strength of its roots. Then, gripping it tightly, she swung her body out over the hole. The air currents tugged ferociously at her, testing the strength of her hands, but she held fast. She carefully worked her way over the hole, hand over hand, using the brush trunks as her anchor. Soon, she crossed the width of it and kicked her leg up onto the edge, sliding her body onto the cool metal on the other side. She sat and rested briefly, catching her breath, only then noticing the dryness of her throat. Fincher had taken her weapons and her canteen, and she had found no sign of water. There would be no relief yet for her thirst.

Far above in the observatory tower, Fincher watched, one brow lifted, as the sightless woman escaped the holding chamber and stumbled her way past the first obstacle of his Mazurin Gon. Rather than send guards in to subdue her, he chose to watch her drama of blind bravery and fortune unfold. Though Fincher had already penned the final chapter of her tale, he found no less amusement in the twists and turns of its telling.

Rosette continued on cautiously as the path sloped upward. She bent her knees, leaning forward to compensate for the increasing angle. Her boot suddenly slid backward on the slippery metal and she caught herself, pausing with fingertips held to the ground. She squeezed her eyes shut, then opened them once more, hoping to shake the blackness that blocked her vision. The halo of light that surrounded the bright pinhole of her vision had expanded slightly, but offered little help.

Rosette lifted one boot, then the other, tentatively climbing once more. Her ears tuned to a barely audible sound ahead, like the rush of a wing through the air. A wave of heat and tingling swept through her, and her gut churning insistently as if to warn her of imminent danger. She slowed her pace, and just as she did, she heard the rushing sound once more and felt a *whoosh* across the path directly in front of her. Rosette stopped awkwardly, then jumped in alarm at the sensation of sharp metal grazing her hand. Rosette grunted and fell backward onto the path, placing her mouth over the wound, wincing more with frustration than pain. Though the wound seemed little more than a scratch, she rightly assumed it could have been much worse.

Rosette sat still for a time, listening to the swishing sounds crossing the path before her. Her pinhole vision offered little in the way of information, so Rosette focused once more on her other senses. She tuned in to the rhythmic sounds and at once visualized what must await her. It seemed an array of blades had been set in motion, swinging ceaselessly back and forth across the path.

In that moment she remembered again the words of Magister Sahler. He had told Rosette that in battle, as in life, there is order, and striking with certain patterns of movement could ensure victory. *Rhythm and pattern,* Rosette thought. She came to stillness within herself, quieting her mind, and soon found that the sound of the swinging blades followed a precise rhythmic pattern. She could hear three blades, spaced one after the other, sweeping across the path in an arc. From the way the first blade had cut her hand, she could tell they swung close to the ground in the middle of the swing, then moved upward at the end of the arc. Rosette moved as close to the first blade as she safely could, feeling it disturb the air as it swung past her face, memorizing its trajectory and its speed.

Rosette listened with her entire body, attuned to the dance of metal through air. She could feel the pattern. *One, one, two, three, one, one, two three.* The first blade would swing twice across the path, then the second blade in one direction, the third in the opposite direction, then the entire pattern would repeat on the opposite side.

Rosette stood, blind eyes shut, counting, feeling, sensing, her body swaying slightly, following as each blade swept across the path. Then she saw it — a break in the pattern where she could slip by unharmed. The only way past the blades would be to crawl, like a serpent on fire, at just the right moment in the sequence, against the pull of gravity on a slippery metal slope. One miscalculation and she could be cut to the bone. Rosette crouched low, breathing deeply, her fingers pulsing with anticipation. She waited for the series of sounds that indicated the break in the pattern approached.

As the moment arrived, she leapt into action, diving past as the first blade swung to her right, then shimmying under the second as it passed overhead, just grazing the back of her vest. Rosette held her breath, listening for the *whoosh* of the third blade moving into its resting position. Fractions of a second stretched to an eternity as time ground to a near halt, affording her time to react. On impulse, she lurched forward, scrambling beyond the third blade just before it reached the midpoint of its swing.

Rosette finally scooted to safety and sat, chest heaving, fingers checking the place where a blade had brushed against her back. Though her vest had been slashed, her skin remained untouched. Rosette blew a strand of dark hair from her face, smoothing it back into place. As she sat catching her breath, she noticed the dark slate of her vision brightening slightly, and amorphous shapes just ahead became visible. Rosette balled her fists and stood once more, moving toward whatever the Gon held next.

After making her way past several more obstacles, Rosette moved into one of the last sectors of the Mazurin Gon, her vision having slowly improved with the completion of each challenge. Though still blurry and dark, she could now make out the shapes of things ahead of her and detect movement with a fair amount of ease. She kept a steady pace, twisting through the maze, moving ever closer to the end.

Just ahead, she heard the agitated voices of men shouting. She stopped her march and tucked her body back against the brush, hiding her form from view. Listening carefully to the voices, she discerned that two guards pursued another prisoner attempting an escape. Rosette squeezed her eyes shut, then opened them once more, peering through the foliage of the brush. She saw the man checking for the guards as he fled. The two guards followed close behind, swords drawn, calling after him to stop. Careless in his haste, the man did not see the danger ahead; just feet away, a pit of quickmetal lay in wait.

Though on the surface it caught the light in much the same way as the surrounding solid metal, when his boot struck the thin crust, it gave way, enveloping him in a suspension of fine metal particles and water. The sleek sides of the pit funneled inward, and the man slid hopelessly down toward his destruction.

"Help! Get me out of here, please!" he screamed as the pursuing guards arrived at the pit. "I promise I won't try to escape again!"

The man sank deeper as he pled, his chin resting just above the surface. "Please!"

The two guards looked at each other, puzzling over whether Fincher would prefer to watch him sink and die, or if he would want them to pull the man out and take him back to the beginning of the maze, where Fincher could watch him struggle through the entire course all over again.

The taller guard elbowed the other. "What do you think, do we pull him out?"

The other cocked his head. "Once he's dead, he's dead. If we pull him out, Fincher can make the final decision."

The other guard shook his head. "But if we interfere, Fincher might not like that. You know he likes to watch what happens naturally."

The man in the pit flailed his arms desperately, spitting out the quickmetal that now coated his lips. "Are you going to just stand there and watch me die?"

The guards glanced down at the man, then at each other in indecision. Before they could come to a verdict, Rosette sprang from the bushes and knocked the guards to the ground with two swirling kicks. As they fell unconscious, she turned her attention to the man trapped in the pit.

"Help, get me out of here!" he pleaded, stretching his hand up to Rosette.

Without hesitation, Rosette knelt down and grasped the man's hand, then tugged him up and out of the pit.

"Oh, thank you, thank goodness you came, those bastards were going to watch me die." The man rolled onto his back and finally sat up, shaking the quickmetal from his hands and arms. He untied and wiped his canteen, and after taking a swig, he offered it to Rosette. Rosette, grateful to finally quench her thirst, gulped eagerly from the canteen before handing it back to the man.

"I'm Dwyer, been here for a long time." Dwyer looked expectantly at Rosette, who sat silently beside him. "Do you have a name?"

Rosette squinted at the man, trying to bring his face into focus. "Rosette."

"Rosette, I owe you my life. Thank you." He took another sip from his canteen before tying it once more to his side. "I've been through the first three sectors of this maze many times. I've almost made it to the end twice, but each time Fincher sent his guards to take me back to the beginning to start all over." The man paused, shaking his head at the perversion of his captor. "I think he likes to watch. Right now, we are very close to the end. That's why Fincher sent his guards, so I wouldn't get too close to this next set of obstacles."

The man flicked a clod of quickmetal from his boot. "I know what's coming next in the Gon. I've made it into the next set of obstacles once, but I couldn't get through it alone. You need two people to really do it." He looked over at Rosette, placing a hand on her shoulder. "If we work together, we have a chance to beat it."

Rosette cringed as the last phrase left Dwyer's mouth. His words reminded her of what Lium had said at the battle of Thatch, how he had convinced her to trust him, to join with him, and then subsequently betrayed her. Rosette pulled away from Dwyer's touch and stood, narrowing her eyes at him. "I work alone."

Dwyer frowned at the woman, then shrugged, only half-disappointed. "Have it your way." He then turned his attention to a fork in the path ahead. A short distance down the left fork, he could just see a familiar foe, waiting as it always was. He called to Rosette, who stood over one of the unconscious guards. "Before you wander off, I will give you a word of advice." Rosette turned her attention from the guard and looked back at Dwyer.

"Take the right fork. The left fork is full of live wires. It's too dangerous, trust me." Dwyer lifted his hand and ran a finger along the scar on his forehead, unaware the woman could not clearly see his gesture. "I've been there."

Rosette thought for a moment about what Dwyer had said, then took the guards' swords and set them at her hips. She turned and walked forward a few paces to where she could make out the fork in the path. Though Dwyer had warned her of the danger on the left fork, she felt strongly compelled to take that direction. She moved toward the head of the left fork, squinting to focus her vision, finally catching a glimpse of what Dwyer had meant by *live wire*. It was not merely a fence through which electricity had been passed; the live wire was a living creature, a serpent wire, whipping and whirling its long, barbed body across the path, writhing on its posts. It hissed as she approached, flinging a section of itself at her with a stern crack. Rosette hesitated, then drew one of the swords and took a step onto the left fork.

Dwyer sat up taller, gaping at the seemingly reckless woman. "You're not seriously going to go down there with that thing, are you?"

Rosette looked at him with flashing eyes, saying nothing. Despite his warning, her intuition told her that the left was her path, the way that she must go. Dwyer stood at the head of the right fork, brushing the last of the quickmetal from his clothing. "You're insane, you know!"

Rosette left Dwyer to his path and strode confidently into the sights of the serpent wire, sword drawn. The creature reared up on its post, hissing and quivering, flicking its barbed body at Rosette. She slashed at the creature, slicing away a section that had stretched toward her. The serpent recoiled in pain, then tore three sections of its body from the posts, whipping toward its enemy. Rosette struck again with her sword. Her vision remained blurry at best, but she could see the creature had no discernible head; each part of its body seemed to function both independently and as part of the whole. She continued cutting through, twirling and ducking as barbed sections viciously whipped at her. She hesitated, and in that brief moment the creature lashed at her, cutting the skin of her arm.

Rosette winced angrily, gritting her teeth as she drew the second sword. She struck vengefully, severing more and more pieces of the animal with each swipe of her blades. Soon, she stood at the end, where the two forks met once more as one. The pruning had been complete; only a few lifeless barbs clung to the posts, and the remains of the serpent wire squirmed helplessly on the path.

Rosette sheathed her swords once more and started forward on the path. Just as she stepped away, she heard Dwyer's panicked shouts, punctuated by a sustained scream. Rosette determined that he had fallen down and away to the sands of the desert below. Had she followed him, she would have met with death as well. The cut she had sustained in her battle with the live wire throbbed painfully and she placed her hand over the wound, grateful for the pain that reminded her she yet lived.

Just then, she felt a shadow press down on her from overhead. She turned her still hazy gaze skyward and saw what had spooked Dwyer into fleeing so carelessly—a hungry male raiku. She ducked into a nearby hollow in the brush wall, hiding her body from the creature's glowing yellow eyes. The raiku circled slowly overhead, its throaty calls reverberating in the metal structure around her. Rosette scanned the area, searching for cover along her planned route of escape.

As the beast reached the far point of its circling path, she snuck out from her niche and tucked herself into a corner where the path turned sharply, hiding under the overhang of foliage. She looked up through the leaves, but the raiku seemed not to have noticed her. She eyed her next hiding place—an area where the brush wall had become especially overgrown, with thick branches covered in dense leaves arching out over the path. Rosette waited until she felt the beast would not catch her movement, then tiptoed out from her hiding place onto the open path. Despite her mindfulness, the raiku spotted her as soon as she moved, and it shrieked in excitement. The creature drew its wings up, terrible claws bared, then pulled them downward with a great thrust as it began its pursuit. Rosette quickly checked her position, then sprinted for the cover she had spotted from her last hide, the awful screeching drawing closer with each step. Though she knew she should not, she turned to check the raiku's proximity and saw a gaping, toothed beak mere feet from her.

She dove under the overhanging branches and rolled her body

in close to the base of a trunk. Just as she did, the creature landed and slid violently to a halt, growling as it lowered its head, peering at its prey. Rosette scooted farther back under the branches, recoiling at the foul breath of the beast. Agitated by her movement, the raiku attempted to wedge its beak under the branches, but found the space too narrow. It stomped its winged forelimbs angrily, scratching at the ground, its claws evoking horrible squealing sounds from the metal.

The animal turned its head, and to Rosette's dismay, the sideways-turned beak just fit under the branches, affording her a distressingly detailed view of the jagged teeth that lined it. Rosette swiftly drew one of her swords and braced herself against the trunk behind her. She thrust the blade deep into the raiku's jaw, twisting it even as the beast retreated, screeching vehemently.

The raiku shook its head in obvious pain, its yellow eyes flashing with fury. In a rage, the raiku then forcefully shoved its beak under the overhanging brush, sending Rosette scampering sideways, entangling itself in the process. As the creature struggled to free its head, Rosette saw that its horn had hung up in the thick branches above. Seizing the moment of advantage, Rosette leapt into action, scrambling out from her hide and jumping astride the creature's neck. The animal bucked and growled in frustration, yanking against the branches that trapped its horn. Rosette fought to stay in place, gripping with her legs as she drew both swords from her hips.

She raised the butts of both weapons high above her, holding the blades so they crossed in an X formation. She took a deep breath, her green glow swirling with jets of red. With a primal grunt, she drove the blades downward through the flesh of the neck, severing the bones beneath. The screeching was silenced as the headless body flopped down onto the path, toppling Rosette from her position.

Panting with relief, she got to her feet and stood next to the carcass, watching as the kumu drained from its body with its blood.

Through her battle with the raiku, Rosette had been unaware that the two guards she had earlier defeated had regained consciousness, and had come around the path just in time to witness the drama. They had seen the raiku's twitching body fall across the path, and the severed head with darkening yellow eyes reflected in the pool of blood below it. Rosette turned toward them, her clothing marked with the blood of the beast, eyes flaming red.

The guards, frozen where they stood, could not find the courage to challenge the woman who had single-handedly defeated them and slaughtered a vicious raiku. The guards looked at each other, nodded, and ran in the opposite direction.

Rosette wiped her blades clean on the surrounding foliage, readying herself for the final test of the Gon, unaware her every move was being watched.

In the observatory platform high above, Fincher watched, incredulous that the woman had killed his raiku and made it farther in his maze than anyone else, despite her visual impairments. He had watched with amusement and increasing alarm as she passed each obstacle, navigating the deadly maze with seemingly psychic precision. Now, she stood on the cusp of victory, mere steps from the final sector of the Mazurin Gon.

In light of her success, Fincher decided to pay her a visit. He stomped out of the room, concealing his concern beneath his usual stoic expression. Much to his aggravation, he would now have to use something he had been holding for a very long time.

Fincher marched into his study in the upper levels of the Palace of Gosai, his silken garment brushing along the polished floor as he went. He went to his writing desk and slid open a hidden drawer on the side, removing a locked chest. He untied a pouch from his waist, unfastened it, and took out a ringlet of three delicate keys, each cut with intricate patterns. He unlocked the chest and took from it a vial of deep green, viscous liquid. He tilted the vial in his fingertips, watching the fluid shifting inside. "Ah, kumain, I regret I must part with you today," he whispered.

The fluid, an incredibly rare serum made by liquefying the kumu crystal used in emanators, was deadly to anyone from the Land in which the crystal was mined. The serum Fincher now held had been made from Verdean crystal, and was therefore deadly to Verdeans, but not to those from other Lands. As an unusual twist, if the Verdean serum were injected into a person from a Land other than Verde, that person became a deadly weapon, capable of killing anyone from the Land of Verde with a single touch. Fincher loved the complexity of this weapon, so clever in its design and effects, with endless possibilities for manipulation. He loaded the vial into a syringe-like device and carefully tucked it away in his pocket. After locking the chest once more, Fincher methodically replaced the keys in his waist pouch and retied it, a half-smile curling one side of his mouth.

Word of War

One hundred riders thundered over the fields outside the village of Cypress, a trail of dust rising into the air behind them. Though Aux and his warriors had come to Cypress to rest before moving on to Samera to bring counsel to King Jonas, they could not know they would find the king right there in the village. Jonas had come to meet with some of his advisors and constituents who warned of unrest on the shores of Verde. Some had even said that Root, the young boy now under Jonas' care, had seen King Jonas devoured by a great blue serpent in a recent dream.

Aux and his men stopped at the crest of the hill where the guard stations of Cypress stood. Woodson and Bract soon greeted him, looking over the gathered riders with eyes wide. Bract descended the stairs from his post in the east tower as Woodson made his way over from the west. Bract approached Aux, nodding respectfully. "Prime Warrior Aux, what brings you and...," Bract paused and glanced back at the group, "...Verdean and Crimsonite riders, *together*, to Cypress?"

Aux grunted. "Trouble, brother. Lapisians are coming aground on the eastern shore. I believe they are going to invade Verde. We warriors have sworn to unite and fight to protect Verde and Graha against this threat."

Bract furrowed his brow. "How many Lapisians have come ashore?"

"Many days ago I saw at least a hundred gathered. There could be thousands by now."

Woodson had arrived from the west tower and overheard the two men talking. "What do we do?"

"Spread word of the coming war and gather as many as you can to ride with us, not only Guardsmen, but all those willing to fight. In the morning we ride for Samera to warn King Jonas of the trouble on his shores."

Woodson shook his head, "King Jonas is here in Cypress. He's meeting with constituents in the town hall."

"Hmf!" Aux chortled. "Finally, a bit of good fortune. In that case, ride into the village with us. King Jonas will give your orders."

Woodson and Bract both nodded dutifully, moving back through the crowd to find someone with whom to ride.

Aux and his riders descended the hill in a wave of pounding hooves and pulsing auras. The village center sprawled out, green and thriving, at the base of the hill. As they turned onto the central road, they found the buildings well tended; new windows gleaming, walkways swept clean. The village hall stood proud once more with regal hardwood pillars and polished stone accented with lush strands of ivy. The streets bustled with people who, though busily tending to their work, made time to smile at passersby.

For Aux, the seemingly idyllic tableau was overshadowed by doom that lurked on not too distant shores.

The warriors caused quite a stir as they rode into the heart of the village. The inhabitants, already uneasy from hearing rumors of unrest, stopped and stared at the numerous trail-sullied men and women galloping in on snorting beasts. Half immediately turned and ran for the safety of their homes, while the others stood watching warily for signs of aggression. Upon arriving in front of the village hall, Aux called for a halt and dismounted his kontross, tying it to a nearby post. He made eye contact with a tall man a few paces from him, but before he could speak, the man took off, sprinting for the hills. Aux huffed in frustration, stowing his whelix in his saddlebag and scanning the area for someone who would not run from him.

Across the road, he spotted a dark-haired woman in a plain brown dress, her countenance as still and calm as a mountain lake. Aux looked at her fair face and she met his eyes without looking away. Feeling hopeful, Aux waved to her and approached in as friendly a manner as possible, with Woodson and Bract in tow. The young woman lifted her chin slightly as she inspected the enormous man. Though she stood on an elevated porch, his eyes were level with her own.

Aux finally spoke. "I am Aux, Prime Warrior of Crimson, and you likely already know Guardsmen Woodson and Bract, who travel with me. I have urgent news for King Jonas."

The young woman blinked thoughtfully. "What news?"

"Verde is in danger. Lapisians are invading the eastern shore and I must see Jonas now."

The woman paused, looking into Aux's eyes as she tuned in to her intuition. "Your words are sincere. I will find King Jonas at once. Wait here."

Aux bowed slightly as the young woman passed, her skirt brushing lightly over the cobbles of the street as she scurried into the village hall. Within minutes, the young woman emerged along with King Jonas, whose aura flashed brightly when he caught sight of Aux and the Guardsmen. "Aux, my friend," Jonas said, offering a warm handshake.

Aux took his hand, but only half-smiled. "King Jonas, I'm afraid I come to you with solemn news."

Jonas nodded knowingly. "My advisors are gathered in the village hall. Come, let us share what we know."

The two Guardsmen and Aux followed Jonas into the hall and down a corridor until they came to the meeting chamber. An ebony table stretched the entire length of the room and colorful tapestries softened the stone walls. A number of Verdeans sat upon the high-backed chairs, while others stood, closely observing the striking newcomer. At once, a wild-haired boy poked his head out from behind one of the chairs. He watched as Aux entered the room, following the giant's movements as he walked to the end of the table.

Jonas took his place at the head. "This is Aux, Prime Warrior of Crimson and friend to Thornhill and me. He has come with news from the eastern shore."

Aux nodded to acknowledge the gathered. "Not ten days ago, I saw many Lapisians coming aground on the eastern shore of Verde. They did not look friendly."

Hushed voices rose in response, and Jonas raised his hands to bring order to the room.

Aux continued, "I believe that Lapis is preparing to invade Verde. Corpus' influence is stronger than ever there. Do not doubt the weight of this matter."

The gathered began quietly speaking amongst themselves once more, and the young boy then went to Jonas, tugging at his sleeve. "Tell them about the monster, Jonas," he whimpered.

Though Jonas had intended to dismiss the boy's request, a gray-haired man took note. "Of what does he speak, Jonas?"

Jonas shook his head. "Root has had a recurring nightmare where I am swallowed up by a great blue serpent, after which everything turns to darkness."

The gray-haired man lifted a brow. "My king, there may be just cause for concern, but let us not base our judgments on the content of a child's dream."

The young boy climbed up and stood on the seat of a nearby chair, and his green aura flushed with shades of aqua. "The *water...* the monster was in the water!" he cried.

"Hush, child!" the gray-haired man scolded. "It was just a bad dream, nothing more."

Jonas held his palms high, his face stern. "Everyone listen now. Verde, by all accounts, is in grave danger. We must gather together all Guardsmen and any others who are willing to fight to defend the eastern shore." Jonas turned to the two Guardsmen near him. "Bract, Woodson, one of you head north and the other, south. Warn all the villages of the coming danger and bring any riders along with you."

Woodson and Bract nodded and left immediately as Aux spoke. "What of Thornhill and Botan, and Highpointe Rosette? Will they join us at the shore?"

Jonas' aura dimmed slightly and shifted to an olive tone as his expression darkened. "Highpointe Rosette is still being held prisoner in Jonquil, somewhere in Selatan territory. Thornhill and Botan have promised to see to her release as they and the Sankari Sano work to restore Queen Zehn to the throne."

Aux lowered his head, tugging at his scruffy beard in thought. "Then let us ride. Every hour we delay is an enemy's arrow."

Jonas nodded in agreement and motioned for his constituents to follow him out of the village hall and onto the central road. As he exited the building, Jonas could sense a gloom descending, an unnatural storm blowing in on dark winds from the sea. Something was already happening on the eastern shore of his creation.

King Jonas and Aux stood together before the gathered, their auras blending in a flurry of scarlet and emerald. Jonas stepped forward. "My friends, I wish to express my deepest gratitude for your loyalty and bravery. Despite the circumstances, it makes my heart light to know that warriors from other Lands have come together to fight for Verde, and for Graha united."

Aux grunted and gripped his whelix. "The time has come for all Lands to unite against this one doom. We cannot defeat Corpus as separate Lands. Though the Sankari Sano has come, as the prophecy promised, unity is our true savior."

Jonas stepped forward. "Raise your weapons now, as pledge and promise, to unite and fight for Graha, to restore this Land and defeat the Dark One!"

The riders, men and women alike, then raised their weapons high, shouting in response to Jonas' call. Jonas turned to Aux, and both men held a long moment of eye contact, knowing that though the odds stacked up against them, they were brothers nonetheless, and if they were to die, it would be for justice.

Aux soon mounted his kontross and organized the riders into ranks. King Jonas turned from the scene and walked a few paces away in contemplation. *Queen Helena's heart would break if she knew that her Land, born of peace, compassion, and respect for life, was now the initiator of a war,* Jonas thought. He knew that in the coming battle, he would face the Dark One, the Deceiver, the one who had cast him to the Inner Realm to be lost for a lifetime.

Where did this evil force come from? In the Beginning, the Four Founders had come together and created a place of harmony, where beings could live in peace above the blight of violence and hate. How had this disease been allowed to invade his creation. How had this come to pass? Jonas turned back to look over the riders whom had gathered in support of Verde. Whatever the odds, they would face Corpus united.

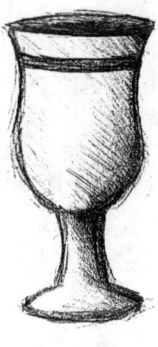

PART 5

THE CUP OF TRUTH

Mila left the heavy sadness of Salvitor's dedication with an urgent mission: to find the map he had left in her realm and return with it to Graha. Without the map and the cache of devices and tools it led to, the group would be left with precious little information on what to do next to restore Queen Zehn to the throne. With watcher minions already reporting the whereabouts of the group to Corpus, time was rapidly ticking away.

Mila stepped through the doorway and back into her bedroom, pausing as her eyes gradually adjusted to the darkness. As she stood, she could just begin to make out the amorphous forms of Sandi and Amy tucked in their sleeping bags next to her own. As her eyes adapted, she suddenly gasped: there before her sat Madison, wide awake and awash in a red glow very similar in shade to Aux's. For a long moment, the two girls stared at each other, unable to speak. Finally, a sleek gray cat awoke and rose slowly from his resting place. "Meow!" he called, tilting his head in curiosity.

The cat broke Madison from her frozen state, and she blinked at Mila in confusion. "What was that I just saw?" she whispered urgently.

"Um..." Mila cut her eyes left, then right, reluctant to reveal details. "What did you see?"

"I saw a doorway, and you walked through the wall!" Madison replied, waving her arms to demonstrate, then noticing something even more unusual. Each time she moved her arms before her, she detected a faint red glow coming from her skin. Madison gasped and her eyes widened. "Oh my gosh, why am I all *red?*" she said loudly.

Amy moaned and turned over in her sleeping bag, disturbed by their noise.

Mila hastily shushed Madison, holding her hands up to quiet her.

Thankfully, Amy soon settled down. Mila blinked slowly as she realized the fullness of what was happening: Madison was *glowing,* and could see her own light. Mila stepped closer to her friend, whispering, "So, you can see that red glow on your skin?" Madison said nothing, but nodded with eyes wide. "And, can you see the glow coming from my skin?"

Madison gathered herself and looked closely at her best friend, only then detecting a white haze of light around her that seemed to pulse as she breathed.

"Oh, whoa...you're glowing white!" Madison began breathing rapidly, and her fair face seemed to grow even paler. "Mila, I feel dizzy..."

Mila grabbed her friend by the hand and gently tugged her toward the door. "Come on, let's go downstairs and get a drink of water. It'll make you feel better." Mila glanced at Amy, ensuring the girl had indeed gone back to sleep. "Just be really quiet, okay?"

Madison nodded weakly, and the two friends tiptoed down the hall to the stairs. Mila's parents had already gone to bed and the house was quiet and dark. Mila did not turn on any lights for fear of waking someone, so they felt their way down the stairs, hands sliding over the smooth oak bannister and bare feet stepping gingerly.

Once in the kitchen, Mila could see fairly well by the light of the range hood, which was always left on—Stephen's late night trips to the fridge resulted in fewer broken dishes that way. Mila took two glasses from the cupboard and filled them with water from the dispenser. The girls sat at the table, sipping at their waters and trying to soothe their frayed nerves. Mila set her glass down, closing her eyes for just a moment. "Okay, so let's just calm down and try to figure this out. Why did you wake up, and what did you see?"

Madison sighed. "I was having that dream again, the one where I'm floating by the mountain and I see the man climbing up the side, and all I'm trying to do is float over to him to tell him to get off the mountain." Madison paused and thumbed her glass. "Well, this time when I saw him, I knew his name was Mason, and I yelled his name as loud as I could, but he couldn't hear me."

Mila lifted a brow. *Mason?* In Graha, the King of Crimson was named Mason; could it be that her best friend was somehow connected with the Outer Realm?

Madison interrupted Mila's thoughts. "And then the man got sucked into that hole, same as always, and I woke up. That's when I saw you." Madison fixed her eyes pointedly on her friend. "You walked right through the wall, like there was a doorway all lit up, and then you disappeared for a second and walked right back out of the wall again. How did you do that?" Madison stared woefully at her arms once more. "And why are we *glowing*?"

Mila exhaled heavily and lowered her head. What had been hidden in the shadows for so long had been brought to light, and from this moment on there could be no more secrets between best friends. It was time for the impossible truth to come out. Mila took both of Madison's hands in hers and looked her directly in the eyes, "Madi, if I tell you this, you have to swear you won't tell anybody, not even your mom."

Madison shrugged. "Okay."

"No. I mean it, Madi, you *have* to keep it a secret." Mila lifted her pinky finger up to Madison. "Pinky swear?"

Madison hooked her pinky finger around her friend's, and they shook on it. "Pinky swear."

"Okay, here goes." Mila took a deep breath. "When we were running to school on the last day of fifth grade, that was the first time I started to glow. When you went on vacation, I mostly just went to the beach every day to run and try to figure out why I was glowing, because at first, running really fast was what made me glow. But one day at the beach, this old man came up to me and gave me this watch." Mila held up her wrist to Madison so she could see the unusual timepiece. "Then he just disappeared into thin air."

"How come you never told me about all this?" Madison asked.

"I tried to tell you, Madi. The first time I started glowing I tried to show you, but you couldn't see it, so I thought it was just my imagination. But while you were at Horseshoe Lake, it kept happening. And then one time, my glow opened the doorway and I...stepped through."

"Stepped through?"

"Madi, it's a doorway to *another world*. I can go there and stay for a while and while I'm gone, the watch freezes time here so nobody knows I left. It's a whole other world with different animals and people, and they need me for something important."

"What?" Madison huffed.

"I know it sounds weird, but it's true."

Madison shook her head. "I can't believe you didn't tell me. I'm your best friend!"

"I'm really sorry, Madi, I thought I was just going crazy. When you came back from your grandma's and you still couldn't see my glow, I was scared to tell you because you might think I'm crazy, too. Until just now, I guess I almost didn't believe it was real, like the whole thing was some kind of dream or something." Mila picked up Madison's glowing arm, smiling. "But now that you can see it too, I *know* it must be real, and now it's our special secret."

Madison shook her head, her complexion turning green. "I don't feel so good, Mila. I gotta go home!"

Madison jumped up from the table and rushed to the front door, storming out into the darkness, shoeless and still in her pajamas. Mila followed, but stopped at the top of the porch steps. "Madi, wait!" she called, but Madison's ruby glow rapidly disappeared down the block like a fading firefly.

Santo soon bounded down the stairs to investigate, meowing in curiosity. He stood up on his hind paws and peered out the screen door at Mila.

She watched until she saw Madison's faint red glow disappear inside the O'Reilly home. Mila went back inside the house, quietly shutting the front door and tiptoeing into the kitchen for one last sip of water with Santo in tow. As she picked up her glass from the table, she saw a strange red cup that she had not noticed before. Finishing her water, she took up the stone vessel, surprised at the weight and coolness of it in her hand. *What the heck happened to Madi's glass? Too* tired to think of an explanation of her own, Mila showed the cup to Santo, as if to ask his opinion. The cat sniffed at the strange cup, bumping it gently with his nose before disregarding it completely. Mila sighed as she set down the cup and motioned to Santo. "Come on, kitty, we have to go back upstairs. Be extra quiet, okay?"

Santo meowed softly and followed Mila as she climbed the stairs with the same cat-like stealth as her furry friend, silently slipping into her room. The restless Amy began to stir once more and then awoke, looking at Mila with one eye half-open, the other shut tight. "What's going on?" she mumbled.

Mila gently closed her bedroom door, thinking quickly. "Madi wasn't feeling so good and she had to go home."

Amy tilted her head inquisitively and scratched her temple.

"You know," Mila continued, pointing behind herself and holding her nose, indicating that Madison had been suffering with intestinal issues.

Amy nodded knowingly. "Oh, that stinks." She smiled to herself as the pun registered in her sleepy brain, slowly lowering her head to her pillow and dozing off again.

Mila breathed a sigh of relief and finally sensed her own exhaustion. She had already experienced a journey in the Outer Realm and had then returned, only to find herself in the hot seat with a mess of explaining to do. She was most certainly ready for sleep. Santo padded to her as she nestled in her sleeping bag, inviting the cat to curl up in the space near her belly. He did so, and purred contentedly as Mila sleepily stroked the length of his back, her hand moving ever slower until she fell fast asleep.

Hiding in Plain Sight

Mila woke with a start and immediately began thinking of Salvitor and the map. She could feel her heart quicken, tuning in to the urgency of the matter. She looked around her room, searching for anything that could either be a clue to its whereabouts, or the map itself. Her eyes came to rest on the mobile of the solar system near her window, the motionless spheres ever awaiting a breeze to set them circling in their orbits. She looked to the battered mermaid clock on her nightstand. Mila had always thought her coy smile seemed to indicate that the mermaid knew some secret, but she dismissed the idea that the clock could somehow be a map of any kind.

Mila spotted Madison's empty sleeping bag. She paused her search and zipped it closed, rolling it up neatly and pulling it into her arms. *I'd better tell Mom about Madi going home,* Mila thought. Still clasping the sleeping bag, she went to her parents' room and found her mother reading in bed. Olivia looked up and smiled, and Mila could hear her father singing in the shower in the adjacent master bath.

"Morning, Mila. Are you girls up already?"

"Kinda. Madi had to go home early, she didn't feel good."

Olivia's brow tightened with concern. "Goodness, did she get home okay? I should call her mother to be sure—"

"Oh, no," Mila interrupted. "I watched her walk into the house, and she's probably still sleeping and trying to feel better. Maybe we should wait to call her."

"All right," Olivia conceded, glancing at her bedside clock. "Are the other girls up yet?"

"No, they're still sleeping."

"Well, Mrs. Moorehouse is coming to pick up Sandi and Amy in an hour. Try to wake them so they will be ready to go when she gets here." Olivia closed her book and sat up on the side of the bed. "And I better get moving myself."

"Okay, Mom, we'll be ready."

Mila left the room and headed down the hall to wake her friends. Not long after, the three trotted down the stairs and into the living room to wait. Mila could hear her mother talking on the phone, or perhaps more appropriately, offering only a few words during long periods of silent listening. The blow of a horn broke her from eavesdropping, and she saw a black sedan pull into the driveway. "Your mom's here," Mila said to Sandi.

Mila followed Sandi and Amy out onto the porch, waving to them as they hopped in the car. She then made her way back into the kitchen, where her mother leaned against the counter, gazing up at the ceiling, phone held slightly away from her tired ear. Olivia glanced at Mila and shook her head, pointing to the phone and the long-winded caller on the other end. Mila laughed to herself and grabbed an apple from the fruit basket before sitting down at the table. The water glass she'd used the night before was still there, along with the strange cup that looked to be made of red stone. Olivia picked up the vessel, turning it in her hand and admiring the artful patterns of the stone. As Mila watched her mother inspect the cup, a flash of realization shot through her, and her glow pulsed in response.

"Mm-hm. You can't control what's going to happen, Mike." Olivia paused, interrupted again by the chatty caller. "Go with the flow, right."

Olivia caught Mila's eye once more and held up the stone vessel, gesturing to it as if inquiring where it came from. Mila shrugged and shook her head; she had her suspicions, but not a word of it could be spoken to her mother.

"Hey...hey, Mike? Mila is up and she wants to talk to you," Olivia nodded enthusiastically to her daughter. "It's your Uncle Mike," she whispered, covering the microphone.

Mila grimaced and reluctantly took the phone. "Hi, Uncle Mike. Yeah, I did get the birthday plane tickets, thanks a lot for those..."

Mila, like her mother, found little pause in the deluge of chatter. She listened for a time, trying in vain to contribute to the conversation, then rested her head in her hand in defeat. Eventually, Uncle Mike did come up for air long enough to wait for answers to a few questions.

"Yeah, school is going good," Mila replied. She looked up at her mother and shrugged, shaking her head slowly. "Um, yeah, I'd like to come visit..." Mila sank lower in her seat, frustrated at yet another interruption. "We'll come soon, I promise. Do you want Mom back?"

Olivia waved her hands wildly and shook her head, mouthing *no* repeatedly.

"Okay, I'll tell her. Bye-bye!" Mila hung up the phone.

"Whew!" Olivia huffed in relief.

"Uncle Mike said to tell you goodbye, and that the twins want us to come visit soon."

"Good grief, that man can talk," Olivia lamented.

Mila giggled. "I know!"

"I don't know how your father got a word in edgewise growing up with Mike." Olivia laughed, then returned her attention to the red stone vessel. She picked it up once more, holding it to the light.

"Mila, do you know where this came from? I've never seen it before."

"Um," Mila hesitated, walking the line between truthfulness and secrecy. "I think it's Madi's."

Olivia cringed. "In that case, I better wash it."

She squirted a generous blob of dish soap into the vessel and gave it a thorough scrubbing, being careful to remove any germs that could have contributed to Madison's sudden illness. Olivia admired the carvings on the vessel as she dried it. "It really is beautiful. I wonder where they got the set?"

Mila scooted her bare feet down the leg of the table, enjoying the smooth texture of the wood on her soles. The sound her skidding feet made was unnerving, and she continued with hope of distracting her mother from the stone cup.

"You know, the weather is supposed to be gorgeous today," Olivia said, glancing out the kitchen window at the bright blue above. "Not a single cloud up there right now."

An idea suddenly popped into Mila's head. Perhaps a walk on the beach would help clear her mind and lead her to the mysterious map she sought. "Is it okay if I go to the beach for a while?"

"You can go right after breakfast if you want. Just be back in time to help me clean out the flower beds."

"Okay, I will," Mila replied, and disappeared up the stairs to her room.

As Olivia had predicted, it was indeed a beautiful day. The mid-morning sun streamed cheerfully from the cloudless sky, sending sparkles across the surface of the sea. The gentlest breeze wafted in from the ocean, and Mila filled her lungs with the salt air. Despite the urgency of her task, she found herself relaxing as she walked along the beach. The warm sand squished between her toes, and a seagull flanked her on the ocean side, hoping to snag a scrap of something edible. The scene reminded her of a day two summers past, when she and Madison had walked along that same stretch, tossing French fries to a group of enthusiastic gulls. They had unintentionally incited a feeding frenzy, and ended up abandoning the container of fries, sprinting to the boardwalk to escape the birds. Mila smiled at the memory. In that moment, she wished Madison could be there with her, not only to help her find the map, but to bear the enormity of all that had been placed on her shoulders on the other side of the doorway. But Madison was already overwhelmed, and would need some time before she could deal with all that she had learned the night before.

Mila sighed and walked on, remembering Thornhill's instructions. He'd told her that she must find the map as quickly as she could, that the group desperately needed Sal's guidance and tools to find Queen Zehn. She had also promised to find Rosette, who'd been captured in Jonquil, and bring her back to Verde. Though Mila didn't know how she would do it, she needed to keep her promises.

Mila kicked a clod of wet sand out before her and watched it break up in the air before splashing down into the surf. She thought of the mysterious old man who had dug the watch out of the sand that day at the beach. Something told her that man must have been Salvitor. Could it be that the map was buried somewhere in the sand as well?

Mila looked out over the vast expanse of beach ahead and thought of the impossible task of finding a buried map. She'd heard somewhere that there were as many grains of sand on the beach as there were stars in the sky, and a cloudless night at her aunt's house in the country had revealed just how futile that search would be.

Mila sighed in resignation and glanced at her watch to check the time, wondering if the watch itself could be a clue. Pixie had dismissed the idea, but Mila unfastened the watch to inspect it anyway. She flipped it over and noted the etching of the eleven symbol. She pressed it hard with her thumb, hoping to stumble upon a secret compartment she'd missed before, but finding none. Mila shrugged and strapped the watch once again to her wrist. She turned from the sea and looked toward the boardwalk and its many shops. Perhaps it was time to take a break from searching to enjoy a treat.

Nearby, she spotted the umber-colored building that housed Go Joe, the coffee shop owned by Vincent's parents. His Aunt Elena had made a delicious frozen drink for Mila earlier in the summer. She jangled the change in her pocket and withdrew a handful to count it. She smiled at the total and eagerly headed for the boardwalk. She jogged through the dunes and onto the boards, now creaking as they grew warm under the influence of the late morning sun.

As she crossed onto the tiled patio of the shop, an elderly woman looked up at her and smiled, and Mila greeted her as she opened the door. The familiar tinkling of the bell rang out overhead, and a young man behind the counter looked up. It was Vincent, working that day at the shop to earn his allowance.

"Oh! Hey Mila!" Vincent barely concealed his excitement.

Mila waved, approaching the counter. "Hi, Vincent. I was just really thirsty and I wanted to try that frozen drink again."

"Okay, I'll get my aunt and she can make it for us," he said, hastily disappearing into the kitchen.

Within moments, Vincent emerged with his Aunt Elena, who flashed her trademark bleached-white smile. "Hi, sweetie! Oh, tell me your name again..."

"Mila."

"Mila! That's right. So, you want another one of my special frozen decaf lattes, huh?" Elena said proudly.

Mila nodded, smiling. "Yes, please, they're really good."

"Coming right up," Aunt Elena shooed Vincent from behind the counter, encouraging him to socialize with his guest.

He came around to the seating area, where Mila had moved to look over some of the art on the walls. A few of Vincent's fractal pictures were featured prominently, their colors especially luminous in the yellow light that streamed in the storefront windows. At the end of the row she noticed one in blue tones that she had not seen before, its flowing colors mimicking swirling ocean water with light reflecting over the surface. She turned to Vincent, who stood fidgeting beside her.

"How do you make these?" she asked.

"I make them on my computer. You can let the computer do it, or you can make your own pattern."

"Yeah, but how do you decide what you want them to look like?"

Vincent shrugged. "I dunno. Sometimes I have a dream about it, and then I just go on my computer and make it like I saw in the dream." Vincent pushed his glasses a bit higher on his nose. "My father says that Neolardo—I mean, Leonardo Da Vinci used to have dreams about his inventions and things, and that's how he came up with all kinds of stuff. I think he's really neat because he was a really famous artist, but he was an inventor, too. My father, he has a picture of the man—" Vincent held his arms out to demonstrate the appearance of the art piece, "—the Vitruvian Man, in his office back there. I like to look at his paintings but I *really* like to look at the drawings he did of all his inventions. I think I would like to invent something someday..."

Vincent cut himself off mid-sentence. He was rambling again. He could almost hear his mother's voice chiding him for going on and on. He looked over at Mila, afraid she would be bored by his chattering, but she simply looked on with interest.

"So, what do you want to invent?" she asked.

Vincent smiled and enthusiastically shoved his hand into his pocket, pulling out a tattered paper that had been folded many times. He unfolded it carefully and held it out to Mila. "I want to invent something like this. It's a flying machine that Da Vinci dreamed up. I think it would be cool."

Mila took the paper from Vincent and glanced at the sketch. Her eyes widened—the depicted machine looked very much like the sanlifter she had flown over Jonquil in the Outer Realm. "Hmm, that would be cool," she said nonchalantly.

Mila handed the paper back to Vincent and returned to looking over the art on the wall. A red "Sold" tag caught Mila's eye, and she studied the picture it marked. It was a painting Elena had sold for one hundred dollars some time ago. "If you don't become an inventor, you could become a famous artist. You already sold one!"

Vincent bashfully lowered his head, smiling. Mila moved closer to the picture, thinking there was something strangely familiar about it. Of course, she'd seen the picture before, but now the swirling patterns of gold and white stood out like neon déjà vu. She traced the curve of one spiral with a finger and at once it struck her—the spirals in the fractal picture looked exactly like the rotating cloud formations she'd seen when ascending into Jonquil.

Her heartbeat quickened; could this be a clue? Thornhill had said Salvitor loved patterns, and Vincent had explained that he used repeating patterns to make the pictures. In light of its striking resemblance to Jonquil's clouds, Mila was almost certain the picture was either a vital clue or the map itself. She turned to Vincent. "Is it okay if I take this up to the counter real quick? I want to ask your aunt something about it."

"Sure," Vincent squeaked, carefully removing the picture from its hook and handing it to her.

Mila walked to the counter where Elena busily wiped the espresso machine. As she approached, Elena smiled and pushed the two frozen drinks across the counter. "Here you go. These are on the house,"

"Oh, thanks, thanks a lot," Mila replied, taking a big slurp through the red spoon-straw, then pointing to the picture she had in hand. "Didn't you say before that somebody bought this picture, and that his friend was going to pick it up?"

Elena glanced at the picture, nodding. "Yeah, that's the one. The name of the guy that's picking it up is on the receipt taped on the back."

Mila felt her heart jump into her throat as she flipped the picture over and thumbed the receipt, almost afraid to see what name had been written there. Finally, she turned the slip over. *Sankari Sano.* Mila froze, eyes fixed on the name as Elena went on. "He hasn't showed up yet, so I figured Mr. Sano must be some foreign fella, you know, maybe Hawaiian or somethin' exotic like that."

Elena sniffed the air and jumped. "Oh goodness, I'll be right back. I gotta get the concentrate off the stove!"

She dashed into the kitchen as Mila gaped in disbelief at the name on the back of the receipt. *Sankari Sano.* This was it, this *must* be the map. Though it didn't look like any map she'd seen in school, the familiar cloud-like swirls would likely mean something to Thornhill or someone else in the group. But how would she get it out of the coffee shop? Surely Aunt Elena would not let her take it.

Just then, a loud crash and a shout burst from the kitchen. Vincent's eyes bugged out. "Oh, man, I'll be right back, that didn't sound so good!"

Mila looked on as Vincent raced into the kitchen to see what all the commotion was about, leaving her alone in the front of the shop. Mila glanced down at the map, then craned her neck to peek through the kitchen door. Vincent and Elena seemed to have a whale of an issue on their hands; she could hear them chattering in between sloshing and banging sounds. It seemed that this was her chance. Mila built her nerve and unhooked the backing from the frame, carefully sliding out the picture. She glanced around once more to be sure no one was looking, then quickly opened a doorway beneath her feet, vanishing through the tile floor and onto the other side. An empty picture frame and a pair of frozen lattes were all that remained, hovering in time.

Assembly of Dark Warriors

Far above the Land of Verde, a malevolent presence hung in the air. Wreathed in shadow and black cloud, Corpus the Dark One looked out over a massive Lapisian army, numbering in the tens of thousands, covering the eastern seaboard. The great army had fallen under his command without so much as a whimper of resistance. Each one, in a singular moment of surrender, had turned from the light and embraced his darkness. With a single touch, Corpus had tainted the very lifeblood of Lapis, the sea, with his poison. He had poured into the waters his hatred, his malice, and his will to destroy all life on Graha. The waters then carried his evil intent into the minds and hearts of the people of Lapis, allowing him to effortlessly seize control of an entire nation with one thought. Most of the people of Lapis, now wholly possessed by this evil, obeyed the will of the Dark One above all. The precious few Lapisians that had escaped this fate fled or went into hiding, refugees in their own Land.

With his army now assembled, Corpus called forth his servant Micca, the Waymaker of Lapis. In the receding breakers near the shore, his mighty figure began to emerge. Seawater dripped from the long black ropes of his hair and streamed from his brown skin. His crooked smile twisted the form of his face, his brows held taut over his haunted eyes as he stood on the Verdean shore, whirlpools curling about his feet. He raised his arms into the air, shouting an incantation in praise of the Dark One. The assembled army responded in a sinister wave of shouts, and a call and response ensued. The voices rolled over the surface of the dark waters, building in a wind that rushed from the sea onto the coast.

Despite the impressive display of allegiance, the Dark One wrestled ceaselessly with his own anger. The young girl had somehow escaped his grasp, finding King Jonas and returning him to the throne in Samera. How was it that a mere child had been able to travel so effortlessly between realms and win victory against him? Perhaps more importantly, could he find a way to extract her powers and use them to amplify his own?

Though the answers yet hid somewhere beyond the reach of his mind, it was no matter; his unstoppable army would now march into Verde, waves of destruction rushing ahead of them, sparing not a spark of life. The people, plants, and animals of the Land would all perish, the landscape wiped clean of all organic disease and made perfectly barren, a blank gray slate on which to exert his influence. Though the timing of his attack was not exactly what he had planned, the massacre would be complete.

The formless shadow hovered high above the scene, observing his tools of destruction. Though they served him without question, he looked upon them with indifference, as disposable things to use and discard. Corpus held no more regard for his soldiers than any other citizen of Graha, the waste that stood in the way of his total domination. The time had come to exterminate the vermin.

Corpus finally descended to where Micca stood awaiting his command. Micca lowered his head as his master approached, then nodded, having received his instructions telepathically. At once, Micca lifted his fist high and shouted, his voice booming out over the waters as he gave the battle cry. The voices of many thousands responded as the soldiers began to march into Verde.

An Uninvited Guest

As the lesser sun slipped below the horizon, a golden streak tore through the deep blue of the Seletan sky. Queen Zehn, in a grand display of her gift of flight, approached the Palace of Gosai after her evening voyage around the boundaries of Jonquil. Each sunrise and sunset, the people of Jonquil came out of their homes and sat in meditation, awaiting the passing of their queen. Through the fleeting sight of her brilliant golden energy, the people felt connected to Zehn, and the queen infused her Land with her energy. Whereas King Jonas of Verde had chosen to connect with his people through the land, Queen Zehn had chosen air.

Zehn ended her flight with a graceful landing in the water gardens outside the palace. Under the watchful eye of her Guardsmen, she entered the lofty edifice and made her way down a grand hall to the royal chamber. Beneath glittering crystal skylights, she walked upon exquisite silk rugs through radentium archways studded with jewels. The polished sandplaster floors glinted in the light, as if impregnated with thousands of tiny diamonds. Zehn sighed as she came to the end of the long corridor; after channeling so much of her energy into her Land and her people, she looked forward to a warm floral bath and cool silk sheets. The queen took great solace in the seclusion of her gleaming chamber, surrounded by order and beauty, soothed by soft music and scent. It was her way.

As Queen Zehn approached her royal chamber, one of her attending Guardsmen engaged the lever system that moved the massive double doors. Each door stood twice Zehn's height and had been crafted of solid radentium adorned with ornate carvings of twin raiku, metallic sentries who guarded her sleep. As the doors swung open, Zehn smiled and nodded at the Guardsmen. They bowed humbly, closing the great doors behind her.

She walked contentedly through her parlor, gently touching each artifact as she passed, shutting her eyes as she resonated with gratitude and appreciation for the divine essence within each precious object. Glittering gems, blown glass sculptures fashioned by renowned artisans, and furnishings almost too fine to sit upon graced the parlor, each one reflecting the soft flickering of the chamber lights in a unique way.

Zehn performed this same ritual every night, each movement a mantra, connecting with the most private energy of her own inner space. Every item had been carefully chosen and thoughtfully placed, amplifying her loving intentions as ruler and creator of Jonquil. Zehn shut her eyes for a moment as she came to the last object, a miniature version of the Palace of Gosai cast in pure radentium. She laid her palms over the central dome, feeling the coolness of the metal against her hands as she infused it with her intentions: wealth, health, and blossoming of spirit.

Concluding her ritual, she passed through an archway graced by a set of floor to ceiling silk drapes that, at night, were pulled shut to separate the parlor from her sleeping and bathing chambers just beyond. The soothing blue and gold hues of the drapes seemed to shift in the light, their slight iridescence highlighted by the glow of the lights. Zehn tugged at the woven cord that held back the drapes on the left, but paused before closing the right. She was not delighted by the opulence of her parlor as she had been so many nights before; despite the sheen of the silk and the sparkling light in her jewels, something seemed ominously dark. Though music drifted sweetly into the chamber from the musician's pit below, the melody brought no solace, and dissonance hung in the air.

The sensitive Zehn paused, sensing the change in the energy of her space. King Jonas had been cast out from Samera over a year before, and though Zehn always felt a certain void in her heart from his absence, tonight the darkness had deepened palpably.

Zehn suddenly detected movement in her parlor. She snapped her head round, focusing her eyes with laser intensity. There was Fincher of Jonquil, stoic and smug, casually strolling through her private parlor. Zehn gasped, shocked and outraged by the presence of the uninvited guest. Valuing her privacy, she ensured her chamber remained heavily guarded at all times, yet Fincher had somehow managed to weasel his way inside. Zehn felt outrage simmering within, and for once, she failed to find the perfect words to say. She stood silently agape for a long moment before finally finding her breath. "How did you get in here?"

The man paused and turned his narrow face toward her, then continued browsing through the treasures in her parlor, unconcerned.

"Why are you here, Fincher?" Zehn said, her voice rising.

This time the man did not even glance her way, but instead picked up a pale blue gem from a prominent display stand, turning it in the light. Despite the queen's demands, no explanations would be made until Fincher felt ready to speak. After inspecting the jewel for some time, Fincher set it back on the display, then clasped his hands behind his back, facing Zehn. "It must be divine to live amongst such treasures."

He glanced down at the gleaming radentium floor and the pale silk rug that covered a length of it. "Even the soles of your feet touch only opulence."

Zehn, having lost her patience, stomped forward. "Answer me now, or answer to my Guardsmen!"

Fincher held up his hands. "My dear lady, please, hear me out. I realize this is a serious intrusion, but I have come with an offer worthy of such an infraction."

Zehn cocked her head, her slanted eyes flashing in agitation.

"I beg of you, Queen Zehn, give me audience."

Zehn eyed Fincher suspiciously, crossing her arms over her chest. In recent years, Fincher had become something of a concern in her court. Though he possessed great gifts and a brilliant mind, Zehn had always sensed that underneath his stoic façade lurked an insidious shadow. Fincher took the Queen's silence as agreement, and spoke once more. "In all your long years on the throne of Gosai, you have never taken a partner. Though you certainly have many years of youth ahead of you, it is wise to plan for future generations."

Zehn looked on in disbelief as Fincher strolled past her and into her bedroom, sitting down on her most sacred and personal space: her bed. He ran his hand over the embroidered silk covers, enjoying the sensation of touching such a forbidden thing.

"I offer myself to you as your companion, that we may rule Jonquil together. I can think of no other Jonquilian as deserving of this honor." Fincher paused, lifting his eyes to Zehn's. "The children born of our union would carry the highest blood, a golden legacy preserved in flesh."

Zehn felt the urge to strike the audacious man, but could only stand seething in silence as Fincher got up and walked toward her once more, running his hand down the seam of the one silk drape she had earlier closed.

"Join with me, Queen Zehn, that we may together elevate Jonquil to the loftiest heights," Fincher said, reaching his slender hand out toward the queen.

Zehn dropped her hands, balling them tightly into fists. Not only had Fincher entered her private chamber without permission, he had sat upon her bed, an act punishable by the highest sentence. As an added insult, he had offered himself up as a gift; surely a mere ploy to take over the throne. Zehn darted into action, snatching a bejeweled dagger from its sheath and racing toward the nefarious intruder.

Fincher did not move, but lightly thumbed the seam of the silk drape beside him. Zehn could not know that Corpus hovered high above the palace and had created a doorway, on Fincher's cue, just behind the drape. As she finally came to Fincher, he swiveled away, pulling back the drape and revealing the doorway just beyond it. Zehn had no time to react; she was pulled through the doorway and into the Inner Realm, where she would be lost for many lifetimes, unaware of her true identity.

Fincher squinted at the bright flash as the queen was cast out and the doorway shut behind her. He stroked the drape and carefully tied it back into place with the rope, fluffing it lightly with his fingertips. He turned and walked slowly into his new bedroom, hands clasped behind him, eyes flashing with satisfaction.

The rewards of serving the Dark One are many, he thought, as he rested upon the bed once more.

PART 6

THE CHAMBER OF LIGHT

Pixie woke early in Salvitor's workshop, as she had so many mornings before. In times past, she had either awakened to an empty room, or to the face of her elderly mentor leaning over her, his wiry brows knitted into a crooked line.

This time, however, she found herself surrounded with many and different companions. Thornhill and Botan slept soundly near the door, and Lium, who had laid his mat down at the very back of the room, now stirred. Pixie sensed a surprising emptiness in the place, though more bodies occupied the room than she had ever seen. Salvitor was palpably absent.

Just then, Lium awoke and sat up straight, eyes fixed on Pixie. "Did you sleep?"

Pixie nodded, wrapping her arms around her knees against the chill. Lium stood and stretched his arms overhead, chasing the stiffness from his lean form and tying his fair hair into a tail. Nearby, Botan then lifted his head, eyes half-open. "Good morning, friend," he croaked.

"It looks to be," Lium replied, observing the clear skies beyond the grimy windows.

Thornhill, restless with thoughts of his dear Salvitor, was soon up and about, rummaging through the closet and muttering under his breath. He eventually emerged with a tray of five drinking cups and a tarnished kettle. Setting the tray on the worktable, he shuffled outside to draw water from the condenser disc, a device that collected moisture from the fog and clouds to provide water for the homes of Jonquil. Thornhill filled the kettle and went back inside, disappearing once more into the closet.

Botan scratched at his side and yawned. "Can I help you with something, Thornhill?"

The old man mumbled something unintelligible, then exclaimed, "Ah! There it is." He burst from the closet, a metallic object cradled in his palm. Botan watched in curiosity as Thornhill placed the ring-like device over the opening of the kettle, allowing the thin metal ribbon in the center to drop into the water. Moments later, steam began to rise from the mouth of the kettle as the water inside heated to near boiling. Thornhill folded over the hem of his jacket a few times and used it to clasp the hot ring, removing it from the kettle. He went to his pack and took out a loosely woven cloth sack filled with dried leaves, dropping it into the water. He picked up the cooled device, smiling. "I've always wanted one of these. Sal used it everyday to make his morning arbata. Quite clever."

"I'll say," Botan said, running a hand through the mess of wavy brown locks atop his head. "After arbata, what is our plan? Are we in agreement that this is the safest place to wait for Mila's return with the map?"

Thornhill gently swirled the kettle, coaxing the essence of the leaves into the hot water. "Yes, I agree. At the very least, we have access to water and a safe place to sleep." Thornhill looked around the room. "And I propose we tidy it up a bit here to make it a proper memorial, out of respect for Salvitor."

Botan nodded and looked to Pixie, whose smile barely masked the sadness beneath. "He would have liked that."

The four soon drank their cups and set to work tidying the workshop. Stray papers were gathered together, dust whisked away, and drawings thoughtfully placed on the worktable. When they were satisfied, Lium, Pixie, and Botan gathered their belongings in their packs and went outside to ensure the grounds were also made respectable.

Thornhill remained inside, savoring his second serving of arbata. He took up the unused fifth cup from the tray and filled it, watching as the steam curled upward in ethereal swirls. He then lifted his own cup, and with a wink, he gave one last toast. "To you, my dear friend."

The last sips passed down into his body, warming an aching heart as Thornhill packed his things.

Just before leaving, a fluttering movement caught Thornhill's eye. A lone silk nondo had made its way into the workshop and now flitted about the model sanlifter that hung from the ceiling. Not wishing to trap the creature inside, Thornhill went to it. "Come now, there is nothing for you in here," he whispered, his hands cupped gently to capture it. The nondo, however, fluttered away from him and came to rest atop a round table nearby. Thornhill approached and saw a parcel, wrapped in silk paper and bound with twine, sitting patiently on the table as if waiting for him to find it.

Thornhill's green aura pulsed as he moved closer; he'd not seen the package before, and none of the others had mentioned it during their morning cleaning. He felt a catch in his throat as he saw the words "For Thornhill" scrawled on the parcel. He quickly took it up and twisted off the twine, his fingers trembling slightly as he lifted the lid and found a mysterious device and a letter.

Thornhill's eyes welled with tears as he recognized the distinctively messy handwriting.

Dearest Thornhill,

As you have found this letter, you must already know that I am gone. I regret that I shall not take arbata with you again in this life, but do take solace in knowing that we will meet again. I wait in the depths of the omniscient sea of the eternal, from which all things are born and to which all things return.

Many times in our youth I tried to convince you to come to the Inner Realm with me. But you, ever plodding and conservative, always refused. You keep too safe, Thornhill the Hesitant!

Thornhill paused. Salvitor had incessantly prodded him to go adventuring, and Thornhill had been reluctant to do so. He continued reading:

We must explore this universe, Thornhill, every crevice and creature. We must know it, for that is how we come to know ourselves. I beg of you, my dear friend, trust me now as you once did. You must see the Inner Realm at least once in your life; its wonders and beauty, and the people so different, yet so much the same. You cannot keep to the stone halls of Samera and the comforting embrace of Mother Graha forever. What is life if not a grand adventure?

I have enclosed a device that will enable your adventuring, and I encourage you to use it. Be sure to obtain key number 29 from the ring, as you will most certainly need it. And remember, Thornhill, experience is everything!

Until we meet again,

Salvitor

Thornhill sighed as he finished reading, a tear drifting down his wrinkled cheek. He paused before slowly folding the letter once more, allowing his eyes more time to drink in the words from his departed friend.

A gust of wind blew open the front door, and the silk nondo flicked its delicate wings and took to the air, fluttering outside. Thornhill followed the creature through the door to the compartment where Salvitor kept his ring of many keys. Thornhill removed number 29 and placed it and the letter in his shirt pocket, securely buttoning the flap. He then tossed the ring of keys back into the compartment and stretched his fingers a few times, the last stiffness of early morning lingering in his tired bones. Smiling despite his pain, Thornhill closed up the workshop and made his way out into the morning.

As Thornhill looked for Botan and the others, he witnessed a bright flash down the path. He paused, cautiously allowing a wave of optimism to flow through him. Could the flash of light mean that Mila had returned after such a brief time away? He turned and looked back at the humble workshop, reached into his jacket, and withdrew a single, oval-shaped leaf. Cradling it carefully in his palm, he blew over it, and the leaf floated upward and forward in gentle arcs, finally coming to rest on the roof of the domed building. At once, the leaf began to tremble and glow, and in the next moment, it split into two, replicating itself exactly. The two leaves began the process anew, trembling and glowing, and when they had been filled with light they burst into four.

In the next moment there were eight, and the leaves continued multiplying exponentially, sealing tightly against one another as they did. Soon the entire domed structure was covered in a green shield of leaves, pulsing with light. Just as the replication ceased, the leaves began to harden, encasing the building in a protective covering, guarding it from intruders and the ravages of the elements. It now stood a silent memorial to the great mind that once paced its floors and filled it with ideas.

Thornhill nodded, satisfied, and turned to head down the path to where he'd seen the flash of light, an expectant smile painted on his face. He rounded a curve in the path and saw, as he had hoped he would, young Mila holding a paper of some kind in her hands. His heart quickened.

Thornhill finally found his breath. "Mila, child, it is good to see you back so soon. Tell me, have you found the map?"

"Well," Mila hesitated as she slowly unrolled the picture she'd taken from the coffee shop, suddenly losing confidence that it could be a map of any kind. "My friend made this on his computer. I don't know if it's the map or not, but it reminded me of the clouds I saw when we first flew into Jonquil." Mila reluctantly held out the picture to the old man. "And it had *Sankari Sano* written on the back."

Thornhill took the picture, and his brows seemed to leap up toward his hairline. "Oh, yes! Yes, child, this is Jonquil, down to the last cloud!" Thornhill ran his fingers over the images, as if retracing a journey. "And yet, I can't see any mark here that would indicate where in Jonquil we need to look...Botan!"

Botan jogged over to meet them, calling to the others in the group to come as well. Thornhill handed the picture to Botan, who took it carefully, his aura shifting to bright green. He hummed thoughtfully, and as he exhaled, threads of jade spiraled round his head.

"Can you see anything, my friend?" Thornhill asked, peering over Botan's shoulder.

"Interesting...this image has hidden dimensions. Most pictures drawn on paper are only two-dimensional, with the illusion of three dimensions being created by the artist's skill. This picture is unique in that it has three actual dimensions. When I look at it using my gift, it is as if I am seeing the real Jonquil, mountains and valleys..."

Botan paused and his eyes widened. "And secret places!" He pointed excitedly at a spot on the map that seemed to jump out at him. Just outside the Kanluran territory was an unusual mark, different from the rest of the patterns of the image. It just looked out of place. "There is a mark, here. I'm sure it was made after the map was created. It doesn't fit. It must be a clue." Botan turned the map ninety degrees and placed it gently on the ground, kneeling before it. Everyone gathered closely around, awaiting his word, and Botan pointed to the center of the map. "This is where we are," he explained, sliding his finger along a swirl of cloud. "And here is where the mark says we need to go."

Thornhill tapped his staff next to the map. "The island of Ispa. How soon can we get there?"

"It looks to be about a day's walk from here," Botan said, tilting the map slightly.

"A day's walk?" Thornhill's voice grew dark with concern. "But will that have us traveling through Kanluran in the dark."

Botan stood, rolling the map carefully in his hands. "If we make good time, we should be there by nightfall. We can find a place to hole up and rest until morning."

Thornhill nodded, leaning on his staff as he addressed the group. "All right, everyone, we have a long trek ahead, and nightfall will be upon us before we know it. We must keep a steady pace while there is light and be ever watchful for danger. Corpus never sleeps."

The group soon headed up the path, past the workshop encased in its protective shield. Botan stopped and turned in surprise at the sight of Thornhill's work. "What's happened here?"

Thornhill came to stand next to Botan. "I've created a barrier that will protect Sal's workshop from intruders." He turned to

Botan, the hint of a smile lifting his face. "A memorial."

Botan hummed and put his arm around Thornhill's shoulder. "That is something. Nothing can get inside?"

Thornhill lifted a brow. "Not without an emanator."

"It's really neat—it looks like a cocoon," Mila added, walking up the path for a closer look.

Pixie followed close behind, then passed Mila and walked up to the structure, gently running her fingers over it. "I guess all his papers are safe now, huh?"

She turned to Thornhill, her aura dimming slightly as she squinted at the bright sky beyond.

"Yes, child, as safe as can be." Thornhill tapped his staff on the ground, turning from the memorial. "But we must go. Daylight slips away as we speak."

"Yes, this way, everyone," Botan said, leading off down the path.

The group soon gathered their packs and headed toward the secret place that, in their sincerest hopes, held the cache of devices and tools they could use to find Rosette and bring Queen Zehn back to the throne in the Palace of Gosai. The gentle blue light of morning washed the eastern catacombs and buttes in an eerie glow, and shadows hovered in every niche and hollow. The dry soil puffed into the air with each boot fall and rose around the group like a dry fog.

Botan and Lium lead the group, their gifts proving particularly helpful in the maze of rock. Thornhill took his position at the rear, watching for minions and keeping a keen eye on the girls in the middle. Pixie marched slightly ahead of Mila, seemingly disinterested, but looking back from time to time to check on her.

Pixie abruptly paused and reached into her vest pocket, withdrawing a long, wispy object. She lifted it to her ear and slid it into place, carefully smoothing the frayed edges of the colorful feathers.

"Cool earring," Mila said.

Pixie nonchalantly stroked the earring and glanced off into the distance. "Thanks."

Mila began thinking of the map, and the amazing coincidence of the whole situation. How was it that a friend from school had somehow crafted a perfect replica of Jonquil, with a mark on the location of a secret stash of treasures? Mila furrowed her brow in confusion. "I just don't get it."

Pixie tugged upward on a strand of her spiky blonde hair. "Don't get what?"

"I don't understand how my friend could have made a map of Jonquil on his computer. He doesn't know anything about it, and he's never been here before," Mila scratched her head. "And how did Salvitor find his picture?"

Pixie kicked a stone out of her path and watched as it rolled into a nearby gulley. "Well, I think I might know how."

Mila jogged to catch up with Pixie and looked up at her in curiosity.

"Toward the end, Sal was going back and forth between your realm and ours all the time, sometimes twice a day." Pixie frowned. "I think it was making him a little bit crazy."

"I know how that feels!"

Pixie picked up a gnarled stick as they walked. "Anyway, Sal was totally impressed with the Inner Realm, and how even though it was so different, both realms seemed to work together in a lot of ways. He was always going on and on about..." Pixie cleared her throat and stood up straight, lowering her voice, "...the consciousness of society."

She laughed, but saw that Mila did not completely understand. "You know, like the ideas of all the people of one world? He always said that those ideas aren't just stuck in their world. He said he noticed that ideas in one realm would cross over to the other one all the time, like it was this collective brain we all share through the subconscious mind, like in dreams."

Mila nodded slowly. "My friend Vincent, the one who made the picture, he told me that sometimes he would have a dream about a picture, and that's how he made up the patterns, from what he saw in the dream."

Pixie nodded excitedly, pointing the stick in the air. "So your friend could have dreamt of the layout of Jonquil without actually knowing what it was. Then he made the picture...and Sal found it." Pixie shook her head. "Nothing ever seemed to amaze Sal. All kinds of crazy things seemed normal to him. But seeing that picture just *had* to melt his brain"

Pixie smiled and broke the stick in two, tossing it to the ground.

Mila giggled at the thought of an old, wild-haired man standing in the Go Joe coffee shop, eyes glued to a picture reflecting the face of his home Land.

* * *

She was quite right about how it happened. Salvitor had found the Sankari Sano in the Inner Realm, and had succeeded in passing the watch to her. He had then visited her hometown once more to complete the final task, without knowing exactly how he would do it.

Late one afternoon, he walked slowly down the beach, taking in the sun and salt air, allowing them to clear his mind. A barking dog soon broke him from his thoughts and he looked to the boardwalk, observing the antics of the creature. The dog bounced along at the end of its leash, pink tongue lolling out, eyes fixed on a group of gulls that had gathered in front of one of the shops. The owner tugged at the leash, but the dog rushed forward, spooking the gulls into flight. Salvitor watched seven gray birds flap into the air, rising in front of the shop's yellow sign, which read *Go Joe*.

I don't have one from there yet, Salvitor thought, rushing excitedly from the beach toward the shop. Despite the seriousness of his mission, he was set on completing his collection. Through all the time he'd spent in the Inner Realm, he had acquired tokens from many of the restaurants and cafes he had visited — metal spoons. Each one similar, yet unique in subtle ways, the simple souvenirs had become an obsession. Salvitor had spoons from every boardwalk cafe he had visited, with the unique, long-handled spoons of the Go Joe coffee shop the only exception.

Salvitor crossed the warm stones of the patio and entered the coffee shop, barely acknowledging the smiling woman behind the counter. He hadn't come to socialize, only to obtain the finishing piece for his collection. As he scanned the room for his quarry he spied some intriguing art pieces on the wall. One in particular was vaguely familiar, and as he focused on it, he was struck by recognition.

There on the wall hung a nearly perfect replica of the layout of the Land of Jonquil. His eyes shot open and his knees weakened as he stumbled over for a closer look. Every swirl of cloud, every landmark, every curve and line was there, down to the tiny island of Ispa outside Kanluran territory. Sal examined every inch of the image, his mouth agape at the staggering example of how two realms indeed shared one consciousness. He removed the picture from the wall with trembling hands, shaking his head in wonder.

"So, you like the picture?" a voice called from the counter.

A startled Salvitor looked up to see the woman, Elena. She had her hands on her hips, white smile flashing.

"It's remarkable!" he stuttered.

"Well," cooed Elena, stroking her dark hair, "make me an offer. It can be yours for the right price."

Salvitor walked to the counter, eyes fixed on the picture in his hands. He looked up at Elena and met her friendly gaze. "I'll give you one hundred dollars for it."

Elena gasped, nearly swallowing her gum. "Oh my, you got a deal, it's all yours!" she squeaked, vigorously shaking his hand.

Salvitor reached in his pocket and withdrew five rumpled bills, handing them to Elena. She smoothed them and put them in an envelope she stuffed under the cash drawer in the register. "Let me get you a receipt. I'll just be a second."

When the woman disappeared into the back room, Salvitor quickly removed the picture from its frame and made a mark on it with a pen-like instrument he took from his pocket. Satisfied, he placed the picture back in the frame and clipped the backing into place just as the woman emerged from the back room. She smiled and handed him the receipt. "Thank you so much!"

Salvitor nodded and took the receipt, scribbling something on the back. "I'm buying this as a gift for a friend, and they will be in to pick it up soon. I will write the name on the back, here."

Elena nodded, noting the exotic-sounding name he'd written as she taped the receipt to the back of the picture. "Okay mister, thank you very much. The artist will be very happy to know he made a sale today. He's my nephew, you know!"

The left side of Salvitor's mouth curved into a faint smile, and he turned and shuffled toward the door. Elena reached into a drawer and withdrew a red "Sold" tag, smiling broadly as she attached it to the picture. She wrote "to" next to the name the man had written on the back of the receipt, but soon realized there would be no corresponding "from." Elena looked up at the sound of the bell ringing as the front door opened. "Hey, mister, what's your name?"

Elena saw only the door slowly closing. It seemed the man had vanished into thin air, along with the long-handled spoon she'd earlier left on the counter.

The group soon stopped at the mouth of a shallow cave dotted with tiny woven nests. As they approached, a wave of winged creatures burst from the cave, chirping excitedly as they flocked out to perch in the twisted branches of a nearby tree. Parched and sun-weary, the group moved inside the cave to rest in the shade and refresh themselves with food and water. Botan took out the map once more, checking to ensure they were on track.

"How are we doing, Botan?" asked Thornhill.

Botan nodded as he nibbled at a turryn. "Just fine. Though once we arrive I'm not sure what we are supposed to do. The island of Ispa is just a featureless wasteland. Pixie, you mentioned that Salvitor's letter said Mila knew where to find this cache of devices. Does it give any other instructions?"

Pixie lowered her eyes. "Well, here," she said. She reached into a vest pocket, withdrawing the letter and handing it to Botan. "It says the stuff is hidden in the *basement*, and that we have to turn on the light to see them."

Thornhill stroked his white beard as he looked over Botan's shoulder. "Sounds like one of Salvitor's riddles to me. Mila, does that mean anything to you?"

Mila shrugged. "Um...I don't know yet."

Thornhill nodded in resignation and took out the canteen from his pack. He took a sip, then passed it to Mila. Hot and thirsty, Mila gulped a healthy swig, caught her breath, and prepared to chug another swallow, but Thornhill placed his palm over the mouth of the canteen before she could. "Sip slowly, child. We may not find anything to eat or drink in this place."

Mila sighed, then rested her head in her palm. At Go Joe, a delicious frozen latte sat waiting for her on the counter. In that moment, it didn't seem completely unreasonable to her to open the doorway and go back to get it.

* * *

The twin suns began their trek downward in the western sky, stretching long shadows out from each traveler. The group walked a silent trail through the flatlands of Kanluran, enveloped in a stillness that felt more ominous than tranquil.

"It's so quiet here, it almost hurts my ears," Botan whispered.

Thornhill nodded. "Yes, it is unnerving, the empty silence of this part of Kanluran. I feel as if we are being watched. But..." Thornhill paused, scanning the landscape, "...I certainly don't see or hear anyone."

Lium coughed and cursed the dusty conditions, hoping to shift the group's focus and avoid any probing questions. He knew what watched them from the shadows. Botan smiled and offered his canteen, which Lium took it with a nod, sipping politely at the water before returning it to Botan.

"Thankfully, we've not much longer to go. According to the map, we should arrive on Ispa just before nightfall," Botan said, taking a swallow of water himself.

Pixie and Mila walked together on the right side of the path, the younger coaxing bits of information from the elder whenever the chance presented itself. Mila had not forgotten how Pixie seemed to walk right through the workshop door when she'd made her escape. "Hey, Pixie? That day when we first met you in Sal's workshop, how did you walk through the door like that?"

"I didn't walk through the door," Pixie said flatly.

"Well, what did you do?"

Pixie twirled the feathers of her earring around her fingertip. "With my gift, as long as I can see through something, I can get my body through it. If there's a crack or hole big enough for me to see through, like a keyhole or anything, I can squish my energy through the hole and teleport to the other side."

Mila's mouth fell open. "Really?"

Pixie rolled her eyes, and a flash of bright gold bolted through her aura. In the next moment, her body seemed to blink out of existence. Mila looked around. "Pixie?"

The other girl materialized behind Mila. "Boo!"

A startled Mila gasped, then nodded slowly in admiration. "*Nice.*"

Hidden Meanings

The suns finally slipped below the horizon and darkness fell over the island of Ispa, bringing a disturbing chill to the air. If the map had been correct, the group now approached their destination, but they found themselves in the middle of an empty stretch of dusty land. No structures stood against the dry winds, no signposts, not a single clue could be found. Botan checked the map once more, then looked around, nodding confidently as his glow swirled brightly around him. "I'm certain this is the place, but there appears to be nothing here."

Thornhill scratched at his temple. "I keep thinking of that word, *basement,* that Sal wrote in the note. It must be a clue."

Mila cocked her head to the side, then pointed at the ground. "Well, I guess he means it's in the basement. You know, the basement?"

She looked up at a puzzled Thornhill.

The word "basement" does not exist in the language of Graha. Of course! While to her it obviously indicated the lower level of a structure, to the others, this simple word was a confounding riddle. Mila began walking carefully over the ground, stamping her feet as she went. "See, in my world, the basement is an underground room below your house. I don't see any houses around here, so maybe Sal just meant that the place we're looking for is underground."

The auras of everyone in the group collectively pulsed brighter as the realization came at once. Thornhill's eyes widened. "Ah! And the door to this place is likely flat on the ground. Look closely, everyone."

The group began checking the ground, sweeping away dirt and searching for the hidden doorway. Pixie kicked away soil with her boot, coughing as clouds of dust rose. Lium used his sight to scan for inconsistencies in the soil, and Thornhill poked at the ground with his staff. Botan scanned the dimensions of the area, tapping the ground as he went. Soon, he walked over an area that felt different to him, and sounded almost hollow as he passed over it. He paused, concentrating the light of his glow downward as he used his gift.

Thornhill took notice. "What is it, my friend?"

"Something. I can sense there is a space below." He swept his boot back and forth, brushing away layers of dry soil and sand. Slowly, the shape of a symbol began to emerge from the dust. He knelt excitedly, sweeping the area clean to reveal a heavy metal disc with a raised carving of the symbol of eleven at its center.

"Look here!" he said, squinting for a better look as the collective glow of the group aura lit up the object. "Could it be a lid to some kind of storage space?"

Thornhill knelt beside the object, nodding. "It has to be something. Let's try to pry it open. I need a blade..."

He looked up at Lium, who reached into his vest and withdrew a sturdy blade. Thornhill took it and worked it back and forth between the metal disc and the smooth stone that surrounded it. Despite his efforts, the hefty disc did not budge. Thornhill huffed. "Perhaps we need to unlock it first. But with what key?" At once he thought of the jumbled ring of keys back at Salvitor's workshop. He hadn't thought to bring them along, and now sorely regretted it.

He stood wringing his hands as Botan carefully ran his fingers over the disc, looking for any opening. "I don't think there are any keyholes, or openings of any kind for that matter." Thornhill paused as an idea lit up his glow. "A password, that's it! We need only to speak the right password, and the disc will unlock."

Botan raised an eyebrow as Thornhill stood tall, clearing his throat. He began to recite the first verse of the prophecy, the one inscribed on the stone he'd carried in his pocket for so long. As he came to the words "Sankari Sano," he spoke them with special emphasis, aiming his voice at the locked disc on the ground before him. Despite the grandeur of his recitation, the heavy disc remained exactly as it was, motionless and securely locked. Botan sighed and looked up at the old sage, who frowned in disappointment. Just then, Mila's aura grew a little brighter.

"What is it, child?"

Mila shook her head. "Oh...probably nothing."

Thornhill knelt beside her, placing his hand on her shoulder. "Come now, we need everyone's ideas."

"Okay, I was just remembering how Sal wrote in the note to turn on the light. Maybe light has something to do with it, like, the light from our glows could open it?"

Thornhill cocked his head. "Mila, do you remember what I told you, that anything you remember that stands out is important?"

"Yeah, I remember."

"This is one of those things, child. Never hold back, do you understand?"

Mila smiled. "Understood."

Thornhill placed his hands on the disc, building his glow to a brilliant emerald as he did. After a few moments, the disc still sat unresponsive.

Mila began to think of what Jonas had said some time ago about her unique glow. He had mentioned that her glow was white because it contained within in it all the colors of light, while the people of the Lands of Graha glowed with only the color of their home Land. Perhaps this unity of light could be the key. Mila then knelt down beside the disc. "Let me try once, Thornhill."

Thornhill stepped back a few paces, watching intently as Mila placed her hands on the symbol of eleven at the center of the disc. Mila took a few deep breaths and closed her eyes, her aura expanding in waves of white light. The brightness of it was almost too much for Thornhill, and Lium shaded his sensitive eyes. As she knelt there, she intended for her glow to flow into the disc, as it had into Jenni the manatee in the quarantine tank, and the tree in the Harita Forest.

Mila felt waves of energy flowing from her body into the disc, and opened her eyes to see that the symbol was now aglow with white light. She then took her hands away, and at once the symbol shifted downward until it was flush with the disc. Mila quickly scrambled up and away, not knowing if the heavy metal disc would move suddenly and hurt her. The symbol then began rotating until it locked into position and the disc itself began to rotate, scraping along the stone sides as it slowly turned upward on its threaded base. As it again came to rest, a puff of stale air audibly vented, like a soda bottle opening, and light streamed out from under the disc.

Mila looked up in surprise at Thornhill, who embraced her tightly. "Remarkable!" He looked upon the open door and the space below, lit by the brilliance of friends both old and new.

Mila smiled and found herself bouncing lightly on her toes. Lium, watching in silent amazement, turned to her and gave a wink. Mila felt her face flush hot, grinning bashfully as she lowered her head, hoping that the dark would hide her blushing. Pixie, however, could see the change in Mila, and rolled her eyes in response.

"Nice work," Botan said, smiling at Mila. "It looks like it should slide right off now." Botan reached down and gave the disc a push, easily moving it aside. Below it stretched a gleaming metal ladder that descended down through a narrow tunnel into a chamber. Thornhill got to his hands and knees and poked his head inside the opening. "Well, let's have a look."

He shimmied down into the opening and onto the ladder, descending cautiously. Pixie and Mila followed, and as Botan attempted to pass through the opening, he found himself a bit pinched. The combination of his stocky frame and his weapons and pack were too wide for passage. "It appears I have a little more flesh on my bones than the rest of you," he laughed, removing his weapons and leaving his pack on the ground beside the opening.

Lium chuckled as Botan finally squeezed through, but took pause before following him. In the far distance, Lium heard the approach of the thing he had set in motion—a thing that could not be stopped. He flinched, attempting to shake the hissing sounds from his ears, a growing sense of anxiety tightening in his chest. Finally, he gathered himself and followed Botan down the ladder into the chamber below.

The ladder led to a cavernous chamber that looked to have been laser-cut into a perfect pyramidal shape. The walls were honed smooth and glowed from within as if alive with light. Along the sides of the pyramid chamber were rectangular radentium tables, equally exacting in their cut, and somehow glowing even more brightly than the walls. Mila turned in circles, taking in the spare splendor of the place. She looked to the gleaming tabletops and found each one covered with all manner of devices, protected under crystal dome enclosures. The space felt like part museum, part secret laboratory, and was absolutely pristine.

Thornhill ran his hand over a nearby table, then inspected his fingertips in wonder. "It seems Salvitor had a secret side, far less dusty than the one we all knew."

Though Salvitor's workshop had been a mess, this chamber seemed a sacred space, his very soul displayed in crystal and light. Even Lium found himself admiring the mechanisms that had been put in place to keep everything so well-preserved. "I know Salvitor was always experimenting, but I had no idea he'd created so many devices," Lium said.

Thornhill smiled, shaking his head. "Neither did I. There must be hundreds here. I recognize some of them, but others are foreign to my eyes." Thornhill turned to the young blonde girl. "Pixie, if you recognize anything that could be of use to us, especially a finder or a—"

"I know what most of these are," Pixie interrupted. "Well, some of them I've only seen the drawings for, but I helped him with a lot of the things he made."

Thornhill placed a hand on Pixie's shoulder, nodding. "Good." He leaned over the table closest to him. "I will see what I can find that may be of use."

As Thornhill explored the chamber, Mila walked closely behind Pixie, carefully looking over the many devices under the glass domes. They all looked valuable, and she was sure they each had an important purpose, but she couldn't understand how they would be used. "I don't really know what to look for. I used a finder once, but it didn't look like any of these things."

Pixie stopped, nudging Mila with an elbow. "Come on, I'll show you what to look for."

The blonde led Mila around the room, pointing out different forms of devices and how they could be recognized. The girls soon came to a group of sparkling objects that looked more like jewelry than tools. "These here," Pixie tapped gently on the glass dome, "are durationals. I know how to use these."

The girls came to the end of the row and moved to where Lium and Thornhill stood looking into one of the domes. Lium pointed a finger at the glass. "Thornhill, are these...envelopers?"

Thornhill nodded. "Indeed they are. One of the most dangerous devices Sal ever created. He had been experimenting with extremely dense matter and created the device more by accident than by intention. Once activated, it will envelope everything around it for nearly a quarter spatial; not even light can escape its grasp."

Thornhill lifted the dome and picked up one of the two devices, which looked to Mila like a hockey puck. "The enveloper draws all surrounding matter into itself until it reaches maximum density, then it closes," Thornhill said, handing the device to Lium. Lium held it in his palm and ran his thumb over the smooth black surface, contemplating its gravity. Once Thornhill had turned and was not looking, Lium slipped the enveloper into his vest pocket and walked away.

Pixie and Mila followed Lium as he strolled past the next table of devices. In the center, a reflective sphere sat among a collection of metal cubes. The sphere had been polished to a high sheen, a bluish hue emanating from its surface. Mila looked into the sphere and smiled; it reminded her of the gazing ball her mother had placed in her garden one summer. Mila moved closer to Lium as she studied the sphere. "Isn't it pretty?"

Lium glanced at Mila, and without thinking, he looked into the sphere. What reflected back to him was a distorted image, one blurred with greed and smeared with deceit. Though he clearly saw his familiar form in the sphere, he could not recognize his own face. The sight of this foreign image drew dark flames through the entirety of Lium's aura, dimming and weakening it. For a fleeting moment, he dropped his guard, his true intentions leaking through the façade he had so carefully cultivated. His thoughts echoed out from the shadows where he'd hidden them and were exposed in this brief flash for the girl to see.

Mila took a step back, startled by what she had learned in the twinkling of an eye. Her face went pale as she saw, for the first time, the one she most admired in the light of truth.

Thornhill, having tuned in to the sudden change in the mood, turned to see Mila's face, and suddenly felt what he had long suspected was true. He walked past Lium to Mila, taking her hand and pulling her a few paces away. The young man said nothing; he only listened to the hissing sounds outside the chamber that he alone could hear. He lowered his head, feeling his breath struggling against the stiffness of his ribs. His eyes burned as he looked at the girl who had admired him so, knowing full well that he would be her undoing. The wheel of inevitability barreled forward, swift and fierce, and he found that he could not meet the girl's eyes.

Lium had led the group into a near perfect trap. Old Thornhill would be powerless in a room with no plants; Botan, having dropped his weapons to squeeze through the entry, was not prepared for battle; and Pixie could not teleport to escape a sealed room with no cracks. Once the disc was closed over the entrance, there would be no escape for any of them. Lium, saying nothing, turned his back on the group and began climbing the ladder.

Mila felt her heart pounding in her chest as she stepped weakly after Lium. "Where are you going?"

Lium paused on a rung and turned to face the group, his eyes flickering as he spoke coldly. "A successful man makes many sacrifices."

Mila blinked in disbelief, standing agape as she watched his silent and perplexing retreat. A dark cloud drifted through her aura, spawned of hurt within, and then drifted out toward Lium. As it engulfed him, he seemed to flinch, having somehow sensed the girl's pain. Then, without a backward glance, he quickly ascended, leaving a stunned group behind in the chamber. He scrambled out of the opening and stood by as Corpus' minions poured into the entrance.

He placed the disc over the entry and turned it into place, feeling the sand scraping harshly against the threaded base.

Soon after, he fled toward the border of Ispa, his body growing heavier with each footstep, his mind burdened with the weight of his own deeds. The brave and selfless girl had been dashed with betrayal, the innocent heart crushed. Lium was hated now, rather than esteemed; he was a man of spoiled integrity. For a Jonquilian, it was a fate worse than death.

Down in the chamber, Mila turned to Thornhill, her eyes moist with pain, her aura dim. Thornhill gripped her hand tighter and watched in wide-eyed horror as nine minions flew down the ladder and into the chamber. They gathered in formation, hissing ominously. By their appearance, Thornhill knew they were not the watchers that had been tracking them through Kanluran: these shadow beings were of a more potent breed, and the group was now in grave danger.

He raised his staff, turning to Botan. "These are no mere watcher minions. Fight!"

The shadows rushed forward, breaking glass domes and crushing the devices underneath. They even overturned two of the tables, ruining the priceless treasures that had once been displayed. Soon the shadows were upon the group, and Thornhill and Botan placed their bodies in front of the girls to protect them. Thornhill lashed out at the shadow before him, twirls of snaking vines shooting out of his staff, but the vines passed through the being as if it were thin air. Thornhill struck again, but could only watch as the minions advanced and finally overtook him and Botan.

Mila cowered with Pixie in a corner behind the men, who now slumped under the influence of the dark beings that attacked them. Mila could see the kumu draining from their bodies as their auras faded and flickered. Heat shot through her body, and panicked breaths came shallow and quick. As she watched her mentors fall into deadly danger, a storm began to build within her. The sting of betrayal fueled the roiling cauldron, rising higher and higher on plumes of anger within.

The shadow beings seemed to enjoy their evil work, chortling excitedly as each glimmer of kumu was taken from the two innocent men. An urgent fire burst forth inside Mila, her glow expanding and intensifying with the desire to save her friends. Without thinking, she stood up and stepped between the attacking shadows. She balled her fists, her jaw tightening just before she found her voice. "Leave them alone!"

Her shout seemed to startle the minions, and they moved away from Thornhill and Botan, distracted. As the men sat gasping, Mila faced the shadows unflinchingly, her eyes glowing with light, her aura brilliant white. Just as the shadows moved to pounce on the girl, a piercingly bright flash shot from the top of her head down to her feet, creating a tube of light along her spine. In the next instant, a translucent field of white light spread out from her form, enveloping everything around her. The others watched in amazement as the minions shrieked and shriveled, disintegrating in the brightness.

Mila stood in a trance-like state, her head tilted upwards, eyes closed, surrounded with light. As the light field continued to grow, the remaining seven minions turned to flee up the ladder, but they, too, were consumed by the light. With the destruction of the last minion, the light field receded, and Mila's glow returned to its normal state. She stood very still, slowly cracking her eyes open to look at Pixie, who still sat dumbfounded in the corner. After a long silence, Pixie finally drew a breath and nodded slowly at Mila.

"Nice."

Mila smiled weakly. "Thanks."

Exhausted by the intense output of energy, she collapsed.

* * *

A few minutes later, Mila had recovered from the incident. Thornhill and Botan both had tended to her, feeding their own light into her body to refresh her. "Remarkable, simply remarkable, Mila," Thornhill said. "Do you remember how you did that?"

Mila shook her head. "I'm not sure how I did it. It kind of happened by itself."

"Well, child, we owe you our lives."

"Yes, we are most grateful," added Botan, patting Mila on the shoulder.

Pixie simply smiled with a nod. Mila thought of the time when her glow burst into Jenni the manatee in the quarantine tank room at the zoo. She hadn't intended for it to happen, yet it seemed that when her light was most needed, it always knew exactly what to do. Thornhill had been right about that.

Thornhill began rummaging around the debris in the room. "I'm afraid we haven't much time. Corpus knows where we are and it won't be long before he creates another group of minions."

"And surely they will find this place again," Botan said. "What if one of these devices falls into the wrong hands?"

Thornhill shook his head vigorously. "We must not let that happen, Botan. We cannot risk Corpus or his cohorts finding any of these devices. We must do an unthinkable thing."

Thornhill paused, and the others looked at him in concern. "We must destroy this place. We must leave no trace of Salvitor's work."

Mila frowned. "But don't we need a finder or something to help us find Queen Zehn?"

"Ah!" Thornhill exclaimed, reaching forward and lifting a familiar device into the air. "Yes, yes we do. And here it is."

Thornhill brought the device over to Mila. It looked identical to the one she'd used to locate Jonas. Thornhill pressed his thumbnail against the tiny button and the drawer popped open, revealing a blue gem inside. "Ah...beautiful," Thornhill whispered, taking the gem between his thumb and finger.

Mila inspected the gem, but was soon distracted, pointing inside the drawer. "Look, there's a little piece of paper in there."

Thornhill blinked, reaching in to retrieve the scrap. He unfolded the paper and read it, nodding. "Yes, according to Sal's note here, this jewel belonged to Queen Zehn." He smiled as he closed the drawer, polishing the glass dome with the hem of his jacket. "Mila can use the jewel with this finder to locate Zehn in the Inner Realm."

"And we can move on to find Rosette." Botan paused, his eyes growing dark. "And Lium...he will stand before Zehn for his crimes."

Mila lowered her head as she remembered what Lium had done, clearing her throat to relieve the growing tightness there. "Now I go back home and try to find Zehn with the finder, just like I did with Jonas?"

Thornhill nodded. "And as quickly as possible, child. Rosette could be in grave danger."

"Okay, I'll find her as soon as I can."

"I think I should go with her," Pixie said.

Thornhill looked at Pixie with a lifted brow.

"I should go with Mila to help her find Queen Zehn," Pixie clarified.

"No, Pixie," Thornhill said. "You cannot cross to the Inner Realm. You would get yourself killed — "

"No, I wouldn't!" Pixie interrupted, jogging to where she had seen a particular device. She opened the cracked dome and grabbed the two durationals on display. She brought them over, turning them in her palm. "These are durationals. I know how to use them. They will let me go to the Inner Realm and back without getting hurt."

Thornhill held his hands up. "Pixie, it is much too dangerous for you to do this. The durationals are very delicate devices — "

"I *know* how to use them! I've done it before! I'm not just some kid, you know!" Pixie took a breath and calmed herself, then stood a bit straighter. "Besides, Zehn is my queen. I should be allowed to help bring her back."

Thornhill narrowed his eyes at the blonde. "Then you accept that by crossing over you may be placing your life in danger?"

"Yeah, I do," Pixie replied.

Thornhill sighed in resignation. "Get yourself prepared to go."

Thornhill turned to sift through the rubble once more, checking for devices still in useable condition, leaving the girls to make their preparations. Mila looked at Pixie. "You know, it's okay to be a kid. Kids can do things, too."

Pixie smiled, gripping the durationals in her palm. "I know." She tucked one of the durationals in her pocket and held the other between two fingers. To Mila, the device looked like a clip earring with a blinking inner light. Pixie turned each of the three tiny dials on the face of the device with her finger, counting to herself as she did. "You gotta be real careful to set the timer right, or things can go bad."

Mila cocked her head to the side. "How bad?"

Pixie gave Mila a sideways glance. "*Bad.*"

Pixie double-checked the timer, ensuring she had set all three dials correctly before clipping it to her free earlobe. She stroked the feathered earring in her other ear and smoothed a stray hair into place atop her head. "Okay, let's go."

Thornhill had made his way back and placed one hand on each of their shoulders. "You two take care. When you return, hopefully we will have found Rosette alive and well."

Mila nodded and turned toward the wall, which still glowed with residual light. She took several deep breaths and watched as the doorway slid open before her. Pixie glanced in surprise at Mila, who held out her hand. "You ready?"

Pixie took her hand. "Always ready."

In a flash of light, the two girls disappeared and traveled to the Inner Realm in search of Zehn. Botan guarded his eyes against the flash, then turned to Thornhill. "Now, what to do about this place?"

Thornhill's shoulders drooped. "We'll need to use an enveloper. It will consume everything—the devices and the chamber." He looked woefully at Botan. "And a good portion of the island of Ispa, as well."

"How will we get away?"

"The device has a timer. We will need to move quickly, but we will have time to get to a safe place."

Thornhill went to the dome where the envelopers had been

displayed. The glass had cracked, but had not been destroyed. Thornhill lifted the dome carefully, his eyes widening. "No..."

"What is it?" Botan walked over.

"Two were here, yet now there is only one. An enveloper has been stolen."

"Lium," Botan growled, jogging toward the ladder as if to pursue the man. "It must have been Lium. The minions were all destroyed."

Thornhill slowly shook his head. "What weakness is it that allows the hearts of men to so easily forget the light?"

"I don't know my friend, I don't know."

As Thornhill took the enveloper and slid it into his pocket, he took note of Botan, who stared up the ladder in dismay. "Nor do I know how we are going to get out of here," Botan said. "It seems Lium has shut us in."

"Are we locked in from the outside?" Thornhill asked.

Botan began ascending the gleaming ladder. "I'm not sure. Let's see."

Thornhill waited at the base of the ladder.

"All right, let's hope for the best," Botan said, reaching for the handle on the bottom of the disc. He grasped the handle, tugging it firmly in a counter-clockwise direction, but it did not budge. Botan sighed, looking down at Thornhill. "It's locked."

As he spoke, the disc suddenly turned and slid away, and a pale hand reached down in front of Botan's face. Startled, he nearly fell from his perch, catching himself as he looked up at the newcomer. "My stars!" he exclaimed, taking the hand in his own and climbing out of the chamber.

"Who is it?" Thornhill called.

Botan pulled himself out onto the sands. "It's Meadow!"

Thornhill chuckled in relief, quickly ascending the ladder to reunite with his friend. He clambered out of the opening, stood, and embraced his rescuer. "Meadow! Your timing, as usual, is impeccable."

Meadow nodded graciously. "I saw in meditation that you and the others had been sent to your graves. In my vision, I saw betrayal and death; I feared the worst had occurred. I am happy to see you still draw breath, but where are the girls?"

"They have gone to the Inner Realm in search of Zehn."

"Together, then?"

Thornhill chuckled. "Yes, they insisted upon it."

"I see. I have recently returned from the shadow plane of Lapis where I had gone in search of Cira. I must tell you, the seas there are disturbed. Dark forces are at work. Something massive is building."

Botan sighed, frowning. "It seems we must be in three places at once to fight this enemy." He found his weapons and strapped them once more to his body. "What do you know of Rosette?"

Meadow offered Botan his canteen as he spoke. "Rosette yet lives. She is being held by Fincher in the Mazurin Gon."

Botan took a long drink, wiping the water that dripped from his stubbly chin as he passed the canteen to Thornhill.

"I propose we trek to Seletan, friends," Thornhill stated, lifting the canteen to his lips. "Rosette is our priority until Mila and Pixie return with Zehn." After drinking, he returned the vessel to Meadow, who nodded in agreement.

"I suggest we travel through the city of Aksini," Botan said. "I have a friend there, and we can refresh ourselves and gather some supplies before we move on to Seletan."

"Agreed," Thornhill said, carefully withdrawing the enveloper from his pocket. "And now…"

Botan and Meadow looked on as Thornhill set the timer and placed the enveloper near the entrance to the chamber. His aura flickered, and as the enveloper lit up briefly to indicate it had been armed, the three men turned and dashed away.

Soon after, Botan, Thornhill, and Meadow ran toward the bridge at the edge of Ispa. As they approached, they heard deafening thunder, and shockwaves of energy blasted past them, nearly knocking them to the ground. Thornhill turned to look and saw a tremendous wound had been torn in the Land, a gaping crater that had indeed enveloped half the island where they had been standing a short time before. Salvitor's secret chamber, the many treasures within, and indeed the very land itself, had simply vanished.

Thornhill gazed mournfully at the spectacle, thinking of all that had been lost. "I'm sorry, my dear friend," he whispered.

Botan rose, pulling Thornhill to his feet, and the three men rushed on toward Aksini.

The Inseparables Part Ways

Bract and Woodson walked together through Cypress as they had so many times before. Though Bract had been commanded to head north to Maru, and Woodson south to Zila to spread word of the impending war, the men decided to walk the path to the stables together. Both sensed the gravity of their missions, and that this short walk together could very well be their last.

They traveled for a time without speaking, but Bract, knowing his companion well, could feel a question brewing in Woodson's mind. Seconds later, as if on cue, Woodson cocked his head and took a deep breath. "Name tags," he said quietly, tugging at his shirt.

Bract rolled his eyes, half-smiling as he tilted his head to the sky.

"Why in the world do we have to wear name tags on our uniforms?" Woodson said, turning to his strapping friend. "Don't we know each other's names by now?"

Bract shook his head. "Woodson, you worry about the strangest things."

Woodson paused for a moment, assessing the validity of his own inquiry, then laughed to himself. Since the Sankari Sano had laid hands on him, much of his timidness and fear had melted away, but it seemed he still found ways to worry himself into a froth.

The two men walked together in silence once more and as always. They had always been tied together; born just three days apart, their paths had consistently intersected as they grew up. They lived close to each other in childhood, though Woodson never found the nerve to speak to Bract, who seemed abnormally large and brutish for a boy of the same age.

As the two reached the turning age of eleven, they were somehow placed in many of the same classes in Develoption. At first Woodson was petrified of Bract, who found Woodson annoyingly timid and anxious, but soon they came to be good friends.

The two did well in Develoption, easily mastering their simple gifts. Bract could dehydrate any organic material with a touch of his hand, and had grown into a steady and patient man of great strength. Woodson had the gift of implantation—he could send a single-word subconscious command to a person, which would cause an instant reaction. Though he could have manipulated others greatly with his gift, he was too afraid of the repercussions he would suffer if he did. Each time he thought to implant a command, he would over-analyze every possible outcome and reaction, worrying himself into such a state that he decided to refrain from using his gift after all.

Bract and Woodson slowed their pace as they came to the stables near the main road that ran from north to south. Each man went inside and obtained a hadra for the long ride ahead. As they led the beasts from their stalls and onto the main road, the animals paused, as if offering a space for benediction. Woodson removed his cap and nervously scratched his head, kicking at a stone in the path. "Well, I guess we split up here. I go south and you go north."

Bract smiled, placing a hand on his friend's shoulder. "Be safe, Woodson."

Woodson replaced his cap and straightened himself once more. "You, too."

Bract took a few steps northward, then paused and turned back. "Woodson?"

The wiry man nearly stumbled as he turned, lifting a brow in curiosity.

"Try not to worry too much."

"I won't...or I mean, I will." Woodson at first cocked his head in confusion, wondering if his words had come out correctly, then smiled and mounted his hadra, galloping off into the south.

Each man rode a path of solitude to his destination. Bract arrived in Maru and found that though the town seemed revitalized by Jonas' return, much tension still hung in the atmosphere. Ill-intentioned Crimsonites still crossed the border with fair regularity, and the border Guardsmen stood ready to react instantly to any threat. Bract traveled along the border stations in Maru, spreading word of Aux of Crimson and how he had united Verde and Crimson as one Guard against the coming peril from Lapis. Bract told of the hope for peace, and that unity would be the only weapon that could defeat their enemy.

* * *

Woodson found Zila surprisingly quiet compared to the days when it was the largest gaming town in all of Graha. The few native residents that remained had gathered together in one community, and Woodson was able to easily warn them of the coming war with Lapis and the dire need for unity.

As each man carried out his assigned task, dark waters rolled onto the shores of Verde and into her deltas, leaving destruction in their wake. The Dark One watched as Micca of Lapis brought the first wave of the plan ashore to Verde, her people unaware that the second wave would be the true harbinger of doom.

Insurmountable

Far below, Rosette approached the final test of the Mazurin Gon. With her sight nearly restored, she raced down a straightaway and rounded a sharp corner, coming to a courtyard flanked by tall brush. At the rear of the yard, an ornate metal building stood in the skeletal shadow of a dead Grapa tree, one that had been gifted to Jonquil by King Jonas himself. Rosette had heard stories of this gift tree and went quickly to lay her palms on it, her fingers coaxing bits of dead bark from the parched trunk. Touching a piece of home and somehow a part of Jonas infused her body with hope and strength, lifting her spirits.

She shifted her focus from the tree to a metal sign that hung above the entry door. Though obscured by heavy oxidation, she could just make out the words *Sala Zagadek*.

Rosette groaned. "This can't be happening," she muttered. Rosette detested riddles, trickery, and games, the very things the sign indicated lay ahead. Jonquilians found a clever puzzle engaging. It was rich food for the ever-hungry mind and a test of the intellect of potential Prime Warriors. Rosette, though, was physical, tactile, and direct to a fault, and playing such games did nothing but waste time and stir up frustration. Jonquilians practiced a twisted way of testing their warriors that, from her perspective, seemed designed to confound rather than assess battle skills.

Despite her ill feelings toward the challenge ahead, Rosette moved forward and pushed on the door, finding that it swung open easily with a soft squeak. She paused to allow her eyes to adjust to the darkness as she stepped inside the metal hall. The walls were stained black as pitch, the only light available squeezing in around the frame of the entry door and a faint glow some distance down the hall. Rosette carefully groped her way to the end of the hall where she found two doors, one on either side, each displaying a hammered metal sign dimly lit from behind. The door sign on the left was marked *kuacha*; the one on the right, *kuendelea*. Rosette scratched at her temple. It had been long years since she studied the ancient language, and the two words were so similar that even then she had often mixed them up. She remembered that one word meant *quit*, and the other, *continue*, but as she looked at them she could not recall which meant what.

Rosette assumed that in the Mazurin Gon, *quit* did not mean to simply go back to the entrance to start over; it meant to quit in a far more inalterable way, one that likely landed you far below on the dunes of Tenpi.

Rosette looked upward, searching her memory, then glanced at the door on the right marked *kuendelea*. She squared off in front of the door, bracing herself. "Let's hope I remembered it right," she said aloud. Rosette took a deep breath and then pushed on the door, finding it did not move. She tilted her head to the side, taking a step backward and then throwing her weight against the door, but it still would not budge.

She pushed upward and even tugged sideways at it, thinking it a sliding type, but the door remained stubbornly closed. Rosette grunted in frustration and banged her fist against the sign, startled by the loud, empty echo the rattling metal made in the hall. Listening to the dramatic effect of sound in the space, she smiled to herself.

"*Kuendelea!*" Her voice rang out in the hall, reverberating against the metal surfaces of the structure. At once, the door slid open before her, revealing yet another dark hall beyond.

"Hmph." Rosette stepped through the doorway. The narrow

space was lit only by a razor-thin opening in the roof through which light cut like a blade, cleaving the hall in two.

Rosette moved to the end of the hall and found another door. Though similar to the one she'd just passed through, Rosette found that this door had a pulley mechanism with a rope attached to a nearby hook and a heavy stone weight on the other end. The stone weight was also tied from behind with another length of rope that went straight through the wall, probably to another part of the mechanism on the other side.

Rosette deduced that the stone weight would probably open the door if she could cut the tie rope and release it from the hook. She took a sword from her hip, stepping back and then striking the rope with all her strength. Though the fiber hummed at her touch, the rope surprisingly did not break. She struck it again, even rasping the sharp blade back and forth across the surface, but the rope remained unscathed.

Perplexed, Rosette sheathed her sword and took the rope between her fingers, inspecting it, then moaning with dismay as she recognized its composition. It was nondo rope. Expertly woven from the strongest vine fiber and nondo silk, the rope would never yield to mere metal blades; there were precious few ways to destroy it. Momentarily distracted from her goal of severing the rope, Rosette noticed that an illuminated metal plaque inscribed with a verse:

> *Feed me and I will live*
> *Give me drink and I die*
> *Sit next to me and I comfort you*
> *But touch me and you cry*

"A *riddle,*" Rosette hissed, furrowing her brow angrily at the seemingly childish game. She paced to and fro and for a moment entertained the idea of gnawing at the rope until either it or her teeth finally yielded. She gathered herself and read the verse once more, relaxing into the questions. Rather than doggedly focusing on finding the answer, driving herself nearly to madness in the process, she decided to do what her Magister had instructed her to do in such situations.

She would clear her mind, allowing the solution to fall into the silent, empty space between thoughts. Rosette took a deep breath and shut her eyes, visualizing the space between her ears as a clear blue sky. As thoughts came into that space, she saw them as passing clouds, drifting gently, barely disturbing the perfect emptiness. As she floated in the ethers, she thought again of the rope, and her eyes popped open at the thought of the one thing that could both answer the riddle and sever the nondo rope.

Rosette stepped up to the door and spoke the answer aloud. "Fire!"

Though the door did not move, to her right an oil torch spontaneously lit, revealing its hiding place in a dark recess beside the door. Rosette's aura flashed and she took up the torch, realizing her task. She held the yellow flame under the nondo rope that fixed the door weight in place. Soon, the nearly indestructible rope began to scorch, then finally gave way, allowing the pulley stone to smoothly drop to the ground with a clunk. As it did, the door slid upward, allowing her to pass into the next hall.

Rosette walked through darkness to the end of the hall and found yet another door. Though it had no visible pulley system, it did have a very conspicuous keyhole. Rosette thumbed the keyhole and peered through it, seeing nothing but blackness inside. She looked around for a key but found none, and so turned her attention to the inscribed metal door plaque:

> I swirl all around yet cannot be seen
> Can be captured but never held
> I have no voice, yet can be heard
> Your sails I long have swelled

Rosette blinked in confusion, shaking her head; what voiceless thing could be heard? She sighed, closing her eyes and visualizing her mind once more as a clear blue sky. She breathed smoothly and easily, relaxing into the quiet space, allowing her guidance to come as it pleased. She opened her eyes and read the verse again, stopping at the last line. *Your sails I long have swelled*, she thought. In a flash, the answer came to her and she spoke it aloud: "Wind!"

As suspected, the door did not move at the speaking of the word, and she figured that, as with the previous door, the mechanism required her to use the element itself to open it. Rosette smoothed her hair back with her palms, exhaling heavily. How would she generate wind powerful enough to blow open a door?

The unusual keyhole caught her interest once more. During her childhood, a group of minstrels had passed her home one summer night, sending sweet music drifting into her room. She'd gone to her window and seen a fair-haired man playing a wooden fife, a mandolin player in a green garment and a plump woman tapping a tambourine against her fleshy hips. The memory of them made her smile, their music inspiring her next move.

She leaned forward and blew into the keyhole. A breathy whistle like that of a primitive flute sounded in response. Rosette lifted a brow in intrigue and took a deeper breath, now realizing the true nature of the key. She blew into the keyhole again, and after refining her embouchure, created a pure tone that resonated in the hall. Within moments, the door slid open and a satisfied Rosette passed eagerly into the hall beyond.

She made her way once more through darkness to the door at the end and found the metal plaque displayed there lit by a pinhole beam of light projected from a high place above. In that light, she could make out the carved relief mounted on the door – the head of a raiku, mouth half open, tongue lashed out. She instinctively recoiled, remembering the beast she'd slain earlier in the Gon, then turning her attention to the plaque:

> *Gentle enough for the skin of queens*
> *Yet I turn rocks to sand*
> *Light enough to caress the sky*
> *Precious to this Land*

"Mercy," whispered Rosette, stroking her brow as she turned the words over in her mind. What could be lighter than air, but strong enough to turn rocks to sand? She paced for a few moments, reducing the potential answers by a process of elimination before finally clearing her mind, imagining again a cloudless sky. This time, though, the clouds kept coming, one after another, until the blue space had nearly been blocked out by white. At first, Rosette felt frustrated by her inability to clear her mind, but then let herself think. *Clouds...clouds caress the sky, and clouds are made of...*

She faced the doorway and spoke her answer aloud. "Water!"

At her words, a trickling sound started. A stream of water steadily poured from the mouth of the raiku and fell into a drain below. Rosette quickly looked around for a vessel to catch the water; perhaps she would need a portion of it to open the door. Glancing downward, she then saw that the water cascaded over a piece of metal that split the stream in two, redirecting the flow around a small light fixture.

The light began flickering as it collected the energy from the passing streams, and within moments, it had gathered enough to illuminate continuously. Rosette heard a click from beyond the door and it slowly began to swing open. The raiku watched coldly as she passed, water dripping from its jaws. Had she given in to the impulse to catch the falling water in a vessel, the door would have remained tightly shut.

Beyond the door, Rosette found herself in an open foyer with perfectly polished walls and shining radentium floor. She looked up and saw above her a domed ceiling softly lit with countless pinhole stars and decorated with forged metal shapes. Unspoiled by tarnish or dust, the room was immaculate. At the back of the foyer stood a magnificent door protected by guards so motionless and so well camouflaged in their armor that she had not even seen them upon entering.

Rosette swiftly drew her swords, taking an offensive posture, but the two guards lifted their hands in surrender and surprise. "No, no, my lady, no need for that!" the guard on the right quickly said. "You see, we are unarmed and do not intend to fight."

"Yes, my lady," said the guard on the left. "We are here to help you."

Rosette lifted a brow. "Help me?"

The guard on the right nodded. "We are the Guards of the Passage, and our only duty is to answer the One Question of those who wish to pass through to the end of the Mazurin Gon, and to victory."

The guard's voice echoed in the chamber as Rosette stowed her swords. The guard on the left said, "It is true, you have won every fight, beaten every obstacle, and solved each riddle to get here, the last challenge of the Mazurin Gon."

"What's the challenge?" Rosette asked sharply.

The right guard continued, "This door is the *only* way to get to the Garden of Victory, the end of the Mazurin Gon, but the door itself is the challenge."

"Indeed," the other guard cut in, "opening it though, is not difficult, for essentially it is unlocked. All one must do is turn this handle and push," he said, gesturing toward the gleaming radentium handle a few feet from him.

"Yes, the true challenge, my dear," the right guard said, shaking his finger in the air, "is to open it without getting chopped to bits."

Rosette rolled her eyes. "What do you mean?"

"If you were to simply push the door open, the blades mounted above and beside the door on both sides would quickly dispatch you," he said, pointing to where sharp blades had been mounted all around. Some were curved and looked to move vertically across the threshold like pendulums, while others were long sabers, designed to sweep horizontally. As she looked over the apparatus, she began to realize that even she could not escape the trap that had been set.

"To pass safely, you must find the *key* to the door and place it in this water." He pointed to a clear vessel of water in an ornate mount, illuminated by a band of light that shone down from the top of the door. "The proper key, and only the proper key, will break this beam of light just so, and trigger the blades."

"Yes, and once triggered, they will remain in their resting position and allow you to pass safely."

Rosette raised a brow. "So, how are you going to help me get past this door?"

The guards snickered, and the right guard said, "Ah, yes, we can help you. We will answer the One Question."

"Yes, and only the One," the left guard added.

"What's the One Question?" Rosette said.

"Only you know it, my lady. The answer to it will tell you what you need to know to find the key," said the right guard.

Rosette cocked her head, confused. "But I have asked you many questions already—"

The left guard interrupted, "Yes, yes, but none have been your One Question specifically about the *key*."

"That's right," the right guard added. "You can ask away all the day about the weather or the Mazurin Gon or even anything you might want to know about me..."

"Oh, stop it!" the left guard barked, shooting a glare at his companion. "It's true, you can ask as many questions as you want about other things, but when it comes to the key—"

Rosette finished for him, "Just the One."

The guards nodded, smiling, and watched as the she began pacing the floor, no doubt formulating her question.

Rosette's mind raced with possible inquiries; if she were to ask how to dodge the blades, the guards would likely tell her there was no way to do so, and she would have wasted her question. The men had already indicated there was no other way out of the Mazurin Gon, so inquiring about alternate routes would also be a waste. Rosette paused, taking a moment to once more clear her mind. She imagined the blue sky within and felt herself being drawn into memories. The first door within the Sala Zagadek had called for the element of fire, the second for wind, and the third for the element of water.

Rosette's eyes flew open as she realized that there was but one door left in the Gon, one element yet to be used, and one element conspicuously and seemingly intentionally absent from the room. She marched to where the guards stood waiting, an idea taking form within her mind. "I have my One Question,"

"Already?" the right guard asked.

"Are you certain?" the left guard added sternly.

Rosette nodded. "Yes."

The guard on the right smiled. "So, what is your One Question, my dear?"

"Yes, and do ask well," the other added.

Rosette stood very still for a moment, then cast her eyes to the ground, tapping the toe of her boot against the pristine floor of the chamber. She would ask the question that would give her the confirmation she sought and the confidence to grasp that handle and open the door, free of the threat of death. Rosette narrowed her eyes at the guard on the left, moving closer to him as she spoke. "Tell me, is the key to the door an element of Graha?"

The guard's eyes flickered for a second as he looked at his partner. Then, as required, he gave his answer. "Yes."

Rosette smiled, rubbing her palms together as she walked a few paces away. She then glanced down at her boots, well coated with soil, sand, and dust from her long journeys, and began stamping her feet hard against the floor.

The left guard frowned. "What are you doing? Stop that noise!"

Rosette ignored the man, continuing to stomp until she finally squatted down, closely inspecting the floor. There underneath her feet lay bits of mud in a pile of dust and Jonquilian sand.

It was her final key, *terra*, the very body of the planet Graha. She gathered up the element in her hands and approached the door, ever wary of the blades that guarded it. "Stand back," she warned.

The guards scuttled a few feet away, watching closely. Rosette lifted her dirt-filled palms, placing them directly over the vessel of water. In one smooth motion, she dropped the soil into the vessel and deftly sprung backwards onto her hands, tumbling away from danger. Blades seemed to swing in from all directions, triggered by the soil particles blocking the light that once shone clearly through the water. Had a weapon or any other substance been placed in the water, it would not have broken the light in just the right way to trigger the door. As the sabers closed in and then came to rest, the pendulum blades swung back and forth, slowly losing momentum as they approached the still point.

Rosette crouched low to the ground, a satisfied smile just breaking her stoic facade; within moments, it would be safe for her to pass through the door without risk of injury.

"Yes!" the right guard exclaimed, obviously and inappropriately happy for his prisoner. "That's the key!"

The left guard moved forward, blocking the door. "It appears you have solved the last riddle. Congratulations," he said grumpily.

Rosette turned to him and gave a half-smile, then lowered her voice. "Let me pass through this door to the end of the Mazurin Gon." Rosette looked the guard in the eye. "To my victory."

The guard bowed slightly, stepping to the side. "As you wish."

Rosette grasped the handle, pushing at the enormous door until it opened, revealing a lovely water garden with charming fountains bubbling on the other side. Gleaming metal sculptures and colorful glass ornaments graced the space, beckoning for her to enter. Rosette took a step forward, exhilarated at the thought of freedom and sweet reunion.

What she could not know was that both of the guards had deceived her, and she would not step foot into the garden this day. Just as she went to move across the threshold, the left guard reached for her arm, and a voice boomed behind her: "Stop her! Do not let her pass!"

Fincher, unwilling to trust his guards to carry out their devious roles, had arrived, intent on stopping the woman himself. Rosette wheeled round and found the two guards upon her, grasping her arms to prevent her passage. She quickly knocked both of the men to the ground with a swirling kick, heading once more for the open door and the garden beyond, but was stopped short by a stabbing pain in her back. Fincher stood behind her, narrow teeth bared, the syringe of kumain in his hand now emptied into her flesh.

Rosette froze where she stood, caught off-guard by the searing pain that quickly spread from the injection site. She turned to strike at Fincher, but the guards had gathered themselves and were upon her once more. Rosette began struggling against them.

Fincher smiled. "I encourage you to give me audience, for King Jonas' life now depends on it."

Rosette paused her struggle, sensing a grain of truth in the man's voice. Fincher replaced the syringe in its protective case and addressed the woman once more. "What you have most hoped for has come to fruition. King Jonas has returned to his throne in Samera, and the whole of the Land of Verde has been restored."

Though Rosette made great effort to conceal her joy at this news, her aura flushed rose red. But Fincher had already been made privy to the secret in her heart.

The Waymakers of each Land did at times communicate, and for Fincher, it had been easy enough to obtain information. He had been in contact with Solanum of Verde, who spoke with disdain of Jonas and Rosette's love. Fincher knew full well why Rosette fought, why she burned with an inextinguishable fire, and why she would never stop.

"The scope of my acumen reaches beyond the boundaries of Jonquil to all Lands," Fincher said. "I know why you joined the resistance, why you love Verde so much." Fincher raised an eyebrow, the hint of a smile on his lips. "You have just been tainted with kumain, a serum that damages specific types of kumu. Verdean kumu, in this case. The poison will not kill you; you are a half-breed, and so it will only cause a slow decay of your vitality over time." Fincher turned his back on the woman, swiveling his head around as he spoke. "However, if you were to so much as lay a fingertip on King Jonas, he would perish instantly at your poisoned touch."

Rosette shook her head, gritting her teeth. "You lie."

Fincher wheeled round to face her once more, frowning in

disgust. "My dear, you insult me. Only the low-minded man has need for lies. Deceit is the cheap trick of those who cannot afford to be clever." Fincher loosed the frown from his brow and looked down his nose at Rosette. "A man of authentic intellect plays the truth to his advantage and avoids the sloppy business of telling lies."

He then looked out over the beauty of the Garden of Victory that yet lay just out of reach of his prisoner. "Oh, the irony. After fighting for Jonas' life for so long," he faced her once more, hands clasped behind his back, "you would now take it with a single embrace."

Rosette balled her hands tightly into fists, fighting the urge to strike at her captor. As she did, she felt a strange weakness in her hands as the kumain began to drain her strength.

Fincher studied her. "If you agree to return to my Mazurin Gon and to make no further attempts at escape, I will give you the antidote to the kumain."

Rosette looked down and laughed aloud in frustration at her predicament. Fincher stepped closer. "Well, do you agree?"

She looked up at Fincher with ruby eyes aglow. "I have no other choice."

Fincher nodded in satisfaction, signaling his guards. "Follow me."

The guards each took one of Rosette's arms, leading her behind Fincher to the solitary holding chamber near the entrance to the Gon. Though defeated in her attempt to escape, Rosette felt a growing warmth within her. Jonas had returned, and by some means she would find her way back to him.

The door lock clicked into place and Rosette found herself alone in silence. The darkness of the chamber closed in around her, reminding her of the blindness she had struggled with during her journey through the maze. In many ways, she was right back where she had begun. She knelt down near the wall, resting against its cool hardness.

She began to think of Jonas, of the sweet scent of grapa tree blossoms that must surely be opening now at his return. She thought of quiet walks in the forest in kinder times and the warmth of Jonas' touch. Just as she remembered these things, she recalled the insidious poison now creeping in her blood, and that a single touch of her hand would mean a lifetime of emptiness. Rosette lifted her head and shut her eyes tight, a single tear drifting down her cheek.

PART 7

THE LOST QUEEN OF JONQUIL

Mila and Pixie came through the doorway and arrived at the coffee shop in a brilliant flash of light. Thankfully, Vincent and his Aunt Elena were still tending to whatever catastrophe had sent them dashing into the kitchen just before Mila had left for the Outer Realm, and the spectacle of their arrival had therefore gone unseen. Pixie swayed back and forth, gathering herself after the din and bright light of the passage.

Mila looked up at her with concern. "I know, it's crazy loud and bright, but you've done it before, right?"

Pixie did not answer Mila, but instead glanced around the room, overwhelmed by her unfamiliar surroundings. Overhead, white tube lights flickered and hummed in rectangular fixtures, and a strong but pleasant aroma filled the air. On the counter, Pixie spotted an object of particular interest: a long-handled spoon with the Go Joe coffee bean logo at the top. Pixie immediately realized the spoon was identical to one from Salvitor's collection. "Hey, it's Sal's spoon..." She stopped herself mid-thought as a dull ache in her earlobe reminded her that she needed to tend the durational. Pixie unclipped the device from her ear, frowning as she massaged the lobe.

"What's wrong with your ear?" Mila asked.

Pixie shook her head. "Sal designed these durationals to be clipped onto your clothes, but I like to wear as an earring. It hurts after a while, though." Pixie carefully adjusted the dials for length of time, going over calculations and settings in her mind.

Mila cocked her head. "What are you doing with it?"

Pixie waved a hand. "It's complicated. You have to use this equation to figure out your settings...you wouldn't get it."

Pixie clicked the dial a few more times, then nodded confidently, her uncertainty veiled beneath a seemingly assured facade. She clipped the device to her ear once more, snapped her fingers, and smiled. "Okay, all set."

Vincent and his aunt emerged from the back room and came up to the counter. Elena's eyes opened wide as she saw the blonde girl, who had not been there a few minutes before. "Oh, I'm so sorry, I didn't hear the bell when you came in, sweetie, I was so caught up back there."

"It's okay," Mila said. "She just popped in a second ago. This is Pixie, Madi's friend—I mean—cousin...from out of town." Mila cringed at the suspicious sound of her own stammering. And what would they think of a name like *Pixie*?

Aunt Elena smiled broadly. "Pixie?" She folded her hands over her heart. "That is so adorable! I had a Chihuahua named Pixie, a feisty little thing. Lived to be eighteen years old. Such a doll." Elena placed her hands on Vincent's shoulders. "Pixie, this is my nephew, Vincent."

"Hi," the boy said, smiling nervously and pushing his glasses up to a more comfortable spot on his nose.

Mila finally spotted her latte waiting for her on the counter. She quickly stepped over to it and took a long sip, then offered some to Pixie. "Here, try this. It's her special flavor mix."

Pixie lowered her head and placed the drinking straw between her lips. As the frozen concoction met her taste buds, her eyes rolled back in her head. "That's the best thing I have ever tasted!"

Aunt Elena giggled. "Oh, thank you, that's what everybody seems to say." She casually pushed her dark hair behind her shoulders, feigning modesty. "I would make you another one, but I can't right now. I'm all out of my secret flavor mix and I just spilled the new batch of concentrate all over the floor back there. I'll have to go to the store and make some more tomorrow. Pixie, can I get you something else to drink?"

Vincent cleared his throat, steeling himself. "You can have mine if you want. I didn't drink out of it yet."

Pixie crossed her arms over her chest, shaking her head. "No thanks, I'm not really that thirsty."

Mila tucked a second spoon straw into the frozen concoction and held it up to Pixie. "We'll just share this one." Mila glanced at the durational clipped to Pixie's ear, a reminder of the time limitation that pressed down upon them. "We have to go now. I told my mom I would be back soon. Thanks for the special drink."

Elena smiled brightly. "Sure, sweetie. Be careful on the way home."

The two girls turned toward the door, walking in tandem.

"It was nice to meet you, Pixie," Elena called after them.

Pixie swiveled round and waved stiffly. "You, too."

Mila glanced back at the counter. "Bye, Vincent."

The young man blushed as he lifted a hand to wave. "Bye, see ya later."

A bell tinkled overhead and the ocean breeze rolled in through the door as the girls made their way out of the shop and into the sunshine.

Pixie was at once transfixed, eyes locked on the ebb and flow of blue water just beyond the boardwalk. Her ears filled with the rush of the waves as she drew a relaxing breath, taking the salt air deep into her lungs. How different it seemed from her arid home of Jonquil, where the thin blue ribbon of the Western Sea rested far below, eternally out of her reach.

The girls left the boardwalk and walked onto the beach, the warm sand engulfing their feet more and more with each step. Mila watched as Pixie awkwardly negotiated the shifting sand in a pair of tall boots, standing out from the other beach visitors like a beacon. "Oh, Pixie?" Mila stopped for a moment to untie her Chucks and roll up her jeans. "It's better if you take off your shoes."

Pixie did as Mila suggested and cautiously moved closer to the ocean, walking out over the damp, compacted sand. She gasped as the chilly water touched her toes for the first time, surprised by the sensation. Ahead, she watched sand crabs scuttling about, expertly outpacing the lapping waves with their sidestepping gait.

Pixie giggled and tiptoed forward in pursuit of the busy crabs, her aura swirling with bright yellow and gold as she went. She looked back to where Mila stood a short distance away. "I've seen the Western Sea from a distance, but I never actually got to walk where the water could touch my feet." She wiggled her toes as a wave receded, feeling the sand squishing between. "This is amazing."

Mila nodded knowingly. She'd seen many remarkable things on the other side of the doorway, yet countless wonders waited, unappreciated, right in her own neighborhood. Though the people of Graha possessed special gifts that a rare few, if any, on Earth could ever know, some of them had lived in isolation or endured great ridicule because of these very gifts. Mila suddenly felt fortunate for her ability to experience both worlds.

She broke from her thoughts and made her way to Pixie, dragging her toes in the sand as she went. "Hey Pixie, try this," Mila said, tapping her friend on the shoulder. Mila faced the sea, ankle-deep in the foamy surf. "Just stay like this and don't move for a minute. It feels like the water is pulling you out to sea even though you're standing still."

Pixie did as Mila suggested, shutting her eyes and lifting her arms for balance. She glanced at Mila, smiling. "It kind of makes me feel dizzy, and I'm sinking lower with each wave."

Mila laughed and splashed forward into deeper water, then hopped back after realizing her jeans were getting wet. Pixie reached down to pick up a seashell. After inspecting it, she heaved it as far as she could into the sea. "So, how does it feel to be the Sankari Sano?"

Mila shrugged. "It feels...big."

Pixie shook her head. "I was picturing the Sankari Sano as some incredible warrior from another planet with serious weapons, and maybe four arms or something." She looked down at Mila. "I can't believe you're just a kid."

Before Mila could respond, a seagull suddenly swooped down at Pixie's head, no doubt intrigued by golden spiky hair that, to hungry gull eyes, could vaguely resemble French fries. Pixie instinctively teleported a few feet away, as she often did when startled, but the bird was undeterred. Pixie called out, flailing her arms wildly, swatting at the bird as if being attacked by a grown raiku. "Get it away from me!"

Mila watched the spectacle, a smile slowly growing on her face. Pixie jogged away in a last attempt to avoid the curious bird, but tripped and fell to her knees instead. As she sat cowering in the sand, Mila finally let out her laughter, trotting over to her frightened friend. "It's gone, he flew away."

Pixie looked up at Mila with furrowed brows. Mila continued giggling. "I might be just a kid, but at least I'm not afraid of a little bird."

Pixie huffed, brushing the clinging particles from her clothing. "I thought something was trying to eat me."

Mila tilted her head. "They mostly just eat French fries and dead stuff. We're safe." Her expression became serious. "But Pixie, make sure you don't use your gifts here. The people in my world don't do things like we do. I don't think anyone can see us glow, but..." Mila looked up and scanned the shoreline for anyone who may have seen Pixie's display. "It's better just to blend in."

Pixie nodded, straightening her blonde spikes. "Okay, I'll try."

The two girls continued walking down the beach in silence, listening to the waves roll onto the shore and back out again. Pixie turned over thoughts in her mind of the fate of her world, her queen, and the direction of her own life. She watched the water move in and out, powered by unseen forces, a seemingly ceaseless cycle that could not be stopped. "So if you are the Sankari Sano, but you're just a kid..." Pixie turned and looked Mila straight in the eyes, "... how are you going to help us?"

Mila sighed and shrugged. "I'm not sure about everything, but I know how to use my glow to heal things, and to help people. I've been doing that for a while." Mila reached down, plucking a half-buried seashell from the sand, then tossing it into the surf. "The new stuff I'm just now learning how to do, well, Thornhill said I will know what to do when the time comes for me to help." Mila remembered many occasions when she seemed to surrender to a higher force within her. "Just like what happened when we were in Salvitor's basement and my glow killed all those shadow things."

Pixie's nodded, eyes wide. "That was something."

"So I guess it doesn't matter that I'm a kid, because I don't think I'm supposed to fight anybody. I think I'm just supposed to show up."

Pixie smiled slightly, gazing at the girl with the unusual white glow. As she looked upon her, Mila's glow began to build, and her face brightened with excitement. Pixie moved closer to her. "What, what is it?"

Mila held her hand to her tummy. "Dave's Dogs!"

She pointed at a silver vendor cart parked farther down the boardwalk. "C'mon, Pixie, if you come to the beach, you gotta get a chili dog!"

Mila took Pixie's hand and began jogging toward the stand. The familiar scent wafted through the air and Mila felt her mouth watering. She dug into her pockets, hoping she had enough money for at least two. As she approached the counter, the chunky man inside smiled knowingly. "Well, hello ladies."

"Hi, we need some chili dogs, please. My friend has never tried them."

"Well, you came to the right place, Dave's makes the best dogs in Ocean City!" the man said proudly.

Mila carefully counted the bills in her hand and laid them on the counter. "Two with everything, please."

"You got it," he replied, turning to fill the order.

The steam rolled out of the bin as he loaded the buns with the famous dogs, chili, and mounds of bright orange cheese. Mila could feel her stomach leaping with joy, and she suddenly wished she'd had enough money for four.

"Here you are, ladies. Enjoy." The man slid the paper plate across the counter as he took the bills from Mila.

"Thanks!" They scurried over to a bench to enjoy their snack.

Pixie seemed somewhat intimidated by the messy creation, holding her palm under it to catch the falling sauce and cheese. Mila eagerly took a big bite, smiling at the cheese that clung to the tip of her nose. Pixie soon followed suit, and was pleasantly surprised by the rich and foreign flavors.

Upon reaching the end of her dog, Mila took the last bit of her bread and tossed it to a waiting pigeon. Pixie did the same, greatly appreciative that these birds didn't seem to want to attack her. She hurriedly swallowed the bite of food in her mouth and turned to Mila. "They remind me of the joli in the Gon."

Mila looked puzzled. "The who in the what?"

Pixie smiled, pointing to the pigeons. "They remind me of the joli in the Mazurin Gon. It's a crazy maze in Jonquil where all the warriors go to be tested. Anyway, the joli that live there are about the same size, but their wings are different. When they fly, their wings move so fast that they almost disappear. The joli carry food through the maze."

"That sounds like a hummingbird. Here we have little birds that flap their wings really fast like that. You can't even see them moving."

Pixie soon slowed her eating pace and set her plate in her lap, sighing. "The food is really good here, but maybe a little heavy." She then held her hand to her stomach, handing Mila the remaining portion of her chili dog.

Mila gobbled it up eagerly, brushing the crumbs and stray strands of cheese from her shirt. "Pixie, do you have school in your world, or do kids just hang out and do whatever they want all the time?"

Pixie looked perplexed. "What do you mean?"

"Here in my world, when you are little, you start going to school." Mila paused, realizing Pixie did not understand what the word meant. "See, school is a place we go to learn things, like how to read and do math and science. Do you go to school?"

Pixie finally nodded in comprehension. "We have Develoption. When you are really young, you learn from your family and from learning groups of other kids around your home. You mostly just play, because that's what little kids need the most to learn, I guess." Pixie fell silent for a moment, remembering the lonely years of her own childhood that differed greatly from the description she had offered Mila. "Then, when you turn eleven, you start going to Develoption to learn about other things."

"Like what?"

"Like how to use your gifts, what kumu is and how to access it, and they teach you about the Four Founders, the kings and queens. You know, all that kind of stuff."

"That's different from school here," Mila explained. "Here, you start going to school when you're only six, and my mom always says that half the stuff they teach doesn't even help us in the real world. She's a teacher."

"Is that like a Magister?"

Mila shrugged. "I guess so. Teachers help kids to learn things their parents don't know how to teach them."

"Yeah, I guess your teachers do the same thing as Magisters. We have four High Magisters, one for each Land, and each Magister has apprentices that learn from them and help them teach. Gishon is the High Magister of Jonquil, Sahler for Verde, Bobbin for Lapis, and for Crimson..." Pixie paused and looked away, obviously hiding something, "...someone else."

Mila cocked her head, noting the slip, but Pixie was talking again already. "I was studying under an apprentice of Gishon. I was doing really good, and I was supposed to move up and start studying under Gishon himself, but...I'm gonna need to start showing up more often for that to happen!"

Mila giggled, tossing the greasy paper plates into a trash bin next to the bench. Pixie stood. "Each Magister trains about ten students at a time, sometimes for just a year or so, sometimes for decades. It all depends."

"Depends on what?"

Pixie rested her hands on her hips. "On how much you got and how fast you learn to use it."

"So how long do you think you will have to train with Gishon?"

"Don't know." Pixie turned her slanted eyes downward and kicked a pebble across the boards. "See, when I was younger, I never really paid attention to the apprentices that tried to teach me. I wanted to learn from the old ones, the wise ones, you know? Not some young apprentice that barely knows more about their own gifts than I do about mine."

Mila flicked a stray piece of cheese from her shirt.

Pixie continued, "The only one I wanted to learn from was Gishon. To me, he was the best because he has the gift of invisibility."

Mila's eyes widened. "You mean he can make himself disappear?"

"Into thin air!" Pixie said. "And he could stay invisible for as long as he wanted! It takes so much energy and control to do that. I wanted to be just like him, so I decided I wasn't going to listen to anybody unless they were as gifted and wise as Gishon."

"Is that why you stopped showing up for lessons?"

Pixie nodded. "One day, Gishon sat me down and talked to me. He said that even though I had strong abilities, I had no discipline. He said I would have to earn the right to study with him by doing better with his apprentice. So, I started showing up more and doing my exercises. Not because I thought I needed to, but because more than anything I wanted to learn from Gishon." Pixie stretched her legs out in front of her. "The apprentice actually turned out to be really good. She even helped me learn to control my gift, so when I get startled, I don't just automatically teleport...sometimes it still happens."

Mila giggled. "Like earlier, with the killer seagull?"

Pixie shrugged, grinning sheepishly.

Mila sighed. "It seems like your school is different from mine. You get all kinds of special training that's meant just for you. In my school they teach everybody the same old stuff." Mila sat up straighter in her chair, finally voicing the question she'd held back for some time. "So, what's the name of the last Magister, the one from Crimson? You didn't say his name."

Pixie cleared her throat, glancing at the ground. "Yeah, I don't remember his name."

For just an instant, Mila felt an uncomfortable tightening in her gut. She could hear a few fragments of Pixie's thoughts, and her new friend seemed to be holding a secret. Mila cleared her throat. "Are you *sure* you don't remember his name?"

Pixie cut Mila a sideways glance. "No one is supposed to say his name...strange things can happen to you."

Mila scooted closer. "What kinds of things?"

Pixie turned and looked toward the sea. "Well, I've only heard rumors, but supposedly he made this spell, so that whenever someone spoke his name, it opened a little portal and he could take part of his mind and put it inside of yours, and then he can hear all your thoughts, know everything you know. He just wanted to learn—I think—but something about the spell went wrong. I heard that if you say his name and he links up with you, it kind of makes you go crazy, because you get some of his thoughts, too. You feel like you are hearing crazy voices all the time."

"Weird," Mila whispered.

"Yeah, and then once the spell got going he couldn't stop it. It just keeps happening."

"Why? Why can't he just undo the spell?"

Pixie shook her head. "He can't undo spells. Everybody has weaknesses, and that is his."

"So, it will just keep happening forever?"

Pixie nodded slowly. "He is the most powerful of all the Magisters, so everyone was already kind of afraid of him anyway. So nobody says his name. Ever."

Mila's eyes widened. "Geez, I hope his name's not Bob or John!"

Pixie smiled at Mila, then squinted as a sparkle of light flashed off the faceted edge of Mila's watch. "How's the timetick working for you?"

"It's good. It stops time while I go to your world, and it always seems to open the doorway on your side close to Thornhill." Mila frowned, recalling her return to Samera and Thornhill's unexplained absence. "But one time I crossed over and Thornhill was nowhere close. I don't know what happened."

"I think I know what happened."

Mila lifted a brow at the blonde, eager for her response.

"See, Salvitor told me about the timetick and the resonator, about how he could wrap a strand of someone's hair around the resonator fork, and then it would help guide the user to that person."

"So, is the resonator in my watch broken or something?"

Pixie shook her head. "Sal also told me that the Sankari Sano has the power not just to open doorways, but to open them wherever you want and have them lead wherever you choose. You don't really need a resonator."

Mila placed her palm over the watch, lowering her hands in front of her. "But how? How do I get a doorway to lead where I want it to?"

Pixie shrugged. "I'm not totally sure, but…"

"But what?"

"Well, you said once before you crossed over to Samera, but Thornhill was far away when you got there. What did you do different that time?"

Mila scratched her temple. "I don't know. Everything seemed normal like the other times I crossed. Except I do remember I was thinking about King Jonas and how pretty the castle was. When I first opened the doorway, I pictured myself landing outside of the castle and looking over the stone wall."

Pixie lifted her index finger. "That might be it. If you have any telepathic gifts at all, you have to be careful what you think about, what you picture in your head. It actually makes things happen. Do you have telepathy? Can you talk without talking, and hear people's thoughts?"

Mila nodded. "Yeah. I have been doing that for a while. Like just a few minutes ago when you said you forgot that one Magister's name, and I knew you really didn't."

Pixie blushed slightly.

Mila's aura swirled energetically. "So I can talk without talking and hear people's thoughts, and now it looks like I can control where the doorway opens, just by picturing a place in my head."

Pixie nodded. "That's what it seems like." She narrowed her eyes at Mila. "You better be careful. Sal always said that thoughts are more powerful than we know."

Mila swallowed hard. "Okay, I will."

Pixie stood up, winked, and turned to the ocean. "Let's walk down there, way down where those people are. I want to see those rocks."

Mila hesitated, observing the dark clouds that had begun to gather over the coast. "It looks like it's going to rain." Just then, thunder rumbled in the distance, and lightning illuminated the hanging clouds. "I think we should go back to my house instead. There might be a bad storm coming."

Pixie sighed. "All right, if we must, we must." She turned from the sea, shoving her feet back into her boots. "So, what are you going to tell everyone about me? I'm sure your mom and dad or whoever is going to wonder."

Mila groaned. "Oh man, I didn't think about that," Mila crossed her hands over her head, then looked up at Pixie, "I know, we should head over to Madi's house first. She's always good at these kinds of things."

Pixie shrugged. "But what are you gonna tell *her* about me?"

Mila looked squarely at Pixie. "Everything."

Pixie's mouth fell open, but before she could protest, Mila patted her shoulder. "Don't worry. I think she will understand."

The two girls left the beach and made their way back into the neighborhood, heavy with the weight of big news.

Journey to Aksini

Bitten by crisp winds and parched as desert sand, Meadow, Thornhill, and Botan at last arrived in the town of Aksini, the closest to the Palace of Gosai. The town sat at a higher elevation than all other places in Jonquil besides the palace island itself, and that, along with exceptionally cool and clear air, meant visitors were afforded incredible views of the surrounding areas. The layout of the buildings and homes was such that one could stand at any point on the main road and get a clear view of the palace floating at the far reaches of Seletan.

Meadow slowed his pace, falling slightly behind as he took in the surprising beauty of it all. "It looks almost as if Corpus has left this place untouched. Much of the metal here is polished, and the windows are still glassed."

Botan nodded. "Yes, the people of Aksini place high value on esthetics and art, even in these times." His aura waxed to a more saturated tone as he entertained a pleasant memory. "Being so close to the palace, they have a special affinity for order and beauty, more so than most Jonquilians. They also deeply believe that one day Queen Zehn will return, and they do not wish to be ashamed of their homes when she does."

Thornhill hummed. "Sounds like what Lium said about their homes being extensions of their sacred selves. Making the home as beautiful as the soul seems part of their desire for authenticity."

"*Lium?*" Botan snapped. "Lium and authenticity should not be uttered in the same breath."

Thornhill grunted in agreement, and the three men continued down the main road. After passing several structures, they approached a sandplaster dome tucked behind a line of trees with twisting branches. Botan felt his heart flutter as he caught sight of it. He wondered if she would still be there, tending the shop, shaping masterpieces and glowing vibrantly as she always did. Though many years had passed since their last visit, the indelible memory of her fair face was as fresh as the first time he'd met her.

Botan stopped, pointing to a path marked with an artfully shaped metal sign that read *Gallery Selin*. "Here we will find my friend Selin. I'm hoping she can give us some more information." Botan's craned his neck in an attempt to see around each coming curve in the serpentine path before they'd come to it. Thornhill smiled, tuning in to his friend's anticipation. Even Corpus himself could not extinguish every flame.

As they approached the radentium front door, they saw it gleamed with high polish and featured the ornately cut design of a tree that echoed those in the yard. To the surprise of all, not a single speck of the tarnish of Corpus' hand could be seen, and the tinted glass in the door and the windows still afforded a clear view of the front gallery space. Within, Botan saw blown glass and metal art pieces, along with a water fountain.

Botan whistled softly. "Remarkable, how pristine the facade is in such dark times." He gently ran his hand over a curve in the trunk of the metal tree design. "This door is as perfectly polished as I remember from the times before Corpus. I hope that means she is still here." Botan tugged at the blown glass door handle and a chime softly rang out. The three men entered the gallery and were immediately soothed by their surroundings. A roaring fire warmed the air, the burning wood sending off an herbaceous scent. To the left of a wide desk stood the blown glass and metal fountain Botan had seen from outside; beyond it was a cozy shop room stocked with various herbs and vegetables. To the right of the door sprawled the gallery space, peppered with colored glass bulbs, lit from within by candles, and on polished metal tables, artful arrangements of glass flowers that shamed the finest of living gardens.

Framed by crystalline flowers and trickling water, a young woman stood behind the desk, twisting a length of wire into a sinuous shape with a tool. Her pale golden aura surrounded her elegant form in a bubble that pulsed as she worked, and her short blond hair stayed slicked back behind her ears.

Her name was Selin, renowned artist and gifted observer. Able to pick up on the finest changes in body language, the timbre of the voice and nearly imperceptible shifts in the aura, Selin detected subtleties that even the best communicators would miss. Her sensitivity allowed her to know the true condition of a person's heart, and to sense when the truth was being disguised. Even the most practiced liar could not fool her. Authenticity was more important to Selin than even Jonquilians of the highest integrity. Botan had always been a breath of fresh, green air, honesty without obligation, admiration without agenda. Had the two not been hopelessly separated by the borders of their Lands, she'd always felt they would come together as more than acquaintances.

Selin looked up from her work at the sound of the door chime. Upon seeing Botan, she dropped her tool, her smile illuminating her face. At the same moment, Botan set eyes on Selin, blushing upon sight of the lovely creature. For long years he had admired her, and her magical brown eyes that seemed to see everything in his heart. To him she seemed an otherworldly being, surrounded by delicate and beautiful things and the sound of water and music.

The woman swept gracefully from behind the counter. "Botan! What a joy!"

Botan took both her hands in his, his eyes drinking in the fairness of her face. "My dear Selin, your façade is as fresh as the day I first beheld it. How do you do it?"

Selin smiled, raising a brow at the double meaning, and glanced behind Botan. "Polishing has become a daily meditation...who are your friends?"

Botan finally took his eyes off Selin and looked to his two companions. "Ah yes, this is Thornhill, Prime Advisor to King Jonas of Verde, and Meadow of Verde."

Selin took each of their hands in her own, meeting their eyes with her bewitching gaze. "I am pleased to meet you." Selin turned back to Botan. "You three must be chilled and parched. May I offer you arbata?"

Thornhill moaned, his body collapsing slightly. "My dear, you are reading my mind."

Botan smiled. "That would be perfect."

Selin turned and opened a drawer in an apothecary chest near the desk, taking out a petite kettle and a cloth bag filled with arbata leaves. She gave each of her guests a dainty cup of colored glass, crumbling the leaves into the kettle and holding it under a cascade of water in the nearby fountain. "I do love the sound of water. It is the finest music." She unhooked a ring-like device from the handle and dropped it into the water. Thornhill took notice: the device was similar to the one he had used not long ago in Salvitor's workshop. His aura flickered slightly as he remembered his friend, and that he would not take arbata with him again in this life.

Selin glanced into the kettle. "To what do I owe this visit, gentlemen?"

"Mostly to weariness," Thornhill quipped. "But we are also here to bring counsel, and perhaps gain some from you."

Selin looked closely at Thornhill, noticing a slight fading in his aura. She returned to the apothecary and took out a few silvery gray leaves, rubbing them between her fingers and allowing the fine particles to drop into Thornhill's cup. "For vitality and strength," she said, returning to the kettle and removing the ring.

Steam rolled from the opening as she carefully poured the hot tea into the men's cups, then into her own.

Thornhill took a whiff of the sweetly pungent drink as it steeped. "Mm, very fresh."

Selin smiled. "Despite the harshness of these times, in Jonquil you will still find the finest medicine plants."

"Indeed," Thornhill held his cup with both hands to warm them.

"Come, sit and take some rest as we drink," Selin said, eyes focused on Thornhill.

The group sat down at the round table in the adjoining shop, and all three men seemed to sag with relief into the comfortable padded chairs. Selin sat back and crossed her long legs, cradling her cup delicately in her fingertips. "Tell me, other than weariness and counsel, what else brings you three to Aksini?"

Botan spoke. "We are here to gather food and supplies before moving on to the palace. A member of our group is being held prisoner there."

Selin shook her head worriedly. "Gosai is under Fincher's control, and it is infested with raiku. How do you plan to do this?"

Meadow spoke up. "I have seen in visions that Highpointe Rosette of Verde is being held in the Mazurin Gon. I have tuned into her dreams and I can sense from them that she fights in every moment to escape, and may be drawing close to breaking out. We want to be there to assist her, or at least meet her if she does succeed."

Thornhill furrowed his brow. "I've heard you speak a number of times about your visions, and now you say that you see into the dreams of others? To be so young a Verdean and already possess such gifts...quite unusual."

Meadow smiled gently. "Yes, it is unusual for a young Verdean, but not for a remshifter like me."

"Remshifter?" Thornhill whispered. "I thought that Corpus had destroyed the last of them long ago."

"Many, but not all. We remshifters have the ability to enter a meditative dream state where we can access the shadow plane. There one can gain much information, from other remshifters or from the dreams and thoughts of others, but it is very dangerous. Corpus himself is an incredibly powerful remshifter, and that is how he has gained so much power in the shadow plane. He can sense the presence of your mind in that realm, and if he is able to find you, he can lock you there against your will. Forever."

Botan and Thornhill looked at each other in surprise, then back at Meadow. Botan spoke quietly: "I had heard of remshifters before, but honestly, I'd thought them more a myth than anything. I had no idea of the depth of your gifts, and the risks you've taken for the good of these missions. Thank you, my brother."

Meadow lowered his head graciously, his black hair cascading over his deep green eyes. "It is the least I can do. I owe my life to King Jonas."

A chime rang in the gallery room, and a gust of chilly air spilled into the shop. Selin set down her cup. "That's the door. Won't you excuse me, gentlemen?"

The men nodded, and Botan watched her every graceful step as she moved into the gallery to greet her guest.

The Fallen

With Selin out of earshot, the men could speak about more private matters. Thornhill in particular had many questions burning in his mind. Having been in hiding for so many years with only occasional messages from the ramara, his ears hungered for news of the fate of friends. His slurped the last of his arbata, set down his cup, and rubbed the symbol imprinted on the back of his neck.

It seemed to call for attention, and so Thornhill turned to Meadow. "My friend, are you aware that we have lost Salvitor of Jonquil?"

Meadow's aura flickered slightly. "Yes, I witnessed his death in the vision I had before I came to release you from Salvitor's chamber in Ispa." Meadow paused, noticing the pain in Thornhill's eyes. "I am very sorry for your loss."

Thornhill lowered his head slightly in acknowledgement. "Have you seen anything of the fate of Bobbin of Lapis and her assistants, the twins Cira and Finn? And what of the Great Magister of Crimson?"

Meadow shook his head slowly. "Both Bobbin and Finn are dead."

Thornhill sat back slowly, emitting a weak groan as he covered his eyes with a gnarled hand.

Meadow continued, "The Great Magister and Cira of Lapis are missing, but I am hopeful for Cira. I have seen in visions that she is yet alive, and that she was able to complete her mission. I believe I will soon be able to locate her."

Thornhill sighed. "Well, at least one other yet lives."

"Have you seen or heard from any of the others?" Botan asked.

Meadow frowned. "Nothing else. I have not been able to tune into individuals as well as I have in the past. There is some form of interference from massive amounts of dark energy that seem to be coming from the sea off the eastern shores of Verde. Something tells me Jonas' kingdom may be in grave danger."

Thornhill grunted. "*Jonas.*" He drew his fingers across his white brows and pinched where they met the bridge of his nose. "I feel as if I am torn in two. On the one hand is the life of King Jonas, and on the other, the lives of Zehn and Rosette, whom Jonas himself has bid us to save."

"I understand how conflicted you must feel right now," Meadow said. "But I believe we must stay with the task at hand—to bring Zehn back from the Inner Realm and meet Mila when she returns."

Botan set his empty cup down, nodding. "Once Zehn is returned to the throne, we will have two Founders back in Graha, and whatever forces that may attack Verde would be less powerful. The more light we shine, the weaker the darkness grows."

The gentle ping of the door chime rang once more, and Selin came back into the shop area, peeking out the window at the man scurrying down the winding path. "That man wanted to trade some metal artifacts for one of my glass pieces," she explained, her melodic laugh echoing in the room. "He claimed they were made of pure radentium, but his eyes and his aura revealed the truth."

Botan chuckled. "No one will ever fool you, dear Selin."

The young woman then glanced worriedly out the front window.

"Has the dishonest merchant returned?" Botan asked.

Selin shook her head, backing slowly away from the window. "No, I thought I saw them again. The shadow watchers have been gathering in greater numbers of late." Selin took her seat once more, sipping at the last of her arbata. "Corpus watches, always."

Botan shot a look at Thornhill, who sat forward, his expression grim. "My dear, while you were tending to your guest, we discussed something you should know about." Thornhill sighed, as if preparing himself for his own words. "Salvitor of Jonquil is dead."

"Salvitor?" Selin gasped. "I *knew* him. He spent much time in Seletan with the queen and often stopped here in Aksini." Selin smiled faintly, her eyes far off in a memory. "I remember the day I met him, at the dedication ceremony for the first art piece I installed at the Palace. He was more nervous than I was!"

Thornhill chuckled. "He never was one for parties."

Selin nodded, "I remember the night of the dedication ceremony for his own art installation in the Palace." Selin shook her head. "He stayed just long enough to say he'd made an appearance."

"He is sorely missed," Botan added. He stood and walked a few paces to the adjoining gallery space, admiring a piece installed on the wall above the fountain. "This place is lovely, Selin. You are a truly gifted artisan."

She smiled, rising from her seat to stand close to Botan. "I am humbled that a larger version of this piece hangs in the queen's own bathing chamber...though I cannot know what has come of it now." She traced the curve of a creamy pink blossom with her fingertip and turned to Botan. Her body just barely brushed against his as she retreated to the shop. "What do you need in the way of supplies? I have some good roots, a few dried meats, and of course, you may fill your canteens from the fountain."

"That will do nicely. Thank you ever so much, Selin," Thornhill said gratefully.

Selin and Botan walked to the bins in which the roots were kept, and Meadow stood. "I must find a quiet place to meditate, Thornhill. I want to see if I can communicate with King Jonas and see if there is anything else we must do."

"Good idea." Thornhill motioned to the gallery area. "I believe I spied a nook off the main gallery room, enclosed by drapes. It should do quite nicely."

Meadow smiled, bowed slightly, and moved off into the gallery. Thornhill sighed deeply, for a weariness persisted in him, deep as bone, that arbata and rest could not seem to touch. He watched Botan and Selin as they laughed and filled the packs with supplies, their auras mixing and blending in a communal shade of golden jade. Thornhill treasured the wisdom of his later years, but how he longed for the vibrance of youth, and the fresh spark that now seemed to fade from his heart.

* * *

After the three men had gathered their supplies and bid their host farewell, they made their way south on the central road to the hangars at the edge of town. Botan's pace was decidedly less energetic than it was on the way to the gallery, and his aura swirled in agitation.

Thornhill took notice and patted his friend on the shoulder. "Take a deep breath, Botan."

Botan shot a glance at Thornhill, then looked down at the ground, sighing heavily.

"I'm sure your paths will cross again," Thornhill said.

Botan smiled at his old friend, and the three walked on into the south.

Shadow Hunters

In the dark of the Pravus caves, Corpus stirred, roused by some disturbance within. Through his watcher minions, he had already learned that the child had survived the ambush in Ispa and had escaped to the Inner Realm. Whispers drifted into his mind, shards of thoughts that were not his own. He had connected with the child, the Sankari Sano, and had caught a glimpse of her intentions.

She has returned to the Inner Realm to rescue the lost queen.

Corpus seethed. His fruitless pursuit of the child who seemed to foil his every plan had grown tiresome. He could not allow another Founder to return to Graha, for it would greatly weaken his grasp on the Land. The child had to be stopped.

Corpus gradually built his energy in pulsing waves, drawing from a deep well of dark forces. Reaching within his own form, he withdrew a portion of shadow, separated it from himself, and threw it to the ground. He focused on the portion and began to shape it into three distinct forms that squirmed and writhed as they grew.

The three shadows soon began to solidify into physicality, with claws and teeth and eyes like black, swirling storms. Bristly hairs sprouted all over the creatures as they took the form of three black wolves, snarling and snapping as they came fully to life.

Satisfied with his creation, Corpus opened the doorway and prepared to send the wolves on their mission. With information gathered from his watcher bird, he had learned that the child lived in Ocean City, Maryland, but this time, there had been no minion there to follow her through the doorway to her exact location. Corpus could only send the wolves through and hope they would meet their mark.

Lightning flashed across the sky over downtown Baltimore, and the rain steadily pounded the asphalt. The wolves came through the doorway and landed in an alley, quickly gathering themselves and inspecting their surroundings. Broken glass, garbage, and empty bottles littered the ground, the heavy rain doing little to rinse away the persistent filth.

The three minions padded to the back of the alley where they came upon a homeless man balled up in a corner. He took a drag from his bottle, then coughed in shock upon sight of the menacing wolves. The man stood, set down his bottle, and held his hands out before him. "Easy now, good dogs, nice doggies…"

The wolves bared their teeth and growled, their neck hairs bristling. The largest wolf stepped forward, lowering its head.

"Nice doggie, c'mon now, I don't have any food or I would give it to ya…"

Despite the man's soothing tone, the wolf lunged forward and pounced on him, and the other two followed suit. He screamed for help, his body dematerializing more and more with each cry.

The wolves held fast, and mere moments later, only a pile of empty clothes remained. The liquor bottle tipped over, and a stream of dark fluid ran into a puddle slicked with oily iridescence, draining away just as the drinker's life had. The minion wolves turned from the scene and loped away, beginning the hunt for the child.

Reconnecting

The weather turned quickly, and Pixie and Mila increased their pace as they made their way up the street to Madison's house. Pixie became increasingly nervous, tuning in to the increased energy in the air. The dark clouds above periodically lit up with brilliant flashes, and as the girls approached Madison's block, an ear-splitting boom sent Pixie scampering into an adjacent yard, covering her head.

"What was that?" she cried.

Mila shook her head. "It's okay, it's just thunder, but we better hurry up and get to Madi's before it starts..."

Before Mila could finish her sentence, fat drops of rain began thudding to the ground, pelting the girls and soaking their clothes and hair. Mila sighed and jogged to Pixie, taking her hand. "Come on, we're almost there."

They ran the short distance to Madison's house, trotting up onto the covered porch and out of the deluge. Another loud crack of thunder boomed overhead, and Pixie flinched. "It's gonna take me a while to get used to that," she said, glancing skyward as another bolt of lightning tore through the clouds above. "We don't have this in Jonquil!"

At once, a pale face framed by flowing strawberry hair poked out through the open screen door. "Mila!"

Mila jumped, startled, then realized it was Madison. "Oh, Madi! You scared me."

Madison locked eyes with Pixie, unsure of what to think of the strange girl with spiked hair and boots. She opened the door wide and motioned to them. "Hurry up, come in."

Mila immediately detected the distinctive scent of tomato sauce and garlic. Though still digesting her chili dogs, Mila suddenly felt hungry.

"Dad, Mila's here, we're going to my room!" Madison yelled into the kitchen, already heading for the stairs.

Madison's father replied, though none of the girls understood what he had said. Madison shrugged. "He's in the kitchen, so he's busy."

Mila laughed, following her friend up the staircase and to her room. After fetching her guests some bath towels, Madison flopped down on her bed, for a time avoiding eye contact with Pixie. "So, Mila, who is this?"

"This is Pixie." Mila paused, searching for the right words. "We met earlier."

Madison glanced suspiciously at the newcomer. "I'm Madison. You can call me Madi."

Mila sat up a bit straighter and decided to dispense with the small talk. "So, I know all the stuff I told you before at my house is a lot to think about."

Madison flicked her gaze up at her best friend, saying nothing.

"And I know you're probably wondering what's going on with the red glow around you."

Madison furrowed her brow, glancing suspiciously at Pixie, then back at Mila again.

"Um, Pixie is from the other world, the other side of that doorway you saw in my room. It's okay, she knows about everything."

Gradually, tears began to well in Madison's brown eyes, her lip quivering almost indiscernibly. "Mila, you have no idea all the stuff that's been happening today!" she blurted, her red glow increasing. "If I feel mad or upset and I touch something, it turns to stone!"

Pixie and Mila stared silently at the strawberry-haired girl as she nervously glanced about, as if looking for something. Madison picked up a tube of lip gloss that lay nearby. It instantly turned to stone. She quickly dropped the object as if it were a small, vicious animal. The tears began falling in earnest, and Madison, now bathed in red light, began sobbing as she sat down on her bed. "*That* is not normal!"

Mila wrapped her arms around Madison. Her own glow seemed to pulse and flow into Madison's body at her touch. "It's okay, Madi. Me and Pixie can do things that aren't normal, either. We're all in this together."

Madison wiped her eyes and sniffled. "Well, I can turn it back, too. All I have to do is touch it again and it goes back the way it was."

Madison got up and found the cylindrical stone that had been her tube of lip gloss. One deep breath later, the tube had returned to its original form.

Pixie nodded slowly in admiration. "*Nice.*"

Mila took the lip gloss from Madison and place it on the vanity, then grasped Madison's hands. "Madi, you need to know that all three of us are more than just regular kids. All kinds of weird stuff is happening, but I have to keep going because the people on the other side need me."

Madison blinked. "I have this funny feeling that somebody needs me, too, for something really important. Is that what you mean?"

Mila let go of Madison's other hand, searching for words. "See, when I crossed over to the other world the first time, I found out I'm this thing called the Sankari Sano, and I'm supposed to help the people there."

Madison stared blankly at Mila.

"Something really bad happened to the Land there, and all their kings and queens got sent to our world. Only they don't know who they are anymore. It's my job to find them and help them remember who they are, so I can take them back home to the other side."

Madison continued staring at Mila, now more curious than confused. "What were you doing when I saw you walk through the wall in your bedroom?"

"I was coming back. I already helped King Jonas get back to his castle. Now me and Pixie have to find Queen Zehn, and take her back to hers."

Madison suddenly sat up straight, hands at her hips. "Why do *you* have to do all this? Why can't they just get a new queen?"

Mila smiled. "That would be a lot easier, but they can't. The kings and queens actually created their worlds and if they leave, their home Land starts to die. Right now, the whole place except for King Jonas' Land looks almost totally dead. If we don't bring back the rest of the kings and queens soon, everything in their world could die."

"Oh," Madison said quietly, her eyes cast downward.

"I know it sounds crazy, but it's true. I don't know how, but the three of us are all in this together somehow. We can't talk about it with anybody except each other, okay?"

"Who would believe me if I did?" Madison huffed.

Mila lifted her little finger. "Pinky swear?"

Madison locked her pinky with Mila's and then looked to Pixie, motioning with her other hand. "You too, Pixie."

All three girls linked pinkies in a vow of secrecy.

"All right, our secret is safe," Mila said. "Now, besides the fact you can turn stuff to stone, what else do you know? Do you remember anything about the other world?"

"I'm not sure." Madison frowned, blinking several times as she searched her memory. "Maybe I do. That dream I keep having, the one where I'm floating by the mountain and trying to tell the man to go back down? Well, I know who he is. His name is Mason, and—"

"Mason?" Pixie cut in. "Like King Mason of Crimson?"

Madison's face lit up. "Yeah, that sounds right."

Mila leaned forward. "Do you remember anything else about the dream?"

Madison nodded. "In the dream, I can see parts of this place around the mountain and it looks really familiar, like I had been there before. But I've never seen real mountains before, and some of these even had lava."

"The Acala fire belt," Pixie whispered in amazement.

"And the place just..." Madison paused, her eyes fixed at a far off point. "It feels like home, like some part of me lives there, but I cant seem to talk to that other part to find out what's going on."

Pixie nodded. "It sounds like you have ties to Crimson somehow. Maybe you're supposed to help us find Mason when it's his turn to go back."

Madison shrugged, feeling overwhelmed. "Maybe."

Mila reached into her pocket and withdrew something, carefully concealing it in her palm. "Well, maybe you will and maybe you won't, but right now, we have to find Queen Zehn as fast as possible, and we're going to need this to do it."

Mila showed the finder to Madison, whose eyes widened. "You have to keep it a secret. Don't let anybody see it, ever."

Madison took the finder in her hand, turning it carefully. The device seemed familiar to her, though she couldn't place why. "I won't."

Mila took the finder from Madison and ran her fingers across the glass dome. The device lit up and the familiar topographical map of North America appeared on the display. "Now, if I keep tapping it, it'll zoom in and show us where Queen Zehn is," Mila said, tapping the display a few times. The girls watched in amazement as the display zoomed smoothly to a view of the eastern states, then zoomed two more times before it finally came to rest. Mila considered the readout. "I think it might be Pennsylvania, but I can't really tell. Madi, let's look on your computer."

Madison hopped off the bed and went to her desk, drawing her finger across the touchpad of her MacBook to wake it from its slumber. She brought it back to the bed where Mila and Pixie waited. After a few minutes of typing and searching, Mila found an online map of the United States, and zoomed in according to the landmarks she saw on the display of the finder. "I think the finder is pointing here. Look, you guys," Mila said, holding the finder up next to the computer screen.

Pixie tapped the computer screen, plainly fascinated by the device. "Yeah, that looks the same." She held her fingertip over the state of Pennsylvania, near Philadelphia. "It looks like the finder is pointing right here,"

"Well, at least she's kinda close, and not on 'the other side of the world' in California, right," Madi?"

Madison frowned at Mila, then smiled, remembering her geographical blunder when planning the trip to see Jenni the manatee. "It's too bad we *don't* have to go to California to find her. Shopping where all the stars shop would be so amazing!"

Mila laughed at her friend, but then fell quiet as she recognized the amazing coincidence unfolding before her. *Philadelphia*, she thought. As luck would have it, her Uncle Mike lived in that very same area. It would not be difficult at all to convince her parents to take her there, as the journey could take place under the guise of a family visit. It all seemed just too perfect.

I wonder if this means something, she thought, pondering the ties between her world and Graha.

"How does this thing work? How does it know where the queen is? And how are you gonna get to Philadelphia?" Madison shook her head, visibly overwhelmed. "I don't know if I can come up with a plan for this one, Mila, I..."

"It's okay, Madi," Mila interrupted. "We'll figure it out together, but I can't explain everything to you right now because we have to hurry up. Pixie can't stay here for very long."

Pixie nodded and lightly touched the durational clipped to her ear.

"I promise I'll explain everything to you as soon as I can, but right now, we gotta convince my parents to take us to Zehn."

Madison smiled half-heartedly. "Then let's go now, while my dad is busy cooking. I know he'll say yes."

The girls then descended the stairs, listening to the loud banging of pans in the kitchen. Madison stopped in the foyer to peer into the kitchen. "Mom's gonna be mad, he's destroying the kitchen again." She held her hands to her mouth and shouted, "Dad, I'm going over to Mila's real quick, okay?"

Mr. O'Reilly mumbled something in response. Madison shrugged and opened the front door, and the girls walked out onto the porch, pausing at the sight of the pouring rain. Madison started down the stairs, but then turned back to her best friend. "I'm sorry I ran out of your house last night, Mila. I didn't mean to leave you alone."

Mila smiled, nodding, then followed Madison out into the rain.

Despite their desire to get out of the rain, the girls carefully tiptoed onto the porch, taking care not to alert Mila's parents to their presence. Mila flicked her fingers through her dark hair, shaking out the excess water and accidentally spraying Madison in the process. Madison flinched, brushing the water droplets from her eyes. "Now, we gotta get a story together. Your parents are going to ask who Pixie is, and we can't tell them for real." She thought for a moment, and her face lit up as she devised another brilliant plan. "I got it! Tell them Pixie ran away from home, and we met her on the beach."

Mila nodded. "Okay, that might work. But how are we going to talk them into bringing her to Philadelphia with us?"

Madison paused, then lifted a finger. "Tell them that's where she ran away from. Tell them Pixie ran away and ended up here."

"But why did she run away? We need a reason."

"Let's say that her dad is really mean," Madison said. "She snuck out of bed one night and took some money out of his wallet and ran away."

"Yeah, and that now I want to go back to Phila-whatever, to live with my grandfather, who is nice." Pixie added.

Mila's eyes shot open. "That's it! We'll tell them you ran away and took a bus here but now you ran out of money and you have to go back home." Mila pinched her chin between her thumb and finger. "I think it just might work."

Before Madison could speak on the finer details, Mila shushed her; she could hear her parents talking in the living room, just feet away. Mila crept over and flattened herself against the siding beside the window, motioning for Pixie to do the same. She leaned as close as she could to the open window, listening intently.

"You know, honey," her mother said, "I saw on Facebook the other day that the twins' birthday is coming up soon. We should send them a gift."

"Hmm, you're right, we should. Mike is always so extravagant with his gifts, like those plane tickets he got us for Mila's birthday. We really ought to send them something," her father said.

"Good, just have it gift-wrapped when you pick it out and I will drop the package at the post office for you."

"Wait...how did I end up volunteering myself for shopping?"

Laughter erupted in the room, and Mila looked at Pixie, smiling broadly. *The twins' birthday,* she thought. This was how she would do it. Mila signaled to Pixie and Madison, and all three girls walked into the house. A sleek gray cat bounded down the stairs, tail held straight up in excitement. Santo bumped Mila's leg with his head in greeting, but soon left her side for Madison's. He stood up on his hind paws, tapping at Madison's kneecaps, meowing loudly. Madison shook her head. "Why does he always want to be on me!"

Cued by the meowing and chatting in the foyer, Mila's parents soon discovered that three had arrived instead of just one.

"Well, hello Mila, Madi. Who is your new friend?" Olivia asked.

"Mom, this is my friend Pixie, we met at the beach." Mila feigned a concerned expression, her voice taking on a serious tone. "Mom, Dad, we need to talk."

Mila led her puzzled parents and the girls into the kitchen and to the table. Olivia fetched a few kitchen towels for the soggy girls and then sat down next to her husband.

Mila cleared her throat. "You guys, Pixie ran away from home. See, she fights with her dad a lot, and one day she decided to get some money from his wallet and just take a bus as far away as she could go, and that's how she got here."

Olivia's eyes softened. "Oh my goodness, how have you been surviving?"

Pixie just shrugged silently, afraid she would say something wrong.

"She wants to go back now, to live at her grandpa's house, cause she doesn't have any more money. And the weird thing is, her grandpa lives in Philadelphia."

Stephen sat up straight. "You took a bus all the way from Philadelphia? Do you have any friends or family here?"

Pixie shook her head. "Just Mila."

Stephen rubbed his face in dismay, turning over possible solutions in his head.

Olivia stood and went to the refrigerator. "Are you hungry? Have you eaten anything at all today?"

Pixie smiled. "Mila shared her chili dogs with me."

Olivia sighed, slightly disappointed in Mila's skewed sense of proper nutrition. "Well, we have plenty of food, so don't be shy about asking, and you are welcome to stay here until we can get you on a bus back home."

"Well, see..." Mila started, her hesitancy alerting her mother to a possible snag.

"What, Mila?" Olivia inquired, her tone shifting.

"Well, see, I was thinking we could give Pixie a ride back to Philadelphia because I...kind of promised Uncle Mike we would come visit soon," Mila said, her voice trailing off.

Stephen's eyes widened. "What do you mean, *promised?*"

Mila swallowed hard. "When I was on the phone with him the other day, he kept saying we should come to visit, and he was talking so much, I just said okay and promised we would."

Stephen laughed aloud, drawing his finger and thumb over his brow line. "Oh, *brother.*"

"You always tell me I should keep my promises, so since I promised Uncle Mike, and the twins' birthday party is coming, and my new friend Pixie needs to go there too, it just seems..."

"Too perfect," Stephen huffed in resignation. "Well, we are due for a trip to see my dear brother anyway," he said, looking woefully at his wife.

"Yes, we are, and if we can help Pixie get back home, it's even better," Olivia said, smiling at the blonde.

"Thank you," Pixie said softly.

"Mike did offer to send his limo driver to come pick us up for the bash. What do you say we take him up on it? No use putting miles on our car if he wants to show off!"

Olivia swatted at his shoulder. "Now, that's just the way he shows that he cares about you, honey."

Stephen smiled and sat up straight in his chair. "What do you think, girls? You want to ride to Philly in a big stretch limousine?"

The three girls smiled, and Madison bobbed up and down in

her seat. "Yeah!"

"All right, I'll set everything up with Uncle Mike. The twins' party is this Saturday afternoon, so we'll need to leave by ten o'clock. Just make sure to have all your laundry and things ready or the trip by Friday night, okay?"

Olivia's expression shifted. "The party is *this* Saturday? Oh, no, I'm going to be in Baltimore with my sister Erica...her oldest daughter is having her baby shower!"

Stephen moaned. "Oh, that's right...looks like I'm on my own with this one, huh?"

"I'm afraid so, honey. I'm sorry, it's just bad timing," Olivia said.

"I know, but, a promise is a promise, and we should always keep our promises." Stephen sighed, lifting an eyebrow at Mila. "Right, pumpkin?"

Mila smiled sheepishly, nodding. "And I promise I won't make any more promises to Uncle Mike without asking you first."

Stephen and Olivia laughed, and a relieved Mila felt a secret sense of satisfaction as their plan rapidly fell into place.

The Two Aspects

The Dark One hovered in the depths of the Pravus caves, his mind filled with voices. He felt the presence of the Sankari Sano as if the child were right before him, glowing defiantly. It was her thought form that drifted into his consciousness, and her voice that unknowingly spoke to him. In a flash, Corpus received a revelation: the child knew the location of the lost Queen Zehn of Jonquil, and had set out to find her.

Corpus' energy blasted the walls of the cave interior, knocking huge boulders from their resting places. He had sent three minions to the Inner Realm to hunt the child, yet now he realized they searched in the wrong place.

Corpus immediately tuned in to the minions he'd released in Baltimore. He would need all his energy to create three more, and could not spare a wisp of nourishment for these first three. He instantly cut them off from their source, knowing full well they faced a painful disintegration. Though the minions had served Corpus faithfully, to him they were disposable things, unworthy of a second thought. As he drew his creative force out of the first pack and channeled it into creating the second, he intended for the beasts to arrive in Philadelphia, where the queen had been discovered. He needed only to release them near Queen Zehn, commanding them to watch and wait—the child would come to them. The doorway soon opened, and the new wolves came bounding through into a wide field, noses to the air, black eyes swirling.

In a Baltimore alley strewn with litter, the first pack of minions paced and whined. With the connection to their creator now cut off, they began rapidly decomposing. The once well-muscled flanks atrophied and tattered skin hung from their shriveling bodies. Fearful and wracked with pain, they cowered together near a dumpster, watching unconcerned passersby with cloudy eyes.

A group of teenagers soon approached, and one of the young men spotted the withering animals. "Hey, look, sick!"

The teenager quickly finished the last slurp of his soda and tossed the empty bottle at the three wolves, who barely had enough energy to flinch in response.

"Are they dead? Maybe we should call animal control," a girl said.

"Nah, they look dead to me, check it out." The young man approached the wolves, carefully poking at one of them with the toe of his sneaker. "See, I told you they're dead."

"Ew, totally unnecessary, Kyle," the girl chided.

The young man laughed coldly as he rejoined the group and they continued down the street. The wolves shivered as their flesh decomposed, exposing bones that dematerialized with each ragged breath. Enveloped in the shadow of their imminent death, the wolves in some way understood the pain of the man they had murdered in callous disregard.

In the kitchen of the Parke home, Mila sat with Pixie, sharing a snack. An inexplicable feeling of loss suddenly came over her, and she had to set down her sandwich to gather herself. She felt as if a part of her had been lost, like a child disowned by its mother. She frowned and held her hand to her tightening belly. Though Pixie inquired with concern, Mila changed the subject. Some things were

PART 8

PURIFICATION

In the empty dark of outer Seletan, Lium wandered, half of him drawn toward his dark benefactor, the other tugging him in the opposite direction. In his mind's eye, the face of the child persisted. Hazel eyes swept with storms of gray stared unblinkingly, boring into his heart. Over and again he saw her young face, tight with pain, and the heavy cloak of betrayal he'd thrown about her. His belly twisted into a knot, and his ribs stiffened so tightly that he could barely draw breath. Lium paused his trek and shook his head in an attempt to clear his mind, wincing as the painful visions continued. He lifted trembling fingers to his neck, rubbing the skin where a burning sensation had begun to grow. It spread to his shoulders, his arms...everywhere that Mila's hands had once touched him. The healing touch burned with truth.

As the fire grew in his body, he began to think on the days of his youth in Aksini, and the smelting of a coin of two sides.

Chanlor of Jonquil, father of Lium, had been a man who sought wealth at any cost. Games of chance and questionable transactions saw him risk much despite the needs of his family. Every move he made was choreographed in a dance to attain status and wealth, the things that Queen Zehn had outlined in her guiding principles as earmarks of success.

But Chanlor had misinterpreted Zehn's principles, not realizing that wealth gained by ill means was not like abundance that flowed naturally from living a purposeful and authentic life. According to the queen, the manifestation of abundance, appreciation of beauty and art, and the development of the intellect were the spiritual duty and destiny of every citizen of Jonquil. In his impatience and foolishness, Chanlor failed to gain a full understanding of these directives, and so had often entangled himself in less than noble situations.

Tela, partner of Chanlor and mother to Lium and his sister Ayla, suffered greatly from her partner's indiscretions. Tela possessed a fuller understanding of Zehn's instruction to live abundantly. She knew that true wealth was not a means to an end, but an end unto itself, a sign that one had been living authentically and contributing to the Land in meaningful and valuable ways. She loved the light of truth, and taught Lium and Ayla that for a Jonquilian, the highest attribute is authenticity. Though she often fell short of her own lofty standards, she imbued her children with what she felt to be the proper interpretation of Zehn's principles of abundance, which stood in stark contrast to her husband's ideals.

Though young Lium had idolized his father, as he matured, he saw clearly the man's transgressions. Lium wanted nothing more than to rescue his mother from Chanlor's wavering ways. Torn by the desire to live authentically for the sake of his mother and to seek wealth and status above all like his father, Lium became a coin of two sides, flipping through life, hurtling toward an unclear destiny.

Floating in such close proximity to the Palace of Gosai, Aksini had been the premier community of the Seletan territory and home to Lium and his family. Chanlor had somehow managed to wiggle his way into Aksini, then drove himself to exhaustion seeking the means to stay. Not fully understanding manifestation, he was often caught up in transactions with unscrupulous men, straining his relationship with Tela and the children. Even as darkness began to creep into Jonquil and all the Lands of Graha, Chanlor ignored the changing times and the influx of evil, bent on his goal of increasing material wealth.

In late summer of a particularly challenging year, a surly trio of Verdeans came into Aksini. The leader was a portly man with a greasy face who appeared at all times to be uncomfortably warm, and his lieutenants were a narrow man in a tableman's uniform and another with dark eyes and neatly cropped hair. The men had learned that Chanlor had been the cause of a suspicious loss they'd suffered in the Verdean gaming town of Zila not long before. Chanlor had fixed a match between two warriors, an inexperienced and timid-looking fellow against a formidable brute of a man. Though obviously outmatched, the inexperienced warrior had somehow emerged victorious, and many a gamer lost his silvers in the process. Chanlor, however, was among the few that fate had seemingly favored, and when inquiries were made of those involved, the men discovered they had been duped. They came to Aksini in search of Chanlor and retribution.

The three men created a game that would lure the player into believing he could outsmart the system and emerge victorious. In reality, no one could win. As the men stepped into the gamehouse, the gathered Jonquilians stared at the newcomers, their auras darkening with the suspicion. The dark-eyed man tapped the portly one on the shoulder. "Over there, that's him, that's Chanlor," he whispered, pointing to a game table near the back of the hall.

The portly man squinted. "Are you sure?"

The dark-eyed man nodded. "I'm positive, I remember seeing him in Zila."

The portly man grunted. "Good, let's get on with it. I want my silvers back."

A young woman with bobbed black hair greeted them, a practiced smile cloaking her apprehension about Verdean visitation. "Good day. Will you gentlemen be joining one of the games in progress?"

The portly man smiled and shook his head. "No, my dear, we wish to speak with the manager of the house concerning…a business matter."

"Certainly," she said, bowing gracefully. She fetched the gamehouse manager, who walked briskly to where the visitors stood in the entrance hall. He bowed to each in acknowledgement, then straightened his jacket. "Gentlemen, may I ask the reason for your visit?"

"We are here to offer a new game of chance for your patrons, one that will engage the player for extended periods of time." A sly smile crossed his round face. "Simply for entertainment, of course."

The manager cocked his head, his aura swirling, "I'm sorry, but I cannot allow outside—"

"My fine sir," the portly man interrupted, "we understand your position, and we are willing to divide any profits to your favor. We only ask a reasonable fee as compensation for providing this... entertainment."

The manager paused in contemplation. "Come with me."

The men disappeared into the adjacent room with the manager and emerged a short time later. The manager smiled broadly, his aura shimmering in sandy golden tones. He motioned to an empty table nearby and the three newcomers went to it, quickly setting up the game.

The portly man blotted his face with a white cloth, then cleared his throat. "Ladies and gentlemen, we present to you a most challenging new game, a game for the intellectual player where the wise win and the foolish loose their silvers."

Every ear in the room tuned to his words, and all eyes were on him as he spoke. "Only a select few have ever won this game, but we've heard rumor tell there may be one here in Jonquil who is clever enough to do it." The portly man shifted his gaze, looking directly at Chanlor. "Will he be brave enough to play?"

Chanlor lifted a brow, then made his way to the table with several curious followers in tow.

The portly man raised his palms, as if to caution Chanlor. "Now, how confident are you in your intellectual capabilities, fine sir?"

Chanlor frowned, his aura whirling with tones of dark gold. "I assure you, my intellect is more than adequate for a simple game of chance. Tell me how it is played."

The tableman said, "The name of the game is Cup of Stones. In this wooden cup, there are twenty-two stones marked with numbers, eleven positive and eleven negative. The cup is shaken and three stones are tumbled out for the tableman and the player. The object is to get a hand of stones that adds up to eleven. You may choose to receive as many stones as you want with each round, or none at all, but if you go over eleven, you automatically lose the round. If the tableman comes closer to eleven with his hand, you also lose."

Chanlor smirked. "Seems simple enough. Why have so few

won this game?"

The portly man smiled. "Most are not clever enough to calculate probabilities for both positive *and* negative numbers. It is more difficult than you might think."

"Not difficult at all, unless you are no smarter than a stone!" Chanlor shot back, reveling in the snickers his comment elicited from the gathered.

The portly man lifted a brow and inched closer to Chanlor. "The minimum wager is fifteen silvers. Are you confident it is worth the risk?"

Without diverting his gaze from the portly man's eyes, Chanlor reached into his jacket and withdrew his coin sack. He reached inside and then stacked twenty silvers on the gametable, glaring at the tableman. Excited cries rose from the gathered crowd as the famed Chanlor began the new game. The portly man laughed, patting Chanlor on the shoulder and nodding to the tableman to begin.

What Chanlor could not know was that the tableman, highly skilled at the sleight of hand, would be the one to determine who won each round. No matter how accurate Chanlor's calculations, they would yield him nothing in return.

The tableman tumbled the first round of stones, and to Chanlor's delight, his hand beat that of the tableman's. Chanlor laughed, leaning back in his chair. "Simple game!" he called to those who had gathered round to observe.

Several young women then moved to stand next to him, watching intently. Cocksure and impatient for larger returns, Chanlor wagered a thick pile of silvers for the second round. The tableman tumbled the stones once more, and then unblinkingly slid the silvers to his side as Chanlor lost the round. Chanlor's aura flickered weakly for a moment, then surged with golden yellow once more. Surely the loss had been a fluke; he had figured out just how to win the game before he had made his first wager, and was sure of his calculations. Chanlor cleared his throat, then confidently wagered an even bigger pile of silvers, sliding them casually across the table. The round was played, and Chanlor's eyes widened in surprise as he realized he'd lost once more. Outraged, he thrust his hand into his pocket, withdrawing coins of a larger denomination — *risk more, win more* was his mantra.

But round after round, the stones tumbled and Chanlor lost again and again, sweat beading on his brow as the stoic tableman carried out his unseen manipulations.

I have to win, Chanlor thought, *I can't lose forever, it goes against the odds.*

And yet, with each passing round, Chanlor lost more and more of his riches, believing his luck would most certainly turn with the tumbling of the next stone. Fueled by anger and embarrassment, he played and lost and played and lost until his silver sack had been emptied, and even his ring and wrist cuff had been taken.

The portly man and his dark-eyed companion looked on from across the table. Though at first the others around the game table snickered in amusement at Chanlor's misfortune, they now looked upon him with pity and concern; the game had taken him. Some felt disgusted by the overt display of desperate greed and addiction, leaving the gamehouse at the sight of a man who had forgotten the value of temperance. Others attempted to pull Chanlor away from the table but he either ignored them or lashed out viciously like a wounded animal. He continued playing, wagering even his sanlifter and his family home.

As the lesser sun slipped below the horizon, Tela arrived at the gamehouse, having heard word of her partner's reckless actions. She found Chanlor hunched over a game table, arguing with the tableman. He still desired to play another round, yet he had nothing of worth left to wager. Chanlor had lost everything—his money, his possessions, even his home. A man possessed, eyes blinded by greed and heart closed to the light that would free him.

Tela stomped to the table, scornful heat flickering in her eyes. "Chanlor! Is it true what I have heard? Have you wagered and lost everything we have?"

Chanlor snatched his arm free from his partner's grasp. "Let me be, woman! I have work to do. I can turn this around."

Tela leaned forward, her voice rising. "You need to come with me now. You have already done enough damage!"

The tableman grew impatient. "What will it be, sir? Do you have something to wager, or do you admit defeat?"

Chanlor shot up from his chair, his jaw clenched tight with rage. "I will *not* admit defeat!" He glanced at the radentium ring that graced Tela's hand, the one he had given her as part of their vows of partnership. He firmly took hold of her hand, causing her to cry out, and yanked the ring from her finger.

"Chanlor!" she shrieked. "Have you gone mad?"

Chanlor snapped his head round and glared at Tela. "Let me work, and get those children out of here!"

Chanlor slammed the ring down on the table as a wager and stared at the tableman with wild eyes. The tableman shrugged and set up another round. It seemed that Chanlor was not able to stop, and as long as there was a wager to be had, the game would go on.

A bewildered Tela backed away, her knees weakening with each step. Living with Chanlor had never been easy, but it now seemed he cared for little else than his obsession, and could soon bring harm to her children. Tela took Lium and Ayla's trembling hands in her own, comforting them. She turned to the man she had once loved and admired, watching as he waited for the results of his final round.

"Goodbye, Chanlor," she said softly.

Chanlor did not so much as glance up from his game to acknowledge her departure, but stayed focused on his undoing.

Tela left the gamehouse, soothing her weeping children, and returned home. She quickly packed their things in the sanlifter and took her children north to Utara. There, she did her best to care for them, to teach them the values she held dear and the true directive that Queen Zehn had given. Though Tela did what she could, she was looked upon with shame, ostracized from her community. A single parent of two children living in the shadow of Chanlor's disgrace had little chance for honor, especially when forced to take the lowest of positions to put food in her children's mouths.

The three Verdeans had taken back what had been stolen and more, leaving their nemesis to sort through the ruins that remained. Chanlor, now broken, destitute, and utterly alone, left the gamehouse and wandered to the edge of the territory, looking out over the silent desolation below. Standing on a knife's edge, the desert beckoned as his only solace, a barren oasis of peace. Chanlor drew in the hot dry air, holding it in his lungs, then jumped to his death on the sands below.

Though Tela later learned of his fate and mourned his passing, she felt relieved in knowing his torture had finally come to an end.

Some years later, Lium's older sister Ayla left home to partner with a good man from Kanluran. Tela's heart broke at the thought that her beloved daughter had moved so far away, likely in part to escape the shame of association with her mother and father. Lium, however, dutifully stayed with his mother, doing his best to help regain some semblance of a respectable family name, and some measure of wealth. Lium vowed to do better than his father did — above all, he would not bring more shame to his downtrodden family.

As a young man, Lium joined the Guard of Jonquil. He excelled in his work, spurred on by his desire to clear his mother's name so that she could walk the streets of Utara with confidence, and so his sister would visit her once again. Though he did well as a Guardsman, he knew that humble rank would not be enough to redeem his mother and his family name; he would need to rise to extraordinary heights. He would need to become a Prime Warrior, like the famed Esod of Jonquil, a man he had long admired. Lium sought out Esod and placed himself in such a way that their paths would cross time and again. Though at first Lium's requests were met with little regard, eventually Esod came to admire the young warrior's drive and vision, and agreed to train him.

Though Lium had at first been ecstatic to train with the most famous of the Prime Warriors of Jonquil, impatience dogged him like an itch that could not be reached. Tired of the shame that had long cast shadows over his family, Lium looked for ways to expedite his rise to fame. He began to lose sight of his mother's teachings, and spiraled ever deeper into the want of material power. The stench of his greed soon drew the attention of Corpus, who came to Lium with an offer he could not refuse.

By joining with Corpus, who almost guaranteed victory, Lium felt he had aligned himself with a path that led to wealth and respect. Certainly his mother would be relieved, his sister would return, and his family would rise once more from the gutters of shame. Blinded by desire, the irony of it all escaped him, and Lium became what he had most feared — a transcription of his father.

* * *

Lium tripped over a chunk of rock in his path and stumbled forward, just catching himself before falling. Having been broken from the memories of his youth, his mind turned to his travels with the group throughout Verde as they sought to return King Jonas to the throne. Though he had worked in shame and secret for Corpus, there were times during the journey where he felt honor filling his heart. They'd come in fleeting moments of illumination—guiding the group through Jonquil to Salvitor's workshop, fighting side by side in battle with warriors from different Lands, and leaping from the very edge of doom to rescue Mila from the wreck of the sanlifter.

He'd felt strength within him in those times, like the vigor his mother often spoke of, that pulse which kept her moving forward in integrity despite the corruption of her husband. She had taught him of the energy she possessed, nourished by authenticity, which allowed her to live in peace each day despite the many glaring eyes directed at her and her children. Lium could now feel it, an ever-hopeful spark which still sought to light the flame of integrity despite having been extinguished so many times. Though he had willingly sworn allegiance to the Dark One, he'd felt more like a prisoner, forced to act against his own true will. He remembered the flame-red eyes of Rosette upon learning of his betrayal, all for a sack of coins. He remembered Mila, the child who fought for the resistance despite no promise of reward, and finally, he remembered his mentor Esod, whom he had most admired and aspired to emulate. Esod, the Prime Warrior now dead at the hand of Lium's master.

The burning sensations grew into fire, filling his heart with white-hot flames of purification. Lium cried out, grasping his chest as he fell to his knees. Blinded by brilliant light and overcome by inner fire, Lium grew fearful. Had Corpus decided to punish him, having discovered the conflicted state of his heart? Through the heat and light, Lium saw in his mind's eye a scale—his heart against a pile of silvers. As the scales began to tip in one direction, Lium realized what he must do.

Gradually, the heat and blinding light subsided, and Lium gathered himself, standing once more. He felt new strength in his legs, and as he drew breath, he found his ribs unencumbered. Lium balled his fists, his eyes glowing with golden yellow tones. In the end, he would do that which brought him feelings of integrity and usefulness, that which brought lightness to his heart, and above all, that which allowed him to die with some measure of honor and a clean conscience.

The seed of light that Mila had planted with a simple touch had blossomed into an inextinguishable flame: Lium had been illuminated. With clear eyes and focused mind, he turned and marched toward the Palace of Gosai and the call of destiny.

A Queen in Disguise

At precisely 9:55 on Saturday morning, a sleek black limousine pulled into the driveway of the Parke home. Inside the house, three eager faces pressed against the window glass, vying for a glimpse of their long-awaited chariot. Upon sight of it, Mila, Pixie, and Madison burst from the front door, hopping excitedly down the stairs.

"Wow!" Madison beamed as she approached the vehicle, completely starstruck.

Mila ran her hand along the smooth curve of the fender, watching her own reflection shift in the freshly waxed paint. Stephen was not far behind her, a childlike look of wonder spreading across his own face as the driver's side window slid down. A man in a dark blue cap waved his hand. Stephen smiled broadly when he saw the driver, a family friend of many years. "Hey, Joe!"

Joe put his hand out the window, revealing the cuff of his starched white shirt. "Hello, my friend! It's been a long time. How've you been?"

Stephen shook Joe's outstretched hand. "Doing just fine, glad to be getting up to see my brother."

"How's Olivia? She coming along?"

Stephen shook his head. "She's great, but she's on her way to Baltimore for her niece's baby shower."

"Oh, I see, it's just you and me and three lovely ladies." Joe waved to the girls, who had cupped their hands around their eyes, peering through the tinted glass for a look at the mysterious interior. "I swear, your daughter has grown a foot since the last time I saw her!"

Stephen laughed. "Yeah, and she'll eat you out of house and home, too." They chuckled together, and Stephen headed toward the front door. "I'll get the house locked up and then we can roll."

Joe nodded, then got out of the limousine and walked to the girls. "Ladies, my name is Joe and I'll be your driver today. Would you like to get in and look around?"

The girls nodded excitedly, and Madison bounced on her toes. "Yeah!"

Joe chuckled and swung open the rear suicide door to *oohs* and *ahhs* from the girls. Madison was the first to claim her star-for-a-day status, hopping into the limousine and nearly dropping her purse at what she saw. Polished hardwoods, ruched white leather seats, and a dazzling light display hit Madison like a Hollywood brick.

"Look, Mila, the lights are changing colors!" Madison exclaimed.

Mila smiled as she poked her head inside and allowed her eyes to adjust to the dark ambiance. The red, green, blue, and yellow LED lights reminded her of the Lands of Graha and their unique and colorful glows. She stepped inside, urging Pixie to follow. "C'mon Pixie, this thing is cool."

Once all three girls were inside, Joe began a brief tour and tutorial. "Now, if you want to turn the lights off, just flip this right here," he explained, pointing out a switch on the wall. He pressed down on a section of the counter and a panel clicked open, revealing a cooler stocked with soda beneath. "And if you get thirsty, just help yourselves."

"Wow, I feel like a movie star!" Madison exclaimed. Stephen stepped into the cabin of the limousine. He shook his head and smiled as he checked out the surroundings. "A little over the top, Mike!" The vehicle featured two flatscreen televisions, a computer, a stocked candy bowl, and a full bar. Stephen opened a small cooler near the end of the bar and found a bottle of Dom Perignon inside, perfectly chilled and waiting to be enjoyed. Stephen shook his head rapidly and slammed the cooler door shut. *I'm not going there,* he thought, remembering how, once opened, the contents of champagne bottles tended to rapidly and inexplicably disappear.

The passengers soon took their seats, and the limousine eased out of the driveway and onto the road. Madison plugged her iPod into the stereo system and chose a playlist for the trip while Mila played with the lights. "Dad, how long is the drive gonna take?" Mila asked.

"About two and a half hours, depending on if we hit traffic on 113." Stephen looked past his daughter at the blonde girl who had joined them for the journey. Though he did not want to pry into what seemed a troubled life, his curiosity soon got the better of him. "So, Pixie, what's your grandfather's name and number? We'll need to get hold of him and let him know you're coming home. I'm sure he's worried sick."

Pixie's heart skipped a beat. "Um, his name is...Salvitor," she said after a pause.

Mila's eyes widened as she continued for Pixie: "Yeah, but he doesn't have a phone, because...he doesn't have a lot of money." Mila's heart pounded; she hadn't thought past how to get Pixie to Philadelphia with her, and they had no story for what they should do with her once they were there. Mila thought fast. "Dad, is it okay if Pixie comes to the party with us? She's probably never seen anything like Uncle Mike's mansion! Please, can she come, too?"

Stephen shrugged. "I don't see why not. We can drop you at your grandfather's after the party."

Mila smiled, greatly relieved. "Thanks, Dad."

"No problem." He looked again at the quiet blonde girl. "I'm just glad you're on your way back to your family, Pixie."

"Yeah, thanks a lot for giving me a ride," she replied. "I do miss him."

Pixie then turned her fair face to the back of the limousine, hiding the sadness that lay just below the surface.

A short time into the ride, Stephen decided to watch a movie and dug through the DVD collection, putting in the earbuds as he searched. He offered a few extra packages of earbuds to the girls, but they waved him off. Mila nudged Madison with her elbow, indicating that their time for private conversation had finally arrived. Sure enough, minutes later Stephen became transfixed as the opening sequence to *Top Gun* played on the flatscreen, the earbuds drowning out any sounds from the cabin.

Mila slid closer to Madison and motioned to Pixie to do the same. The girls turned their bodies so their backs faced Stephen. Mila reached into her pocket and withdrew the finder, sliding her thumb over the glass display. "We have to keep checking this, so we know if we are heading in the right direction." She looked toward the front of the cabin, making sure her father was not watching or listening. "Especially once we start getting close to Philadelphia."

Madison leaned over and inspected the finder, watching the dots blinking on the display. "What do these dots mean, Mila?"

"They tell you how far away from Queen Zehn you are." Mila tapped the display and pointed to the blinking dots. "See, this dot right here is Zehn, and this one is us. See how it's moving?"

Madison nodded, moving closer to get a better look.

"Well, after a while, the dots will look like they become one, and then you know that Zehn is really close."

"But what if Zehn is far away from the party? And how will we get your dad to take us to her?"

Mila sighed. "I'm not sure, but don't worry. Things always seem to work out somehow."

As time ticked away and the limousine neared the outskirts of Philadelphia, Mila periodically checked the finder and each time was heartened that they seemed to be drawing closer to Queen Zehn. She began to think once more on the many amazing coincidences that seemed to drive her forward in her quest to help the people of Graha. What force choreographed the movements of people and events and allowed her to end up right where she needed to be at just the right time? Out of the corner of her eye, Mila saw her father shift in his seat and pull out his earbuds. She slipped the finder back into her pocket and tapped the other girls to warn them.

"One of my favorite movies!" Stephen said as he shut off the DVD player.

Madison looked quizzically at Mila, who shrugged in response. As the limousine marked off the final miles before their exit, Mila wondered where the finder would take her, and how she would accomplish the complicated task of retrieving and returning a queen who had forgotten herself...all in total secrecy.

She smiled as she looked around the cabin and realized that for the first time since her adventures began, she was not alone in her task. Her best friend and a new companion now travelled with her, and she relaxed into the feeling of support their presence provided.

* * *

Michael Parke had truly outdone himself. Though well known for sparing no expense, especially when it came to the twins, this particular party was unendingly lavish, seemingly fit for royalty. Hordes of children in their best finery dashed about a gallery of ice sculptures and grazed amid tables loaded with elaborate confections of all kinds. As Mila followed her father through the garden, a group of young boys bounded past, their hair askew, curls toppling from sweaty heads, wild eyes dancing at the opportunity to play unsupervised.

Mila smiled and thought of young Root, and how he would have loved to play in a place such as this.

The group rounded a corner and came into the central commons of the garden where they found Michael and his twin daughters, Annabelle and Gabrielle, posing for a photograph. The twins wore matching dresses with airy chiffon skirts in a range of pastels, their long blonde hair adorned with fresh orchids. While Michael smiled broadly as the photo was snapped, the twins wore stoic expressions, looking bored to tears by the whole affair. Michael saw his brother and the girls approaching, and his smile grew even larger. "Steve!"

Stephen jogged to his brother and the two embraced briefly. He then introduced Pixie and Madison, and Mila hugged her uncle as well.

Stephen tugged at his khakis. "We feel a little underdressed!"

Michael waved his brother off. "Sometimes things get a little too fancy around here. So, how have you been? How's work?"

Stephen nodded slowly. "Good, good. I tell you, I can't believe how big the twins are getting." He turned to address the girls directly, and they stared blankly back at him. "You are becoming lovely young ladies."

Michael sighed. "They look more and more like Nora everyday."

Annabelle huffed in exasperation, crossing her arms over her chest. "Daddy, you said you were going to get a pony for the party. Where is it?"

"Yeah, why can't we have a pony?" Gabrielle added.

Michael rolled his eyes. "And they act more and more like Nora everyday, too," he whispered to his brother.

Stephen fought the urge to laugh and simply patted his sibling on the back. Two young girls, friends from the boarding school the twins attended, approached. The taller girl flipped her dark brown curls behind her shoulder and fanned her face. "It's so hot out here, let's go inside and get ice cream."

Gabrielle and Annabelle looked at each other, at Mila and the girls, then promptly walked off with their friends without saying a word.

"Where is Nora?" Stephen asked.

"Inside...*managing*," Michael shook his head and rubbed his brow. Stephen took note. "Mila, why don't you and Madi and Pixie hang out and mingle for a while. I want to talk with Uncle Mike for a bit."

Mila smiled. Dad was making this far too easy. "I guess we can do that. C'mon guys."

The three girls moved deeper into the garden, past artful arrangements of elegant cakes and pastries to the end of a hedgerow, where a punch fountain ran over with exotic fruit juices. Mila took a cup from a hook and dipped the ladle in the ruby pool at the bottom, carefully pouring a drink. Pixie and Madison did the same, and the girls stood sipping their punch, trying to look natural.

Mila looked around, then pulled the finder from her pocket. She tapped the screen of the finder and her eyes nearly popped out of her head. The two dots had grown even closer since she'd last checked in the limo; it appeared that Zehn must be at the very same party. Goosebumps erupted on Mila's arms. The machinery of time and space had again aligned everything in perfect order for her mission. Madison moved in for a closer look at the finder. "So how are we going to find Zehn?"

Mila tapped the screen once more. "We watch the finder until the two dots look like one, and then we just have to look around for who's nearby." She glanced around at the many groups of children and adults clustered throughout the garden. "Hopefully she's not in the middle of a big group. I don't know how we'd be able to tell which one she is!"

"Is she gonna be a girl or a boy? Adult or kid?" Madison asked.

Mila sighed, "I don't know. Jonas was a man, but I don't know if it always works the same."

"Okay, let's just start looking around," Pixie suggested.

The girls agreed and set off to find the veiled queen.

* * *

In a quiet corner of the garden, Zoe Chen plucked the blossom heads from a rosebush, tucking them into her handbag. A privileged child of high society, her parents had sought to buy her affection with things, rather than to earn it with discipline and love. They traveled extensively, and as they viewed bringing a child along as an inconvenience, they left Zoe with her nanny whenever they took another of their extended vacations. Her parents mistakenly and lazily assumed that all a child needed for a happy childhood was to have anything her heart desired. What she needed most, though, was her parents' presence. Though her family was rich beyond measure, Zoe lived in abject poverty.

When Zoe was five years old, her parents were lost at sea during a private cruise, their yacht never found. In the years to follow, her caretaker often became so preoccupied with spending her inheritance that she failed to properly attend to Zoe. The child had become a monster.

And so she stood, carelessly picking the fragrant blooms, a deep sense of alienation eating away at her young heart. Though many children laughed and played around her, somehow she could not join their dance.

Not far away from Zoe, Pixie followed Mila and Madison through the maze of hedges in the formal area of the garden. The dense foliage had been shaped into walls and niches, providing a dark backdrop for the many pale sculptures that graced the garden. Immediately, she thought of the Mazurin Gon. Though she'd never seen it in person, images of the place had been etched in her mind by tales and art, and she'd often dreamt of seeing it for herself. Pixie ran her fingertips along the manicured edge of a nearby brush wall. "This reminds me of the Mazurin Gon of Jonquil."

Madison cocked her head so suddenly she looked like confused puppy. "The *who* in the *what?*"

Pixie smiled. "It's a maze in Jonquil. I bet it looks a lot like this, except there aren't any deadly obstacles here." She looked around the area, suddenly a little concerned. "I hope!"

The girls continued winding through the topiaries and hedges, searching for their quarry. They passed a number of children and adults, and though all of the guests in attendance were wealthy and well dressed, one child stood out from the rest. Her silk dress draped gracefully in opulent shades of gold and sky blue. Though she looked to be only seven or eight years of age, an almost regal air of maturity followed her. Pixie found herself staring, entranced by something in the girl's eyes and the inky black hair that fell just below her chin.

Pixie tapped Mila, pointing. "I think we need to go talk to that girl over there."

"The one picking the flowers?"

"Yeah, something seems different about her. She just sticks out."

"Well, Thornhill always says you should pay attention when you notice stuff like that." Mila waved to the girl, but received no response. She pulled the finder from her pocket and noticed that the two dots were tantalizingly close. Her eyes widened. "Yeah, we better go talk to her."

The three then made their way to the girl. When they finally came face to face, Pixie cleared her throat, unsure of how to break the ice.

"I saw you staring at me," the girl said pointedly.

Pixie fidgeted. "Um, yeah, sorry…I just think your dress is really pretty."

The girl cocked her head, and her black hair shifted slightly. "It's Thai silk."

Pixie nodded. "Oh, I see. Yeah, I like the—"

"And," the girl interrupted, "I have another one that's red and black, and it's silk, too."

"I bet it's nice," Pixie said.

Before she could steer the conversation away from apparel, the little girl crossed her arms over her chest and lifted her chin. "My nanny Em says I can have any dress I want. I can have anything that I want because my parents were so rich."

Pixie, having given up on genuine conversation, raised a brow in feigned interest. "Really?"

The girl unfolded her arms and placed her hands on her hips. "And I'm the fastest runner in the whole boarding school. I'm faster than *everyone*, even the boys."

Pixie stood tall, emphasizing her height advantage. "You're not faster than me."

The girl stood on her tiptoes and frowned at Pixie. "Oh, yes I am!"

Pixie crossed her arms over her chest. "Prove it."

Without warning, the girl took off like a shot, black hair flowing behind her. Pixie looked at Mila, then followed in pursuit. The girl, without breaking stride, called back to her pursuers, "First one out of the maze wins!"

The girl sprinted on, cornering like a cheetah. Pixie, surprised by her speed, stretched her long legs and picked up her pace. Mila and Madison followed behind, keeping the racing girls within sight. As they rounded an arc-shaped path of the brush maze, a man holding a silver tray appeared before them. He shouted in surprise, nearly dropping the delicate pastries he carried as the girls ran around him. Pixie looked back at Mila and winked, then seemed to shift into a higher gear. She passed the girl and crossed out of the maze and into the open yard. Pixie took a victory lap, slowing herself and smiling as she came back to the group at the maze exit. The exasperated girl stood, chest heaving, eyes focused on Pixie with laser-hot intensity. "It was that man's fault!" the girl whined.

Pixie shook her head, panting. "Nope, I'm just faster, that's all. So what's your name?"

"Zoe."

"Okay, Zoe, I'm Pixie, and this is Mila and Madison."

Mila waved, stepping closer to the girl. "Hi, Zoe."

The girl glanced at her briefly, then returned to glaring at Pixie. Mila took the opportunity to peek once more at the finder; the dots had become one, and the display blinked brightly. Mila's heart skipped a beat. *How can this little brat be Queen Zehn?* Putting her opinions aside, Mila looked out over the yard to the woods at the back of the property, remembering a long walk on the winding paths among the trees two years before, when her family had last visited. The dense vegetation acted as a privacy screen, and the quiet shade would make the perfect place to talk to Zoe and try to get her to remember herself.

Mila cleared her throat. "Hey, guys, why don't we take a walk in the woods? Last time I was here I found a bunch of raspberries back there."

Zoe narrowed her eyes. "I'm not hungry."

Before Mila could offer a rebuttal, Pixie cut in. "Well, I won the race, so I get to pick what we do next. And I say we go into the woods."

The girl huffed, frowning as she crossed her arms over her chest once more.

Mila tilted her head and smiled. "C'mon, Zoe, it'll be fun."

Though the defeated Zoe rolled her eyes in protest, she did follow, and the girls made their way to the heavily wooded area at the rear of the property. The estate sat on almost twenty-five acres of native Pennsylvania forest, only a few acres of which had been cleared for the building of the home and the outbuildings. The place held a mysterious darkness, and Mila had felt as if she were in another world the last time she explored it. The girls kept a crisp pace as they approached and entered the woods, then slowed to enjoy the cool shade provided by the canopy above. Mila began deliberately scanning the brush along the side of the path, pretending to look for raspberries. "I think they were farther in than this. Let's keep walking."

As the four continued deeper into the forest, three black wolves skulked out of the shadows, bodies hunched, black eyes swirling. They sniffed the air around the head of the trail where the girls had entered the woods, searching for their scent. The largest of the three paused, growling, then padded into the forest with the other two close behind. The minions of Corpus had found the Sankari Sano once more, and the girls were in grave danger.

Mila walked next to Zoe, who seemed horribly disinterested with their forest quest. Mila's mind raced, searching for ways she could possibly trigger the girl to remember something about Jonquil. When she'd met Jonas, she had a ring that had belonged to him to help the process along, but she had no such ring for Zoe to wear. Jonas, though, had seemed to awaken at her touch. Maybe the same thing would work with Zoe. Mila moved closer to the girl, inspecting the embroidered patterns on her dress. "That really is a nice dress. Are those dragons?" she asked, carefully placing both hands on Zoe's back.

"Don't touch!" the girl snapped. "It's silk, remember?"

Mila sagged slightly in defeat. "Oh, sorry." It took Mila a second to remember the crystal blue gem in the drawer of the finder, the very object that had led her to Zehn. Perhaps if Zoe held it in her hand, It would help lift the veil, and she would remember herself once more.

Mila fumbled the finder out of her pocket. "Hey Zoe, I have this really pretty jewel that matches your dress perfectly." She popped open the drawer as the young girl turned to peer inside.

"See? It's the same blue," she said, carefully placing the gem in Zoe's palm. The girl seemed at first stunned, then delighted, and for the very first time that day, Zoe smiled, her tense lips finally lifting to reveal teeth like dainty pearls.

The girl's expression shifted, and a hint of gold flashed behind her dark brown eyes. "Where did you get this?"

Before Mila could answer, she spotted movement from the corner of her eye. From around a curve in the woodland trail, the black wolves swiftly approached, tarry foam dripping from bared teeth as black as pitch, ears flattened against lowered heads. Though at first glance they took on the appearance of earthly wolves, the girls detected an eerie translucence to their flesh, and their black eyes swirled with sinister storms.

The largest wolf stepped forward and barked viciously at Mila. She recoiled. "Run!"

The girls sprinted off. Rather than give chase right away, the wolves argued amongst themselves, growling and snapping viciously, as if reprimanding one another for failing to pounce quickly enough. The largest wolf soon ended the quarrel, and headed off in pursuit of the girls with the other two in tow.

The girls stumbled down a steep, winding trail crisscrossed with gnarled roots, and soon found themselves coming out of the woods and into a clearing. A meadow of wildflowers and tall grasses lay before them; grateful for easier terrain, the girls dashed into the clearing, brushing their way past lashing sedges and patrolling bumblebees. A scarlet tanager rose just ahead of them, its red and black plumage starkly contrasting against the green backdrop of the tall grasses. It flapped wildly as it returned to the forest canopy, as if waving a red flag of alarm before the fleeing girls.

Mila glanced upward to watch it and realized the sky was swiftly darkening. A vortex of clouds had gathered over the meadow, and lightning licked across the sky. Mila turned to Madison, who displayed an ever-growing aura of red. "Something's happening," Mila warned. "I can feel it."

At once, the three wolves came crashing toward the girls, circling and growling. The girls huddled together and surrounded Zoe, who squealed and shook with fear, her sheltered life having left her unprepared for such danger. Zoe looked out from behind Mila and Madison at the largest wolf, meeting its stormy black eyes for one frightening instant. "There's something wrong with those dogs!" she whimpered, clinging to the back of Mila's shirt.

Mila took a deep breath, resisting the urge to panic. She sensed the animals were not of this realm, and perhaps she could do something to help, as she had done in Salvitor's chamber when the shadow minions attacked. Mila tried to establish eye contact with the largest wolf, but it seemed focused on Madison, who stood frozen and silent beside her. The wolf glanced at its two companions, then became deathly still, a dark shadow shifting around its body. In the next instant, the crouching beast launched itself into the air and pounced on Madison, knocking her to the ground.

Though her screams rang out over the meadow and echoed through the forest, the sound was muffled by the trees and the commotion of the party.

Mila's body flushed with panic and she could feel herself glowing brightly. The wolf stood astride Madison, dark froth dripping from its black fangs onto her skirt. Before Mila could move a muscle, Madison's glow pulsed bright red, and she punched the wolf in the chest. "No!"

The instant Madison's hand met the wolf's flesh, the creature froze, its black eyes growing still. Despite the close proximity of the other two wolves, all four girls stared in disbelief at Madison — the wolf that attacked her had turned to stone.

Zoe looked up at Mila pleadingly, but had not the strength to ask for help. At last she fainted, dropping to the grass like a felled sapling. Mila quickly knelt to protect her, not forgetting two other wolves were right there waiting to attack. Madison appeared to be more afraid of what she had just done than she had been of the live wolf. She wriggled frantically beneath the stone artifact until she got herself free. "Mila! Did you see that?"

Mila did not respond. The second wolf came closer, a throaty growl rumbling from its open jaws. The wolf tentatively padded to the stone version of its pack leader and sniffed the strange statue. At once, it seemed the animal realized what had happened, and began growling and barking ferociously, its dark eyes pinned on the girls.

"Easy now," Mila spoke soothingly to the beast. "Just relax."

Mila held up her hands and her glow began pulsing intensely. White light flooded from her aura and washed over the angry wolf in gentle waves, as if to rock it to sleep. The snarling jaws began to relax and close, and the growls were reduced to mere grumbles. The wolf began swaying back and forth, as if carried on the currents of Mila's glow. The creature soon closed its eyes.

"That's right, just go to sleep, boy," Mila said, turning to Madison, who stood beside her in disbelief. "Madi, turn it to stone!" she whispered.

Madison hesitated for a split second, but quickly gathered herself and stepped toward the sleeping animal. She reached out her hand and noticed how tiny it appeared next to the enormous beast, like a doll's hand on a carnival stuffed animal. Finally, Madison pushed herself forward, laying her palm flat on the head of the slumbering wolf. A flash of crimson burst from her skin and into the wolf, and before it could wake from its trance, its flesh was turned to stone, forever locked in placid sleep.

Madison backed away from the animal, still only half-believing what she was seeing, then turned to Mila, who stood in a brilliant orb of white light. "Mila—"

Madison was interrupted by the cries of Pixie. They turned and saw Pixie teleport from one part of the meadow to another, staying just out of the reach of the frustrated beast. Each time it would come close enough to attack, Pixie would disappear in a flash of bright yellow, leaving the wolf with a mouthful of nothing. "Hey, a little help over here?" she called.

Mila and Madison dashed to where Pixie materialized, hoping they would not be attacked in the process of helping their friend. Of equal importance was keeping the wolf away from Zoe, who still lay unconscious in the grass.

Mila thought quickly. "Pixie, just stand still for a minute and let the wolf come close to you. We will hide over here in the long grass. When it gets close enough, Madi can turn it to stone."

Madison's eyes widened. "What if it sees us first?"

Thunder blasted overhead. The sky had continued darkening, and a tempest roiled above the meadow, ripe with rotating clouds and lightning. Mila took Madison's hand and crouched down into the cover of the tall grasses. The wolf approached.

Frothing with anger and having tired of the game of chase, the animal marched toward Pixie, who stood still and faced her foe rather than teleporting away.

The wolf became visibly excited; perhaps it had exhausted its prey and could now clamp its jaws around her, draining her essence and sending that energy back to its master. Pixie faced the beast, backing away a few paces to give her hidden friends more time to react. The wolf crept closer and closer to where Mila and Madison lay hidden. Soon, its black eye was within a foot of their faces.

The wolf began growling and snapping its jaws, its attention fixed on Pixie. Her aura flashed in alarm. "Uh...guys?"

Madison reached a slender arm through the grasses and poked the beast with the tip of her finger. Though the animal reacted, turning to snap at whatever had touched it, it was instantly immobilized, a look of surprise forever etched on its face.

Madison flopped down in relief next to Mila in the grass. Pixie jogged to them. "Thanks, Madi, I was starting to get tired." She casually thumbed a strand of hair, tugging it upward into place. "Can't keep doing that forever, you know."

The meadow fell silent and the scarlet tanager dipped through the air once more.

Mila finally spoke. "See, Madi? At first you didn't like that you could turn things to stone, but now you just saved our lives by doing it."

Madison nodded, eyes wide and chest heaving. With the intense use of her gifts, Madison was flooded with memories of her life in Graha, and bits of the recurring dream she had been visited with began arranging themselves into coherence. As the pieces fell into place, Madison began to understand that somehow she was supposed to protect Mila from danger.

"Oh my gosh, Zoe!" Mila gasped. They had forgotten all about her.

Zoe lay facing the sky, eyes half open. The sky above the meadow cleared rapidly, and Zoe looked upon the drifting swirls of white clouds on a canvas of pale blue. Memories of a Land of clouds and sky—lofty and surreal, with dry cool winds sweeping through open spaces—swept through her mind. A feeling of freedom and light washed over her, and a burden that had pressed upon her heart for what seemed longer than she'd been alive lifted. The fine silk of her dress began to feel like that of a royal garment, and the coolness of the jewel she still gripped in her palm seemed to penetrate her being, running through her veins like blue ice.

The girls soon arrived at Zoe's side, and Mila knelt down to check on her. "Zoe, are you okay?" She brushed a blade of grass away from the girl's face. "Don't be scared, the wolves can't hurt you now."

The girl blinked her slanted eyes and Mila took a deep, slow breath, sensing that the time for full transformation had arrived. "Here, let me help you up." She reached for Zoe's hands with one of her palms turned up, the other down.

Zoe at first seemed confused, then instinctively moved her palms to meet Mila's. Just as they made contact, a flash of white light dashed from Mila's aura and entered Zoe's body. The girl gasped in shock, then relaxed once more as the energy worked its way through her form. In her mind's eye, Zoe began to see visions—the same memories that Thornhill had shared with Mila at the beginning of her journey, the same memories she had shared with Jonas at the zoo. Zoe witnessed Mila's travels through Graha with the group, and how King Jonas had been restored to the throne in Samera. Zoe watched the destruction of the Land of Jonquil, once an endless panorama of order and beauty—now razed to ruins. The creeping evil had invaded every haven and quiet place in Jonquil, and Zoe sensed that somehow, as it penetrated the Land, it infected her own body as well. In her heart she began to understand that Jonquil was *her* Land, and with her departure, it had fallen into darkness.

Zoe opened her eyes, now moist with tears, and looked tenderly upon Mila, who knelt before her awash in white light. She sat up slowly, squinting at the light of the sun that poured down on the meadow through the parting clouds. She looked at Mila and smiled knowingly, her eyes sparkling with golden light. "Mila," she said softly, "I know who you are."

Mila noticed that the timbre of Zoe's voice had changed; she sounded more mature, and her words had taken on a more formal air.

Mila smiled broadly. "Do you know who you are?"

A golden orb began to expand around Zoe. Bright tendrils twisted above her and then down into the earth. Her face shone, placid and full with the understanding of something that had made her feel different all her life, and in fact, for many lives. Zoe drew a deep breath, standing tall as she began to realize she was not just a little princess like her nanny had always told her. She was a queen—Queen Zehn, the rightful ruler of the Land of Jonquil.

Incredibly, the transformation from Zoe to Zehn had taken mere minutes. As Mila's powers had grown over time, Zehn did not need an overnight visit with the jewel as Jonas had with the ring. A simple touch of Mila's hand had done the trick.

Finally, the girl spoke: "I am Zehn, queen of the Land of Jonquil."

Zoe found the blue gem she'd dropped next to her in the grass, gazing into its depths before tucking it into a pocket in her dress. She got to her feet and stood what seemed at least a foot taller than she had before, her eyes sparkling with golden light.

Mila smiled and felt excitement bubbling in her aura. She nudged Pixie with an elbow, ensuring she was fully aware of the miraculous transformation occurring before them. Pixie, at first awestruck, soon shifted into a place of respect and reverence; this was her queen. Pixie knelt before Zoe, acknowledging her. "Welcome back, Queen Zehn."

A frantic beeping sound brought Pixie back to her feet. Her eyes flashed as she realized the source — the durational had reached critical levels. Pixie had ignored a number of warning tones from the device during the wolf incident, and now she was almost out of time.

"Oh, no, we gotta go back right now," Pixie said, plucking the device from her ear and checking the time dials. "I'm almost out of time!"

"Um..." Mila took stock of the situation and decided to go with her gut. "I think I'm gonna stay here with Madi for a while. I'll open the doorway. You take Zehn and go back now."

Pixie looked concerned. "I don't think we should split up."

Mila didn't answer.

Pixie sighed. "If you have to stay, just make sure that when you go through the doorway that you picture yourself arriving close to us."

"Like we talked about on the beach when we had chili dogs?" Mila asked.

Pixie nodded. "Yeah, that way we can all be together again." The durational kept beeping. "All right. We've got to go."

Mila quickly took three deep breaths, and before she could think of how to do it, she had opened a doorway in midair, with no door or floor behind it at all. Zoe looked at her with golden eyes, pleasantly surprised.

"All right, let's go," Pixie said, hand outstretched. "Take my hand, Queen Zehn." The girl reached out, and Pixie clasped her hand with a smile. "I'm honored to bring you back to your kingdom."

The girl nodded graciously, and the two then stepped through the doorway in a brilliant flash of light.

In the tall grass of the meadow beyond the forest, three stone statues crumbled to dust, their spent essence trailing away on the wind and falling to the earth like ashes. Having sensed their failure, Corpus had once more removed his energy from his minions, leaving their remains to decay in a foreign realm.

Out of The Forest

In the middle of the balloon artist's grand performance, a woman came screaming from around the side of the garden, a group of men in tow. "There, over there! That's where I saw the wolves, they were going into the woods after the girls!"

Overhead, thunder clapped forcefully, and rain began to pour from the darkening sky. The storm was back, and one by one, the attendees began to panic, scattering in all directions, herding children into the house and away from the rain and the possible wolves. Ice sculptures melted in the deluge, their shapes shifting and smoothing, water pooling on the stone walkways underneath. Stephen and his brother overheard the screaming woman and jogged to her.

"Ma'am? Did you say you saw *wolves* following some girls?" Stephen asked.

The woman nodded fearfully. "Yes, the three girls that came with you. Zoe Chen was with them. I saw all four of them walk into the woods and then three wolves went in after them."

Michael and Stephen forgot the storm and dashed toward the woods, fearing what they might find. If wolves were in fact running loose in the forest, Mila and the other girls could be in danger.

The brothers ran toward the entry path, but before they could reach the treeline, Mila and Madison came jogging out, unharmed. Michael slowed, nearly collapsing with relief, while Stephen ran to his daughter, panting. "Mila!" He grasped her shoulders and led her and the others under the canopy of a nearby tent. "Are Pixie and Zoe still in the woods? When did you see them last?"

A startled Mila shook her head, thinking fast. "Pixie never went into the woods with us. We went inside the house and she called her friend to come get her and take her to her grandpa's house."

Stephen cocked his head, but before he could question Mila, she continued, "See, Pixie felt really embarrassed to be around so many rich people. She just wanted to leave."

Stephen lowered his head. "Oh, I see…but where is Zoe?"

Mila shrugged, unable to think of a proper story, "We don't know where Zoe went, but she's probably just pouting somewhere or hiding from the rain. We tried to play a game with her, but she didn't want to play."

"Zoe…*Zoe Chen* is missing?" Michael held his hands to his head, looking to be on the edge of implosion. "Oh no, no, no. Please tell me this is not happening."

"Don't panic, Mike," Stephen insisted, "she's probably just hiding somewhere. Now Mila, did you see the wolves in the woods?"

"Wolves?" Mila paused, trying to look as surprised as she could. "We never saw any wolves."

"A lady here at the party said she saw three black wolves go into the forest not long after you girls. You didn't get chased by wolves, or dogs?"

Mila shook her head. "They must have been chasing rabbits or something."

Stephen took a deep breath. "All right, maybe they were just a couple of stray dogs."

Michael huffed dramatically. "I don't care. If there's any chance there are wolves on the loose and Zoe friggin' Chen is out there, I want every cop, animal control officer, and crocodile hunter I can get out here right now!" Michael marched off toward the house, water dripping steadily from his chin. "I gotta make some phone calls!"

Stephen sighed. "Looks like I need to make a phone call, too." He pulled his mobile from his pocket. "Mila, Madi, I'm going to have to stay here with Uncle Mike and help him sort out this mess. I'm gonna send you back home with Joe."

Mila blinked. "Why can't we just stay here with you?"

"No," Stephen insisted. "If there *are* wolves running around here, it's not safe for you to stay. Besides..." He glanced in a nearby window, observing his brother gesticulating wildly as he talked on his phone inside. "Uncle Mike is flipping out right now. He's in no condition to entertain company."

Stephen wiped his fingers dry and tapped the screen of his phone, dialing his wife. "I'll just get a rental car and come back home as soon as Mike and I find Zoe and get this all straightened out, okay pumpkin?"

Mila sighed. "Okay, Dad."

Stephen led the girls inside to the safety of the house while all the arrangements were made. Olivia, though concerned, agreed with his decision to stay behind and support his brother. The disappearance of a high-profile child like Zoe Chen could cause quite a stir, and Stephen needed to be there to calm the storm.

Mila and Madison sat dazed in the back of the limo. Though the storm raged on outside the privacy of the cabin, the only detectable sign of the bad weather was the sound of raindrops on the roof. Madison, still reeling over the incident with the wolves, shook her head. "What happened in that field, Mila?"

"I think those wolves were minions, made by this evil thing from the other realm. Somehow they must have found out where I was, or where Zehn was, and they came to kill us."

"The wolves were from the other world?"

Mila nodded. "Their eyes were weird and they just looked... wrong. I'm pretty sure they were not normal wolves."

"All I know is they were so big, and I was so scared, but something made me feel like I had to protect you. That's what made the wolves turn to stone, when I touched them with that feeling."

"You really did save our lives, Madi." Mila took a breath and felt the tension in her belly finally release. "Thanks."

Madison leaned her head back against the soft ruched leather of the seat, closing her eyes for just a moment before opening them again in alarm. "Mila," she turned her head slowly to face her friend, eyes wide. "Every time I close my eyes, I see pictures from another life. That dream I kept having seems so real. In the dream place, my name is Maddox, and it feels more like my real name than Madison." Her brow tightened. "What does that mean?"

"I don't know," Mila said, "but at least we're together."

Madison smiled, then turned her face away from her friend once more. Exhausted from using her newfound gifts so intensively, she leaned her head back once more and soon fell into a deep sleep.

Mila stared at the blank television screen mounted on the wall, listening to drumming of raindrops on the metal roof of the limo. During her fight with the wolves, a new gift she had not yet discovered within herself had emerged at just the right moment. Not so long ago, she'd discovered a strange glow that could open a doorway to another realm. Though she'd first crossed in search of finding her birth parents, her identity, or some sense of self and a reference point for where she belonged in the world, she had discovered a much broader perspective. Mila had learned that a single wish could send her on an unimaginable journey.

Though still in the dark as to her origins, Mila basked in the light of her own illumination, satisfied that she had at least come to know a special part of herself, if not her birth parents. She could not know that as the next layer of the onion was peeled away, her world would again be turned upside down.

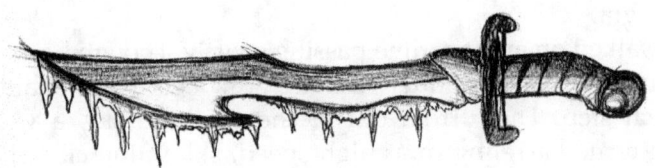

PART 9

THE PLANE OF SHADOWS

King Jonas lay in a bed in Cypress, drifting across the nearly imperceptible line between rest and slumber. He breathed gently, focusing on the feeling of existing in two states at once while he searched for the remshifter. In evenings past it had always been Meadow who sought out the king on the plane of shadows, his skill as a remshifter allowing him to navigate in that dark place. This night, Jonas entered the darkness of his own volition, urgently seeking counsel. The dissonance between Lapis and Verde grew with each passing hour and the fate of his friends—and his heart—was yet unknown. Jonas held a picture of Meadow in his mind as he at last let go and slipped into a dream.

Jonas found himself standing in a spring meadow filled with hari flowers in bloom. The pink blossoms perched atop thin, wavering stems, appearing to hover over the greenery below. The field stretched endlessly in all directions, and Jonas began to walk toward the rising suns in the eastern horizon. With each step, the rosy color of the blooms danced upward and entered his heart space, filling it to near overflowing. Jonas smiled at the fullness of the sensation, the warmth of it, and felt that if even one more particle of adoration had entered his being, his heart would burst from delight.

He walked on and on, time passing swiftly. Though he walked in beauty, the silence of utter solitude grew ever more deafening with each step. Then, from out of the southern sky, a winged creature came barreling in at high speed, skimming close to the ground, setting hari flowers quivering in its wake. Jonas stopped and squinted into the distance, trying to make out the nature of the beast. As it neared, he saw it was a hoverdale. Atop the animal, to his joy, was Rosette.

At once the doors of his heart flung wide open, tinting his aura with rose pink as it expanded in a supernova of emerald tones. The hoverdale began to slow, and before it could make landing, Rosette leapt from its back and stood just feet from the king, staring at him in disbelief. Jonas' heart pounded wildly in his chest, his eyes wide with wonder. For a moment, neither of them could move or speak, spellbound by the charge of their reunion. Then, as if suddenly broken from that spell, they rushed together and met in an embrace of red rose and green, their light growing with each joyous breath.

Rosette laughed aloud as the tears came, warm and fresh, washing away the ache that had frozen her heart for so long. Jonas lifted her into the air, spinning giddily, twirling into weightlessness. As they came to rest, Jonas looked into the deep green pools of her eyes, finally finding his words therein. "No longer will we be relegated to shadows of secrecy. I will declare my love for you before all of Verde, all of Graha. This I promise you, Rosette."

Rosette's eyes flashed with concern. "I was born to a Crimsonite father and a Verdean mother. You know what people will say." Rosette lowered her head, speaking softly. "I cannot bring shame to the throne."

Jonas smiled and lifted her chin with a finger. "There can be no shame in true love."

He tenderly wiped away the tears that fell, looking deeply within her. Reflections of sunlight shifted swiftly in her eyes, and Jonas turned his face to the sky. The suns had already made their westward trek through the heavens and were now setting, casting a warm glow over the meadow. Jonas felt a heaviness in his chest as he remembered that one passes only briefly through the dream plane before entering the plane of shadows. Jonas let go of his embrace and took a few steps back from Rosette, pained by the reminder that the most beautiful things in creation were often the most short-lived.

Rosette blinked in confusion. "Jonas, where are you going?"

Jonas paused, smiling. "Hari flowers bloom only for a day." He reached down and plucked one of the delicate blossoms, then stepped forward, placing it in her palm. "Far too short a time, my love."

He watched the sadness fall as she glanced down at the petals in her hand. He felt himself drifting away from her, drawn by some force seemingly within himself. The lovely meadow faded rapidly into dark fog and shadows that mimicked the landscape of Cypress. He had entered the shadow plane.

Through working with Meadow in dreams and meditation, Jonas had trained himself to awaken within his dreams and enter this plane. He now entered the shadows without the assistance of his faithful remshifter and could only hope he would not lose himself in the dark. Jonas soon found himself floating high above Cypress. Unsure of how to find Meadow, he called out his name, though his voice dissipated as soon as it left his lips. The spoken name morphed from sound to a luminous green thread that curled out before him, drifting through shadows in search of the remshifter's consciousness.

As Jonas waited in the darkness for a response, he recalled his first meeting with Meadow. Jonas had invited the young man to Samera a number of times, having heard of the power of his gifts and his willingness to be of service. Remshifters were precious and few, and Jonas wished to give him guidance in finding the highest and best way to use his gifts. Quiet and gentle, Meadow could never have enjoyed the life of a Guardsman, no matter how great his desire to serve the Land of Verde.

In his wisdom, Jonas devised a way for Meadow to use his gifts and his stealthy stoicism—and his ability to seemingly disappear—to his advantage. He appointed Meadow to a secret position, the only one of its kind. Meadow would use his remshifting gifts to gather information from the shadow plane and then report directly to Jonas, revealing nothing of his mission to the rest of the kingdom.

Perfectly suited to solitude and secrecy, Meadow served Jonas well, the king's trust in him growing with the passage of time. Jonas eventually came to rely on Meadow, steady and faithful, as a second set of eyes, one that he would need ever more desperately as evil spread and chaos descended throughout the Lands. In this pivotal moment, Jonas needed Meadow more than ever.

High above the desert in the Land of Jonquil, Meadow entered an evening meditation, intending to call Jonas out of his dreams and into the shadow plane for a conversation. He expanded his awareness to panoramic observation, searching for any indication of his king's presence. At once, he heard a faint call in the distance and swiftly focused his attention on the origin of the voice. To his surprise, he saw the emerald thread twisting in the fog over Cypress, searching for a connection. With an exhale, Meadow spun his consciousness into a similar thread of deep green that stretched out from his mouth like a serpent, searching until it finally connected with Jonas'.

As the streams of consciousness met, a burst of light sprang out of the fog. Meadow, without effort of any kind, moved at what seemed the speed of light over a shadow version of the Land. Every landmark, every tree and river were represented in shadow form, as was the dark traveller hurtling toward Cypress. Meadow soon found his pace slowing and saw King Jonas waiting in the shadows.

"Meadow!" Jonas called, drifting closer to his confidant. "I had so hoped to find you here, my friend."

The two men soon came face to face, and Meadow spoke urgently. "We must be brief, my king. This plane is more dangerous than ever. Corpus watches always."

Jonas nodded. "What word do you have for me?"

"I travel now with Botan and Thornhill in Aksini. We are very close to the Palace of Gosai, but the Land is becoming ever more unstable. Several of the lesser islands are crumbling so badly that they are too dangerous to traverse in darkness. We chose to make camp and wait for the light of morning."

"I see. What of Rosette? Is she still being held in the palace?"

"Yes, I have seen it in meditation." Meadow narrowed his eyes at Jonas, observing the fresh radiance that illuminated the King's glow while speaking of Rosette. Meadow considered asking a question, but opted to hold his tongue.

"And Salvitor," the king went on, "he chose to stay behind in Seletan?"

Meadow lowered his head. "In a way, yes." Meadow paused, searching for gentle words. "Jonas...Salvitor has passed into spirit."

Jonas' eyes widened. "What?"

"Minions of Corpus had been stalking Salvitor for some time. They finally caught up with him when he could find no escape."

Jonas silently scanned the gray landscape of amorphous shapes shifting in and out of form, thinking of the pain that must have descended upon his friend at Salvitor's passing. "Thornhill," he whispered.

"Thornhill of Verde is great of heart and luminous in spirit. He will get through."

Jonas nodded. "What word do you have from the eastern shore and the trouble with Lapis?"

Meadow shook his head. "I have searched for Cira and though I feel that she yet lives, I have not been able to locate her. Massive amounts of dark energy are interfering with my vision in the shadow plane of Lapis. Jonas..." Meadow paused, forcing a stiff breath. "Bobbin and Finn have also passed."

Jonas winced and looked away from Meadow, staring blankly out over the bleak fog below. "So much death..."

Before Meadow could speak any words of condolence, Jonas snapped his head to the right, having noticed a shadow moving from the corner of his eye. "I fear our time is up, Meadow. Thank you for your service. Your counsel is a great help and comfort to me."

Though Jonas did not fully explain, Meadow understood the meaning of his words and chose not to pry. Keeping to his station as a faithful servant of the throne of Samera, he allowed the king's private thoughts and his heart to remain his own.

Without a word, Meadow lowered his head in humility, then raced away to the east. Jonas watched his retreat, then quickly drew himself back through the luminous doorway to the dream plane, and then to the waking world. His eyes shot open, and he sat up straight in his bed, his rapid breaths the only sound in the dark and silent room. As he lay back onto the pillows, he closed his eyes once more, noticing the faintest scent of hari blossoms in the air.

* * *

Near the eastern shore of Verde, Meadow searched the sea of the shadow plane for Cira of Lapis. Having felt her presence in meditation, he held high hope that she yet lived, and scanned the sea for her light. The seas had been made shallow by the dark forces, as if layers of the waters of Lapis had been peeled back and laid upon the shores. Meadow could now see clearly through the shadow waters as he skimmed over the surface and descended to walk the sea floor.

Meadow searched every corner and low place, finding no signs of light that had not been shaded by Corpus' influence; the few citizens that remained in Lapis were dim shells of their former brilliance.

Despite appearances, Meadow felt closer to Cira than ever before, and a tangible sense of her presence urged him forward through the darkness. He moved over the sea floor until he came to the base of a majestic undersea mountain range, black monoliths stretching across his entire field of vision. Meadow shifted his focus to panorama, and as his awareness expanded up over the tallest summit, he caught sight of an azure light pulsing in the northern territory.

Meadow swiftly moved toward the light, his energy expanding hopefully as he went. *By the light of Graha, let it be Cira!* Over mountains and submerged trenches he raced, one eye turned toward the blue light of hope, the other ever watchful for the Dark One.

A Time to Prepare

Jonas awoke at sunrise, energized by the hope that the group stood on the brink of freeing Rosette and bringing Zehn back to reclaim the throne of Gosai. A vision flashed in his mind of Rosette, trapped in a holding cell, waiting for the others to come save her. She was one who had never needed saving, and he could imagine she did not like the position one bit. Jonas almost chuckled to himself as he thought of it, sliding his body out of bed and dressing quickly. Despite his hopeful mood, danger loomed on the shores of Verde, and there was much work to be done. Sunlight streamed out from behind a thick gray cloud as Jonas and two of his Guardsmen rode into the town center of Cypress. The walkways and streets had been swept clean of debris and lined with blooming plants and fruiting trees. Shops bustled with customers, arms loaded with fresh foods and goods that had for so long been scarce, laughing as they talked with one another. Further down the main road, stately buildings framed by carved wooden columns stood silently, observing the comings and goings of the townspeople. Many seemed busy at work, while others strolled casually along, joyfully basking in the glow of their newly rejuvenated town center and the rebirth of hope itself. For Jonas, the sight was bittersweet; while the music of joy now danced in the heart of Cypress, darkness threatened to silence that melody.

Jonas and his Guardsmen tied their hadras and went into the hall, where Aux and a number of other Guardsmen of Verde and Crimson awaited their arrival. Jonas walked the marble floors of the hall and went into the meeting room where he found Aux, his crimson glow contrasting against the muted tapestry that hung behind him. Despite his tremendous size, he seemed smaller than the last time Jonas had seen him, and dimness haunted the edges of his aura.

"Aux," Jonas said, extending his hand. "What news do you have for me?"

Aux took the king's hand firmly in his own, then placed a rolled scroll on the table. "We got word that the Lapisians have come ashore, bringing flooding to the eastern seaboard," Aux cleared his throat. "Many thousands of them."

Jonas furrowed his brow, then looked carefully at Aux. "Are you all right, Aux?'

"I'm fine," Aux shot back. He then lowered his voice. "I haven't slept a wink, been all night coming up with this plan." He unrolled the scroll to reveal a map of Verde and the adjacent seas of Lapis.

"We're fighting Lapis, which means we'll be fighting water. I say we build dams and walls wherever we can to control the flow and stop them from taking the Fodlas River."

Jonas nodded. "If they reach the river, they will have easy access to the Jala swamplands, and then—"

"Samera," Aux interrupted, his voice dropping.

"We cannot allow them to reach Samera. Let our first order of business be to dam the Fodlas to prevent them from using it as a

Clouds of Solitude

238

path to Samera."

Aux nodded, placing a mark on the map in the corresponding place.

Jonas continued, "Woodson and Bract have organized the building of walls and dams in Maru and Zila. We will need the same protection here. Have the builders create water walls at intervals of one half spatial throughout the inland areas along the eastern border of the Seros forest and Cypress itself. I will personally assist with moving the heaviest of the materials."

"Good," Aux grunted.

Jonas walked to a nearby window and looked out over a field dotted with Guardsmen, their red and green auras blending and swirling as they worked as one. "Remarkable...in all my days I have not seen such cooperation between Verde and Crimson."

Aux stepped to the window and got a look at the Guardsmen below. "Jonas, all of them seem to understand that if we don't cooperate, we will die."

Jonas turned to Aux, his eyes flickering. "Why must our very lives be threatened before we see the value of unity?"

Aux lifted his brows and turned once more to the scene outside the window. Who could explain mysteries unknown to a Founder of Graha?

Aux left the hall and returned to the fields where the Guardsmen and others had gathered. There he found Blitz managing the construction of the ramparts. Over and again, he raised his hands into the air, his red aura flashing, then drove his fists of stone down onto boulders at his feet. Bits and pieces flew about, and Blitz himself seemed to vibrate from the force of the impact. Yet he tarried on, dutifully carrying out his task of building up the stone foundation of the barricade.

Satisfied with the progress of construction, Aux moved on to a field just west of the ramparts, where one-eyed Charg had gathered a group of Verdeans for training. As he approached, Aux could see Charg's wild, ruddy hair flicking about his face like flames, a lone streak of gray showing his age and experience.

Charg gave Aux a nod of acknowledgement and continued with his lesson. "Now this," he said, lifting a handful of leather straps in one hand and several round metal objects in the other, "is a slingow, the best weapon to fight the Lapisians who have the power to change to water. They can only do it for a moment and then they turn back, but that's all it takes to give them an advantage and get away."

"Can all Lapisians turn to water? How will we fight such slippery people?" a young man asked.

"No," Charg growled. "Only some can do it, but you need to be ready. Take the slingow and load it, like this." He placed the heavy balls in the catch basket. "Then you fling it like this," Charg took a number of steps away from the group and began swinging the weapon around in wide arcs, increasing the speed with every turn. When he unloaded, the metal balls flung out in different directions before him, thudding to the ground a good distance away.

"Hmf!" Aux huffed. "Nice throw."

"They go in many directions, so the enemy cannot know which way to move." Charg handed the straps to the young man who had inquired. "Practice with it, you're going to need it."

The young man at first paled, but then took the straps and jogged off to gather the balls from where they'd fallen. Aux planted his hand on Charg's shoulder. "Tell me, where are Tannis and Bronnis?"

Charg turned, pointing southward. "Over there...with the tender ones."

"Carry on," Aux said.

A group of inexperienced fighters had gathered for training in sword combat with Bronnis. His skill and patience proved invaluable in the endeavor, not only in dealing with his trainees, but with his brother Tannis as well. While Bronnis ran the trainees through drills, Tannis stood off to the side, plucking stones from the soil and tossing them as far as he could, feeling the heat in his palms build with each volley. He picked up a smooth stone and held it in his hand, allowing his anger to build, focusing it onto the stone. Within moments, flames burst from its surface and Tannis launched the stone, watching it tumble and burn like a falling meteorite. Bored with his game, he stomped over to where his brother worked. "Bronnis, why are we wasting time with exercises? We need to meet them head-on before they destroy half the forest."

Bronnis shook his head slowly. "Patience, brother. This hour is a blessing. It gives us time to prepare and plan."

Tannis snatched up another stone in frustration, his heat building once more. "Patience? Patience will not save us from Lapis!"

Bronnis held up his hands, calming his brother. "Patience and preparation will. We cannot clash with this enemy without a plan."

Tannis frowned and hurled the stone past his brother, spitting on the ground in disgust. Though Bronnis dutifully turned his focus back to his trainees, his brother's volatility haunted him like an ember in dry brush.

A Storm Comes Ashore

On the eastern banks of Verde, a storm came ashore. Under Corpus' influence, the dark army of Lapis crossed over the reefs and came onto the land, bringing flooding and destruction with them. The surge rushed inland, flooding many miles of coastline with dark water.

The army steadily waded forward, eventually entering the Sero forest, pristine and newly rejuvenated by Jonas' return. The army came with biting blades and gnashing blows, trampling the delicate flowers and ferns that huddled at the bases of the great trees. One by one, each giant was toppled into the muddy waters that surrounded the forest. Every place that the water flowed, destruction followed, and all that King Jonas had set right was once more fouled by evil. The Lapisian soldiers advanced easily in the flooded forest, naturally attuned to the medium in which they moved. Though a handful of Verdean Guardsmen had come out to meet the army head-on at the border of the forest, they'd been hopelessly outnumbered, quickly meeting their deaths at the hands of an army overcome by darkness.

In a cruel twist, it had been the very water itself that lent ease to their corruption. Though Corpus had been able to influence certain numbers of citizens in each Land to serve him, his influence in Lapis had spread like a virus, rapidly inserting itself into the matrix of the Land. The very thing that nourished the Lapisians, which gave them life, shelter, and food, had been turned against them, for the waters of the sea not only held living bounty, but *information*.

Indeed, the water itself had memory, the ability to be imprinted, and Corpus used this quality to his advantage. He had injected the waters of Lapis with his malice, his evil intent, and his desire to destroy all of Graha. As each Lapisian touched and took in the waters that surrounded them, they became possessed by that evil, and soon nearly every Lapisian, save a few refugees, had been turned into a servant of the Dark One. In the ultimate blaspheme, Mother Sea had become an agent of destruction.

A mile inland, a second wave of Verdean Guardsmen met with the Lapisian army, sloshing through flooded fields and dunes, working in vain to hold together the crumbling ramparts. A great river of water flowed in from the sea and onto the Land, providing Corpus with the means to influence his army and for the Lapisians to exert their force on Verde. Without the water, they would lose most of their power and advantage.

Leading the Lapisians were two men, dark skin gleaming as water dripped from their frames. As a Verdean guardsman approached, one soldier created a deep depression in the Land that rapidly filled with swirling water. The vortex sucked in the Verdean soldier and held him beneath the surface until he finally succumbed, a thin trail of bubbles the only trace of the location of his body.

The other soldier approached a brave Verdean Guardsman of size and strength. The Guardsman stood his ground, facing his foe unflinchingly. The Lapisian soldier looked at him with interest, part of him approving of the courage displayed and not wishing to engage such a formidable man in hand-to-hand battle. The Lapisian raised his arms above his head in a sweeping motion, and as he did, the waters around him lurched in response.

A great column of water rose before him, and before the Verdean could move or even blink, the water coiled about him like a serpent, binding his arms and legs and crushing the breath from his lungs. The Guardsman weakened more and more, then fell to the flooded ground, the kumu draining from his form.

Micca, the Waymaker of Lapis, charged forward to where the man had fallen, checking to ensure he'd been exterminated. Once satisfied, he stood and looked out over the flooded landscape, a tight grin creeping across his face. Soon all of Verde would be drowned and broken, and his master would keep his word: the throne of Venelia would be Micca's.

Several Lapisian soldiers approached on Micca's left, breathless and dripping wet, holding two wounded Verdeans. "Micca, we have captured these Verdeans as prisoners, where do you want them taken?"

Micca's face twisted with disbelief. "Prisoners? We don't have prisoners, only kraktau bait!"

He drew an icy blade from his belt and slashed the prisoners open, their blood staining the water around them.

Micca turned toward the sea and gave a grating call, his voice trilling even over the din of the battle. As his cold breath left his lips, it created a cloud of condensation in the warm air about him, exposing the condition of his heart. Within moments, the kraktau began to emerge from the water, huge claws snapping and eyestalks waving. The crab-like creatures shuffled forward, following the scent of fresh blood. As they found the bodies, bones snapped and flesh was torn away until the kraktau had devoured every morsel of evidence.

Micca turned from the scene, a sickening grin splitting his face. "If there are any other prisoners, do the same with them!"

The soldier nodded and dove into the water, disappearing in the murk.

Clarity

Mila leaned against the plush leather seats of the limousine, her mind drifting. Madison still slept, her head lolling gently with each bump in the road. Mila had thought to wake her; there was much to talk about, after all, but she probably needed to rest and find a way to absorb the unbelievable occurrences of the day. Mila had just decided to close her own eyes when Madison woke with a start, her glow whirling round her in ruby ribbons.

"Are you okay?" Mila asked.

"I had that dream again." Madison took a deep breath, glancing to the front of the cabin to be sure the partition was closed. "The one where I'm trying to get the man to go back down the mountain and he gets taken away, but..."

Mila sat forward. "But what?"

"Now I know it's not just a dream, Mila. It was *real*. I don't know how to explain it, but it really happened to me...maybe a long, long time ago."

"And you think your name was Maddox back then, right?"

Madison nodded slowly.

"Do you remember anything else about the man you saw?"

"He was Mason, he was..." Madison paused, her eyes flickering with realization. "*My* king." Madison lifted her arms, staring at the red glow that now pulsed from them. "I am from Crimson," she stuttered, slowly turning her gaze to Mila. "And I'm supposed to protect you from some kind of evil."

"Corpus?" Mila asked expectantly.

Madison tilted her head, frowning in frustration as she searched her memory. "Corpus..."

"Corpus is the bad guy, the one who's destroying all the Lands and killing the people. I've never seen him," Mila swallowed hard, leaning back on the seat once more, "but I know he's there."

Madison shrugged. "I don't remember the name, but it seems like we're talking about the same thing."

"Do you remember any other people, or what your home was like in Crimson?"

A slight smile crept across Madison's lips, her eyes twinkling as she explored a far away memory. She told Mila of the Land she had known: dark and jagged mountains, some crowned with fire and smoke, standing guard over canyons and sprawling valleys, villages in the green foothills bustling with life and strength, and the mines of the south, rich with natural treasure.

Madison paused and tucked a ringlet of strawberry blond hair behind her ear. "Mila, this is all so weird."

"Believe me, I know." Mila sat forward expectantly. "Do you remember anything about other people you used to know?"

Madison nodded, lifting a finger. "The thing I remember most, just like it happened yesterday, is standing in this big room, and this man, my teacher, was right in front of me, holding up this little round thing."

"What was it?"

"I dunno for sure, but I know that I was getting ready to use it, and once I used it, I would forget everything. So, first I wrote a letter to myself," Madison stared at the floor. "I wrote down really important stuff that I would need to know, and then I hid the letter someplace safe, but..."

Madison looked up at Mila, moist-eyed and forlorn. "I can't remember where I hid it."

Mila slumped in her chair, tapping the toes of her worn Chucks together a few times before smiling optimistically at her best friend. "Don't worry, Madi. When you really need to, you'll remember."

The girls fell silent for a time, listening to the hum of the wheels on the road. As the mile markers flew by, Mila soon found herself thinking of food. They hadn't had time to eat much at the party, and her rumbling belly reminded her of that misstep. She glanced at the bowl of candy across from her; a Kit-Kat might be just enough to hold her over until she could get some good hot food.

Just as Mila started to get up, the limousine began to slow, and Joe guided the vehicle off the freeway at the next exit. Mila at first wondered about the reason for the stop, but had her question answered as they pulled into a nearby gas station. Just as her attention turned from candy to gas station hot dogs, she was broken from her thoughts.

"Poe!" Madison blurted, suddenly sitting straight up.

A startled Mila nearly fell out of her seat. "What?"

"Poe! I remember that Poe has something to do with this."

"Oh, good!" Mila said excitedly. "Is Poe a place or a..."

"The warrior Poe," Madison interrupted. "Maybe he has the letter!"

Mila was at once surprised and intrigued by Madison's words. Though she had at first thought that she would have a lot of explaining to do, it appeared that Madison held a great many pieces of the puzzle. How was it that Madison knew so much, and what, if anything, did she know of the days before her adoption and how her life began?

Madison lowered her voice. "I think I know what you need to do next in the other world, Mila."

Mila lifted a brow. "You do?"

"You gotta find that letter. I know I wrote something super important in it, and you need to find it as fast as you can."

"So I *shouldn't* go to Pixie and Queen Zehn first?"

Madison shrugged helplessly. "All I know is the letter is really important and you gotta find it, Mila. You gotta go now."

Mila blinked. "Like, *right* now?"

The limousine eased to a stop at pump number seven, and Madison watched as Joe emerged from the cab, stretching himself as he stood and pulled his wallet from his back pocket.

"Well, we're stopped. Do you have to be inside a house to open that doorway thing?"

Mila shook her head. "No, the doorway can be anywhere I want it to be."

Despite Madison's call to action, Mila sat perfectly still, her mind racing with possible explanations of her origins, her unique gifts, and her very reason for being. The idea that a letter, one that her own best friend somehow penned in another world at an earlier point in time, waited to give up its secrets was almost too tantalizing to believe. She felt excitedly foggy, like a sleeper becoming aware that she walked in a dream. Mila wrinkled her nose as a strand of her hair fell into her face. She took a red band from her pocket and smoothed her dark hair into a little ponytail. *I do need to get back to Graha.* Pixie had explained that Mila could control where the doorway opened by using her thoughts, and the resonator only acted by default to bring her to Thornhill if she did not intentionally visualize a place to land on the other side. Mila sighed. "Okay, I'm gonna picture where I want to end up. Hang on a second, Madi."

Mila closed her eyes and thought of the one person she knew who could help her in the Land of Crimson: Aux.

As she visualized, she began to see him clearly, standing strong and tall, whelix in hand, and could even hear his voice as he smiled and said, "Hello, little lady." Once Mila felt she had focused sufficiently on her target, she opened her eyes once more and turned to Madison. "Okay, Madi, I'll find the letter and come back as soon as I can...but I guess it doesn't matter how long it takes, because you'll be frozen anyway!" Madison cocked her head to the side, somewhat confused, but Mila decided not to explain. She took a deep breath and opened the doorway below, noticing that it adjusted in size to fit perfectly onto a section of the limo floor. Madison drew her legs up onto her chair in alarm, gasping. Her eyes widened as she gaped at the anomaly, then back at her friend. Mila smiled and focused once more on Aux.

"See you soon!" Mila said, and hopped into the bright void.

Illumination of Jonquil

In a flash of white light, Pixie and Queen Zehn stumbled through the doorway and onto the dry soil of Niso Island in Jonquil. Before they could even get their bearings, Pixie heard the insistent beep of the durational on her ear. She quickly pulled it off to check its status, but it went dark, having run out of power.

Pixie exhaled slowly, realizing how close she'd come to disaster. If they had been delayed even a moment more at the Parke home, she and Zehn would have met their deaths between worlds.

Refreshed by the crisp air of her true home Land, Zoe began to glow brightly, and her body entered metamorphosis. She grew rapidly to adult height, and though her appearance changed drastically, her inky black hair and elegantly slanted eyes remained the same. Within moments, little Zoe had fully become Queen Zehn of Jonquil, triumphantly returning in a swirling orb of brilliant golden yellow.

Pixie watched the transformation, frozen with awe, until the queen turned her shining face to look at her. Pixie quickly bowed low, acknowledging her queen once more. "Welcome home, Queen Zehn."

Zehn smiled, but her expression quickly shifted as she and Pixie realized that her dress had not come so gracefully through the transformation. What had once been a long and flowing silk gown was now torn at the seams, and to Zehn's dismay, obscenely tight. Pixie heard footsteps nearby. She turned around and saw, to her relief, the familiar emerald aura and warm smile of Botan. He had seen the brilliant glow of the queen, like an evening sun, from where they had made camp, and had come to greet the new arrivals.

"Queen Zehn..." he whispered, almost in disbelief, and dropped to one knee in reverence.

"Botan of Verde, it is wonderful to see you again." Zehn looked down, tugging at the remains of the silk dress. "Though I must apologize; I am not dressed for the occasion."

Botan looked up at her and fought the urge to smile, quickly turning his attention to Pixie. "Ah, Pixie, I'm so glad you made it back safely, but where is Mila?"

"She stayed back to help her friend Madison with something. She said she would come back as soon as she could."

Botan nodded, "I see. Well, dear queen, if you will wait here for just a moment, I will go back to camp and find something a bit more..." he paused, trying not to stare at the numerous patches of her exposed skin, "...comfortable for you to wear."

"I thank you, Botan," Zehn replied, bowing her head slightly.

Minutes later, Botan returned with clothing for Zehn, then went back to camp to allow her some privacy while changing. Though baggy and plain, the garments were still better than the silken shreds in which she had arrived. She and Pixie then followed the light of a collective green glow, and soon found Thornhill and Botan camped nearby. Thornhill lit up when he laid eyes on Zehn, rising from where he rested only to lower himself once more before her. "My stars, Queen Zehn!"

Zehn smiled serenely and placed her palms on either side of his face, lifting it gently. "Thornhill of Verde, I am so very pleased you are here."

Thornhill stood slowly and with great effort, having left his staff on the ground. "As am I, Zehn, as am I," He looked at Pixie and winked. "Very nice work, Miss Pixie. Your mentor would be most proud."

Pixie smiled and crossed her arms over her chest. "Thanks."

Botan joined the conversation. "Queen Zehn, we have so much to tell you, but I am not sure where to begin."

Zehn turned to Botan, her eyes glowing thoughtfully. "When the child found me, she shared with me the memories of all that has come to pass in Graha." She paused, her aura shifting slightly in tone. "I have seen much—the hardships you have endured in the absence of the Founders, your constant battles against dark forces, and how you have worked to restore the Lands. I owe a debt of gratitude to you all," she said, bowing.

Thornhill huffed. "Dear Zehn, you owe us nothing. All that we do is in appreciation for the Land that nourishes us, for the wisdom and compassion of the Founders, and for our very lives. No work we can do will ever outshine these gifts."

Zehn nodded slightly, a faint smile curving her thin lips.

Botan continued, "My lady, some things have come to pass that the child, Mila, is not aware of. Fincher has usurped the throne of the Palace of Gosai and has surrounded himself with raiku. He has allowed most of the kingdom to fall into disrepair and is now using your Mazurin Gon as a prison." Botan paused, his mouth dry with bitterness. "It is also a tool of execution."

Zehn's eyes flashed and her aura simmered with golden fury. She clenched her fists tightly, feeling the strength retuning to her body. "*Fincher,*" she hissed, the memories of his betrayal flooding her mind once more. "He will pay for what he has done. He will be removed." Thornhill glanced at Pixie and sighed. "And I'm afraid we have one less ally to help us in ousting Fincher." He rested his palms atop his staff. "My dear Zehn, Salvitor of Jonquil is dead."

Zehn's eyes shifted in tone, and a ghost of sadness drifted across her stoic facade. She quickly turned her gaze to the west. "This is a dark hour for my kingdom. Salvitor was a true Jonquilian; high in character, rich in mind, and fervent of heart." Her voice quivered as she spoke, like ripples on a pond disturbed by a stone. "His brilliance shall never be matched."

Pixie hesitated, then finally spoke up. "We all miss him." Thornhill sagged, feeling the weight of his own remembrance. "My lady, how I wish that I could give you more time to grieve, but I cannot." He stepped toward Zehn, his voice low. "We are not safe in this place. Minions of Corpus pursue us and with your return, we will not be difficult to find."

Zehn tilted her head. "Minions of Corpus?"

"They are shadow servants of the enemy; watchers and destroyers with them," Botan said. "We encountered some not long ago and Mila was able to eradicate them, but she is yet to return...Zehn, I know you have only just arrived, but by your light, by your very presence, there must be some way to stop these minions, to give us a chance to remove Fincher and restore you to the throne."

Zehn stood taller, her aura brightening and her calm expression growing stern. "I know what I must do."

Thornhill and Botan looked at each other, green eyes flashing with curiosity, and Pixie felt a sly smile cross her lips. The glimmer of hope had at last returned to the Land of Jonquil.

* * *

Not far from camp, Meadow still sat in meditation. Having located the one he hoped was Cira, he then travelled in shadow to Jonquil, noticing that the Land appeared to hover higher in the sky than it had when he left to search Lapis. The island they had chosen for their campsite had somehow been elevated to an altitude near its original position in the days before the fall. Tentatively optimistic, Meadow raced through the shadow plane back to his body, and quickly pulled himself into consciousness. His eyes flew open and he looked around, somewhat bewildered by the physical reality that surrounded him. With a few breaths, Meadow gathered himself and made his way back to camp, hope lightening his steps.

Meadow walked into the collective light of the group, a broad smile brightening his mysterious countenance. Having enjoyed only a precious few opportunities to see Queen Zehn in the past, this meeting, for him, was particularly joyful. Pixie was the first to spot his approach, and she tapped Botan on the shoulder to alert him to his presence. Botan saw Meadow's beaming smile and laughed aloud. "Goodness, Meadow, I think that's the first time I've seen all your teeth!"

Thornhill chuckled and watched as Botan ushered Zehn to meet the young man. "Zehn, this is Meadow of Verde. He assisted Thornhill and I in protecting Mila and rescuing King Jonas from the Inner Realm."

Queen Zehn bowed graciously to Meadow, who dropped to one knee in respect. "I'm honored to meet you, Queen Zehn." He stood and looked to Thornhill, his deep green eyes glinting. "Thornhill, I have happy but urgent news. I believe I have located Cira."

Thornhill's face brightened in surprise, and he stepped closer to Meadow, leaning heavily on his staff. "Where?" he asked breathlessly.

"I traveled in the plane of shadows and found her in the far northern sea of Lapis. We must free her before harm comes to her at the hand of Micca or the Dark One."

Thornhill pulled at a white strand of his beard in thought. "Yes, we must not delay. Trouble brews in those seas, and every moment that passes is a danger to anyone that remains in the waters."

"And yet the need to reach the palace is equally urgent," Botan added, his aura pulsing as he spoke. "It's unfortunate we're forced to wait out the night before traveling because of the crumbling of the Land."

Zehn lifted her hands gracefully, as if to calm the fears of the gathered. "My dears, you are safe now. I can feel my Land stabilizing and elevating beneath me as Niso and all of Jonquil restores itself. I believe all danger of landslide has passed, and you may begin the next leg of your quest right now."

"Yes, it's true," Meadow cut in. "I saw in the shadow plane that all of Jonquil is raising higher. The Land responds even now to your presence, Queen Zehn."

Pixie felt her heart lift at the news; it seemed hope had not been entirely extinguished in her home Land.

Thornhill nodded. "Well, in light of this new development, let us gather ourselves and head for Gosai."

The group packed up and moved in darkness toward the Palace of Gosai. As they traveled, Zehn continued to gain power, her glow waxing ever more brilliant with each spatial they covered. The group heard great cracking and grinding as the very rocks beneath them melded together and once more formed an unbreakable crust over the radentium discs that crept ever higher in the atmosphere. The now rarified air grew cooler, and mist began to roll in around them, becoming just visible in the first light of dawn.

As the group approached the edge of Niso, the lesser sun fully crested the horizon, washing the landscape in cool blue light. The ruined Palace of Gosai stood starkly against the serene indigo sky. Upon sight of it, Zehn froze, unable to take another step toward the home she no longer recognized. Her breath became constricted by stiffening ribs, and her belly ached from shock. Though tears formed in her eyes, they were quickly consumed in the fuming anger that flared within her. *Someone will pay for this.*

Startled by movement, Thornhill looked to a rocky outcropping nearby and saw that watcher minions followed them, tracking their movements and no doubt reporting the group's location to their dark master. He lifted his staff, pointing. "Zehn, they have found us, look there!"

Zehn whipped her head round at Thornhill's warning, focusing her eyes on the place where he'd pointed.

Thornhill groaned faintly, somewhat relieved. "It appears they are only watcher minions. They cannot harm us, but where watchers go, destroyers are not long to follow." Thornhill continued walking, motioning for the others to follow. "We must hurry."

Zehn stood her ground. "These are the agents of Corpus." She cocked her head to the side, her nostrils flaring slightly. "The beings responsible for the destruction of my Land?"

Thornhill turned round. "In part, yes. They show Corpus our movements and he then sends the destroyer minions."

Pixie chimed in, "The destroyers ruined Salvitor's secret chamber...and all but a couple of his devices."

Zehn's jaw tightened as she fought to control the rage that boiled within her. She could feel the presence of the minions on the Land as if they trampled over her own body. As her anger rose, Zehn felt a contrasting lightness in her form as it began to resonate with a familiar frequency. Zehn turned to the group, her aura expanding by the moment. "Please excuse me; it is time to clean my house."

She then ascended, riding a pulsing wave of energy into the air, radiant golden plumes lifting her higher with each breath. When she had reached a certain altitude, she called down to the group, "Hold your ears, dears!" Zehn suddenly took off on a burst of sonic energy, a deafening boom cracking at her departure. She circled high above the group in ever-widening arcs, eventually covering the entire circumference of the island. At once, Zehn let out a high-pitched scream, the sound of which shook the very Land itself. As the call rang out in powerful waves, every minion within range instantly disintegrated in its wake.

Upon completing her task, Zehn drifted out of orbit and back down toward the group, who still held their hands clasped over their ears. Her glow flickered rapidly as it receded to its normal shape and size, and she gently touched down before the group, her eyes glassy. "Now *that*," she whispered, her voice low and husky, "was satisfying."

Her knees buckled, and Botan and Meadow rushed to support her. Having expended incredible amounts of energy eradicating the minions, she now found herself too exhausted to stand unassisted.

"Goodness, what in the world was that?" Botan asked, gently fanning Zehn's flushed face.

Zehn moaned, leaning on Meadow's shoulder as she gathered herself. "Banshee...sound weapon. It is one of my natural gifts." She paused, shaking her head. "Though I have never before been forced to use it."

Zehn stood tall, finding her strength once more.

Thornhill chuckled. "Even after all these long years, you still have the power to surprise me, Zehn."

Pixie stood close to the queen, her eyes still wide with amazement. "How come it didn't kill us?"

"Frequency," Zehn stated matter-of-factly. "The minions are very dark, and the discrepancy between their vibration and mine is great. The high frequency sound was too dissonant and foreign for them to tolerate. For you, it was merely uncomfortable; for them, it proved deadly."

Pixie nodded slowly. "*Nice.*"

Meadow said, "Now that dawn has come and the immediate danger has passed, I must depart for the northern seas of Lapis to find Cira. We must remove her from any potential harm due to the conflict between Lapis and Verde."

"Yes," Thornhill said. "It seems we must be in several places at once."

"I will need a flyer or preferably a sanlifter for my journey." Meadow turned to Zehn. "Do you know where I can find one?"

Zehn smiled. "Indeed, we are very close to a flight yard." She lifted her arm and pointed into the distance. "Simply walk east and just over that hill you will find it."

Meadow looked to where Zehn had pointed, noting the hill in the distance, then lowered his head and bowed graciously. "Thank you, Queen Zehn." He then turned to Thornhill and Botan. "When I have word, I will find King Jonas on the shadow plane, and he can then give counsel on your next meeting." Meadow pulled his hood further down over his face. "Farewell, friends."

"Thank you, Meadow, journey safely," Zehn said.

Botan and Thornhill both said their goodbyes, and Pixie

waved as Meadow turned and walked off to the east, seemingly disappearing in the soft light of dawn.

Zehn sighed. "I'm afraid I've used up much of my energy, I will need to walk with you to the Palace rather than use my flight."

Thornhill nodded. "Very well. Let us all put one foot in front of the other until we arrive."

Pixie smiled up at Thornhill, and he winked back, sliding his arm under Zehn's for support. Botan took Zehn's other arm in the same way, and the four moved toward Gosai, one step at a time.

The Letter

Moments after leaving Madison behind in the limousine, Mila stumbled through the doorway and found herself in the midst of chaos. She stood in the middle of an open field where groups of men and women rushed about, most barely acknowledging her, others failing to notice her at all. Some of them glowed in tones of red, while others shone green.

As she observed her surroundings, Mila felt tears welling in her eyes. Unbeknownst to her, her powers of empathy had grown much since her last visit, and she did not understand the influx of strong emotions in her heart. Fear, doubt, and even terror washed over her as she tuned in to the Guardsmen and citizens now bracing for war. Bewildered by the intensity of the emotions, she walked aimlessly in circles, soon drawing stares from passing Guardsmen. What business did a child have in the middle of battle preparations in Cypress?

A female Guardsman of Crimson grabbed her by the arm. "Child, what are you doing here?"

Mila gasped, broken from her empathic trance but not yet able to respond verbally. The brutish woman tightened her grip. "All of the children have long gone into the high caves to hide. Tell me, why are you here?"

"I..." Mila stammered, "...I'm looking for Aux."

The Guardsman huffed, her brows leaping upward. "Aux? How do you know him?"

Mila frowned. "It's kind of a long story."

The woman leaned down, eyeing Mila carefully. Though the girl had a strange white glow, something about her seemed to soothe any suspicion. "Come with me."

The Guardsman led Mila to where a group of Crimsonites gathered around a honing station. As she approached, the crowd parted, and there before an immense disc of stone sat Aux, sharpening his whelix.

"Aux, do you know this child?" the Guardsman asked.

Aux looked up from the grinding wheel and his eyes widened, "Mila! What are you doing here?" He quickly set down his whelix and stepped toward her, waving off the Guardsman.

"Well, I came here to you because I need your help."

Aux furrowed his brow. "*My* help?"

"Yeah, see, there's this letter that I have to find. It's really important and my friend said that I have to find the warrior Poe in Crimson, because he might know something about it." Aux shook his head, his aura dimming slightly. "I'm sorry, little lady. Poe died long ago in battle."

Mila drooped and felt her energy collapse, like a sail that had lost the wind.

"All that's left of Poe is his legacy, and a monument statue in Vires."

Mila's ears tingled. "There's a statue of Poe?" she said hopefully.

Aux nodded. "In Vires."

Mila rubbed her palms together, her glow brightening. "Maybe that's what she meant, maybe she meant for me to go to the *statue* of Poe."

Aux lifted a brow, eyeing Mila. "She who?"

Several of the gathered Guardsmen abruptly stood and gave nods of acknowledgement. Aux turned round to see King Jonas approaching, flushes of jade highlighting his smiling face. "My stars, Mila!"

Mila smiled. "Hi, King Jonas."

"Tell me, where is Queen Zehn? Have you not yet found her?"

"Oh, I found her! Pixie and Queen Zehn both went back to Jonquil to meet Thornhill."

Jonas displayed a concerned look. "And why did you not go with them?"

"I had the feeling I should stay back in my world for a while to talk to my friend." Mila paused, unsure of the best way to explain the situation. "See, my friend Madison thinks she used to live here, and she started remembering all this stuff about her old life. She remembered that a long time ago she was about to do something that would make her forget everything, and so she wrote a letter to herself with really important stuff in it. And now I have to find the letter, and the only clue I have is that Poe has something to do with it."

Aux cocked his head. "Your friend is from here?"

Mila nodded. "Yeah, from Crimson, and back then her name was Maddox."

Aux's glow lit up, flashing shades of maroon and scarlet. "You've seen Maddox of Crimson?" he said, nearly choking on the words.

"Um...kinda," Mila replied, shrugging. "Did you know Maddox?"

Aux spoke reverently. "She was a promising young warrior, about my age. I knew of her."

Mila shook her head, her aura whirling in dizzying spirals around her head. "This is just way too weird."

Jonas said, "It seems that we are all strangely connected. I do not understand it completely, but I believe we can trust what Mila says. If she needs assistance in finding the letter, she shall have it."

"Galt!" Aux shouted toward the group of Guardsmen gathered nearby.

At once, a strapping young man came bounding up from the back of the group. "Yes, Aux?"

"Do you remember when I told you that I had seen the Sankari Sano with my own eyes?"

"Yes, I remember," Galt replied.

"Well, now you can say the same." Aux gestured to Mila.

Galt at first appeared confused, his eyes flicking back and forth between Aux and the child with the white glow, but he soon realized the meaning of Aux's words and dropped to one knee before Mila, removing his helmet in a gesture of respect.

Aux spoke sternly. "I need you to take her to Vires, and by your sword or your life, see to it that she finds this letter she is looking for. Let no harm come to her."

"I understand," Galt said dutifully. He held out his hand to Mila. "I am Galt of Crimson. It is my honor to take you to Vires."

Mila smiled and reached out to shake his hand. "I'm Mila."

As their palms met, Mila was afforded a glimpse into the young man's life. She felt the love and reverence for his father, for the

Guard, and for Crimson. She felt his strength and certainty and above all, the goodness of his heart. In that moment, she knew she would be safe with him.

Jonas patted the young Guardsmen on the shoulder, then lifted him from his kneeling position. "Then let us quickly make any necessary preparations. It is not safe for Mila to linger here."

"Oh, Aux?" Mila asked, holding back a smile. "Before I go, can you give me that whelix lesson you promised me? I might need it."

Aux thumbed his ruddy beard, saying nothing, while Jonas chuckled aloud. "Mila, your presence can lighten the mood most anywhere." He then escorted Mila inside a shelter to prepare for the long road ahead.

PART 10

RECLAIMING GOSAI

After a seemingly endless journey with precious little food or comfort, Mila and Galt arrived safely in Vires. The kontross stomped to a halt, dust flying from its cleft hooves, panting with exhaustion. Galt dismounted with a thump, arched his back to chase away the stiffness, then lifted a hand. "Let me help you down, we can walk from here and let her rest."

Mila took Galt's hand and slid off the kontross, taking what felt like a two-story drop to the ground. As she took the first few steps, her feet felt unsteady, if she'd become a baby just learning to walk. She tuned in to the sensation and could feel part of her energy rooting down into the ground, then back up again into her body. As she did, visions of Crimson in her prime flashed through Mila's mind— majestic peaks standing guard over valleys tinged with green, hearty people gathering in groups to feast, and a vibrant aura of crimson red pulsing from the Land. Mila blinked and scanned the area, her surroundings a stark contrast to the visions she'd just experienced.

"Are you ready?" Galt asked, smoothing his brown hair back before replacing his helmet.

Mila nodded. "Yeah, I'm ready."

Mila found her legs once more and the two picked up the pace, heading toward the memorial. They found the center of Vires quiet

Clouds of Solitude

and stark, wisps of dust blowing across the worn cobbles as the wind sang mournfully in the courtyard. Mila looked toward the memorial area and saw an imposing stone statue. Her glow lit up, and she tapped Galt on the arm. "Is that it? Is that the statue of Poe?"

Galt nodded, wiping the dust from his eyes. "Yes, great warrior he was."

As Mila and Galt approached the statue, it grew forebodingly larger with each forward step. When they arrived at its base, Mila looked down and saw that litter and rubble had gathered in the basin; it looked to have been largely ignored for a very long time. The likeness of Poe stood proudly in full armor despite that, with a grim stiffness to his face that went beyond the hardness of the stone.

Mila frowned. "He looks...mean."

Galt huffed. "Poe was all fight. Harsh, maybe, but his focus is what made him great." He looked down at Mila, raising a finger. "To be really good at one thing, you have to sacrifice being good at anything else."

"Yeah, I guess you're right."

"So, what exactly are we looking for?" He looked at the battered monument before them. "Aux spoke of a letter, but a scrap of paper would not survive long exposed to the elements."

Mila groaned. "You're probably right." She walked around the statue, inspecting the basin and the writing on the plaque, but finding nothing indicative of a letter, or even a clue as to where it might be found. "I'm not sure what I'm supposed to be looking for. I just know I have to find this old letter and somehow Poe is a clue."

Galt hummed, conducting his own inspection at the same time. The two circled the statue, investigating every crack, lifting each rock and bit of rubble, peering into every hole and crevice, but finding nothing. Frustrated, Mila sat down on the edge of the basin, and Galt came to join her. "Don't worry, we'll figure it out. By my honor I swore to help you find the letter. I will do it somehow."

Mila smiled. "Thanks." She blew the dust off her fingers. "Thornhill said once that everything I need will come from inside me right when I need it. So far it has happened just like he said, but now...I don't know."

Galt suddenly sat up straighter. "Inside..."

Mila glanced up. "What?"

"Inside." Galt stood, tapping his fist in his palm. "This monument was built to honor Poe, but long ago there were rumors that it was built not so much in Poe's honor, but to hide something where no one would dare look." Galt turned to face the statue, his voice low. "To look for it would have defaced the only monument to one of the greatest warriors of Crimson."

Mila's face brightened. "You think there's something inside the statue?"

Galt paused, his gaze falling on the stone face of Poe. "There is but one way to know for certain."

"Are you gonna break the statue?"

"We must." He turned quickly to Mila. "I will take the blame for defiling this monument, if there is any to be had. You will be held innocent." Galt then took a few paces backward. "Stand back."

Mila hopped behind Galt and watched as his glow began to build, vertical lines of light rutilating the reddish orb as he breathed. Suddenly, a jagged stone spike rose sharply from the ground, splitting the monument asunder, the halves of the body falling to either side. As the statue crumbled, Mila caught a flash of red within the rubble at the bottom of the basin. As the dust cleared and Galt's aura returned to normal, Mila squinted her eyes, looking for it once more. There in the center, a corner of bright scarlet emerged from the debris. "Look!" she exclaimed, pointing.

Galt looked to where Mila pointed. "What is it?"

The girl had already rushed forward, clearing away the pieces of rubble to uncover what had been revealed. After a few moments, Mila retrieved a box carved from red stone that somehow felt familiar to her. Mila ran her thumb over the top of the box, brushing away the dust and finding the stone smooth as honed granite. "It's a box, I can see the lid here." Mila pulled at the top of the box, but it did not budge. "But I can't get it open."

"Let me look," Galt said, carefully taking the object from her hand and inspecting it. "I don't see a keyhole, or anywhere to slide even a fingernail in the seams." Galt paused in thought, glanced at the remains of the statue, then handed the box back to Mila. "But something tells me I shouldn't smash this one to open it."

"Yeah, maybe not." As Mila took the stone box in her hands once more, her mind raced back to the night when she and Madison sat at her kitchen table, sipping water and trying to make sense of the strange things that had happened. After Madison had gone home, a drinking vessel crafted of a similar red stone had mysteriously appeared where an ordinary water glass had once been. "Something tells me Madi would know how to open this."

Galt sat on the edge of the basin to rest. "Who?"

"My friend, the one who told me to find the letter and bring it back to her."

"Do you think the letter is inside?"

Mila nodded. "I have to go back and see if Madi knows what to do next." Mila looked around the site, her eyes falling on the rubble in the monument basin. "Because I sure don't."

Galt sighed, his head held low. "Neither do I. I promised Aux that I would help you find the letter you seek. I feel I have let you both down."

"Don't worry." Mila patted the strapping Guardsman on the back, smiling. "Somehow everything works out the way it's supposed to." She looked at Galt, gratitude brightening her face. "Thank you for bringing me here, and for helping me and protecting me."

Galt moved from his seat and knelt on one knee before Mila. "It was my honor to take part in such a mission. I hope one day to see Crimson and all of Graha restored, but a Guardsman could ask for no more than to have been a part of the effort. I know my father now looks well upon his son. Thank you, Mila."

Mila smiled and embraced her protector, then took a few steps backward. "Okay, I'm gonna open the doorway. Make sure you don't get too close to it."

Galt stood and took a step back, unsure of how to best prepare himself for what he was about to witness. With a single breath, Mila opened the doorway, and Galt squinted in astonishment at the mystery before him.

"Goodbye, Galt, thanks again."

Mila stepped through the doorway, and Galt held his hand to his eyes to shade them from the flash. Moments later, the girl was gone and it was only Galt and the shattered remains of the monument in the cold and silent courtyard of Vires. Galt went to the ruined statue once more, placing his hand over the pile of rubble in the basin. "Forgive me, Poe. All was done for the good of Graha."

After paying his respects, Galt returned to his kontross. The animal at first snorted and tossed her head in protest, but Galt spoke to her in soothing tones. "Easy, girl, the road is long, but you'll be home soon enough." He patted her massive shoulder and the beast seemed to calm, lowering her head in submission. He mounted once more and turned her head toward Verde, not knowing what he would find upon his return.

Lium Returns

After an arduous journey in the cold and dry of Jonquil, Lium finally landed his sanlifter at the flight yard near the Palace of Gosai. He turned the craft sharply at the end of the landing path and pointed it back into the wind for takeoff. He then went inside the hangar and found another sanlifter, rolling it out and positioning it in the same way. Once his plan had been initiated, a swift escape would be their only hope.

Lium entered the palace and made his way to the royal chamber, where he found Fincher pacing restlessly, his tail of dark hair flicking back and forth behind him as he went.

"Lium!" he barked, walking briskly to the young man. "Under the circumstances, it is very good that you have returned."

"What is it?"

Fincher's face crumpled in disgust. "Queen Zehn has returned to Graha."

Lium's aura flashed bright gold, and his eyes sparked. "Are you certain?"

"I am." Fincher winced. "I heard an unmistakable cry in the distance. She has indeed returned and I suspect she brought the group of resisters with her."

Lium tried to hide his joy at the news, covering his smile with feigned concern. "We cannot allow her to reclaim the throne."

"No," Fincher coughed the word. "She must be removed from the equation. Zehn must die."

Lium gulped, finding it ever more difficult to stuff his feelings. Fincher pointed his gaze at him, narrow eyes shaded with darkness. "And I want the rest of the resistance dead along with her, including the child."

Lium lowered his eyes and nodded, not wishing to give away his compassion toward the girl, who had given him the gift of clarity and a chance at redemption. Fincher went on. "Once these obstacles are removed, I will rule Jonquil for good. The highest position at my right hand will be awarded to you, along with more wealth than you can comprehend. The rewards of serving the Dark One are great, Lium," he said, almost managing a smile.

Fincher's words echoed slightly in Lium's mind. All his life he had struggled to attune to wealth and power, yet now that they were freely offered to him, the idea of accepting them seemed intolerably discordant. The disease that Lium had suffered, the one that had been his father's undoing, had passed, and for perhaps the first time, his heart was illuminated with the light of clarity.

"Ah," Fincher called, suddenly remembering. "The scrappy woman." He turned his slanted eyes upward, searching for the name. "Rosette. She is in the solitary holding chamber of my Mazurin Gon. She nearly escaped once, so I poisoned her with kumain." He nearly sang the word, savoring its sweetness as it crossed his tongue. "She won't be going anywhere, at least, not without the antidote." Fincher opened his coat and withdrew a vial of green fluid, pressing it carefully between his thumb and forefinger. "I have not yet decided if I will give it to her, or watch what unfolds if I do not."

Fincher slipped the vial back into his pocket, Lium's keen eyes watching his every move. "It is most probable that Zehn will come first to the Palace. We must set a trap to hold her and the group until they can be dealt with." Fincher clasped his hands behind his back and strode to the door, cracking it slightly. "Avel!"

Within moments, the door swung open and a young Guardsman appeared. "Yes, Fincher?"

Lium looked past Fincher and made brief eye contact with the Guardsman. He seemed eager to serve, but also reluctant to be in a position that required he serve such a man, a conflict Lium well understood. To him, the young man looked much like his late mentor, Esod, with long dark hair and glinting, slanted eyes. Lium's aura swirled as emotions rose, but he quickly gathered himself as Fincher spoke. "I have received word that enemies approach the Palace. You must set up a trap directly in front of the main entry doors in the grand hall. Make it sufficiently wide to cover the entire area so that if anyone enters, they will surely be caught in it. Do it quickly."

"As you wish, Fincher," Avel replied, hastily making his way down toward the entry hall.

Lium watched the young man leave, knowing what he must be feeling—such desire to serve, yet integrity tugging at him to resist the false ruler of Jonquil. Lium felt his stomach turn. "I will go with him. We need to be prepared in case the intruders have already arrived."

Fincher nodded. "Very well, do so."

Lium saw his opportunity. He bowed to Fincher, a little lower than usual, and flicked his hand, unseen, over one of the blades in his vest. The weapon tumbled out and hit the ground, pinging loudly against the polished floor.

"Oh!" Lium exclaimed, quickly reaching for the blade and pretending to stumble forward as he did. He reached out and caught hold of Fincher's waist and coat hem to steady himself, knowing full well how Fincher despised being touched.

Fincher recoiled, yet simultaneously tried to help Lium up, if for no other reason than to get Lium to stop touching him. Unbeknownst to Fincher, Lium had slipped his fingers into Fincher's waist pouch, undetected. He clasped the vial of antidote deftly between two fingers, reaching clumsily for his blade with the other. As he replaced the blade in its hold, he slyly slipped the vial into his vest pocket. Distracted by the physical contact, Fincher remained unaware that the antidote had been stolen.

"Please forgive my clumsiness, Fincher," Lium said dryly, adjusting his clothing.

Fincher nodded, his aura swirling in agitation. "Do let me know when our guests arrive."

"I will." Lium bowed slightly, then swiftly left the room. With each step, his heart expanded in golden waves so intensely that he feared Fincher would see the changes in his glow. Lium held his breath, stuffing his laughter as he shuffled out of the room.

* * *

Rosette's Dream

Rosette found herself strolling through an endless field of hari blossoms. She checked for her belt and found herself unarmed and dressed in a soft, flowing garment. The fragrance of the blossoms drifted up and around her, so sweet as to be intoxicating, and she felt herself spinning giddily where she stood. She at once realized that she must be in a dream, for no circumstance such as this had ever occurred in her waking life. She remembered then a similar dream, one in which she and Jonas reunited in just such a field of flowers. She felt her heart quicken and she looked around in all directions; could he have somehow called her out of the ethers to meet once more?

She held her hands around her mouth and called into the distance, "Jonas?"

She listened and watched for a few moments, but only the blossoms were there. She blinked and looked to the horizon; had she seen a man's form moving? Just as a hopeful smile began, she felt herself jarred to wakefulness by the sound of a nearby explosion.

Rosette hopped to her feet, waiting out the agonizingly long moments for her eyes to adjust to her surroundings. Soon, she realized the chamber had been blown apart; the door and the entire wall that surrounded it had been torn away by force, and clouds of dust and pulverized rock rose around her. The blast had come from an emanator that the great Prime Warrior Esod had given to his only pupil. As the dust began to settle, Rosette saw the pupil standing before her, golden eyes flashing, a strand of blond hair blowing gently in the breeze.

"Lium!" she growled, every muscle in her body instantly tensing with rage. She lurched at him, fully intent on taking his life with her bare hands, despite the promise she'd made to Jonas so long ago. As she took another step toward her nemesis, her boot slid on a chunk of metal, forcing her to break stride and slow her attack.

"Wait!" Lium called out. "I'm here to help you!"

Regaining her balance, Rosette looked into Lium's eyes and was compelled to take pause; something had changed within him. His eyes were new, freshened somehow, and the veil of secrecy and aloofness he'd always held that bothered her so had been lifted. A genuine glow of light came from his body, untainted by the muddy shades of conflicting thoughts, and all about him flowed an air of purity. Rosette narrowed her eyes. "What have you done?"

It was then that the tears came, not from Rosette after so much suffering and betrayal, but from Lium. His eyes welled with them, a single line of salty regret drifting down the left side of his face. "Rosette, I have betrayed you and many others. I have no right to enjoy any piece of goodness that may come from this resistance, but what I do know is this: I see clearly now, and I know exactly what I must do. Freeing you is only a part of it."

Slowly but surely, the desire to kill Lium left Rosette, and she began to relax. "I've trusted you before and regretted it," she snapped.

"I'm not asking you to trust me." His voice quivered with emotion. "I'm simply setting you free. You can take my life right now if you want, but I beg of you, let me complete my work. Let me set right the wrongs I have done." Lium held out his palm and the vial of antidote he had stolen from Fincher.

"What is that?"

"It's the antidote to the poison that Fincher has given you. I took it from his coat." He stepped closer to Rosette, palm still extended. "Use it and be free."

"Why should I believe you?"

"By all rights you shouldn't, but you don't have a choice."

Rosette glared at the man she'd come to despise, her eyes shooting hot daggers of hatred and pain, yet he did not turn from her gaze. He looked back at her unflinchingly, with a peace in his heart that even Rosette herself had not yet found. It seemed that her medicine would come in more than one dose.

True Allegiance

In the grand entry hall of the Palace, Avel made preparations to create the trap as Fincher had ordered. Though Fincher had not specified, Avel knew full well what kind of trap he had intended to set. Avel possessed the gift of transmuting metals, dematerializing them into any form that he wished, including the deadly quickmetal that dotted the Mazurin Gon. He knew Fincher wanted him to create a quickmetal pit in which the intruders would be hopelessly drawn to their deaths.

Avel stood back several paces from the entry doors and closed his eyes. He breathed deeply for a time, his yellow glow building with his energy. When currents of amber began circling his head, he finally opened his eyes and focused his energy on the Palace floor. Within moments, the floor began to quiver, waves passing over its surface as on a body of water. Avel kept his focus, and soon the area in front of the doors had been transformed into a deep pit of quickmetal that, unless disturbed, remained almost undetectable to the eye. Satisfied with his work, Avel took up a position nearby and hid himself, waiting to pounce on any intruders who tried to escape the deadly pit.

Avel finally heard the voices of people approaching. His back stiffened and the hairs on his nape stood on end; would today see his first battle? Avel palmed his sword, readying himself to draw it if so called. As the entry door swung open, the supposed enemies were revealed — an old man, a Verdean man with dark hair, a young Jonquilian girl, and to his utter shock, Queen Zehn herself.

Shame and anger flushed through Avel's heart as he fully realized his own dire contribution to the evil unfolding before him. Fincher, false ruler of Jonquil, had known full well the queen had somehow been rescued and brought back to Graha, and now sought to destroy her for his own benefit. Panic soon displaced the anger and shame, for in moments, the group would step over the threshold and fall to their deaths in the pit he had created. Though only following the orders of the current ruler of his Land, Avel could not stand by and watch the true queen perish. He shot out from his hiding place, his glow blasting outward in bright yellow tones. "No, stop!"

Despite his warning, boots fell on a floor that gave way like liquid, and each of them dropped hopelessly into the pit. Avel rushed forward to where Queen Zehn bobbed, half-surprised, half-enraged. "Take my hand, queen!"

The young Guardsman held out his hand until Zehn found it, hauling her up and out of the quickmetal.

"Help!" a frail voice called.

Avel whipped his head round and saw the old man sinking. He would need to act quickly. Avel launched his body sideways and grasped the white hair at the back of Thornhill's head, tugging him to the side of the pit and lifting him out.

"Thank you, good man," Thornhill said breathlessly. "There are others...two others."

"I'm out. Help Botan!" Pixie called, having already teleported out to safety.

Avel turned from the girl and looked to see Botan swimming with all his might toward the side, yet sinking with each stroke. Avel cantilevered his body out over the pit, his core muscles straining, arms extended toward Botan. "Reach, I've almost got you!" Avel shouted, encouraging the man to keep fighting.

With a final heave, Botan lifted his arm up and out of the pit and took hold of Avel's hand. Avel quickly pulled him out to safety.

Having rescued his alleged enemies, Avel fell to his knees before the queen. "Please forgive me. I didn't know it was you!"

Thornhill stood unsteadily. "Young man, you have just saved our lives. You have done nothing for which to seek forgiveness!"

Avel shook his head. "You don't understand," he panted, swallowing hard. "The quickmetal pit—I created it. Fincher told me enemies were coming and to set a trap. So I just did as I was told because it was all I knew how to do." Avel looked up at the queen and spoke with resolve. "I know better now."

At once, the group heard an ominous crack, like a great seal releasing, and a humming sound coming from above. They looked up and saw that the crystal dome of the palace was opening.

From the window of the royal chamber, Fincher had seen the sanlifter circling the Palace and had decided to add his own twist to the trap that Avel had set. He'd scuttled down to the control box that opened the dome and now watched for the creature he suspected would soon arrive to investigate. The noise, the smell of flesh, the scent of fear—all were irresistible to it, and Fincher knew full well it would come. After initiating the opening sequence, Fincher left the control box and took up a hiding place across the hall where he could watch the fate of the group unfold.

Crystal shattered violently and fell like piercing rain as a giant raiku crashed through the narrow opening in the dome before it had fully opened. The creature landed heavily, cracking the floor and sending a cloud of pulverized stone and crystal into the air. Having heard the din of the raiku's entry, two Guardsmen came running into the entry hall, weapons drawn. The raiku whipped its head round and instantly snatched up one the Guardsmen, severing the man in two. The animal hungrily gulped down half of the body and then turned its attention to the other Guardsman.

The young man dropped his weapon and bolted for a nearby door, but did not reach the safety of the room beyond. The raiku tore into his flesh, making short work of its second victim. Avel watched in horror as the insatiable beast then locked its eyes on the group and lowered its head, letting out a horrible screech that threatened to shatter any remaining glass in the room.

"Everyone get back, stay along the edges!" Avel shouted, shimmying his body along the wall at the sides of the quickmetal pit, where a narrow edge of solid floor remained.

The group followed suit, carefully inching away from the creature while avoiding falling to certain death in the pit. Thornhill's foot slipped, and the elder man nearly lost his balance, grasping at the smooth wall as if some fingerhold would miraculously make itself known. Botan held his hand up against Thornhill's back to steady him, feeling his breath rasping through his lungs. The raiku stomped forward awkwardly on all fours, growling as it approached. To their dismay, the group soon learned that the length of the creature's head and neck allowed it to stand on the edge of the pit and snap its jaws dangerously close to each one of them. It was only a matter of time before someone was taken.

"Avel, hurry, you must get rid of the quickmetal!" Botan called.

Avel squeezed his eyes shut for an instant, then glanced fearfully at Botan. "I *can't*...I can't change it back!"

Botan's heart sank and he glanced at Thornhill, who wore an equally hopeless expression. All the while, the raiku eagerly clawed and screeched, each snap of its jaws inching ever closer to its prey.

* * *

Maddox Awakes

Mila dropped through the bright opening in the ceiling and landed in a crouched position on the floor of the limo. Madison gasped loudly, not expecting her friend to return so quickly and in that way. "You're back...but you just left?"

"I know." Mila straightened herself and came to sit beside Madison. "The time thing is...weird."

She held out the red stone box she'd taken from the monument in Vires. "But I think I found what you needed."

"A box?" Madison gazed at it, and although she was certain she'd never seen it before, it was somehow familiar to her.

"I think the letter you want might be inside it. We found the box inside a statue of Poe."

Madison took the box from Mila and turned it carefully in her hands. "How do we get it open?"

Mila sighed. "I was hoping you would know."

Madison pulled at the seam where the lid had been secured, but it would not budge. "Maybe we need a key."

Mila's mind suddenly clicked, remembering the time when she and the group were struggling with opening the lid to Salvitor's chamber. They had tried in vain to open it by a number of means, and in the end, she herself had been the key. "Madi, let's try this..."

She turned to her friend, unsure of how to explain what she would need to do. "Just hold the box in your hands, like this, and close your eyes. Just keep taking deep breaths and try to imagine yourself glowing red, really bright."

Madison furrowed her brow. "But I don't want to glow!"

The rise in her emotions triggered that very glow, and crimson light began to emanate from her skin. "Oh no," she whined.

"It's okay, that's good! Just take deep breaths and hold on to the box."

Madison rolled her eyes. "All right, here goes."

With each breath, Madison's glow expanded, its brightness focusing between her hands. Within moments, Madison felt tingling, then a shift beneath her fingers. "I think something just happened," she said, her glow receding. Madison moved her hand and saw that the stone box had been transformed into wood.

"Ah!" she yelped, dropping the box.

As it hit the floor, Mila saw that the lid had come loose. "Madi, I think you did it!"

Madison sat forward. "I did?"

"Yeah, look." Mila reached down and picked up the box, easily sliding off the top. "It's open!"

"Is the letter inside?" Madison peeked inside the box.

Mila smiled as she found the folded piece of silk paper and handed it to Madison. "This has to be it."

Madison carefully unfolded the delicate paper and scanned it. "Somehow I recognize this handwriting," she mumbled. "This must be the one."

"What does it say? Read it!"

Madison cleared her throat. "If you are reading this letter, take heart that you have followed the instructions of your Magister and hope is yet alive. Thus far, your memories have been hidden from you, but you must now read these words and remember the truth. You were sent to the Inner Realm to protect the Sankari Sano from evil forces. Though many have assisted the Guild and risked or even lost their lives, she is the key and must now take her place as the Eleventh Member of the Guild. Keep her close, keep her safe, and help her understand what she must do. Signed, Guild Member Number Three," Madison looked at Mila with eyes wide, "Maddox of Crimson."

She looked back to the letter, observing a mark that had been stamped underneath the signature. "The symbol of the Guild..." Her finger trembled as she traced the outline of the shape. In an instant, a rush of memories then flooded over Madison, nearly taking her breath away. Visions flickered in her mind like pages of a picture book, each a record of a life event.

After the wave passed and the pictures faded from her mind, a bewildered Madison glanced at Mila, then hurriedly removed her shoe, peering at the bottom of her foot as if expecting to find something. She ran her hand over her sole, yet her foot remained as it always had been.

Mila shook her head in concern. "Madi, what are you doing with your foot?"

Before their eyes, an area of shading then began to grow on the bottom of Madison's foot. In a matter of moments, a clear outline of the symbol of eleven appeared on her sole.

"Oh my gosh, Mila, look!"

Mila moved in for a closer look. "I know that symbol. I've seen it before." Mila thought of her adoption letter, the table in Sukai, and all of the other occasions on which she had seen the curious symbol of eleven. The strange connections linked up in a tangled web of coincidence and relativity, tying her world together with one beyond a bright doorway and fusing an ever-stronger bond between the two girls.

Madison replaced her shoe and paused, blinking at the curious sensations sweeping over her. With the influx of memories, the fog in her mind began to lift and pieces of the puzzle that had long vexed and confused her fell into place. Suddenly, Madison began to laugh.

Mila cocked her head. "Madi, are you okay?"

Madison nodded. "I'm better than okay, I'm feeling..."

"What?"

"Peaceful." she turned to Mila, her red glow pulsing gently. "Peace comes with knowing."

"What are you talking about, Madi?" Mila leaned closer to her friend's face. "What does all this mean?"

Madison smiled, holding her hands out to Mila, one palm up and the other down. "Let me show you."

Mila then placed her palms over Madison's just so, as she had done a number of times with Thornhill and others, and at once was swept into the memories of Maddox of Crimson.

Years ago, the Great Magister of Crimson sent his student Maddox to find and protect the Sankari Sano in the Inner Realm. With the last Lapisian member of the resistance murdered and Salvitor of Jonquil missing, she represented the last spark of the resistance and hope for Graha.

The Great Magister had used his gift to create a kind of spell that allowed Maddox to come to the Inner Realm and live out an entire lifetime, a feat otherwise impossible for people of Graha. Maddox had willingly accepted her task knowing full well if she crossed back to the Outer Realm she would be destroyed, the particles of her existence flung to the far reaches of the universe. Once she stepped over that threshold of light, she could never return.

* * *

Startled at the realization of her friend's identity and her sacrifice, Mila pulled her hands away from Madison's. She sat silent for a moment, staring at her best friend and now, apparently, her guardian. "You came here just to help protect me? Like when those wolves attacked us in the woods?"

Madison nodded slowly, her eyes flashing as she remembered the beasts.

Mila furrowed her brow. "And you can never go back? But I can go back and forth whenever I want—"

"You're special, Mila," Madison interrupted. "No one else can do what you can."

Mila sat back in her chair. "But..."

Just then, Joe returned from inside the gas station with an armful of snacks. Mila watched as he wrestled with his keys and tried to open the door without dropping anything. Once inside, he opened the partition, handing a few bags of chips to the girls. "Ladies, I got you some chips. I only have sweet treats in that snack bowl back there so I thought you might want something salty, too."

Mila smiled, hopping forward to claim the chips. "Thanks, Joe!"

"All right, let's get back on the road and get you home. Won't be long now."

The partition then slid back into place, and Mila turned and looked back at Madison, who sat near the back of the limo. She seemed so far away, yet at once she felt closer to her than she ever had before.

* * *

Resolution

As Fincher watched the raiku snapping ferociously at the trapped group, he looked closer, frowning when he realized Lium was not among them. Had he moved off to some other area of the palace?

The raiku let out an ear-shattering shriek, distracting Fincher from his thoughts. The beast lunged at Pixie, jaws wide open and tongue lashing, but just as the creature went to snap its jaws closed, the body of its victim seemed to disappear.

Pixie had teleported behind the beast and now crouched near its tail, hoping to remain undetected. The frustrated animal called out and dove for Thornhill, extending its neck over the pit. Before it could seize the helpless old man, Avel drew his sword and in a single swift motion, threw it at the beast.

The blade pierced through one eye and went right out through the other, killing the raiku instantly. It splashed headfirst into the pool of quickmetal, a trail of bubbles marking its descent. The surface of the pool shimmered slightly, then returned to stillness, a silent and fathomless grave.

Fincher stumbled out from his hiding place, shaking with rage. His carefully calculated trap had been spoiled and his raiku defeated. He looked down the hall and saw yet another variable he had not expected: Rosette had been freed and now entered the room, fully equipped with all her weapons.

"Impossible!" Fincher gasped, his mind whirling with factors and probabilities. How could the woman have escaped a second time without alerting his guards, and furthermore, why would she do so, knowing she would be doomed to a life of weakness and misery without the antidote?

"The *antidote*," Fincher whispered, frantically checking his coat, only then realizing that the precious vial had been stolen.

As if on cue, Lium arrived on the scene, standing calmly next to Rosette, making no attempt to capture her. In fact, Fincher realized, he seemed to be *assisting* her.

"Traitor!" Fincher screamed. "You will pay for this!"

"Don't look his way!" Rosette warned. "He can blind you

with his hands."

Hopelessly outnumbered and somehow outsmarted, Fincher fully realized his dilemma. With the formidable Rosette and an angry Queen Zehn standing against him in the same space, he had little chance for victory. Fearing for his life, Fincher fled toward the royal chamber. Lium took a few steps after him, then stopped and called for the others in the group to wait as well. He reached into his vest pocket and withdrew a black, puck-shaped object, cradling it briefly in his palm before looking back up to the group. "You must get as far away from the Palace as you can. Find the two sanlifters I've made ready in the flight yard. You have only minutes, go now!"

Lium gripped the puck tightly in his fist and took off to pursue Fincher. Thornhill, having spied what Lium held in his palm, spoke quickly. "I know what he's going to do...to the flight yard, quickly!"

The group carefully picked their way back along the edges of the quickmetal pit and then out the front door. Grateful for solid ground underfoot, they sped toward the flight yard as fast as their feet would carry them. Just ahead, they could see the two sanlifters that Lium had mentioned, perfectly positioned for takeoff. Breathless and nearly out of time, they scrambled into their seats and Botan and Avel quickly prepared their craft.

"Pedal as fast as you can!" Thornhill shouted across the runway.

As the pilots pedaled, their sanlifters seemed to creep down the runway in slow motion. Though valiant, Thornhill soon realized their efforts would not be enough; they were not going to make it into the air in time. "Faster, we must hurry!"

Queen Zehn, though unaware of the reason, tuned into the urgency of the moment. "I can help. Everyone hold on tight!"

Though not yet fully restored in her power, Zehn quickly built what energy she had, her aura expanding in a brilliant orb that encompassed the whole of the sanlifter. The margins of her glow scintillated with golden rays, like a noon sun, and suddenly a sonic wave burst from her body, rushing toward the hangar, bouncing off the wide doors and then racing back toward the creeping sanlifters. As the wave hit, the crafts were lofted instantly into the air, and took off at a speed that never would have been attained using only the onboard power.

"Ha!" Botan laughed, hoisting his fist into the air as his craft sped forward ever faster.

Satisfied with the takeoff, Queen Zehn turned round in her seat, curious as to the fate of her home; what had been the reason for all the rushing?

In the palace, Lium raced to the royal chamber and found the door securely locked. He took a blade, swiftly picked the lock, and opened the door.

As Lium burst into the room, Fincher wheeled round, palms out and eyes glaring, fully intent on blinding the young traitor. Lium did not look his way. Fincher clenched his fists. "I cannot comprehend what has happened here."

"That is because your mind is narrow and dark," Lium shot back.

Fincher boiled inside, yet contained his emotions. "The path of least resistance to obtain the wealth and power you desire was cooperation with Corpus, with me. Tell me, what calculation have you used to arrive at *this* outcome?"

Lium lifted his chin and spoke with resolve. "A true Jonquilian lives authentically in abundance. He does not allow the love of beauty and wealth to become a disease in his heart. The value of my life cannot be counted in silvers. After all," Lium chuckled and held out his palm, cradling a black puck that blinked insistently, "you can't calculate everything."

Fincher's expression tightened, and his eyes grew wide as he recognized the device and his own fate in the same instant. The next moment, the enveloper opened and the unfathomable power of the infinite made itself known.

Just as Lium surrendered to that pull, he thought of his mother, her struggles, her love for integrity, and hoped that by way of his final works, she could look upon him with pride and live out her days in peace.

The enveloper took Fincher, Lium, and most of the Palace of Gosai down into the singularity, the point of infinite density, at its core, leaving only emptiness in its wake.

* * *

A short distance away, two sanlifters circled higher into the endless blue of the Jonquilian sky, their passengers agape at what they had just witnessed. For the good of Jonquil and all of Graha, a traitor had made the highest sacrifice for the resistance. Unaware of the fullness of the drama, Zehn could only gaze upon the nothingness below. Where once had been her opulent palace, the queen now circled above a black and empty place, and she felt the void within her very heart. She folded her hands over her breast and wept.

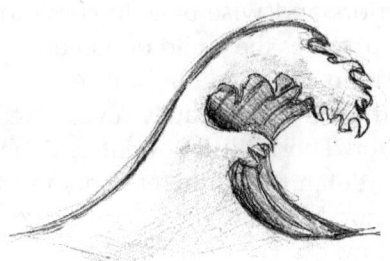

PART 11

THE UNRAVELING

Mila and Madison sat in the back of the limousine, eating the potato chips that Joe had given them, discussing the evermore complicated situation in which they found themselves. A distracted Madison finished her bag and mindlessly opened another.

"Ew," Mila groaned. "You like sour cream and cheddar?" She wrinkled her nose. "Those always smell like feet to me."

Madison paused, lifted a finger coated with orange dust to her nose, and giggled. "No, they don't!"

Mila laughed and pointed at some of the dust stuck to her friend. "It's on your nose!" She sighed, growing somber. "Madi, I wish you could have been with me through all of this from the very beginning, when I first started to glow."

Madison blinked thoughtfully, brushing the orange coating from her nose. "But I have been."

"What do you mean?"

Madison sat forward, for a moment forgetting her snack. "Mila, this thing started long before your glow. It started before you were even born, way back when the prophecy was discovered by my teacher, the Great Magister of Crimson."

Mila focused on her friend, listening intently.

"He told lots of people about the prophecy, but he chose just a few special warriors and wise ones to come together and save Graha. We called ourselves the Guild of Eleven."

"Who's we? I mean, who's in the Guild?"

Madison breathed in deliberately, eyes fixed on Mila. "My Magister the Creator, Thornhill the Mentor, Bobbin the Collector, Salvitor the Guide, Botan the Gatherer, Finn and Cira the Decoys, Maddox the Protector, Meadow the Informer, Poe the Defender… and you, Mila the Key."

Mila whistled. "How did you just remember all that?"

"I'm not sure." Madison blinked. "It feels like I've known it forever."

"Madi…" Mila struggled for words. "You seem different somehow, like…older, or smarter!"

Madison laughed aloud. "I think it's because I'm remembering everything that I knew when I was Maddox. It's like having a little adult inside me."

A worried expression washed over Mila's face, and her aura flickered slightly. "But are you still Madi, my best friend?"

Madison playfully shoved a chip in her mouth and crossed her eyes. "Duh!"

Mila laughed in relief, turning to place the empty chip bags in the canister beside the drink cabinet. Madison cleared her throat. "Mila, how many people do you know in Graha? I want to know who is still alive."

Mila nodded. "I know Thornhill, Aux, Botan, Meadow, and Pixie are still alive. I've talked to them recently."

Madison smiled. "I'm glad they're alive. Once I saw the memories you showed me, I was afraid that everyone would be dead. Do you know if the Great Magister of Crimson is still alive?

"What's his name?"

"Hmm," Madison paused, suddenly lost in thought. "I wonder what will happen if I say his name *here*…"

"Wait a minute." Mila cocked her head, searching her memory. "Is this the same guy Pixie was talking about, that if you say his name he gets in your head and makes you go crazy?"

Madison smiled. "I guess that could happen, but he was my Magister, and I said his name a thousand times before. If your mind is strong, you should be safe. After all," she looked around the cabin, as if checking for some hidden eavesdropper, "we're not even in the same world."

"So, you can tell me his name?" Mila asked expectantly.

Madison scooted close and lowered her voice. "His name is Otnas, Great Magister of Crimson."

"Otnas?" Mila held her breath, her eyes darting around the cabin, ears straining to pick up any new voices within that did not belong. After a few uneventful moments, she let go of her breath. "Well, I feel normal." She peered at Madison. "Are you normal?"

"Probably not," Madison laughed, playfully jabbing her friend's arm. Her expression suddenly shifted. "I hope Otnas is still alive. I remember that I was always able to hear his voice in my head whenever I said his name. It feels kind of lonely not to hear it."

Mila pushed a stray piece of dark hair behind her ears. "So, why did you guys start the Guild?"

Madison licked the remaining dusty orange residue from her fingertips, then crumpled the empty chip bag in her hands. "To find the eleventh member so they could help us bring back the kings and queens and save Graha." She tossed the empty bag into the canister beside the cabinet. "We had a meeting and we decided what each member's job was. After that, we weren't allowed to say anything about the Guild or what we had to do. It was all in secret."

Mila shook her head. "This is so big, and I don't even know exactly what I'm supposed to do." Mila blinked at her friend. "It all seems like a really long dream."

Madison smiled. Mila stared at her, lost in thought, not realizing her gaze had become so intensely fixed.

"Hello, Mila?" Madison waved her hand before her friend's face.

Mila blinked. "Madi, it seems like you know a lot of things." She clasped her hands together, leaned forward, and rested her elbows on her knees. "Tell me...do you know who my birth parents are?"

Madison's eyes softened. "No, I'm sorry. Bobbin would be the one to ask, she was the most gifted seer, other than Helena... *Helena!*" Madison suddenly jumped up in her seat. "Yes, you need to find Queen Helena, she would know."

"Helena knows who my parents are?" Mila's voice rose with excitement. "Where is she?"

Madison held her hands out, as to calm Mila. "She *might* know, but I don't know where she is, and on top of that, we don't have time to talk about all this right now. You have to go back."

"Go back? But I just got here—"

"I know, I know," Madison interrupted. "But I know now that time is running out, and you have to go back and keep going with the mission."

"I'm not sure where to go next." Mila tapped her fingers together. "I guess I can go back to Jonquil and find Thornhill and Pixie and everyone."

Madison nodded. "At least they can help you decide what to do."

"Okay, then that's what I'll do," Mila said, briefly glancing around before finding her pack nearby. She reached into the snack bowl and took a handful of candy bars. "For the road," she said, smiling.

Madison giggled, handing Mila the last bag of chips. "Here, take these, too. Don't worry, they're barbeque, not cheddar and sour cream."

Mila smiled, gesturing toward the floor. "Watch your feet, Madi."

Madison quickly drew her legs up onto her seat, clasping her knees tightly. "Okay, go ahead."

"See you soon," Mila said. A breath later, she opened the doorway on the floor of the limo. In a flash, she tumbled through to the other side, leaving Madison to wait for her, crystallized in a moment, not knowing that as they had shared knowledge with each other, the Dark One learned of those things as well.

The Dark One Appears

Two sanlifters touched down in a flight yard outside the town of Aksini, their passengers still reeling after witnessing the destruction of the Palace of Gosai. The two craft came to a stop and Queen Zehn rose from her seat, wiping the last of the tears from her eyes as she stepped out of the sanlifter. Thornhill went to her, placing his arm around her shoulders in comfort, and the others soon gathered closely around them.

"Are you hurt, Zehn?" Thornhill asked.

Zehn shook her head. "The jewel of Delora, the Gamchok dagger of Crimson, and countless silks and treasures crafted by the finest artisans in Jonquil. All these and more...lost." She turned her face into the west, gazing at the suns that moved ever downward in the Jonquilian sky. "And yet, those are only things." She looked at Thornhill and smiled hopefully. "I am most grateful for my life, my Land, and this chance to heal."

Thornhill bowed slightly, then turned from the queen to address the gathered. "We have now brought back two Founders, and soon, two Lands will be restored to their full strength and glory. The resistance is gaining momentum."

Botan nodded. "Yes, despite what we have seen, and what has been lost, Lium's sacrifice has allowed us to move forward unimpeded by Fincher and Corpus' influence. Jonquil will shine again."

"Redemption comes at a price," Thornhill said, looking toward the remains of the royal island where the Palace once stood. "Yet its worth cannot be measured. I, too, am grateful."

"I feel that we Verdeans must now return home and advise Jonas of Zehn's return. He will be pleased for a bit of good news."

Rosette's aura pulsed, and a tinge of rose red flushed its edges at the prospect of a possible reunion with Jonas. Lium had given her the antidote to the poison that would have kept her from Jonas forever, and gratitude and sadness at once filled her heart, startling her. Though full of emotion, she remained silent.

"Agreed, though..." Thornhill thumbed his beard, "...we don't have much in the way of supplies or food, and the Verdean border is a long journey from here."

"I can help you reach Verde in less than half the time," Zehn said. Both men turned to her.

"I can send a sonic accelerator behind you that will push your sanlifters at high speed, just like I did outside the palace."

"Ah," Thornhill sighed. "That would help us greatly, my lady."

Zehn turned to the young Guardsman, his body held taut as if awaiting orders. "Avel, I want you to help them navigate through Jonquil. It is important they reach Jonas with counsel as soon as possible."

The young man nodded, his black hair shifting behind his shoulders. "At your service, Queen Zehn."

Pixie stepped forward, her head held low. "Um, Queen Zehn?" She hesitated, uncertain of her level of importance in the mission. "Where do I belong?"

Zehn blinked her slanted eyes thoughtfully. "You will come with me to the remains of the Palace. I will need your help inspecting what is left and beginning the restoration of my Land."

Pixie's expression lifted, and a smile lit up her young face. "Thank you, Zehn. I would be honored to help."

"Then it appears all is settled," Thornhill said, smiling. "Let's get the sanlifters prepared for flight."

The Verdeans and Avel pointed the sanlifters for takeoff, leaving Pixie and the queen behind at the head of the runway. As the craft crept forward and finally took to the air, Pixie watched in wonder as Zehn's aura began to grow, intense rays of gold shimmering all about her. The queen breathed deliberately in and out, eyes shut, black hair rising slightly as if influenced by static electricity. Zehn opened her eyes, and as she exhaled, a wave of energy burst from her body, undulating down the runway toward the sanlifters. As the wave arrived at the stern of the craft, they were lofted and accelerated at high speed, surfing the energy wave like ships taken by a powerful current. Zehn let out another breath, her aura settling somewhat from its former excited state.

Pixie nodded in admiration. "*Nice.*"

Zehn tilted her head and took the young girl's hand in her own. "Hold tight, Pixie. I won't go at full speed, but it will still be faster than you've ever gone before."

Before Pixie could ask for an explanation, the queen's aura burst into brilliance once more, and her body lifted from the ground, bringing Pixie along. Startled, Pixie kicked her feet and squirmed, but Zehn held fast, waiting for the girl to realize she could float effortlessly next to her within the field of quiet energy she'd created. Pixie soon calmed herself and held her body still, watching as the ground fell away beneath them.

Zehn turned to her. "Are you ready?"

"Yes?"

Zehn smiled, and in the next instant, their bodies tore through the air, pushed along by a wave similar to the one Zehn had created for the sanlifters. The two hurtled over the edge of Aksini toward the royal island to the south, a roaring wake forming behind them. Though Pixie felt herself moving at breakneck speed, she encountered little air resistance within the pocket Zehn had created around them. She cracked one eye open and then the other, and got a breathtaking view of Jonquil. The shimmering sands raced by below, the passing crests of dunes marking off their progress. Upon arrival at Gosai, Zehn shot straight up, parting the clouds and racing into the crystal blue, twirling dizzying simply for the sheer joy of flying. Just as Pixie began to feel disoriented, the queen ceased her spiraling and slowed, floating gently downward to make landfall once more.

As their feet touched, Zehn's aura settled and she released Pixie's hand, which had turned white with shock during the trip. Pixie looked up at her queen with sparkling eyes. "Double nice!"

Zehn laughed aloud, patted the young girl on the shoulder, and then turned toward the ruins of her Palace. They had much work to do.

Far away, over Utara territory near the Verdean border, the sanlifters came into heavy cloud cover. The winds of Tenpi proved more treacherous than usual, and seemed to reach upward into the highest elevations, making flight dangerous at even high altitude. The winds were so disruptive that the craft broke away from their link with the accelerator wave Zehn had created. The travelers found themselves slowing, buffeted by the violent air currents coming up from below.

Avel grappled with the yoke of his craft, fighting to keep level flight, finally realizing his efforts were futile. They needed to land. He turned and signaled Botan, indicating they should touch down at the edge of Utara and wait for the unusual winds to pass. The sanlifters soon dipped downward below the thick clouds, skimming dangerously close to the disc of Utara in search of a landing place with some visibility. With a timely stroke of good fortune, the pilots soon found a clearing and landed on a stretch of empty sand near the edge of Utara. The crafts bumped awkwardly to a stop, their tired passengers jarred by the rough landing. They all paused for a moment, enjoying the moment of stillness, then disembarked.

Thornhill placed his hands on his lower back and turned to Botan. "What a landing."

Botan groaned, stretching the stiffness from his own back. "Your pilot apologizes profusely for the rough flight."

Rosette smiled faintly, and Thornhill chuckled. "I wonder what could be causing such a turn in the weather?"

"It is unusual for the clouds to hang at such high elevation." Botan steadied himself against a sudden gust. "And for the winds to be this strong."

A bright flash of light nearby cut through the fog, and each of the travelers turned toward it in curiosity. A young, dark-haired girl appeared where the flash had been, taking a few halting steps forward as she regained her balance.

"Mila!" Thornhill called, walking quickly toward her.

Mila waved and jogged to the old man, pressing her face into his long white beard as she embraced him. "Hi Thornhill. I'm glad all of you guys are here." She looked around at the faces of each member of the group. "Did you go to the palace to find Pixie and Zehn yet?"

Botan cleared his throat. "Mila, the palace is, well…it's gone."

"Gone?"

"In the end, Lium decided to help us. He used an enveloper to kill Fincher and it took nearly the entire palace." Botan lowered his voice. "And his own life, as well."

Mila frowned. "Lium's dead?" Her voice quivered; despite his betrayal, she found it hard to bear the thought of his passing. "And Zehn's home is just gone?"

Thornhill placed a hand on her shoulder. "Do not despair, Mila. The palace can be rebuilt, in the same way that Zehn first created it and the whole of Jonquil." Thornhill lifted her chin with a finger. "She needs only time to set things right."

Mila smiled, somewhat soothed, followed Thornhill as he gestured for her and the others to sit on a group of boulders nearby for rest.

"Tell me, child, why did you stay behind and not come back with Pixie after you found Zehn in your world?" Thornhill asked.

"Well, I had a feeling that I should stay, and you always tell me to pay attention to feelings like that." She glanced at her elderly mentor, who nodded approvingly. "It turns out my friend Madi started remembering things about when she used to live here, when her name was Maddox."

Thornhill coughed. "A friend of yours from the Inner Realm *remembers* a time when she lived as Maddox," he leaned toward Mila, "of Crimson?"

Mila nodded. "She thinks it was a long time ago, and she remembered she wrote this letter to help herself remember important things, because she would forget everything once she came to my world."

"Could it be?" Botan whispered.

Thornhill huffed, nodding rapidly. "How, I do not know, but it seems that one other has escaped to the Inner Realm!" He took her hand and patted it excitedly. "Mila, do go on."

Mila straightened up. "She told me I had to hurry and find the letter, so I went to Crimson and asked Aux to help me find it."

"My stars, *Crimson*?" Thornhill gasped. "Thank goodness you are safe now."

Mila shrugged casually. "It was fine. Aux told his soldier Galt to take me and keep me safe while I looked for the letter."

Thornhill exhaled, his body slumping slightly. "Did you find this letter you sought?"

"Yes, and I went back and gave it to my friend and when she read it, she remembered all of these things from her life here. She said she was a part of a Guild of Eleven, with you and Botan."

Thornhill's brows leapt upward in shock. "How could you know these secret things? Your friend must truly be one of *us*." He glanced at Botan, who cocked his head in response.

Mila continued, "And she said that we need to find Queen Helena next. Thornhill..." Mila paused, unsure if her personal desires carried any weight in this circumstance. "She says that Helena might know who my real parents are." She looked up at him pleadingly. "Can we look for her now, please?"

Thornhill's eyes softened, and he put his arm around the child's shoulder. "Yes, Mila; in fact, we have no other choice. The sea must be reclaimed first if we are to have any hope of restoring Crimson in the future."

"Yes, we will need every advantage to fight Corpus in that harsh and unforgiving place," Botan added.

A wide smile began to bloom on Mila's face, but quickly faded as she caught sight of something ominous; not far off, the dark shadow form of a man loomed out of the fog. "Who is that?" she asked, pointing.

The others turned to where she pointed and saw the form, which was now almost upon them. At first, they surrounded Mila to protect her, but something compelled the girl to step beyond that protective barrier. The shadow being came face to face with Mila, mere feet away, and she knew at once that it was Corpus.

The black maelstroms in his eyes swirled as he looked upon the child, the healer, the one who had somehow evaded him at every turn. Corpus hissed as he spoke. "Child, how is it that you cross from this realm to the next without being destroyed?" He leaned down toward Mila. "Tell me now and I will do you no harm."

Mila did not answer, but felt her glow pulse strongly in response, increasing to nearly the same size as that of the kings and queens. Corpus seemed greatly affected by the change and backed away from her a few paces, growling. "No matter. I will know soon enough. I have many ways to manipulate and overpower those who would stand against me, just as I used my servant Lium to capture Rosette as a diversion to divide your group between Verde and Jonquil."

Botan glanced at Thornhill, both men only then realizing they'd left many people vulnerable while rescuing Rosette. Rosette listened to the Dark One's words, her jaw tight with rage, her mind churning with visions of finally destroying the being that had taken Briar, her finest warrior, and cast out King Jonas, her love. Flashes of hot red tore through her aura as she glared at her enemy, thumbing her emanator, awaiting the perfect moment.

"You care too much for others," Corpus chided coldly. "You should have let the woman perish and turned your focus to Verde, but your caring made you weak."

Botan stepped forward. "We believe that compassion is a tonic and love makes us strong. You will not succeed, Corpus."

Corpus laughed. "I have already succeeded, foolish ones. Even as we speak, my Lapisian forces are destroying Verde."

The Dark One then lifted his arms, swirling them rapidly at his sides. As he did, powerful air currents jetted from his form and the cloud cover began clearing rapidly, revealing the cliffs of Sukai below and the Verdean border just beyond. In place of the familiar desert landscape and barren cliffs, a great waterfall now tumbled over the cliffs of Sukai, churning the sands of Tenpi below into a violent sea. Mist and turbulent air rose from the site and shot high into the air, contributing to the unusual weather patterns they had encountered. All across the horizon, water fell over the cliffs in such volume that only one conclusion could be drawn: Corpus had somehow moved the waters of Lapis and flooded the whole of Verde.

Botan's aura flashed, and he shot a panicked glance at Thornhill, who stood like stone, mouth hanging open.

"Using Lapis to crush the central heart of Graha, I cut off all paths to other Lands and gained control over the two largest populations of Graha," Corpus growled, his black eyes fixed on Mila. "You will not unify, and you will never defeat me."

As Corpus spoke, Mila's glow began pulsing once more. As they stood before one another, a powerful feedback loop formed between their two energies, crackling around the area like static. Corpus began moving toward Mila and as he did, an orb of white light discharged from Mila's aura and burst in front of Corpus, splintering into a thousand fingers of lightning that fanned in all directions before him.

Her light seemed to pull at him, but he quickly withdrew, his energy contracting as, for the first time in his existence, he experienced a feeling of vulnerability. Corpus howled angrily as he fled, his form dissolving into the dark clouds above that then moved off to the north. Though shaken, exhilaration raced through him at the prospect of learning to use the child's power to his advantage, just as he had used the Prime Advisor of Jonquil so long ago. For in the days before the kingdoms fell, Salvitor, Prime Advisor to the Queen of Jonquil, unknowingly betrayed the throne to which he had pledged his allegiance.

Overwhelmed

When Corpus first became aware of his own existence, his natural desire for expansion also came forth, as it does in all conscious beings. As his awareness grew, he learned of the doorways and sensed their power, but could not find a way to manipulate them to his advantage. He sought other ways to gain control and influence in Graha, creeping about the Lands in ethereal form, haunting the halls of weak and idle minds. Held in check by the light of the Founders, Corpus could only pick away at the underbelly of society, causing brief periods of discord that would eventually resolve, the chaos each time returning to order. He would then resurface, stirring up hate, greed, and jealousy, preying on the darkest emotions of the people of the Land, turning their faces from the light, causing them to forget love and brotherhood.

With calculating collusion and methodical persistence, Corpus eventually began to gain ground, and the evil force grew stronger. In certain places and times, shadows blocked out any semblance of light, and the people lapsed into the madness of fear, dogged by phantoms of their own making, unaware that a single choice would bring them back to wholeness. They began to forget themselves and doubt their strength, and as they did, Corpus drew even more power from their delusion.

Yet despite his successes, he could not sway the opinions of all the masses, and he could never reach the Founders, assured in their positions as creators. Corpus was left to slink about in dark places, recoiling from illumination.

But before Graha could return to order, the pinnacle of chaos would be reached. Corpus abandoned his attempts to corrupt the Founders directly and instead turned to those closest to them, their advisors and trusted ones, to carry out his machinations. He learned of Salvitor of Jonquil, Prime Advisor to Queen Zehn, and began spying on his movements and studies. He observed Salvitor's fascination with the doorways and his travels from Graha to the Inner Realm. Corpus learned that the doorways opened at 11:11 in random places throughout Graha, and anyone who passed through them without proper protections would be lost in that other realm, forgetting their identity and assuming another, or simply being annihilated in the process of crossing.

Through Salvitor, he also learned that the doorways could be manipulated, opened and closed at will, and could be used to travel back and forth between realms, for those with the knowledge to do so safely. Somehow the brilliant Salvitor had devised a way to come and go between realms unharmed, with his memory and identity intact, and Corpus followed Salvitor's studies closely, coveting the knowledge and abilities the old man had gained. He knew that if he could somehow cast the Founders into the Inner Realm, they would not even know they had been displaced, they would forget their divinity, thinking themselves mere ordinary citizens of a foreign realm. They would live out many lifetimes oblivious to the secret in their hearts.

Corpus could then rule over all of Graha unopposed, as the strength would quickly drain from the Lands without the presence of the Founders.

Though Salvitor at first continued his work, unaware of Corpus' activities, he eventually became aware that through his studies and travels, he had inadvertently placed a tool of destruction in evil hands. In the days following this realization, Salvitor grew ever more despondent and obsessed, guilt gnawing at the hollows of his old bones. No matter what he accomplished, what mysteries he unraveled, or what discoveries he made, no advancement could shed enough light to eliminate the shadow that stalked him — that he himself had made a way for Corpus to cast out the Founders of Graha.

Metastasis

As Corpus retreated, shaken by his encounter with Mila, the child herself became dizzy, her knees wobbling as she teetered on the verge of collapse. Though Rosette sprang forward and reached for her, she could not catch hold of her in time, and Mila fell to the ground near the boulders upon which they had been sitting.

As she fell, her wrist smacked against a jagged stone, shattering the face of the watch, sending shards of glass and bits of metal falling to the ground. Without this device, time in her world would march on in her absence, and every minute spent on the other side of the doorway put her at risk of being discovered.

Unaware of this temporal dilemma, Rosette crouched at Mila's side, cradling the girl's head. She noticed the wound that now stained her fingers red. "She's hurt." She looked up at Thornhill. "We need to get something for the bleeding."

Thornhill knelt beside them, taking a strip of cloth from his pocket. "Use this for now. We'll need to find some styptic herbs."

"I have some darah in my pouch." Avel took out a rolled cloth sack from his jacket, untying it and offering it to Thornhill. "Only a pinch, but it may be just enough."

"Thank you, Avel." The old man eagerly took the dried leaves and rubbed them in his palm until powdered, then dabbed it onto Mila's wound. "She's had quite a bump on the head, but I think

Corpus may have drained her strength as well. We need to get her someplace safe." He squinted as a gust of wind blew strands of white hair into his face. "She cannot go into Verde with us."

"I can take her back to Zehn. She will be safe, and the queen can help her heal," Avel said.

Thornhill considered. "But such a long journey with no supplies or rest—"

"We can stop for rest and supplies in my home of Fuzei," Avel interrupted. "I have friends and family there that will help us."

Thornhill nodded. "Yes, good. Go quickly now and spread word of the trouble in Verde to any you meet. If what we have seen is any indication of Corpus' plan, Jonas will need all the help he can get."

"I understand. Help me get her into the sanlifter. We will leave immediately."

Botan and Avel lifted the unconscious Mila into the sanlifter, carefully propping her up so she would be safe. Avel prepared the craft for takeoff and soon took to the air, battling the winds as he climbed ever higher above Utara. Soon the craft rose above the treacherous currents, and Avel and his precious cargo headed for Fuzei.

Thornhill, Rosette, and Botan prepared their own craft for the journey into Verde. Though the winds still swirled, their intensity had somewhat lessened, and the group decided to take advantage of the opportunity. Jonas and his Verde were in dire need of their help, and not a moment could be spared to wait for fairer weather. The three soon took off from the edge of Utara, passing in and out of ethereal columns of vapor as they went.

The diving sanlifter rode the wild turbulence beneath the clouds and finally broke through, finding calmer conditions in the higher elevation. Botan turned round and called to his passengers, "It's much quieter up here. I think we should make it over the border safely, so sit tight."

As Utara disappeared behind them, Botan spotted a great shadow looming in the clouds. The dark form crested with white rose above the cloud bank, moving slowly westward. Botan blinked, not believing what he saw. He leaned over the yoke and pointed out the window. "What is *that*?"

Thornhill gasped. "My stars..."

Through a break in the clouds the Verdeans then clearly saw that the shadow was the crest of an enormous wave, a veritable wall of water that had been lifted from the seas of Lapis and drawn over the eastern shore of Verde. Corpus had not chosen to simply flood Verde; it seemed he sought to wipe it from the very face of Graha.

Botan's hands tightened on the yoke. "Hold on!"

The pilot banked hard to port in a desperate attempt to circle back and retreat from the great wave. The craft dipped violently, tossed by unnatural winds, rapidly losing precious altitude. The flooded sands of Tenpi waited below, churning angrily under the influence of the dark waters that flowed. Botan watched as the sands drew ever closer, the craft now spiraling downward, out of his control. "We're going to crash!" he shouted.

The sanlifter pirouetted ever downward in a dizzying dance, tilting and turning in the air and then finally diving below the surface of the churning waters below. What had once been bone-dry desert swallowed the sanlifter and its occupants in a watery embrace. It seemed that all had been lost.

The great wave moved westward across the Land of Verde, leaving death in its wake. Though Verdean and Crimsonite Guardsmen fought bravely, valor would be no match for evil this day. Despite his great gifts, King Jonas could not stop the destruction. He had no influence over the waters of Lapis, or the evil that now tainted them. Only Queen Helena of Lapis herself had the power to stop Micca and his army from extending Corpus' reach once more into Verde, and she, like the other Founders, had been cast into the Inner Realm, yet to be found.

The wall of water soon broke and curled over, falling steadily forward and finally crashing to the ground near the Jala Swamplands. Sprays of white shot high into the air and foam engulfed all that lay before the wave, pounding the flesh of the land until it surrendered itself to the flow. Crops and wild meadows turned to black lakes, and the forests trembled. While some of the grandest trees held fast, the lesser ones toppled, their shallow roots unable to grip the saturated soil. Swollen rivers were soon choked with their bodies, crashing downstream in mighty currents, scouring chunks of rock and mud from the banks.

Villages and towns all across Verde yielded to dark water. Houses were swept from their foundations and families left clinging to floating debris. In peaceful times, the low position of the Verdean valley had been an advantage; many rivers, fertile soil, and fair winds had long graced the lovely green Land. Now, the low elevation had become a liability, and ruin poured into the lowlands. The floodwaters spread for hundreds of spatials, threatening man and beast alike, immersing and erasing all that which had been set right by King Jonas upon his return.

The Lapisian army moved along with the deadly waters, conquering as they went, unharmed by the waters.

It seemed the nightmares of the child Root had come to pass. A great blue serpent had indeed risen from the waters to consume the king of Verde, bringing darkness to the Land. Root's warning had come too late.

At the foot of the Samera Kingdom, a single yellow flower floated down the central road in the town of Thatch. The blossom lifted its face toward the castle, which seemed to look upon the flooded town below with great sadness. Its high position left it untouched by the waters, so the castle of Samera stood as a beacon of hope, though King Jonas did not move within her halls. Jonas had been in Cypress, helping the Guardsmen prepare for the coming invasion; did he yet live?

Dark Fathoms

As Verde lay submerged in dark waters, Meadow fought his own sodden battle with the Lapisian seas of the north. Steering his longboat into black and angry swells, he braved the icy depths in search of Cira. Having seen that azure light in the plane of shadows, he'd set out to find her at any cost, perhaps that even of his own life. Meadow sailed on, numb fingers clumsily clamped around the rudder of his modest vessel, shivering uncontrollably. He cringed as another frigid gust blasted over him, catching his hood like a sail and filling it with frosty air. He hunched forward, drawing his hood in close to his face and tying it tightly. Though chilled to the very bone, he was heartened. The high winds could mean only one thing: he had moved into the Ilma Stream and was closing in on his destination.

Seeking escape from the bleak surroundings, Meadow's mind returned to his travels since leaving Queen Zehn and the others in Jonquil. He'd taken his sanlifter over land and sea, finally making a night landing at Kardia, the northernmost Lapisian island large enough to house a flight yard. After landing, he'd entered a building near the hangars for cover. He moved with caution; though the island had long been deserted, danger lurked in every corner of Lapis, regardless of any facade of desolation.

Meadow crept into the building, gently sliding the door shut behind him. Inside, he found a room with a wide wooden table and bench, and a mural of a nautical map of Graha on the wall behind it. Meadow sat down on the bench and settled in, preparing himself to enter the shadow plane. If he were to succeed in his mission, he would need Mimpi's help, and knew of but one way to contact her.

Meadow breathed deeply, his eyes fluttering shut as he fell easily into a well-practiced state of meditation. He felt his consciousness rise high above the building, overlooking the landscape of amorphous shadows below. Within moments, he saw a deep blue glow nearby, shining encouragingly—the remshifter Mimpi. He sent a brief message to her, then pulled his consciousness back to the room, blinking slowly to attune himself once more to wakefulness. Though soothed by what he had seen in the shadow plane, Meadow fought the urge to relax; this was no place to become too comfortable.

Suddenly, Meadow drew a breath and held it, whipping his head round in alarm. He heard footsteps in the adjacent room. Meadow stood and silently stalked to the door, hiding his body behind the jamb, exposing only half of his face to view. The chairs across the room were awash in a dim blue glow, as if illuminated by some unseen light. His pulse quickened, and a smile tugged at the side of his mouth. Could she have found him so quickly? A figure in a long, hooded cloak came into view, a deep blue glow emanating from within. Meadow stepped from his hiding place, now almost certain of the identity of the intruder. "Mimpi?"

The figure jumped and twirled around, weapon drawn, and the hooded face of a young woman then became visible in the glow of Meadow's aura.

"Meadow!" The woman came quickly forward, stowing her weapon. "You nearly scared the life out of me!"

The two embraced, laughing in relief. Meadow sighed. "It is good to see you, friend. I so hoped to find you well."

The woman pulled back, looking over Meadow. "Yes. For now, I am well, but things are grim here. Scarcely a safe space to hide anymore. Corpus' influence is everywhere and his agents are always watching, though now most have moved off toward Verde."

Meadow nodded. "Yes, I have seen darkness moving there. I can only hope that Jonas is prepared for whatever comes ashore." Meadow took a step away from Mimpi, turning his face to a sliver of moonlight that struggled through a dirty window nearby. "But that is not what I am here. I seek your counsel for other reasons, Mimpi."

The woman sat down at the table, removing her hooded cloak and revealing bronzed skin and a cascade of wavy black hair that fell nearly to her waist. "What reasons?"

Meadow turned toward her. "I am in search of Cira of Lapis. I traveled in the shadow plane and found her in the far northern seas. She must be a prisoner of Micca; no one would choose to stay in that place."

"Unless they were possessed by evil."

Meadow shook his head. "No, my friend, I saw her light, bright and blue as it ever was. She is unchanged."

She nodded, twirling a lock of black hair around her fingers.

"I must free her, Mimpi," Meadow said, coming to sit with her at the table. "Tell me the safest passage to the isles of the northern seas."

Mimpi frowned. "The northern seas are treacherous and cruel."

"Yes," Meadow said, placing his hand over hers, "and that is why I need your help."

Mimpi smiled, clasping both her hands round his. "If you promise to take care."

"I promise."

"All right." Mimpi sat up, lowering her voice. "Take your sanlifter to the city of Parvati in Crimson. From there, you must get a longboat with thick sails and stock it with food and water. Do not be tempted to take a smaller vessel. You will not survive."

"Could I not fly all the way? Are there no flight yards in the northern isles?"

She shook her head. "The isles are tiny; there's nowhere to land. You will have to sail there from Parvati." She pointed to the map of Graha on the wall behind them. "You must sail due north, staying close to the shore. Keep the land within your sight as you sail. If you go too far out, you will be caught and taken out to sea by a powerful current, the Azure Ring." She traced a circular pattern over an open expanse of the northern sea between the inhabited and uninhabited continents of Graha. "You will circle endlessly in that current—for a vessel such as a longboat, there is no escape from it. You will never be found."

Meadow lowered his head and the woman continued, "Keep sailing until you come into the Ilma Stream. You will know when you have found it; the winds are fierce and cold, but they will carry you directly to the isles of the northern seas, which lie just east of the northernmost part of Crimson. As you get closer, you will find more and more ice in the water, so take care to avoid a major collision."

"It appears I have a difficult journey ahead of me," Meadow said grimly.

The woman's eyes softened with concern. "Meadow, let me join you. It is too dangerous to go alone."

"No, Mimpi," Meadow said quickly. "We are two of just a few remaining remshifters. If we die together on a dangerous mission, the Founders will then have very little help in fighting Corpus." He leaned back against the wall, his deep green aura flickering. "We must stay solitary, stay safe."

Mimpi smiled knowingly. "You are right, as always." She reached out and gently palmed the side of his face. "Do take care, Meadow."

Meadow stood and put up his hood. "I must go. Where can I find food and supplies?"

Mimpi took both his hands in hers, gazing up at him with

concern. "Stay here tonight. A few of us are in hiding not far away." She looked him over. "You look as if you need a hot meal and a night of deep sleep anyway."

Meadow tilted his head. "But I—"

"Gather your strength tonight," Mimpi interrupted. "You can head for Parvati in the morning."

Meadow sighed, smiling. "An offer I cannot refuse."

The two soon headed toward the secret hide of the Lapisian refugees. That night, Meadow enjoyed a hearty stew, the company of friends, a warm bed, and a brief time of peace between two arduous journeys.

Meadow was shaken from his memories by a blast of wind. The jib strained against the flow and the fabric began to tear at the base. The gusts rapidly intensified, and before he could catch his bearings, a snow squall blew in out of nowhere, pouncing on the small vessel like a predator on prey. Meadow rushed to pull in his sails and release the jib, but it was too late. Another ferocious blast caught the mainsail, and the longboat overturned, sending Meadow crashing into the icy waters.

The intense cold stabbed through his body and his muscles locked, unable to release for a breath of air. Meadow flailed, grasping at chunks of ice that seemed to intentionally bob and duck away out of his grasp, taunting him. He finally reached the listing boat and grasped the side, barely able to hold himself up out of the bone chilling water. With the very last of his strength, Meadow flung a leg up over the side of the boat, hoping to clamber inside. To his horror, the added weight caused the unstable craft to list even further, and before he could react, it overturned. The mast bashed against him, opening a gash in his head and knocking him unconscious. His body drifted downward into the icy black, so still and silent as to appear almost peaceful, leaving only a faint ribbon of pink to mark his descent.

* * *

Surfacing

And it seemed the breath of hope had drowned, and all light had been obscured by dark cloud. Bodies yielded their kumu to the cycle of birth and death in ways they could not have imagined in kinder times. Corpus had once again claimed the Land of Verde, this time stealing her right from the king's grasp, tearing the very land from under his feet. Though Queen Zehn had indeed returned to her Jonquil, she had not yet regained enough power to heal her own Land and also assist another. In the fight against Lapis, Verde surrendered to darkness as Corpus grew ever more powerful.

It seemed that no one, not even a Founder, could stand against him.

To be continued...

MAP OF THE
LANDS OF GRAHA

PRAVUS CAVES

KINGDOM OF RUTILUS

FORBIDDEN LANDS

IGNIX TRAILS

RUDHAS MOUNTAINS

SULIX

NOMEN

ROBIR

VIRES

CRIMSON

PARVATI

VAUX

ACALA MOUNTAINS

ANALA MOUNTAINS

IGNIX TRAILS

FLUX

IGNIX TRAILS

SOZA RIVER

MARU

VERDE

KARDIA

LAPIS

SURUTA LAKES

CYPRESS

PARNA

ROAD OF DARWOOD

SERO FOREST

FODLAS RIVER

ERAS BRIDGE

PADMA ISLAND

PHOS

VENELIA KINGDOM

JALA SWAMP

EMU LAKE

FAGE

JIVSA

HARITA FOREST

SAMERA KINGDOM

THATCH

DESERT OF TENPI

ZILA

JONQUIL

FUZEI

SUKAI

SALVITOR'S WORKSHOP

PALACE OF GOSAI

ABOUT THE AUTHORS

J.J. Bende has always had a strong passion for fantasy and science fiction stories. Early in life, he began crafting the story of Eleven in his mind, and the tale has grown and evolved with him through the years. Sharing this story with the world is another gratifying outlet for him in addition to his design work, paintings, and photography.

J.J. was born and raised in Ohio. He studied fine art at Bowling Green State University, specializing in drawing and photography.

He currently lives in Columbus, Ohio with his wife and young son.

Carisa Holmes was born in Dayton, Ohio and attended Colonel White High School for the Arts, moving on to study vocal performance at Wright State University.

Carisa has always been a lover of all forms of art and creative expression. Music and the written word, however, are her true loves. She began with poetry and short stories, moved on to songwriting and now with Eleven: Shadow and Light, has co-authored her first novel.

She lives in Columbus, Ohio and works as a writer and holistic health advocate.

www.ingramcontent.com/pod-product-compliance
Lightning Source LLC
Chambersburg PA
CBHW070738180626
46818CB00007B/2898